THE COLOSSUS

Book 1 in The Red Scarf Series

Simon Wright

Copyright © 2023 Simon Wright

This novel is entirely a work of fiction. The names, characters and incidents portrayed in it are the work of the author's imagination. Any resemblance to actual persons, living or dead, events or localities is entirely coincidental.

The right of Simon Wright to be identified as the author of this work has been asserted in accordance with the Copyright, Design and Patents Act, 1988.

Simon Wright asserts the moral right to be identified as the author of this work.

For Mac
Who threw me the lifeline.

Who walkedst on the foaming deep,
and calm amidst its rage didst sleep;
O hear us when we cry to Thee,
for those in peril on the sea.

WILLIAM WHITING,
'ETERNAL FATHER, STRONG TO SAVE'

PROLOGUE

September 7, 1566

Hungary

It had been a long, brutal month. The longest of his forty-six-year reign. And it would also be his last. Suleiman the Magnificent knew he was now close to death. Illness had ravaged him in recent years, but this hadn't kept him from the field. Now, lying on a grand bed in his battle tent, he reflected on his reign. He had much to be proud of. He had conquered lands from Hungary to Persia, from Portugal to Somalia. He counted over twenty-five million people under his rule. And here he was, back in Hungary once again. Had it all been worth it, or was it just a never-ending cycle of lands gained and souls lost?

He listened to raindrops tapping on the tent canvas. A cool breeze blew through the opening, briefly teasing his long white beard, even as life crept from his body. His tall, muscular stature had been eroded by his slow sickness. His gentle hazel eyes had lost their light. All that he had been was leaving him now.

'Where is my grand vizier?' Suleiman wheezed to his servant kneeling nearby.

'He is still at the front, Your Imperial Majesty.'

Sokollu Mehmed Pasha had taken much of the burden of leadership off the shoulders of his sultan in recent weeks. They were camped at Szigetvár, no more than ten miles from the southern Hungarian border.

In the last days of this siege against the stronghold, the vizier had taken to sleeping in the trenches with his men. Such was his drive to conclude this battle and get his sultan back into the recuperating arms of Constantinople.

This was an unusual approach for any officer, let alone a grand vizier, but Mehmed was a warrior at heart. His had not been the political upbringing of so many of his predecessors. He had been pressed into military service as a young boy called Sokollu, through the devşirme system of child slavery. There he became a Janissary, part of a small elite force who moulded their conscripts into ruthless fighting machines. He was renamed Mehmed, and it wasn't long before he started moving through the ranks. In many ways, he was still at his most comfortable leading men into battle.

That very night he had put an audacious new plan in place. If it worked, it would bring this bloody battle to a rapid and timely conclusion. Both sides had seen many men fall. Far too many. It was time to finish this.

Suleiman valued his grand vizier. In his long reign, Mehmed had been his most loyal servant and greatest adviser, except for Suleiman's cherished wife, of course. With great will and effort, he mustered the energy to respond to his servant.

'Send for him ... and tell him to make haste. Our time is short. I need him, now more than ever.' This last part was barely more than a whisper. A personal admission perhaps.

As the servant dashed from the tent into the brooding, wet night, Suleiman relaxed a little. His fight was almost done. His thoughts turned, as they did every night when he closed his eyes, to his beloved Hurrem.

The love of his life. Of course, there had been others. Many, many others, but none that had commanded his heart so completely.

When she'd passed away, Suleiman had also started a long, slow decline. Without her at his side, everything seemed a little less vital, a little less important. The people would gossip that he was dying the slow death of a broken heart, and secretly Suleiman shared that view.

His sunken eyes dampened at the thought of his wife, and some words from a poem he had written to her came to his mind.

He murmured, 'My woman of the beautiful hair, my love of the slanted brow, my love of eyes full of misery … I'll sing your praises always. I, lover of the tormented heart, Muhibbi of the eyes full of tears, I am happy.'

Mehmed, who had stepped unnoticed and unannounced into the tent, made out his sultan's mournful voice, and a lump came to his throat. He looked at his master now, and he saw the power that had once been. Yes, the magnificence. In his simple white robes, complete with long, flowing white hair and beard, he seemed to shine with some divine light. Mehmed knew that he had been privileged to walk the same earth as this great leader and that none would see his like again.

'Your Majesty, I came as quickly as I could. I bring good news: we are close to a wonderful victory in your name. Another great stride in your empire's growth.'

'My friend, come closer. Let us speak no more of magnificent victories. This battle, like so many before it, has come at a heavy price.'

'But Your Majesty …'

'Please, Mehmed, enough. Let us now talk not as

leaders or rulers but as men. As friends.'

Mehmed stepped closer to the bed and into the lamplight that told him the truth of his friend's condition. He was close to death. Mehmed had to control his tears. He would not insult his ruler with some indulgent show of emotion. His friend deserved a more dignified end than that.

'Your Majesty, I have no doubt that your greatest battles still lie ahead. You are Suleiman the Magnificent, you, you ...' Mehmed searched for the message that would reassure his friend and leader.

'Shush now. Sit here and hold an old man's hand. Listen to what I have to say.'

Mehmed acquiesced and sat on the bed next to his dying friend. Suleiman stilled his heavy breathing a little, ordered his thoughts, and summoned the energy to say what still needed to be said.

'Mehmed, hear me now. No protestations or objections. Just hear what I have to say. There are things, protocols that will need to be put in place. There are plans that will need careful management in the weeks ahead, and I am entrusting this to you. I need to know that I can rely on you, that I can release my hold on this life secure in the knowledge that my wishes will be observed. To the letter, no deviations or amendments ... to the letter, mind. Do I have your commitment, my friend? Can you make that promise to me?'

'Your Majesty, I will always endeavour to ...'

'No. None of your endeavouring now. I don't need to know that you will try. I need to know it will be done. It *will* be done. Yes, or no. Can you make that promise?'

'Yes, my friend. I serve at your pleasure. I always have. The answer is yes, of course.'

'Good. That's good. Much rests on this. More than you realise. Not just our future, but the future of many generations to come will be determined by my choices and your actions. Now'—he paused, gathering some last vestiges of breath and strength—'how am I to be judged, Mehmed? How will I be remembered?'

Mehmed started to open his mouth, a eulogy already forming, but Suleiman squeezed his hand.

'No. I will tell you. I'll be remembered well by some, not so kindly by others. Mehmed, my friend, I have done some terrible things in my life. Horrendous things. It seems that in the moment of our most difficult choices, we find a reason, an excuse, rationalisations for our terrible deeds. But when we look back upon these endeavours, when we assess them with the clarity of time passed, well, then we see them for what they really are. Dreadful acts. Atrocities. Unforgivable choices. I have invaded many countries, taken many children from their fathers. I have orphaned many more. I have killed my own sons. My *own sons*, Mehmed. Mustafa strangled in front of me. Bayezid executed. And his sons. My grandsons. How can Allah ever forgive me?' Suleiman's throat choked up with emotion.

Mehmed hesitated momentarily but then could hold himself back no longer. 'Your Majesty, the fading light is playing tricks on you. That is not the legacy I see. Not at all. You will be remembered as the benefactor of the golden age of Ottoman rule. You will be remembered for the military might you have wielded. You will be remembered for building a wealth in our economy that is unsurpassed. One that has benefitted every one of your subjects. You will be remembered for bringing culture where there was ignorance and humanity where there was barbarism. You will be remembered for law reform, for education reform, and for social reform. You *are* the Lawgiver. You will be remembered as a patron of the arts and literature. You will be remembered as one of our great poets. One of the greatest ever. You will be remembered for making Constantinople the finest city in the world. You are the religious leader of Islam and the earthly leader of all Muslims.'

Mehmed paused. He felt he had still barely scratched the surface of his master's achievements. There was so much still to be said, but the sands of time were down to the final grains. The distant sound of battle threatened to intrude, but Mehmed blocked it out. He needed to focus. There would be time for glorious eulogies later, but right now, what should this man hear in his darkest moment? What did he *need* to hear?

'But, my friend, most of all, you are loved. You are loved by your people. You *will* be remembered. You will be remembered forever.'

Suleiman was still. Had he slipped away while Mehmed had been struggling to honour him? But no, his hand rose slowly and beckoned Mehmed closer.

'I hope you are right, my faithful servant. Inshallah. Inshallah. Now, listen carefully. I haven't long; you must take careful note of these, my final wishes.'

Mehmed knew the time for conversation was at an end. He now had to listen and listen well.

'I wish I was back home, Mehmed, back in the arms of my beloved Hurrem. She would take this pain away. Would that she were with us still. She'd know what to do. Instead, I have chosen to die in this godforsaken field of mud and blood, this plain of sacrifice and surrender.

Fighting yet another battle. Laying siege to another stronghold. Damn this place all to Jahannam. This castle has burned my heart. I beg of God it will descend into flames.' His breathing grew more harsh, more urgent. 'Sulem will need much support in his accession. You must buy him time, protect him, and guide him. Don't allow any panic to set in. I will not have the work we have done become undone. I have laboured too hard for too long to let everything just crumble. Do you understand me?'

Suleiman grabbed Mehmed's robe with as much urgency as his frail hand could muster at this point.

'Yes, Your Majesty, of course. I will devote the rest of my life to your legacy. I will protect and guide your son in the days and weeks to come.'

'Good. Good. Now, there is one more thing. This is most important, Mehmed, so hear me well. I want to be buried in Constantinople.'

'Of course, Your Majesty. Plans are already in place. A tomb is already built. A magnificent mosque is planned in your honour. But you know this.'

'Yes, yes, I know. My body will be interred there, as it should be. But that is not all I am.'

Mehmed held his breath as Suleiman paused.

'The Prophet has spoken to me, Mehmed. As I stood in the palace, touching his mantle and standard, he spoke to me as plain as I am now speaking to you. He told me that my soul will enter Barzakh upon my death. But it will also continue to reside within my burnished heart until Judgement Day cometh.'

Mehmed stilled even further at the mention of the Prophet Muhammad. Like all Muslims, Mehmed was most familiar with Barzakh, the holy place where souls wait for Judgement Day. Yet this talk of Suleiman's heart was already a radical departure from Muslim belief.

'He told me that my heart will continue to command the devotion of our people, even after I am gone. Whosoever shall control my heart shall also have dominion over my people. Do you understand, Mehmed? Do you see? My heart shall become a holy relic, second only to those of the Prophet Muhammad —Alayhi as-salam. In the right hands it will ensure a golden age for our empire for centuries to come, until the day of judgement. My reign will continue forever. Forever.'

Mehmed stared at his ruler in disbelief. Had Suleiman's fever made him mad? What was this blasphemy? What was he being asked to do?

'Your Magnificence,' Mehmed started, using the epithet that he knew Suleiman secretly delighted in. 'Your Magnificence, I have no doubt of your place in heaven, as I have absolute conviction that the Prophet Muhammad—Alayhi as-salam—will be overseeing your soul's journey to Allah.' He steeled himself. 'But, but this talk of your soul residing in your heart, that can't be right. That isn't right.'

Suleiman's eyes blazed in anger and desperation.

'Listen,' he hissed, 'my heart *will* endure, and it *will* command the faith and dedication of the people. It has been foretold to me, and now I am sharing this prophecy with you. Do you understand?'

Mehmed cowered before Suleiman's resurgent authority.

'Yes, Your Imperial Majesty. Yes, I understand.'

'When I am gone, you must arrange for my heart to be removed and embalmed. And then, you must take responsibility for its safety. You will know when the time is right for it to be reunited with the sacred position of sultan. I am entrusting you with this, Mehmed. You and you alone. No one else must know of this. No one. Do you understand what I am asking of you? Tell me you understand. Tell me you will comply.'

Mehmed shook his head imperceptibly. This was an impossible choice. To make a sacrilegious promise or deny his friend this dying wish?

'I serve at your pleasure, Your Majesty. It will be done. I vow to you in this moment, it will be done.'

His final words were overwhelmed by a gigantic explosion that drowned out the general cacophony of battle. Mehmed allowed himself a small smile as he walked over to the tent opening to get visual confirmation. His plan had been executed.

Only hours earlier he had briefed one of his bodyguards to take a bomb and scale the castle walls with it. Create enough of a gap to house the explosive device and then detonate it, forming an accessible breach for the Ottoman soldiers to gain entrance. This was the beginning of the end of this bloody siege. He strode back to his sultan's side with the joyful news.

'Your Imperial Majesty, the castle defence is broken. Victory will soon be ours.'

He smiled down at his master, but Suleiman lay still. The sultan's final battle was at an end. His heart beat no longer. Mehmed placed his hand on the sultan's chest and prayed for the strength he would need to keep his promise.

PART 1
VENTURER

1

May 22, 2012
London

'So, what did he do?'
Daniel Fairlight let the question hang in the air of the packed hall. After all, it was a good question. *The* question. Daniel always enjoyed this juncture in his lecture. As a professor of Ottoman studies specialising in the so-called golden age, Daniel always felt this was a pivotal moment. One that shone a light on the prosperity of the Ottoman Empire and anticipated the slow decline to come.

'Professor? Sir?'

Professor Fairlight came back into the room. 'Can you repeat your question, miss?'

It hadn't escaped Daniel's notice that a good 70 per cent of the room was female. His colleagues often joked that his students were more interested in the magnificent Daniel than in Suleiman the Magnificent. Daniel was just over six feet tall, with a kind, tanned face, piercing blue eyes, and an unkempt mop of dark-brown hair. His athletic good looks, which he'd sustained even though he wouldn't be seeing forty again anytime soon, had attracted attention that he'd struggled to manage on numerous occasions in the past. He secretly looked forward to hitting that certain age where you kind of became invisible to the other sex, regardless of your pedigree.

'Well, you can't just leave us there, Professor, with some kind of Indiana Jones cliffhanger. What did Mehmed do when Suleiman died?'

'Hmmm. Yes, quite. What *did* he do? Well, before I attempt to answer that, let me ask *you* a question first, Miss ... Miss?'

The student who had asked the question stood up. The audience quietly murmured, observing how stunning she was. But it was her piercing gaze that most struck Daniel. It was knowing. Daniel sensed that this was a formidable woman. One to be taken seriously.

'My name is Banu,' she said.

'Nice to meet you, Banu, and thank you for your question. It's a great one. So, my question is ...' Daniel paused, the audience hanging on his every word. 'My question is, what would *you* do?'

Without missing a beat, Banu responded confidently, 'I would have to give it very careful consideration, Professor.'

'No time to think, Banu. Word will get out in a matter of minutes of the passing of Suleiman the Magnificent. There is much that needs to be done and little time in which to complete it. You need to decide, and you need to decide now. Do you honour your friend and ruler's final wishes, or do you dismiss his confession as the feverish rantings of an old dying man? What's it to be, Banu?'

The young woman was still standing, her eyes locked on Daniel. She gave a hint of a smile. 'All right, Professor. If nothing else, then out of respect for one of the greatest leaders the world has ever seen, I would be faithful to his request.'

'Ah. So, you will cover up his death, cut out his heart,

and—what, hide it somewhere? Or maybe keep hold of it. Keep it for yourself, Banu. Is that it?'

She flinched slightly; her certainty wavered. 'I didn't say that. I'm just saying I would want to honour his wishes. That seems like the right thing to do.'

'You may be correct, but let's see what your fellow students think. Anyone?'

Arms shot up across the room. Initially people had been relieved that Banu was taking the heat, but now everyone had a view. Daniel pointed quickly around the room, keen to get a groundswell of opinion out.

'Of course he should honour his master's wishes. Anything else would be a betrayal.'

'No. He shouldn't be distracted by all this heart nonsense. He just needs to manage how the news gets out and then shift his focus to supporting Sulem.'

'No way, man, the dude has to take his responsibilities seriously. The whole future of the empire was at stake, right?'

'None of this is of any relevance,' an authoritative voice asserted from the shadows at the back of the room, not waiting for Daniel to invite his input. 'To suggest that Suleiman the Magnificent was on speaking terms with the Prophet Muhammad is preposterous. To propound that he had immortal dominion over our kingdom is sacrilege.'

Daniel noticed Banu turn and scowl at the rear of the hall. He sensed the debate escalating. This wasn't uncommon. Muslim history and beliefs could be a very divisive subject. More now than ever, maybe. Daniel had the utmost respect for the Muslim faith, but it was still all too easy to find yourself giving unintended offence.

'Okay. Let's rein it in there. We all need to be mindful

of the fact that we are inevitably blurring fact and mythology at this point. It is very difficult to assert with any absolute authority what happened in Suleiman's tent that night. So, let us look at the facts first.'

Daniel could see he was in danger of losing the room. Conflicting opinions had triggered heated side discussions that threatened to get out of hand.

'All right, back in the room. You can debate the finer points of Ottoman rule in the Shovel in a few minutes' time. I may even allow one or two of you to buy me a pint.' Cheers went up at this point. Daniel learnt a long time ago that the best way to a student's heart invariably involved alcohol.

'The facts,' he boomed across the room. 'Fact. Suleiman was gravely ill before he set out on what would become his final campaign. Fact. On the night of the seventh of September, 1566, Suleiman *did* die as the Siege of Szigetvár was drawing to its bloody conclusion. Fact. The "dude" in question, as my learned friend so eloquently described him, was the grand vizier Sokollu Mehmed Pasha. He *was* a key architect in establishing a breakthrough in that assault. Fact, and this one is a doozy, the grand vizier *did* hide the news of the sultan's death for forty-eight days. He was trying to protect the morale of his troops and put plans in place for Sulem's accession. He even arranged for another servant to lie on Suleiman's bed as a body double. And I'll give you one more fact. His heart, along with other internal organs, *was* removed from the body before it was taken back to Constantinople for a state burial.'

Daniel paused to let that last fact sink in. He had another bombshell to drop. A fact that continued to keep him up at night.

'And to this day Suleiman's heart has never been found.'

The audience stared back, dumbstruck.

'So, back to Banu's particularly salient question'— Banu bowed her head, seemingly regretting the profile her question had prompted—'what did Mehmed do? Well, there are many stories that try to answer that question, mostly hyperbole and fanciful conjecture. I'll leave you with the mythology that I find most credible and, well, intriguing.

'Mehmed involved a very small group in his deception. Two, maybe three men, including Suleiman's physician. He arranged for the sultan's internal organs to be removed, embalmed with musk and amber, and then sealed. He held a secret funeral service in the tent. Next, he ordered that the heart be placed in a golden casket that had been used for the sultan's correspondence. The casket was of the most intricate design, decorated with many jewels. Priceless, even then. Finally, he ordered the men to dig a makeshift tomb, where the heart could be given a resting place, directly below the tent.'

Daniel paused once more before delivering the final sucker punch.

'Once all this work had been completed ... Mehmed executed the group so that the secret would be sealed along with the casket.'

There was a collective gasp.

'As he travelled back to Constantinople, one can only guess how heavily this secret weighed upon him. What was his intention? To return at some future point. To wait until he could find a way of sharing this deception with the new sultan. Or maybe to retrieve the heart, with all its promised power, for his own glory. All we do know is that at some later point, a more fitting tomb and mosque were built at the site where Suleiman's internal organs were purported to be buried. Even as we speak, work continues trying to identify the exact location of this tomb, which, as we anthropologists are wont to say, has been lost in the mists of time. And if that isn't Indy enough for you budding archaeologists, then I don't know what is.'

The room burst into appreciative laughter.

'Meanwhile, as for Mehmed, we will never know whether he returned to the tomb with some dark personal agenda. What we *do* know is that he himself was the subject of an assassination thirteen years and two sultans later. It is rumoured that the assassin was a Janissary, which has a certain irony given his own beginnings in that elite infantry force. But don't get me started on the Janissaries.'

Some more polite smiles.

'Thank you all for your attention and engagement, and thanks to the dean for inviting me to give this guest lecture. And if I may paraphrase the professor of archaeology that my bright young inquisitor mentioned earlier'—he nodded deferentially in Banu's direction—'I will leave you with this piece of advice: if you want to be a good anthropologist, you gotta get out of the library. And that's my cue. Good night, all.'

As Daniel left the stage, he allowed himself a small smile. It was a privilege to lecture on a subject that had become his life's work, but if he was being honest, he still hoped beyond hope for a proper ending to his own story. He knew deep down that he would be prepared to surrender everything, all that he had accumulated and achieved, for even the slightest chance of discovering Suleiman's heart and revealing the truth behind the mythology.

2

November 11, 1629

Constantinople

The young boy peered through a slit in the rough woollen drapes hanging over his bed. The room was dark but for the light of a lone candle flickering in the corner. The flame danced with the cool breeze coming through the single window. It made the space ebb in and out of darkness, but the boy could still see the familiar ritual playing out across the room.

Emir wanted to look away, bury his head into the pillow, but he couldn't tear his eyes from the brutal scene.

'Kneel down, bitch.' The man was forty, maybe fifty, difficult to tell. He had a huge belly that stretched his shirt to its bursting point. His trousers were around his ankles. He swayed like some mighty ship, correcting against the waves. He was quite intoxicated; even the boy could see that.

'Perhaps I can administer some help first, sir,' the woman replied.

The man reflexively struck her face, the vulgar rings on his right hand slashing her cheek.

'Don't talk back at me, you whore. I'm going to give you the fiercest seeing to you've ever had.'

She glanced down between his legs, and despite herself, a look of scepticism briefly crossed her face. *No, Mama*, the boy thought. *Please don't do that. You know what will happen.* But it was too late.

Enraged, the man grabbed her neck and pinned her to the nearest wall.

'You filthy harlot. How dare you?'

The boy's mother knew she'd lost control of the situation. She stared wildly at the man, unable to utter any of the pacifying thoughts that came to her. As he saw her alarm, her terror, he hardened immediately.

'See, all you needed was to show a little respect. Now I'm going to give you a clipping you won't quickly forget.'

The boy turned away now, tears falling down his face. He had seen this dance many times before. He could blank out the image if he squeezed his eyes shut really tight, but he couldn't deafen himself to the sound of his mother's pain. He knew that she was doing everything in her power to suppress her screams, muffle her cries of anguish, so as not to wake her son.

He gritted his teeth and forced his feelings back down. Eventually sleep started to descend, and the sounds of brutal violation, mere steps away from where he lay, dimmed. Sleep was a welcome release for Emir. The only time he didn't worry about his mother.

As he drifted down, his thoughts turned, as they invariably did, to his father, Berkant. It was nearly two years now since Papa had left. Left his wife, left his family, left the city. Initially the boy had been upset. Devastated. How could his father leave? And how could he leave him? They were as thick as thieves.

Emir had idolised his father. This man who answered to no one. Walked his own path. Not for him a life of serving and scraping. He was too good for that —better than that. Berkant was a charismatic man. A trader and a hustler. He enjoyed operating between the lines, blurring the boundaries, using his quick mind to outwit others. Sure, he dreamt of making a fortune, but in truth, it was the chase that appealed more than the outcome. Every day brought a fresh opportunity for Berkant to pit his wits against the world. Take on all comers. It had the daring of a high-wire act, which was where the attraction lay. In the risk.

Emir would follow his father all day long. Watch him work his little deals with traders and travellers. When Berkant was closing a deal, there was nothing better to behold in all the world. He even taught Emir something of the art of deception through a few disappearing-coin tricks. Emir practised these, entertaining his friends with his sleight-of-hand skills.

And in truth, this devilment was what first attracted the young Esmeray, Emir's mother. Who wouldn't fall for the charms of this trickster? Over time, though, the tightrope drama ceased to appeal to Esmeray. They had talked about starting a family. Surely now was the time he would settle down. Seek out gainful employment which could provide regular income.

Berkant didn't see it that way. She'd married him for what he was, and now she wanted to change him. Esmeray said she had fallen in love with the man he was, and married the man she thought he could become, but this fell on deaf ears. So, she waited and hoped he would come round. By the time she realised it wasn't going to happen, she had a child on the way. And so, the rot started to set in.

Over time her frustration started to show. She told Emir that his father was nothing but an idle layabout. Conning people out of a few akçes. Selling an idea or a promise that was rarely backed up with any actual goods. Plenty of talk but not much action. On the streets *and* in the bedroom, he would hear her mutter. But Emir didn't care. Papa seemed like some kind of prince as he spun his webs around unsuspecting prey. Sure, he would sometimes disappear for a few days, maybe a couple of weeks, if he got wind that a Janissary was on his tail, but he always came back.

Not that Emir hadn't seen it coming. In the preceding months before the huge argument, he had watched his parents fighting more and more. He was unusually observant for a young boy, and he picked up on little signals. Silences. Mood swings. Pleasantries laced with sarcasm. By the end they didn't even try to hide it. This was worse. At least before, he could pretend that things would work out eventually; now he knew they never would.

The night his father left, the storm that raged outside their dwelling was no match for the one within. Mama had found out that her husband was having a dalliance with 'some strumpet' who worked with a travelling theatre group. She confronted him, and instead of being contrite, trying to fix things, he went on the attack. Said he didn't love her anymore. That she was holding him back, dragging him down, suffocating him. He had grand designs. Big plans. But he had sacrificed everything for her. Well, now it was *his* time.

Once he ran out of justifications, he made for the door. Mama didn't even try to stop him. Emir remembered all this, but the image he recalled most vividly was the moment his enraged father stood at the doorway. He turned and looked right at his boy. His expression was one of guilt, laced with loss, anger, and defeat. It was the most distressing thing the boy had ever seen. His father, so utterly beaten down.

So, yes, initially Emir had been upset. But now as his own heartache and dreams swirled around inside him, he felt nothing but a gnawing sense of bitterness and anger towards his father. Berkant had walked away from his responsibilities, but he had also stolen Emir's innocence. The world looked much fiercer from that day forth. And his life was harsher too. As his friends played in the street, he headed to the market every morning at sunrise, looking for work or scraps of discarded food.

His mother also tried everything to gain work, but with a young child there wasn't much she could offer. In the end, she gave the only thing she had left. She was a striking woman whose appearance transcended her circumstances. But Emir watched her in those first few months, and he saw the light leave her eyes. It was almost unbearable to witness. He was prouder of his mother in the hard months that followed his father's devastating exit than he had ever been. Prouder than *any* boy had ever been.

And one day, he was going to make her just as proud.

***

Emir woke early the next day. He saw his own breath as he hurried to get dressed, before venturing out of the makeshift tent that constituted his bedroom.

Thankfully, his mother's last client of the night had gone. She tended to a small fire in the kitchen area of the room, above which a pot was boiling. This was the only source of warmth they had, but it still had to be employed judiciously. Only lit when hot food or drink was required.

One of Emir's many duties was to collect water. He counted himself lucky that their home was downhill from the well. The thought of carrying full pails uphill didn't appeal at all. Once water had been sufficiently heated, Esmeray extinguished the fire. It wouldn't be lit again until the following morning, even in the winter months. The wooden slats of the building were old, and on blustery days the wind blew right through the dwelling. Evenings were the worst. During the night they huddled close together under a blanket for warmth, but as the sun went down, they really felt the temperature drop.

Emir slipped silently up behind his mother and wrapped his arms tightly around her waist.

'Morning, Mama. You look more beautiful than ever today.'

This was a well-trodden line. She stiffened a little but smiled too.

'Emie. I must examine your eyes later; I am worried that you are going blind.'

Emir smiled at his mother's pet name. As a very young boy he had struggled to pronounce his name, saying *Emie* instead of *Emir*. And so the unusual phrasing had stuck.

With this daily ritual completed, they started the struggle of another day. He didn't resent his chores—they were his duty now, as the man of the house. But, at times, it felt an overwhelming burden that stretched ahead as far as any young boy could see. What if he let his mother down? What if he turned out like his father? What if he couldn't find work? What would become of them then?

His mother watched him wrestle with these demons

whilst sipping his coffee. Not for the first time she reflected on how mature he appeared as he blew steam from his cup. He was small for his age, and slight, but his responsibilities had also made him tough. He had sinewy arm and leg muscles that were unusual in a boy his age and helped give the appearance of someone older. Sometimes, though, in his dark-brown eyes she saw the mischief of a child still shining through. His dark hair and tanned skin gave him a Mediterranean look, almost Italian.

Esmeray had always had a mystical connection with her son. It seemed sometimes that she knew what he was thinking before he did. She hated to see him so tormented, but she could do little to alleviate the pressures. She needed him to shoulder some of the weight. She hated herself for this, but she hated her husband more. As she watched Emir, she noticed him gently biting on his lower lip. He did it when he was worrying or concentrating. Berkant would do the exact same thing. It broke her heart. She struck up some conversation to stop her tears coming.

'You should make the most of that coffee. The rumour is that our sultan intends to prohibit the drinking of coffee in our homes as well as on the streets. If you are caught drinking, it will be punishable by death.'

'What is "prohibit"?' Emir asked curiously.

'It means that it would become forbidden. Not allowed.'

'Have you gone mad, Mama? No more coffee? No chance. We are well known for our coffee-houses. I'm sure this will blow over.' Emir couldn't comprehend how such a vital presence in Constantinople could possibly be banned.

The truth was that Sultan Murad IV was already outlawing the ever-popular gathering places. The young sultan was increasingly alarmed by the rebellious and insurgent Janissaries, who would congregate over coffee to plot revolution. Talk circulated claiming that Murad, merely sixteen years old, was patrolling the streets of Constantinople at night, dressed in civilian clothes, enforcing his policy. One rumour asserted that he had caught a man drinking in one of these establishments and beheaded him with his own hands. Emir's mother didn't share this last part with her son. In so many ways he had matured beyond his years, and yet, he was still only thirteen.

Instead Esmeray murmured, 'I swear by the heart of Suleiman, it's true.'

Emir smiled at this idle exclamation. He was fascinated by stories concerning the heart of Suleiman the Magnificent. If you found it, you would become immortal. If you held it, your hand would turn to gold. If you owned it, you would become a powerful sorcerer. If you kept it, you would become ruler of the world. Although Suleiman had died more than seventy years ago, the tale showed no sign of abating, instead becoming more and more fanciful. Emir was obsessed with the legend.

The boy glanced at his mother, sensing that she was worrying about him again. He started to whistle. She had a hard enough life without him adding to her woes.

'I'm off now. Wish me luck. I think today is the day when all our fortunes will change, Mama.'

'I think so too, Emie.'

With that exchange, another daily ritual, she kissed him lovingly on the forehead. He pushed through the door into the cold November air, unaware of just how much his fortunes *were* going to change that day.

3

May 22, 2012
London

Daniel went through his usual warm-up routine below the distinctive concrete buttresses of Brunel's Lecture Centre. He wasn't really a fan of the brutalist movement, especially in university architecture, being a true-blue Oxford man, but he had to admit that there was something quite challenging and purposeful about this particular building. Not bad traits for a seat of learning. And it had featured in *A Clockwork Orange*, one of Daniel's favourite films, so he harboured a secret little affection for it.

An old college friend had asked him if he would deliver the Suleiman lecture as a favour. Brunel had an anthropology course but was much better known as an engineering college. The idea was to make it a public lecture, and charge, to generate some funds. A Daniel Fairlight lecture was always a draw, so a sell-out was pretty much guaranteed.

Daniel ran a small consultancy business, and he had arranged for the operation's project manager to take his business materials home with him, allowing Daniel to change into his running gear and jog the twenty kilometres to his home in northwest London.

He loved Notting Hill. He couldn't imagine living anywhere else. It was a giddy ethnic melting pot, hallmarked by palaces, mosques, temples, and embassies of nationalities and faiths from around the world. The restaurant and bar scene reflected this cosmopolitan feel, as did the world-famous Portobello Road market. There were worse places for an anthropologist to hang out.

It was late May and uncommonly mild, so Daniel was looking forward to the two-hour run. With a following wind he'd be home around nine, just before the last vestiges of the sun slipped away. He was about to set off across the quad when a straggler from the lecture bounced down the stairs.

'Hey, Professor, you sure you don't want a drink? I'm buying.'

'As much as I am flabbergasted to hear a student offer to buy a drink, I'm afraid I'll have to decline your gracious offer this time. Banu, isn't it?'

'Well remembered, although I'm not a student, Professor, just a fan. So, can I just ask, how do you think Suleiman stacks up as a leader? Is he one of the greats?'

Daniel smiled to himself. 'Another smart question, Banu. I wish I had time to get into it, but ...'

'You don't believe the heart legend, do you?'

Daniel was thrown by the bluntness of this challenge. He stared curiously at the striking Middle Eastern woman.

'May I ask, are you of Turkish descent?'

'Yes. Yes, I am.'

'I can see that this is a very important subject to you. One that deserves an honest and considered response. Sadly, I really haven't got time to offer that now, so instead I'll give you the short answer.'

Daniel summoned up all his conviction for this theme: 'I want to. I really do.'

He smiled with a mix of wistfulness and regret. She smiled back.

'And now, I really must leave you. I hope our paths might cross again, Banu, so we can finish this conversation. Night, now.'

'Me too, Professor. Night.'

***

The first couple of kilometres were always hard for Daniel. He felt the jar of the pavement in his feet, his knees, his back, pretty much everywhere. After that he would invariably find a rhythm, and some dynamo inside him would start to tick over. Then, he would feel that he could run forever. Well, at least twenty kilometres, anyway. But it was the initial section that always proved the hard yards.

Whilst he waited for his internal metronome to kick in, he pictured the run in his mind. This was more than just the celebrated visioning technique favoured by many sportsmen to help them realise their goals. It wasn't even a technique in any traditional sense of the word. For as long as Daniel could remember, certainly back into childhood, when he was faced with any challenge, problem, or threat, his mind would still to an almost trancelike state, and then the pictures would resolve.

He would see a blank chalkboard. Then white lines would start to appear. Keylines, elevations, dimension lines, schematics, scale indicators, and contour lines would all weave around each other like some grand design. The drawings, which most closely resembled technical blueprints, explored answers, alternatives, or approaches to tackle whatever situation Daniel found himself in.

It always helped him order his thinking and solve problems with amazing speed. He got his head down and quickly ran the route in his mind. The mess of lines, arrows, and notations on Daniel's inner chalkboard resolved into the optimum route. He smiled. There was something reassuring about the white lines. They would always see him home.

Daniel lived alone in a well-appointed and sought-after mansion apartment block. He enjoyed bachelorhood but couldn't help feeling that if he were going to find a life partner, it would have to be pretty soon. He had briefly been engaged once, but that had ended badly, and his subsequent relationships had all been short lived. Maybe it was because he'd got his fingers burnt, or perhaps it was because any woman he met soon realised that they were competing with a long-dead sultan for Daniel's attentions.

As he started to get into his stride, his thoughts drifted back to the lecture and more particularly, to Banu. He was having trouble getting her out of his mind. Sure, she was captivating to look at, but that wasn't it. She had an assuredness about her. A defiance, almost. It had been a while since Daniel had come across anyone who seemed as obsessed with Suleiman as he was. As he ran, he reflected on her parting questions, regret creeping in that he hadn't made more time for her. He could have at least offered his card.

How should Suleiman the Magnificent be judged? Daniel often argued that leaders could not be judged in their own time, but needed to be considered from a historical perspective, once their legacy had fully revealed itself. However, one could equally assert that one should not apply today's moral compass when considering historical figures. It was, as they say, a different time. And surely that is what Suleiman would say if he could be his own advocate today. *You have to understand I was operating within a different set of rules, a different set of expectations and priorities. And furthermore, so were my enemies. Extreme times require extreme leadership.* Sometimes Daniel could almost hear Suleiman's voice. His tone, cadence, timbre.

In the end, Daniel concluded, he was both catalyst of and benefactor to the golden age of the Ottoman Empire. There were few aspects of the culture and society that he did not profoundly and positively influence. His means were questionable at best, but, one could say, his heart was in the right place.

Once again, Banu's words ruffled his subconscious. *You don't believe the heart legend, do you?* If one was to believe the mythology, Suleiman's heart most definitely wasn't in the right place. Like so many before him, the more Daniel studied the golden age of the Ottoman Empire, the more he became drawn to the mythology surrounding Suleiman's death and subsequent legacy.

Five years earlier, he had taken a sabbatical to search for the heart of Suleiman. It was on that pilgrimage that he'd met, and subsequently proposed to, Maria. Both the relationship and the expedition had ended in failure and frustration. Dealing with the fallout of depression and disappointment, Daniel had started, for the first time, to allow some chinks of doubt regarding the heart legend to creep in.

His answer to Banu had been an honest one. He still desperately wanted to believe that somewhere in the world, the preserved remnants of Suleiman's heart still resided within his golden casket. As to the relic's potential supernatural powers, well, that was quite another matter.

He glanced down at his Fitbit, a present from work colleagues. A self-confessed technophobe, Daniel suspected that tech malfunctioned in direct proportion to his proximity. He pushed buttons randomly trying to get the time, but instead a new figure came up: 193 bpm. That couldn't be right. Was that his heart rate?

He stepped off the pavement, oblivious to the black London taxi bearing down on him. The driver hit his horn and swerved. Daniel fell back, feeling the breeze of the car's drag on his legs. He tumbled to the ground in shock. A couple of passers-by made to help him up again, but most just stared. More embarrassed than anything, Daniel quickly pulled himself to his feet. The sound of rushing water in his head anticipated a set of all-too-familiar symptoms starting to trigger.

Daniel had suffered with panic attacks since childhood. The sensation was always the same. It felt like he was drowning. His body became agitated, restless. His breathing, shallow. It was difficult to swallow and almost impossible to calm himself. The sound of crashing waves became deafening. He had to extricate himself from whatever situation he was in—a theatre row, an aeroplane seat, a car journey, or simply a bed—and move. Then keep moving for as long as it took for things to de-escalate. Many flights were spent walking the aisles. Many nights pacing between the kitchen and the lounge. Valium helped, but his doctor and friend, Paul Atterbury, was increasingly reluctant to prescribe it. Meanwhile, Daniel managed it as best he could. What he did know was that sometimes, just occasionally, he could nip an attack in the bud. Snuff it out before the flame took hold. He focussed on doing that right now.

'I'm fine, honest, I'm fine,' he said to no one in particular.

Twenty yards back another runner slowed and started jogging on the spot. The young athletic man pulled out his phone to make a call. Daniel was oblivious to this. He was having enough trouble focusing on what was ahead of him. Cautiously, after looking both ways a couple of times, he crossed the road and resumed his jog. The young man pulled up his hoodie and followed.

***

As he approached Ealing, Daniel's heart rate finally came down. Not that his Fitbit notified him of this. *See*, he thought, *technology is trying to kill me. Will no one believe me?*

Daniel wondered, not for the first time, whether the new running programme was doing more harm than good. His friend Paul had been pushing him to make exercise a more intrinsic part of his lifestyle. He argued that a proper fitness regime would prove much more effective at aiding sleep and reducing the panic attacks than any number of pills could do.

It was a pretty easy sell to Daniel. When he was younger, fitness and health had been central to his lifestyle, so getting back into the habit felt a bit like meeting an old friend. Daniel shook his head. What was he worrying about? This had been a good call. It felt like he was taking charge of his issues for the first time in a long time. Things were going to be okay …

The motorbike came out of nowhere and knocked

him high into the air as it flew past before accelerating away. The last thing Daniel remembered was hearing the screams of onlookers, and then everything went blank.

A young dark-skinned jogger ran up to Daniel's still form and checked his pulse. Shaking his head, the runner stood up, quickly looked around to assess the situation, dialled a number on his phone, and slipped invisibly into the crowd.

Later, witnesses would say he looked Mediterranean. Middle Eastern maybe. Possibly Turkish.

4

November 12, 1629

Constantinople

Such is the resilient nature of children that, despite the most distressing of circumstances, they can sometimes still find or create an escape to a more carefree and safe space. And so it was with Emir that morning. His worries were bigger than any thirteen-year-old boy should ever have to endure. Would he and his mother have to choose between heat and food again? It had already been two days since his last proper meal. Would he find work? Would they lose their home if he didn't?

These most fundamental of life's challenges—shelter, warmth, sustenance, safety—were rarely far from Emir's mind. Yet as he walked towards the great Faith District market, his heart lifted a tad. It was a new day. A fresh chance to make something happen. As the saying went, hope springs eternal. Perhaps most eternally in the young.

The Faith District was an area of teeming activity and contradictory characteristics, a melting pot of cultures and nationalities arriving daily on merchant ships. First impressions were of a vibrant, energetic culture, but beneath the surface lay festering resentment and agitation. Since the plague of Bayrampaşa a few years earlier, which had threatened to overwhelm the city, there had been increasing unrest amongst the citizens.

These flames were further fanned by a Janissary presence which was both intimidating and unpredictable. The Janissaries had long been a problem to the city, indeed to Turkey as a whole, following a failed attempt by Osman II to disband them a few years earlier. Since then, they had become a law unto themselves, assassinating and extorting sultans and merchants alike. They still provided a policing presence in the city, but such was the level of corruption that many wondered whether an entirely unpoliced city would be more favourable.

Emir was attuned to these issues without really troubling himself with the political details. He knew where to go, and where not to go, whom to trust and whom to avoid, and there was some comfort in that familiarity. Despite everything, Constantinople was still his home.

As he approached, the noise level grew. Alongside the combative sounds and distinctive thrum emanating from the market, the exotic bouquet of myriad spices and herbs battled for attention. The rich, sweet, and bitter aromas were underpinned by a faint suggestion of sewage, one that resulted in a pervading odour that could leave the uninitiated feeling queasy.

Traders and peddlers vied for attention, proclaiming their wares and special prices for one day only. Their voices competed with the inevitable sound of masonry being hammered in the name of some fresh construction, and copper and brass vessels of all descriptions clinking and clanging together. Merchants shouted protestations to tradesman at prices being quoted, eliciting even louder outraged responses. The market throbbed and pulsed like a beating heart, and Emir found the extravagant sights and sounds a welcome distraction from his daily worries.

He walked the periphery of the market, checking for where the best employment opportunities lay. Single traders attracting significant custom were always a good place to start. They would already be stressed by the prospect of losing impatient customers to more available competitors. Emir also noted traders who dressed well, as they were probably successful and may throw an enthusiastic boy a couple of coins to help them out. It didn't always work out that way, but Emir had to try.

As Emir did his well-practised perambulating assessment, his gaze fell on a repugnant-looking trader manning a fine garments store. His belly hung out below his shirt, which itself was already sweat drenched despite the early hour. His face was a mess of carbuncular scars and broken veins. His three remaining teeth protruded out in varying directions like jaundiced tombstones. He was unaware of Emir as he stared at a young woman shopping at the next stall along. His leer betrayed his thoughts. Emir remembered him from the previous week. He had put in a fourteen-hour shift with the promise of an akçe for his day's work. But the trader had said that he was disappointed with how Emir had spoken to the customers and wouldn't pay him. No number of protestations would change his mind. He'd just smiled, knowing that Emir had little recourse. An exhausted Emir had fallen into bed that night and cried himself to sleep. The pain of that memory came back to Emir now, and it stung his eyes.

As he stared at the huge, repulsive excuse for a man, thinking of all the clever things he wished he'd said at the time, his eyes were drawn to an item on the trader's stall—a beautiful red silk scarf. Decorated with the most intricate black stitching, enhanced with a shining gloss, it fluttered in the early-morning breeze, dancing to the pulse of the market and flirting with potential customers. The scarf's pirouettes momentarily mesmerised him, and a mischievous thought insinuated itself into his mind. That was his scarf. He was owed that. At least that. This revolting trader had cheated him; it was only fair to seek recompense. He imagined giving this scarf as a gift to his mother. How moved she would be; how proud of him she would be. And, in that moment, although he had never thieved so much as a slice of bread in his life, he resolved to steal the scarf.

If a friend had called his name in that second, or a stranger had bumped into him, or a bell had chimed, he might have been jolted from this reverie, thought better of his perilous thoughts, and gone about his day. But none of these things happened. As is often the way of the world, Emir nonchalantly made what would prove to be one of the most far-reaching decisions of his life, without even the slightest awareness of how significant the moment was.

He sauntered over to the stall, making sure that he didn't distract the trader from his lecherous thoughts, and then he waited. He would know when the moment came. He had watched how the trader operated the previous week, so he knew exactly what he was waiting for. Barely a minute had passed before his opportunity presented itself. The trader, unable to resist the temptation, and unwilling to recognise the futility of his actions, called to the young woman he had been admiring. He made a lewd action towards her in what presumably was an attempt to present his credentials in the best possible light. As the woman screamed her disgust at him, Emir slowly removed the scarf from its hook, examined it, and then quietly started to tuck it inside his shirt. The trader was still trying to close the most optimistic deal on earth. Emir was in the clear.

Just as he turned to innocently wander off, the woman who had been the focus of the trader's attention pointed at Emir.

'If you spent a little less time forcing your loathsome advances on me, and a little more time minding your stall, you wouldn't be prey to market vermin like him.'

The trader turned, enraged, and instantly recognised the boy holding his merchandise. 'I give you work and money out of my own pocket, and this is how you repay me, you little runt.'

Emir had no time to think. He knew how this was going to play out if he stayed, and it wouldn't end well for him. But the trader was overweight and unfit, and more importantly he was manning his stall alone. He wouldn't dare leave it to embark on a chase he knew he couldn't win. It was clear what Emir had to do. Run.

He turned on his toes, already starting to sprint, and instantly collided full-on with a giant of a man, knocking Emir clean off his feet and to the ground. As Emir peered up at his adversary, he recognised the colourful garb. A Janissary. He was done for.

PART 2
ENTERPRISE

5

May 22, 2012
Oxford

The same afternoon that Daniel was preparing to deliver his Suleiman lecture in London, a young rower powered his way along the River Isis in Oxford. He glanced up at two elderly gentlemen sitting on a bench on the west bank. Neither of them looked his way. One of them, the white guy, looked upset; the other, a dark-skinned fellow, showed no emotion at all. Not boat lovers then, the student thought, and rowed on.

As it happened, one of them was a seasoned rower, having competed for Oxford in the 1958 Boat Race. Sadly, a loss by three and a half lengths, but still. On occasion he could still be seen having a leisurely row early in the mornings. The other man had no interest in boats or any seafaring vessels whatsoever. With one significant exception.

'I won't ask you again, Randolph. Will you do this favour for us? You owe us. *You owe me.* You know you do.' For unnerving emphasis, the words *You owe me* were accompanied by the splintering and cracking sound of breaking macadamia shells.

Not for the first time, Randolph bitterly regretted this debt. A lifetime ago, he had needed to assert some physical intimidation on a business competitor, and a friend had introduced him to Osman. The job had been done very professionally, if a little enthusiastically for Randolph's liking. They'd continued to do business together whenever Randolph needed solutions that potentially extended beyond the law, and slowly but inexorably he'd become indebted to this man. It hung over him like some terrible Sword of Damocles. And now Osman was finally here to collect.

'I can't. You know I can't. This is personal, Duman. This isn't business. This is unfair. Ask anything else of me, but not this.'

Randolph, who was well into his seventies, seemed to be aging as the conversation progressed. His tall, lean frame was that of an older man who still maintained a regular exercise regimen. But his face was heavily creased and wrinkled, betraying what his body was trying so hard to hide. His full head of hair had gone grey in his forties and was now white. He removed his spectacles as he was talking, something he had done since childhood whenever he felt intimidated. All the imposing presence that he had once possessed seemed to have evaporated in recent years.

Osman provided a stark contrast in every respect. His dark, tanned skin was unlined. His short, well-groomed hair had early suggestions of grey breaking up the black. His goatee also carried a little grey, giving him a distinguished look and framing a smile that had caught the eye of many women over the years. That, and his penetrating jet-black eyes. He was of a similar height to Randolph, around six four, but he filled out every inch of it with dense muscle, not an ounce of fat in sight. Any way you looked at it, Osman struck an imposing figure. He shook his head at Randolph's plea.

'We don't need anything else from you, old man.

We need this. It's not like we're asking you to kill someone. If your son takes this job offer, which we know is coming, that will make things, how do you say, complicated for me. And, as you very well know, Randolph, my old friend, I don't like complicated. Just block this move. You have the necessary influence over him. You've always had your way with him in the past, so why not now? You can stop this.'

'No, no. You don't understand. We barely talk anymore. Since his mother …' Randolph momentarily drifted away, then snapped back.

'I said some terrible things. Did some terrible things. After everything that has gone on between the two of us, I can't intervene. I simply can't.' Randolph shook his head as he reflected on his relationship with his son. They were long since estranged. Randolph had imposed his will on the boy from a very young age, but he had paid a heavy price. He couldn't stop thinking that although he may have won many battles in this relationship, he had definitely lost the war. And now, in his dotage, the guilt was devouring him. He would give anything—all of his wealth—to do it over. Or even simply gain some forgiveness. But it was too late for that. All he could do now was respect his son's wishes and stay away. He looked down again and hung his head.

Osman put a cigarette in his mouth, expertly opened and lit his Zippo lighter in one movement, and took a long drag on the Maltepe. He'd tried Camels for a while, but he didn't get the same kick. If a cigarette was going to kill you, you wanted to feel it killing you. He stared out across the river.

'Last chance, Randolph. We only ask for a favour to

be returned once. We won't ask again.'

'I have failed him so many times. I can't do it this time. This burden is already too much to bear. I would surrender every penny of my fortune if I thought I could fix this, but I know I can't. Please understand, if it was anything else, anything.'

Randolph's pleas petered out.

There was a long silence. To Randolph it seemed interminably long. He stared down at his feet and waited.

Finally, Osman responded, his tone noticeably lighter. 'Okay, my friend. Not to worry. I had to ask. You understand that, don't you?'

'Of course, of course.'

'No problem. We have another way we can go.' Osman got to his feet as he brought the meeting to a close, dropped his cigarette, and extinguished it with a heavy boot. 'All I ask is that you are discreet about this conversation. Strictly between us, right? Our alternatives will be severely undermined if you share any of what we've discussed. With anyone. You understand, right?'

Again, 'Of course, of course.'

'I must return to London immediately. Take good care of yourself, Randolph; you don't look so well to me. I'd hate to hear that something had befallen you. Allah'a Ismarladik.'

Randolph offered up a hand, forgetting that Osman never shook hands. He stared despondently down at the small pile of nut shells on the ground.

Osman was already striding away without looking back, speed dialling a number as he went.

'Yes. No. Yes, that's right. Plan B. You know what to

do. Let me know when it's done.'

He crossed the gravelled car park, unlocking his gunmetal grey Porsche Cayenne as he went. He had little time for Germans but had to begrudgingly admire the engineering of this luxury SUV. He jumped in and punched a destination into his satnav. His finger wavered over the 'set' button, but then he decided to select the non-motorway option before activating the route choice.

Despite the unsatisfactory conclusion to the meeting, Osman felt strangely calm. Reflecting on his conversation, he thought in many ways this was probably better. A cleaner solution. Nevertheless, he knew that Randolph would talk—he couldn't help himself. That would need tidying up. A more rural drive back to London would give him some time to think about next steps and avoid the mounting road rage that always came with rush-hour motorway traffic.

He threw the gearstick into first—he couldn't abide automatic transmissions; if you're gonna drive, drive—and squealed out of the car park, spraying a plume of gravel as he departed.

Thirty minutes later he had left Oxford behind and was now cruising along tree-lined lanes, deep in thought. The sun occasionally strobed through the leaves, so he reached for his Wayfarers. Another concession to the West, but, not unlike Porsche, a classic brand, nevertheless.

He had waited most of his life for a sign, a specific set of stars to align, and now he could see that moment was tantalisingly close. All of a sudden, plans had become a bit rushed. Osman hated hasty execution. That's how mistakes were made, how important details got overlooked. But that wasn't going to happen on his watch.

'We've come too far, sacrificed too much,' he muttered to himself. 'This is our moment. Our time.'

His iPhone bleeped. It was a message from his right-hand man, Serkan, together with an audio file. Osman reached over to open the attachment.

At the shocking sound of a car horn, he yanked the steering wheel. In his distraction, the Porsche had drifted across the road. It was a narrow lane anyway, and Osman barely managed to avoid a crash. He glanced in the rearview mirror, just in time to see the other driver offering some feedback by way of a universal hand gesture.

He eased off the gas and made a point of calming himself. Just like that, it all could have been over. His life was too important. Osman knew he had a destiny to fulfil. He had to be better than this. Focussed. Prepared. Indestructible.

Having resumed some control, he selected the file on his phone, opened it, and pressed play. After returning the phone to his jacket pocket, he turned up the volume on his in-car sound system.

'... including Suleiman's physician. He arranged for the sultan's internal organs to be removed, embalmed with musk and amber, and then sealed. He then held a secret funeral service ...'

Osman had to admit the professor certainly knew his stuff. There was no denying his credentials. He had listened to this guy's lectures many times before, sometimes in person. His knowledge of the Ottoman Empire, in particular the golden age, was unsurpassed, Osman begrudgingly acknowledged. However, his interpretation and assessment of some of the facts was much more questionable.

In particular, the professor's outspoken views on the Janissaries had incensed Osman. How dare he speak so ignorantly and yet so authoritatively on something he clearly didn't understand. The Janissaries were a noble and elite infantry corps that created the blueprint for all subsequent special fighting forces. They were quite simply the best of the best. And yet history had not been kind to them. Time after time they were undermined, disrespected, and betrayed. By the time of the Auspicious Incident, the Janissaries had been totally rejected by their own people. The very people they had given centuries of faithful service to.

Osman felt his fingers tightening on the wheel as he listened to the professor's lecture. The despicable treatment of the Janissaries was a theme that always lit a fire in Osman. The recording was suddenly interrupted as a call came through. He hit the answer button on the centre console. 'Speak to me.'

Serkan's voice came over the car audio system. 'Sir, not good news, I'm afraid.'

Osman waited.

'Sir?'

'Spit it out, Serkan.'

Serkan had served under him since childhood, and, following Serkan's father's untimely death, Duman Osman had become a replacement parent. More than that. The parent Serkan had truly been waiting for. He idolised Osman and would have gladly given his life in service of the man. But he also feared him. He had seen first hand what Osman was capable of, and when his fury took hold, no one was safe. Delivering bad news to

Duman Osman was a dangerous thing. In the last year or two, Serkan had reluctantly started to question the sanity of his master, but even that didn't undermine his loyalty. Nevertheless, he was grateful to be on a phone line rather than sitting in the passenger seat of Osman's Porsche at this precise moment.

'I'm afraid the hit wasn't a complete success, sir. He was injured, but not fatally. Just too many variables. Too rushed, sir.'

Osman listened as Serkan shared his news. He wanted to be understanding, accepting of the ineptitude that was being described, but the red mist descended.

Even without the blind rage consuming Osman, he probably wouldn't have had time to react as the stag appeared in his headlights. It stood in the middle of the road staring right at him. It didn't even flinch as the Cayenne bore down. The impact felt like ploughing headlong into a brick wall at fifty miles per hour. As the airbag deployed, Osman vaguely had a sense of the animal being flung high above his vehicle. He hit the brakes and skidded thirty yards farther down the road.

As the car rocked to a stop, Osman was already unbuckling his seat belt, puncturing the airbag, and opening the driver's side door. He leapt from the vehicle without taking a moment to check for personal injury. Osman knew all about personal injury, and none of those warning lights were flashing. His training and his discipline took over in moments of high adrenaline. He paused for a moment before letting out a shriek of almost primeval rage. The white heat coursed through his veins as he strode back up the road towards the horrific sound somewhere between a bark, a howl, and a scream.

Osman didn't slow his stride until he was standing directly over the distressed animal. The stag's eyes were wide and wet as it desperately kicked its front legs in a futile attempt to stand up. The noise coming from the dying animal was hard to believe and even harder to bear. It was clearly in agony.

Osman dropped to his knees, kneeling directly on the flank of the majestic beast. He reached down to the antlers, held one side with his left hand, and wrenched violently with his right. The animal was all muscle and must have weighed around 180 kilos. The stag's neck broke instantly, the antler disintegrating in Osman's impossible grip. Osman's eyes momentarily flared with a hellish mixture of excitement and pure hatred. Not for the first time he gave an internal nod of appreciation to the team of doctors who had, through a series of ethically questionable operations, given his prosthetic right arm a superhuman performance level. Actions such as crushing macadamia nuts and breaking a stag's neck were frighteningly within his strength thresholds.

He got back to his feet, absently wiping the animal's blood onto his jeans before reaching for his phone. The rage was already dissipating. An act of absolute dominance and brutality always had this effect on Osman. The anger would disperse like cloud breaking. He redialled the last number.

'Boss, are you okay? What happened? I heard a massive crash, and you just went dead. Is everything all right?'

Osman took a deep breath. He could feel his equilibrium returning. 'Everything is fine, Serkan. We will achieve our goal a different way. Now, I have another job for you. In Oxford.'

***

Thirty-six hours later Daniel woke up in West Middlesex Hospital with a start. He desperately fought to get some air into his lungs as he scanned the room. Daniel was unable to comprehend where he was or why he was there, and thus his panic started to tighten its grip.

The familiar sound of rushing water echoed in his ears as he tried futilely to sit up. Over the cacophony of splashing and crashing, an urgent beeping noise pierced through his head. Desperately Daniel tried to contain the mounting hysteria. He closed his eyes and focussed on his breathing. Breathe in the light, breathe out the doubt. Slowly. Breathe in, breathe out. In. Out.

Gradually, Daniel felt the tempest in his head start to calm. The room came into focus. Someone in medical uniform stood at his side. She was studying a machine by his bed and adjusting the drip that he was attached to.

'Maria? Is that you?' Daniel croaked through his parched throat.

'No sir, I'm one of the staff here,' the doctor responded as she offered Daniel some water through a straw. 'You've been in a bad road accident. Nothing to worry about, but you're quite beaten up. You've been our guest for a couple of nights now. Is Maria your partner? Can we notify her or anyone that you are staying with us at the moment?'

Daniel shook his head as he tried to remember what had happened.

'You didn't have any ID on you, sir, so we haven't

been able to identify you. Can you tell me your name?'

Daniel stared at the doctor, trying to process the information he was getting. He'd been running. He'd delivered a keynote speech, and then he was running home. And then, blank.

'My name is Daniel. Daniel Fairlight.'

'Pleased to meet you, Mr. Fairlight.'

'Actually, if you're going to be trying to identify me to the authorities, it's Professor Fairlight. Sorry, that makes me sound like a dick. Just call me Dan.'

The doctor hid a smile. 'Pleased to meet you, Dan. How do you feel? Are you in any pain?'

Daniel wrestled with confusion and exhaustion, but as soon as the concept of discomfort was broached, he realised that, yes, he was in very real pain. He nodded.

'Okay. I need you to sleep a little longer while we monitor your vitals. I'm going to give you something for the pain now, and we'll talk a bit later. Don't worry about a thing, Dan; you're in good hands. Here comes the gin and tonic.'

As the morphine started to kick in, Daniel drifted back into the dream he had awoken from. It was a recurring theme, a defining moment, and a memory tinged with guilt and regret. Back he went. Back to Istanbul. Back to her.

***

'I'm sorry, Maria. I can't leave now. This is just too important. This just might be the lead I've been looking for all my life. The clue that will finally show us where the heart of Suleiman is buried.'

'I'm telling you now, Danny: you need to make a choice. You can't just put a ring on my finger and then carry on living your own life like I'm nothing more than an accessory. I have my own career, my own ambitions. We need to build a life together, and that means making some choices, and some sacrifices ... together.'

'Please, Maria, don't turn this into something it's not. I just need to see this through, and then we can talk about the future.'

She stared incredulously at him. He could see her assessing the hand in her head, deciding what cards to play next.

'You need to decide, and you need to decide now. Which heart is more important to you? That of an Ottoman sultan who's been dead for nearly five hundred years, or the heart of the woman you said you wanted to marry?'

Even in the dream Daniel tried to make a different choice. Tried to repair the damage. But he couldn't. He just stared mutely at the girl he loved, even as the tears ran down her cheeks. She turned and walked out of the room.

6

November 12, 1629

Constantinople

Emir stared up at the soldier with genuine awe. He had never seen a Janissary this close. In truth, you didn't want to. The soldier was attired in a long red tunic and a cloth belt that held a horn-handled dagger in place. On his head he wore the distinctive börk, a tall hat with a jewel in the middle and a long flap at the back. Even in his terror, Emir couldn't help but be impressed by the sheer stature and grandeur of the warrior.

The Janissary picked him up off the ground like he was an inconsequential insect. Even if the officer had been alone, escape was clearly futile. As it was, he was accompanied by two further soldiers, also formidably garbed. The Janissary sneered at the writhing boy in his hand.

'This is exactly what I've been talking about, brothers. They really should clean up this market; just look what I've trodden in.'

The soldiers laughed.

'Kazim, let him go—you don't know what you might catch.'

The looks on the men's faces hardened as a new voice chimed in. 'Allah be praised that you valiant and courageous men have come along at this moment. This boy was trying to rob me blind. He is a pestilence in this honest market. You should execute him on the spot.'

Kazim, the senior of the three, glared at the trader. He looked every inch the warrior that he was: well over six feet tall, with a long mane of jet-black hair. His well-groomed black beard was braided and accessorised with colourful beads. His extravagant bushy eyebrows rose as he held the trader in his gaze.

'Are you telling us what to do, fat man? Is that an instruction you are giving me? Do you have the temerity to command me, a chorbaji of the noble Janissary corps? Have I got that right, you foul scum? Speak. Tell me I'm wrong.'

The trader, eager to comply, quickly offered up the suggested assertion. 'You are wrong, sir.'

'*What?*' The junior soldiers guffawed loudly as Kazim toyed with the pathetic man. 'One more word from you. One more. Go on, I dare you. Give me just one more word of disrespect. Please.'

The marketeer opened and closed his mouth a couple of times, but his strong survival instinct kicked in, and he went silent.

Kazim spun on his heels and marched off, dragging Emir in his wake.

'Come, gentlemen, let us deposit this master criminal with the appropriate authorities and be about our duties.'

As the Janissaries strode through a crowd that parted quickly to make way, the purveyor of fine garments looked on remorsefully. He hadn't even had time to retrieve the scarf from the boy.

***

Emir was unceremoniously handed over to local police

agents stationed on the other side of the Kuliyessi. Kazim had instructed one of his reports, a giant of a man called Fazil, to fill out the paperwork and then find them at the usual coffee-house. The head Janissary had suggested to his junior officers that he had revolutionary plans to share with them. Unhappy with this menial duty, and worried that he might miss some of the promised plotting, Fazil sought to make the transfer as quickly as possible.

'This boy has been thieving in the market. We have had multiple complaints. He looks like a pauper to me, so there will be no fine dividend for you. My advice? Just get rid of him into the system as quick as you can.'

With the paperwork completed, the Janissary exited. The agents looked at the boy wearily.

'Have you eaten today?' one of them said.

Maybe this isn't going to be so bad, Emir thought. 'No sir, I have not.'

'Take this bread and find yourself a seat in that cell. Eat well, boy—it may be your last meal for a while. If you can't find somewhere to sit, don't worry. You won't be here long. They're overdue to collect the next batch of juveniles already.'

Emir wondered what a juvenile might be. As one of the agents handed him the food, the other unlocked a cell and pushed him inside. The cell was maybe four yards by six, with benches around the perimeter and running across the middle. To keep his mind off the fear pooling in his stomach, Emir took in every detail he could. He estimated maybe twenty people in the cell, a mixture of men and boys not much older than him. Not one of them so much as looked up at him as he walked across to a space on one of the side benches.

He was still finishing his small hunk of bread when the clatter of the keys in the cell lock drew everyone's attention. One of the officers stepped in.

'Hands up, all those under the age of sixteen.'

Several hands went up.

'Follow me.'

Outside the cell, the boys were all manacled together. If a kid was going to run, this was when he would do it, but being chained to a wider group of hardened criminals somewhat limited prisoners' options. Once they were in the court, any last chance of escape was lost. They were led across the road, drawing looks that ranged from disgust and disapproval through to sympathy and resignation. Emir felt inside his shirt, and for the first time since his capture in the market, he realised he still had the stolen goods on his person. He glanced down, and the red scarf screamed *thief* back at him. No one had thought to ask him for the cloth, and he had forgotten he even had it. Something told him this was not the time to volunteer this piece of information. He looked at his fellow prisoners. Each one betrayed the exact feelings that Emir was experiencing: confusion laced with hopelessness and terror. He called to the lead officer.

'Sir. How will I let my mother know where to collect me?'

The officer behind leant forward and struck him over the head.

'Silence now, boy. You'll not be seeing your mother anytime soon.'

For the first time Emir started to grasp just how much trouble he was in.

Once inside the public building, the boys were

ushered into a courtroom. Far from the hushed and calm climate they might have expected, the room was pandemonium. Men exchanged insults, officials shouted for order, one man tried vainly to silence a chicken, while a collection of men and women tried to catch the attention of family members from a gallery at the rear. Many of the women were sobbing and shrieking in anguish. Emir wondered how any consideration at all would be possible in such a place, and at that moment his answer arrived.

The kadi appeared from a door at the rear of the court and banged a staff three times on the floor. As people turned to identify the sound, they quickly quieted. Within ten seconds the room had gone completely silent. The judge slowly scanned the room with an air of repulsion, then one man shouted, 'Your Honour, Your Honour, there has been a travesty of justice here.'

And the room erupted once again.

'*Silence*,' the judge boomed. 'The next person I hear will be given one hundred lashes before they are executed. Does anyone want to test my resolve in this matter?'

This time the silence remained. The kadi walked slowly to his chair, which was raised high on a pedestal. Finally, he settled and glared down at a nervous looking official. 'What's first on the scroll?'

'Your Honour. We have a juvenile group first. A group of seven boys, all caught stealing at various shops and stalls around the district. None of them can pay any fine. I suggest floggings, Your Honour.'

'Yes, let it be so. Actually, no—no. Hold. I have exhausted my patience with the juvenile crime in my district. Where are the arresting officers?'

'Here, Your Honour. We arrested all but one of these vagrants. Mainly petty theft, but I agree, Your Honour, it is sad to see.'

'It isn't sad, sir. It's a disgrace. An affront against Allah. What are you doing to drive this plague out?'

The officer looked across at the court official, searching for some support, but the official suddenly took an uncommon interest in the paperwork in front of him.

'I see. That was very illuminating. I'm sure we shall all sleep a little sounder tonight knowing that you are securing our welfare, Officer.'

A small ripple of titters started around the room, only to be severed by a blazing look from the judge.

'What about the one you didn't arrest?'

'This one here, Your Honour,' the officer blurted out, pointing at Emir. 'He was brought in by the Janissary Kazim.'

'Kazim, eh? Well, this one must have committed some terrible infringement to have warranted Kazim's attention.'

No one said anything. The kadi stared at Emir for an age, before nodding slightly.

'I will make an example of you, boy. One that I hope will resonate across the district, if not the whole of Constantinople. Floggings for those six; five years in the zindan for that one.'

The official looked shocked. 'Surely Your Honour means five weeks. Am I right, five weeks?'

'Are you questioning my authority, sir?'

'Absolutely not, Your Honour. A thousand thank-yous for your wise judgement. Officer, take these boys away.'

The official looked guiltily at Emir before casting his gaze down to his case files. Emir's eyes shot desperately around the court. Could no one help him? Surely, he would wake up momentarily to find this to be a nightmare. *Zindan.* Just the word summoned up terror in the hearts of men, let alone boys. A visit to one of the dungeons of Constantinople was notoriously a one-way trip.

***

Emir had heard wild stories of how the zindan operated. It was referred to grimly by its inmates as the Bug Pit. Situated on the fringes of the city, it was little more than a giant hole in the ground. The entrance to the abyss was twenty yards across, the drop maybe sixty yards. Even at high noon, no sun reached the base of the pit. At the bottom it spread out into a labyrinthine series of caverns, nooks, and crannies. The only way in was via a rope-and-chain pulley system controlling a giant cage. There was no way out.

Prisoners were lowered down into the depths in the cage, where they were met by inmate guards. These guards were themselves prisoners but had been given certain privileges, including jurisdiction over the other prisoners. Like the worst kind of turned poachers, they were more zealous in their control of the pit than any law enforcement officer would have been. They were reviled and feared in equal measure. They were called the Bloodguard because of the blood on their hands.

If you were appointed to this privileged position, you were tattooed with a red blood drop under your eye and assigned a long red frock coat. Then you were one of the Bloodguard. They were protected by the zindan laws. If you killed a Bloodguard, you were executed in the pit. No trial, no nothing. What the Bloodguard never realised was that if any of them completed their sentence, they would last no more than a couple of days on the outside, as they were literally marked men.

The Bloodguard's main responsibility was to manage the cage activity. In the morning it would come down to collect the dead that had accumulated overnight. It wasn't called the Bug Pit for nothing. The caverns were infested with every kind of venomous creature you could imagine. Scorpions were by no means the king of this particular jungle. Prisoners who didn't die of starvation, dysentery, or malnutrition either died at the hands of another inmate or through the poison of one of the myriad bugs. Sometimes the cage would make two or even three morning trips, loaded with the Bug Pit's gruesome daily toll. A Bloodguard would pull on a rope to indicate that the cage needed to come back down. At the surface of the pit, guards would stab each of the bodies as they were unloaded to ensure no stowaways were hiding among the dead.

In the afternoon the cage returned with a paltry amount of food, which was distributed by the Bloodguard in accordance with who had offered the most compelling sexual favours. Sordid acts of indecency were the only real currency available in the pit. The only form of bribery.

In the early evening the cage would make its next trip of the day, bringing down new prisoners, sometimes only one or two, sometimes upwards of a dozen. The cage would land in a large central space known simply as the core. It was sealed off from the rest of the dungeon by a dome constructed of iron bars and acacia thorns. The Bloodguard lived within the core, whilst all the other inmates were outside the perimeter. Arrivals would be greeted by a low cry of *New blood, new blood*, which they heard long before they reached the bottom. Many would be screaming for some kind of salvation well before the cage emerged into the dim torchlight within the core. A Bloodguard would then allocate the arrivals to one of the seven sections around the core, called 'the territories,' according to where the dead bodies had been retrieved from, earlier that day.

If any of the territories had additional dead, they were then loaded onto the cage for its return journey. Each of the territories had an informal leader, a Number One, who was responsible for identifying and handing over any dead in their area. The Number One changed hands with alarming regularity, as inmates fought for what little authority and privilege was on offer.

Eventually, towards midnight, the cage would make a final visit, this time to collect a passenger. Each day one of the Bloodguard was allowed to work aboveground, dealing with the carcasses that came up and preparing the fresh prisoners for their journey down. They were then allowed to rest in the evening, eat a real meal, and maybe even walk under the stars, supervised of course, before returning to the hellhole of the pit. For a few hours they tasted the slightest morsel of freedom. It was this incentive that really made the Bloodguard position such a sought-after one.

Finally, the new topside man would operate the cage back down with the returning Bloodguard, before bringing the empty cage up to the surface, where it would stay until the following day.

In the pit, this was the circle of life. And so it was that Emir found himself in some dark corner of one of the dungeon's seven hell-holes. He stroked the scarf inside his shirt, hoping for some kind of comfort, but none came. Thinking back on the day's events, Emir was suddenly completely and utterly overcome, and slowly, quietly, he started to weep. He knew in his heart that this was where he was going to die.

***

Exhausted and bereft, Emir finally slipped into a fitful sleep. His fatigue was so extreme that, despite the terrible sense of threat and dread, he would probably have slept through the night if he hadn't felt something, or someone, pulling at him. Initially he thought it was the giant Janissary that was attacking him in his nightmare, but as he came to, he saw a man with a face that resembled a weasel's staring right back at him.

Emir glanced down and saw that the man was tugging on the scarf knotted into his shirt. Another few seconds and he would have freed it.

'Fuck off, you sewer rat,' Emir shouted, using the most abusive word he knew, and trying to sound considerably stronger than he felt.

A few men in the vicinity chuckled humourlessly and offered up their own assessments.

'He's pegged you, friend. You really are a sewer rat.'

'You must be slipping, brother, losing your touch.'

The rat spoke up indignantly. 'If I had wanted to steal the item, boy, it would now be in my possession. I was merely admiring the fine handiwork.'

More chuckles and dismissals.

'Enough,' a fresh voice bellowed. 'Leave the boy alone.'

'Hello. Looks like you've got yourself a bodyguard, boy. You need to be careful, Jabari may be wanting to do more than just guard your body, if you get my meaning.'

'You son of a whore,' the man called Jabari spat out. 'How dare you sully my reputation with your filthy innuendos. As every man here knows, I am the most famous swordsman this city has ever known. Word of my exploits is legend in Constantinople. Why, there are literally hundreds of women crying themselves to sleep this very night because I won't be bedding them. It is a heavy burden I have to bear.'

The men roared with laughter. Emir thought how incongruous it was to hear laughter in a place like this but couldn't resist a small smile himself. This man had a certain theatricality that reminded him of his father when he used to be in full flow.

'Now shut up, you bunch of sodomites, and let me give this boy some much-needed comfort.'

An uneasy silence descended.

He turned his attention to the boy. Sitting down alongside him, he put a hand on Emir's shoulder, and attempted, without total success, his most reassuring smile.

Emir retreated a little, looking doubtfully at his new champion. Neither fat nor thin, Jabari had a big round face which was dark with an almost red hue. His lips were prominent and glistening. His eyes also glittered mischievously. His hair was shaved close, apart from a short tail of hennaed hair tied at the back. Emir thought him funny looking, but wondered if attaching himself to this man might prove his best chance of surviving this ordeal.

'My boy. You're safe now. Nothing to worry about. So first, some civilised introductions, I think. After all, we are not gutter rats like this lot, you and me: we are gentlemen. I will go first. My name is Jabari, but everyone calls me Jaba. I am a great prince, descended from the mighty pharaohs of Egypt, and have royal blood coursing through my veins. Of course, you're not catching me at my best in this moment. However, once I have overcome this unfortunate setback, I intend to sail back to the land of my forefathers and reclaim my birthright. Now you. Whom do I have the privilege of addressing?'

'My name is Emir. I live with my mother on the outskirts of the Faith District.' Emir paused and thought for a second, before adding, 'I don't think I have any royal blood coursing through my veins.'

Jabari chuckled warmly. 'Well, I am not so sure about that. We shall see. Now, first I must apologise for my cellmates down here. Especially the scumbag you encountered.' He glanced at Emir. 'Seriously, my friend, it may come as a surprise to you, but pickpockets *are* operating in this area. If that piece of cloth is important to you, then you need to keep it out of sight and out of reach.'

Emir considered this for a moment. The scarf was important to him. Picturing the moment when he would gift it to his mother was all that was sustaining him right now. He nodded gravely at Jabari.

Jabari pointed at the scarf. 'Is that how you came to find yourself in such unfortunate circumstances, my friend?'

Emir blushed. He felt ashamed and embarrassed.

Reluctantly he nodded, not offering up any explanation.

Jabari shook his head ruefully. 'What were they thinking, sending a boy down here for petty theft. Have they no shame? Maggots, the lot of them.' He continued shaking his head, as if trying to divine how such a travesty of justice could have occurred. Finally, he looked back into Emir's eyes. 'Now, you should rest. Tomorrow I will show you the ropes, but for now you need to regain your strength. We will talk more in the morning.'

Emir still felt wary, but sleep was already invading him at the mention of the word.

'I will watch over you tonight, Emie. Sleep well.'

Emir smiled.

'Why do you smile?'

'My mother calls me Emie, but I have never heard anyone else call me that.'

Jabari gave him a wistful look. 'We had a brother who died not much older than you. We called him Emie.'

Emir wanted to know more of Jabari's surprising disclosure, but already felt his eyelids becoming heavy. Jabari placed a hand gently on his forehead.

'In here, I am your mother. Sleep.'

***

Sometime later Emir partially woke and looked around. Jabari was as good as his word and sat there, wide awake, watching him.

'Sir,' Emir whispered drowsily, 'Why are you helping me? Why are you looking after me?'

Jabari leant over and whispered back conspiratorially, 'I have been waiting for one such as you, Emir. You are a gift that has come down to me from the heavens. And you come to me at the eleventh hour. Another day and it would have been too late. Surely it is fate, my boy. You and I are destined for better things. Tomorrow I will tell you everything and, if it is Allah's will, you may yet feel the sun on your face before the week is out. Now sleep.'

7

June 3, 2012
London

'Not good news I'm afraid, Dan.'

Daniel Fairlight looked across the desk at his doctor with an expression of bitter resignation. He had known Paul Atterbury for twenty years as his doctor, fifteen as his friend. Over the last seven years Paul had also provided private consultations to Daniel's mother as her health deteriorated. Daniel trusted him implicitly. Second opinions would be pointless.

Daniel composed himself. 'That's a bit blunt. You could have bought me some flowers or chocolates or something. Sometimes I think you don't care about my feelings at all.'

Paul played along, knowing full well that this bravado was part of Dan's coping mechanism. 'The truth is, dude, I've never liked you. You're charming, popular, handsome, brilliant, athletic—well, not at the minute, obviously. It's time you heard the truth, Professor: I hate your guts. We all do.'

Daniel smiled half-heartedly. 'All right, lay it out for me. Where do I stand?'

'Well, that's part of the problem. You can't stand.'

Dan winced.

'What, too early? Yeah, too early. I get it. All right, serious now.'

Paul would flip a switch when the professional man was required. Daniel sometimes thought that there were two completely different Pauls: the slightly mad friend and the brilliant doctor. It was brilliant doctor time, unfortunately.

'Let's start with the ankle. As you are only too painfully aware, you have a grade two sprain in the right ankle. The problem with this is that it takes time to ensure a good mend. You know all this, Dan. There's no way round the RICE mantra here. Rest, ice, compression, and elevation. I recommend that you alternate the ice with some heat, at least four times a day, but you must keep that leg above heart level for as much of the day as you can.'

'How long before I can run again?'

'Oh, c'mon, Dan. That's weeks away, maybe months. You know this. You could rush it back. In three or four weeks it will start to feel "fine."' Paul did the accompanying speech marks hand signal that Daniel detested. 'But it won't be. If you want it to come back to roughly the same strength, balance, and flexibility, you *mustn't* rush it. If you weren't already in a wheelchair, I'd have put your foot in a boot for at least another week.

'Listen, mate. If it was just your ankle, maybe we could talk about some accelerating strategies, but as it is, I can't even get you onto crutches anytime soon. It's not the ankle that's the showstopper here, it's your arm.'

'And the hits just keep coming.'

'Well, again, no new news here. The cast on your lower arm should help stabilise the wrist and elbow fractures. The op went well on the radius, and I'm optimistic that the screws we've put in will take. With a following wind we could have you out of that cast in six weeks. But the humerus break, well, that's a different story.'

Daniel stared wistfully out of the window.

'If the arm hadn't previously been broken, then, again, maybe we could have tried to push things along. But the upper arm is now seriously compromised. If we want to get any level of normal functionality back into it, we're gonna have to be very cautious. I'm sorry, but I have to ask again, when did you first break it? What happened?'

Daniel continued to stare away as if lost in thought. 'It's a long story,' he muttered. And then, after another long pause, 'You know my latest *SOS* trip is coming up in a couple of weeks. Is that still an option?'

Daniel had started referring to his obsessive Suleiman expeditions by the acronym some years back to avoid the inevitable eye rolling that often ensued. So, *Search Out Suleiman* had become *SOS*. Paul was familiar with the cryptic code. He covered Daniel's care home visits to his mother whenever the professor was off on one of his *SOS* trips. He stared dispassionately back at Daniel.

'No. I'm so sorry, Dan—I know how much it means to you, but no, it's not going to happen.'

The two friends sat in the office, not catching each other's eyes for a while. Letting the implications of what had been said settle. Sink in. They had known each other for a long time. Silence between them wasn't uncomfortable, but Daniel's disappointment was palpable.

'Listen, mate, I've only got one more appointment this afternoon, then I'm done. If you can just hang on in the waiting room for twenty minutes, I'll run you home, maybe stop off for a couple of pints at the Duke on the way. What d'ya say?'

'You know what? I'm gonna take you up on that. I definitely need a drink. Take your time, I'll clear some mail, reach out to Istanbul. Turn off a few taps. They're going to need to know ASAP. Anyway, you owe me more than just a drink. You got me on to this running lark. You're meant to be looking after my welfare, but I'm beginning to wonder if you're actually trying to kill me.'

Paul smiled as he wheeled Daniel back into the waiting area. 'Rumbled at last. With you out of the way, no one will be able to foil my cunning plans for world domination.'

'You really need to work on that God complex of yours, you know.'

Paul laughed maniacally as he wandered back toward his office. 'You just don't appreciate how good I am to you,' he shouted over his shoulder. 'In the future I'm saving myself for patients who really deserve me. And talking of deserving patients, here is the delightful Mrs MacLeod. How lovely to see you, Mrs MacLeod, especially after my last patient—please come through.'

Daniel sat in his wheelchair, feeling imprisoned by his injuries, and stared disconsolately at his ghostly reflection in the smoked glass reception screen. His mind went back to Paul's question. What happened? It wasn't really that long of a story, but it certainly cast a long shadow. Would he ever truly put the events of that spring day behind him?

***

September 1987. Daniel was visiting his parents at their ancestral home. Returning there had become a bittersweet experience for him. 1987 had closed the first part of his life in spectacular fashion. He was the strangest of creatures, an Oxford student who hailed from Oxford. He had graduated with first-class honours in anthropology and had fully embraced university life, living in student accommodation rather than at his parents'. He'd wanted the whole uni experience but also, if he was honest, to get away from his father.

But Daniel couldn't escape him entirely. His father had been an Oxford rower—not that anyone had made the connection, Daniel made sure of that. He was determined to stay away from the sport. He didn't care for water and also couldn't swim. But an enthusiastic recruiter wrangled Daniel into his first lesson. What followed probably didn't raise an eyebrow with anyone else in the family, given their pedigree, but it caught Daniel completely by surprise. Not only was he an absolute natural, but he caught the bug, big time. And that was how it came to be that Daniel Fairlight was on the winning team for Oxford in the Boat Race by four lengths on the March 29, 1987.

The sheer elation of the day was stolen from Daniel later that evening, when he caught up with his parents in the Green Man in Putney. Daniel had visited most of the hostelries between the river and the top of the hill en route and was in fine cheer when he arrived. His mother was effusive and emotional, fluctuating wildly between shrieks of laughter and tears of proud emotion. His father had maintained a stony silence. Finally, against the advice of his better angels, Daniel actively sought out the positive reinforcement he so desperately craved.

'Well, Father, what did you think?'

Randolph Fairlight stared coldly at his son for a long time before finally delivering his verdict: 'You were lucky. You wouldn't have even made the cut if it hadn't been for the crew mutiny. Any idiot could see that Cambridge were the better drilled team. You won the race because you won the toss. Pure and simple.'

Daniel flushed with embarrassment and long-held rage. 'You just can't bear to see me achieve something that you never did.' As soon as the words left his mouth, he regretted them. It was the kind of statement you could spend a lifetime trying to repress, and another lifetime trying to retract. His father stared at him with cool disdain.

'No son,' Randolph retorted, 'If Oxford had won the toss in '58, we would have won. Everyone agrees on that. You're just showing your ignorance now. Anyway, it's time I took your mother back. Enjoy your moment in the sun. Now you've got this nonsense out of your system, starting tomorrow, we shall start to refocus you on your studies.' And with that he left.

Daniel told himself that he wasn't going to allow his father to ruin this for him, like he had ruined everything else. But, despite his best efforts, he knew that his father had already stolen the achievement from him.

Over the ensuing months, visits back home became rare. On this occasion his mother greeted him with the usual heady mix of emotions, but now she seemed hollower, more haunted somehow. It hurt him to witness this, and although he had no doubt who had stolen his mother's light, he also knew he shared in that. In withdrawing from his father, it was his mother he had inadvertently punished.

As Daniel went to see his father, he thought back on the events of the Boat Race earlier that year. Maybe this time would be different. Surely even he would be pleased and proud to hear Daniel's news.

He entered the pavilion and took a seat on one of the benches. He placed the portfolio case containing his offer paperwork down beside him as he watched his father complete his swim. Daniel had learnt at a very young age not to interrupt his old man during his swimming regimen. He had to admit that his father still looked very athletic for his age. Finally, Randolph pulled himself from the pool and grabbed a towel.

Without even looking in Daniel's direction, he called across the pool, 'Would you like a dip? Oh sorry, I forgot —you can't swim, can you.'

Daniel stared down at his feet and slowly shook his head. Why had he thought that anything would be different?

'Afternoon, Father. Nice to see you. Tell me, have you ever once been tempted to give me words of support? Maybe some approval, or just a little praise?'

'What are you talking about? I have done nothing but support you in your endeavours. Oxford isn't cheap, you know.'

'That's not what I ... oh, y'know what, forget it. Let me just say what I came here to say. I wanted to let you know that I have a place in one of the qualifying regattas for next year's Olympics in Seoul. The coaches say that with my times I've got a really good chance of getting a place in the coxless four. I just thought that, well, well, actually, I'm not sure what I thought.'

Randolph continued towelling his hair as he walked slowly round the pool to where Daniel was standing.

'Well, that's not happening.'

'I'm sorry?'

'We've been through this, Daniel. Your mother and I are agreed: it's time you returned to your studies and stopped these flights of fancy.'

'Sorry, Father. I didn't come to you for permission. This was more of a courtesy visit really. And what the hell do you mean by flights of fancy? You may not remember, but I was on the winning team in the Boat Race.'

'That was boys, lad. And most of them carried you anyway. The Olympics is men. They're in a different league to you, and we both know that you don't cope well when you're out of your depth.'

Daniel flinched. He knew exactly what his father was referring to. He felt himself losing control, a lifetime of resentment and bitterness welling up inside him. 'You sick old man. Your need to control and dominate everything has left you with no one. Even Mother only stays here out of fear. You're nothing but a bitter, twisted, lonely man who is utterly unloved. I pity you.'

'Watch your tone, son. I'm still fit enough to teach you a lesson on how to respect your elders.'

As Daniel reached down to the bench to pick up the clearly redundant case, he muttered, 'I'd like to see you fucking try.'

He never saw the swinging arm coming. The punch lifted him completely off the ground, and he went flying into the pool. Panic enshrouded him as he hit the water. As he desperately flailed about, he could see his father lighting a cigar and staring down at him disdainfully. As Daniel went under, he wondered how his mother would take this.

Suddenly he felt a hand around his wrist, pulling him up above the surface. He gasped for air, genuinely shocked that his father had even bothered to save him. Randolph started to pull Daniel out of the pool by his right arm, leveraging Daniel's dead weight with his arm against the side of the pool. Daniel felt real pain shoot down the arm and realised that it was shifting into an unnatural position against the pool edge. Then he heard a sickening crack, and the pain turned into searing fire down his arm.

The last thing he remembered before he passed out was his body being pulled clear of the water.

***

'Dan, Dan.' It was Paul. Professional Paul. Deadly serious Paul.

'Sorry, I was miles away. What is it?'

'I've got the office on the phone for you. They say it's urgent.'

Daniel grabbed the phone. 'Daniel Fairlight speaking.'

He heard the familiar voice of his project manager. 'Dan, I've got the police here. They've been trying to reach you ever since the story broke in the press.'

'The police? What story?'

'I'm sorry to be telling you like this, Dan, but it's all over the news, and I thought you should hear it from someone you know rather than just getting the shock of a TV announcement.'

'Hear what?' Daniel's tone hardened.

There was a long pause.

'It's your father, Dan. There's been some kind of

accident. I'm afraid he's, well, he's dead. It's all over the news.'

'Paul, can you turn that TV on please. A news channel.'

Paul grabbed the remote and brought up the BBC News channel. A picture of Sir Randolph Fairlight was splashed across the screen.

'... near to a capsized rowing boat. The cause of death is still unknown, but police on the scene are treating this as an unfortunate accident, and say they are not looking for anyone in connection with this incident. Sir Randolph was formerly ambassador to the United Arab Emirates, Iraq, and Turkey, but in recent years there have been calls for Sir Randolph's knighthood to be stripped amidst ongoing accusations of illegal arms trading in the Middle East. He is survived by his wife and son. In other news ...'

'Switch it off, Paul.'

Paul looked across at Daniel and saw that he was going into shock. What Paul didn't know, couldn't have known, was that Daniel's shock was not at the loss of his father but at the thought that he had been wishing him dead at the exact moment he'd received the news. Daniel thought, *Is this some fresh purgatory he is giving me? A lifetime of guilt from beyond the grave.*

'First my accident and now this,' Daniel murmured to himself, as the sound of crashing water started to rush into his head.

8

November 13, 1629

Constantinople

It may have been the notion of a guardian angel watching over him, or simply sheer cumulative exhaustion kicking in. Whatever it was, Emir slept through the rest of the night. Not that morning looked any different from any other part of the day in the pit. Maybe a few degrees cooler—it was unbearable by late afternoon—but it may as well have been the dead of night for all the available light.

As soon as he woke, Emir saw Jabari's eyes twinkling in the light of the candle he held up. Jabari carried a permanent expression suggesting some mischief afoot. He gave his winning smile another run. Emir thought about offering up some advice that involved maybe not smiling but thought better of it. He looked at the floor beside him. There were over a dozen dead bugs and insects littered around, including a particularly gruesome-looking scorpion and two of the biggest cockroaches that Emir had ever seen. He recoiled with a mixture of loathing and genuine horror. Jabari reached out to reassure him.

'No need to worry, my boy. I made sure that none of them touched you. They're all dead. See how Jaba looks after you? We won't see any more now. Once some of the, er, larger cockroaches start moving around'— he gestured with his head towards a group of inmates standing and talking—'the bugs go to ground. They feed at night.' Jabari brushed the dead carcasses away casually and pulled himself a little closer to Emir.

'Just be glad there wasn't a black assassin spider among them. A bite from one of those bastards and you're paralysed in three minutes'—he clapped his hands loudly to emphasise the finality of this outcome, making Emir jump—'dead in five. Anyway, enough of that. Bet you're hungry, Emie. Look, I have saved you a biscuit.'

Emir hadn't really thought about food, but the moment Jaba made the offer, he felt his stomach clench with hunger. He reached out for the piece of oatcake Jaba was holding.

'Thank you, sir. I am most grateful.'

'No more of this "sir" now. "Your Majesty" is just fine.' Jabari gave him a conspiratorial wink, one that said, *You and me, kid.*

Emir stood up, bowed, and doffed an imaginary hat. 'Of course, Your Majesty. I am your humble servant.'

The two of them smiled, enjoying this piece of theatre.

'Then let us away, and I shall show you the delights of my kingdom.'

And so, this incongruous couple perambulated around the territories, looking for all the world like a tour guide with a party of one, marvelling at the myriad wonders the Bug Pit had to offer.

Emir slowly got his bearings. The base of the pit was arranged in a series of concentric circles. The bars of the domed core dominated the centre. There was a gap at the top of the dome large enough to allow for the cage to enter and exit. This aperture was adorned with nails and blades to dissuade anyone from attempting to climb up the bars and into the core.

Around the core was a ring of barren ground. Emir shuddered, overhearing someone call it 'dead-man's land.' The core had four entrance gates, each under the lock and key of the Bloodguard. Around no-man's land there was another ring of metal bars, this one with seven gates, each accessing one of the seven territories. The territories broke down into a multitude of tunnels and caverns the farther away you retreated from the core. Emir saw these recessed areas had become sleeping quarters for the prisoners. He swallowed down the fear that bubbled inside him again. This was the stuff of nightmares.

As Jabari brought Emir back towards the core, he sensed his guardian's disposition darken. He had experienced mood shifts in adults and knew when to act, and when to be still. When to speak, and when to listen.

Being careful not to get too close to the bars and attract attention, Jabari pointed towards the three Bloodguard busying themselves within the core.

'These are the real scum down here, Emie. Prisoners that have turned on their own. Miserable wretches who have sold their souls for an easy ride. The lowest of the low.'

Jabari spat at the ground as he sneered. Emir attempted a spit also. He noticed men from around the core pulling dead bodies up to the inner sanctum.

'What are they doing, sir?'

Jabari surveyed the scene with a grim expression, 'They are bringing out their dead, Emie. Every morning the Number One from each territory checks to see whether any inmates have died on his patch. If they have, he must bring them to the core. The gates are opened one at a time, and the Number One pulls his dead into the core and then loads them onto the cage. The Bloodguard don't even help. They just stand back like the roaches they are.'

'Where are your dead, sir?'

'I have none today, praise be to Allah. But all the Number Ones come to the core to offer a silent prayer before the cage ascends.'

Emir stared upward. 'Do you believe in a heaven?'

'I hope so, Emie. I hope so.' Jabari wiped his eyes and looked away, but when he looked back, they were sparkling with rascality once more. 'Now, we don't have long. The cage will be making its journey back down in a few minutes. Come over here.'

Jabari held the boy's hand and pulled him urgently out of the light surrounding the core and into the shadows of the pit edge. His tone became more hushed. Conspiratorial.

'I want to show you something, Emie. This is the highlight of my little tour. I think you're gonna like it.' His eyes twinkled with even more devilment. He glanced upward. 'Tell me. What can you see up there?'

Emir peered into the darkness. At first, he just saw blackness. He shielded his eyes from the dim core light, and slowly something started to take shape. As his eyes adjusted, it became clearer. That couldn't be right.

'Well, it looks a little bit like ... a ship's anchor?'

'Yes, Emie. Good boy. That is *exactly* what it is. A giant ship's anchor.'

Emir's eyes were wide with amazement. How could this be?

'I don't understand.' Emir looked up to the spot of daylight sixty yards away. 'Is there a ship up there? I don't remember seeing it.'

Jabari chuckled quietly. 'No, there is no ship. Well, not there, anyway. More of that later. So, this anchor is what they call a counterweight.'

Emir looked blank.

'This anchor is suspended by a chain. Can you see the chain, Emie?'

'Yes, I see it.'

'Well, that chain goes all the way to the top where it wraps round a wheel, and then it is attached to the cage. When they try and pull the cage up, the anchor comes down, which makes it easier to pull up the weight of the cage. You see?'

Emir looked doubtful. All he could see was a heavy cage and a heavy weight. Two lots of heavy instead of one. How could that be helpful?

'Never mind. It's not important. What *is* important is the game.'

Emir's attention was immediately re-established. 'What game?'

'Ah, it's nothing. You wouldn't be interested.'

'Sir, please sir, I think I would be very interested. The thing that I am most interested in, in all the world, is games, so you can tell me. Please, please.'

'I don't know. It's not really a game for little urchins like you … but you know what? You are my special guest, so yes, I will let you in on it. Here's how it works. Every day, the fittest men amongst us'—Jabari ruefully surveyed the inmates around him, mindful of the irony in his words—'only the very best of us, mind, compete to see who can climb the wall and jump onto the anchor.'

Emir's eyes grew ever wider.

'And do you know how many men have been able to do it, Emie? Do you? Have a guess?'

'I have no idea. Tell me.'

'Exactly none.' Jabari paused for effect. 'Not one man has been able to achieve this Herculean task. It's impossible. It simply cannot be done.'

Emir felt calm and focussed. This wasn't like when the Janissary had scared him or when he was brought down to the Bug Pit; then panic had blurred his thoughts. Now, he scanned the height of the anchor and the distance between it and the bare rock face of the wall. The anchor hung about twenty feet up, swinging rhythmically, catching its breath from its most recent cage exertions. At its closest point, it was still a good ten feet away from the side wall. After a minute or so of mesmeric study, Emir nodded.

'I can do it.'

'You?' Jabari gave a mocking laugh. 'I'm sorry, little one. I don't mean to offend, but you're wrong. You could never do it. Not in a hundred attempts.'

'Just try me. I know I can do it. I've seen the way.'

Jabari looked wistfully at the boy, up to the swinging anchor, and then back down to Emir.

'I do believe you just might be able to, Emie.' Jabari held the boy by the shoulders, then pulled him into a tight hug. 'You may just be the saviour I have been waiting for.'

**

Jabari spent the next few hours sharing his escape plan with Emir. As the boy started to realise the magnitude of what Jabari was suggesting, fear took hold. Each time Jabari spotted Emir's doubts, he would let Emir share his misgivings and reassure the boy.

In truth, this was a desperate play on the Egyptian's part. Yesterday, intel from another new blood inmate revealed that he'd run out of time. It was now or never. He had the accomplice he'd needed for so long. Emir was small, agile, and perhaps most importantly, easily manipulated. The risks were still manifold, but Jabari knew that he had nothing to lose now. He was using the boy, but he was also giving Emir a lifeline. Surely that made it all right.

'You are doing very well, Emie, very well. Now listen, do you remember a man that came down with you? A fellow prisoner.'

Emir nodded.

'Well, he is a friend of mine, and he brought me some very exciting news. Do you want to know what he said?'

Emir nodded again, happy to be distracted by Jabari's conversation.

'He told me that my brother is waiting for us, and he has arranged for us to have first-class cabins on a giant sailing ship. Doesn't that sound splendid, Emie?'

Emir looked doubtful. 'But I need to get home to Mama, sir. She will be so worried about me. I can't go on any ship. I must go home.'

Jabari paused, trying to weigh up how much burden he could place on this young boy's shoulders.

'Of course. How foolish of me. Of course, you must get home. But me, Emie, I have to be on that ship. If they capture me again, they will execute me for sure. And your cage partner brought me news that the ship sails tomorrow.' He paused to let this sink in. 'So you see,

Emie, we have to go tonight.'

Emir stared into Jabari's eyes for a long time. Jabari knew that a lot rested on this moment. If the boy hesitated, or slipped into panic, it would take a long time to get him back to this point.

Finally, Emir nodded, 'I understand, sir. Then tonight it is.'

Jabari hugged him again, shedding a few tears of euphoria and pride for this brave child. When they let go of each other, Jabari suggested that Emir go and study the wall he would be climbing later that night. Emir nodded earnestly and headed for the giant counterweight, which had reappeared after the cage had delivered some food and returned to the surface.

Emir stared at the wall as if it were some grand masterpiece in a museum. He allowed himself to become consumed by it, and in this reverie, he charted the climbing routes available to him. This had long been Emir's way of problem-solving. His mother thought he was some kind of genius, but his father had always dismissed these episodes as the daydreaming of an imbecile.

Each potential route was scribed onto the wall in Emir's thoughts, and as it reached a dead end, it would be erased to be replaced by a new possibility. Lines, arcs, and arrows covered the wall quickly, and were erased with similar speed. After an hour, Emir narrowed down two options. The paths were clear. In Emir's head the jump had already been executed.

He hurried back to Jabari, eager to share his newfound confidence. As he approached, Jabari hurriedly wrapped a small metal box with some old cloth. Emir saw it but instinctively knew not to ask.

Jabari looked up and smiled at Emir, patting the ground next to him.

'Sit here, Emie, we must talk seriously. Let us speak man to man.' Jabari furtively looked in all directions, reassuring himself that there were no prying eyes, no eavesdropping ears. Emir sat down and looked gravely up at Jabari.

'Listen. When this plan goes into motion tonight, things are going to move very quickly. I am completely confident that our plan cannot fail, but if anything were to happen, there is something I need you to do for me. I have an ancient Egyptian ring that I must get to my brother.' Jabari pulled an unusually shaped, ornate ring off his little finger. 'It is a long story, perhaps for another time, but it is very important that he gets this ring. Vitally important. What I'm saying, Emie, is if I don't make it—which of course I will, but *if* for any unforeseen reason I don't—then I need you to get this ring to my brother, Shabaka. You will find him on board a ship called the *Colossus*. You can't miss it—it's, well, colossal. You know, big. And you can't miss him. Everyone knows Shaba. Shabaka. Now, Emie, will you do this for me?'

Emir looked down at the beautiful gold ring. It dipped down into a 'V' shape at the front and was carved with hieroglyphics all the way round. He looked back up at Jabari and sensed the import of this request.

'We're both going to be fine, sir. I know we are.'

'I'm sure you're right, Emie, but just in case, you see, just in case.'

Again, Emir looked at the ring. Finally, he shrugged, picked it up, and secured it in his shirt. Jabari stared longingly at Emir's pocket, as if regretting his decision, or at least assessing the wisdom of it. He started to reach out.

'You *can* trust me, sir,' Emir said assertively. He paused for a moment, thinking, then returned Jabari's gaze. 'I also have a request. If I don't make it, I want you to promise me that you will get this scarf to my mother and explain everything that happened. Our house is not far from the port, sir. You'll have time before your ship leaves. Can you tell her, tell her ...' Emir started to choke up.

Jabari took the scarf and held Emir's hand. 'I will tell her how brave you are and how wronged you have been. You have my word, Emir. She will know of your valour and your character, I promise.'

The Egyptian man and his young Turkish charge hugged once more and waited for night to come.

9

November 13, 1629

Constantinople Port

Even as Jabari and Emir made their pact in the Bug Pit, the ship that Jabari had spoken of was busily being prepared for departure. Waves gently lapped up against the high port walls. This soothing sound of the ocean gently flexing its muscle provided a constant background thrum to the myriad sights and sounds at play in the quays of Constantinople. Dominating the dockside, rocking gently in the breeze, rested the *Colossus*.

She was a galleon, styled like the famous pirate ships and Spanish warships of the previous century, but she was grander. A man could walk alongside the ship for two hundred paces and not reach one end from the other. Two normal-size ships would have comfortably fitted on her deck. Rumours claimed the ship could carry over one thousand tons of cargo. Some said she would travel with under half of that burden on her Mediterranean journey but would return fully loaded from Alexandria. Everyone conjectured about what those goods would be, where they were sourced, and, of course, what their value might be.

Everything about the ship spoke of romance and adventure. Four masts gave a sense of majesty. Three decks, the low forecastle, the aggressive bowsprit projecting forward like a giant lance, and the distinctive buttressed stern gave the ship a mythological quality.

A small group of sailors shaded themselves behind the last cargo boxes to be loaded. They waited for the sun to drop in the sky before the final push. One had a set of dice and tried to encourage the others to play. The stranger wouldn't take no for an answer, even though many of the sailors were Muslim.

It was a well-accepted fact that some of the laws laid down in the Qur'an were not adhered to as religiously at sea as on land. For a start the main drink on board, especially on ocean journeys, was ale. Simply put, the alcohol in the beer would help it keep, whereas water would spoil far more quickly. This reality, and a prolonged sense of isolation, meant that many of the Muslim crew, though by no means all, would relax the protocols of their faith a little. Beer was drunk and games of chance were played.

But they weren't on board yet, and the *Colossus* definitely hadn't set sail.

The stranger was now baiting the crew. 'Come on, you weak, sad excuses for sailors. Are you men, or are you women in disguise? I can't tell.'

'We don't know you, stranger,' Shabaka, the foreman of the crew, responded with agitation. 'You should be more respectful to those of us who host you as a guest in our fair city.'

'I mean you no ill will, my companions.' The stranger suddenly became more congenial. 'After all, we are to set sail together on a great adventure tomorrow. I want to know that all of you will have my back, as I have yours. You have my word on this. I, Mustafa, am committing my life, here and now, to save each and every one of you once we are at sea. Now come on, let me take a few coins off you before I save your wretched lives.'

A few of the group had been wavering with temptation for a while, and this show of bravado tipped the balance.

Shabaka stepped away a little to check on the sun's progress. There was still a shift to put in, and he didn't want to be working in the dark—but he was stalling as much as he could. As foreman of the group, it was his responsibility, and indeed his neck on the line, if loading delayed departure. But his brother was still in the wind. Shabaka felt in his heart that Jabari would make it. He had to.

Shabaka returned to the men, who were systematically being stripped of their signing-on bonuses by the troubling Mustafa. The gambler, spotting the foreman's return, stood to address him.

'Mr. Foreman,' Mustafa said. 'I understand you are the man to see about positions. I have a man, a great sailor and a tireless worker. His name is Onur. He wishes to join me on this adventure. Can you find a place for him? I'd be prepared to put up a lot of coin.'

'I'm sorry, friend. There are no places left.' Shabaka knew this wasn't exactly true.

Mustafa pressed, 'I understand you have been saving a place for someone. Well, what if that someone doesn't turn up?'

'He will.'

'Yes, but what if he doesn't?'

Shabaka grabbed the Turk by his lapels and threw him against the nearest wall.

'He. Will.' The two men glared at each other for a moment, before Shabaka looked around at the other sailors. 'Right, enough of this horseplay. There is work still to be done. Now you've finished losing your money to this charlatan, perhaps you could think about doing what you are actually being paid to do. Now.'

'Shaba. Where do you want us to start?'

'With the box that is currently supporting your lazy arse. Where do you think?'

Shabaka left them moving the pulley system back into place to load the remaining crates. He wandered out onto the dockside and stared across the city into the rapidly setting sun. Had his brother got word that they were sailing tomorrow morning? Did he really have an escape plan? He absently reached down to the ornate ring on his little finger. As he twisted it anxiously round, he felt a chill settle on him.

'Jaba, my brother, keep safe and, by the heart of Suleiman, Godspeed.'

***

Even as Shabaka intoned Suleiman's prayer, seven hundred miles away plans were afoot to liberate the revered sultan's heart. For sixty-three years it had rested securely where Suleiman's grand vizier had buried it. A garrison of some eighty men guarded the mausoleum that had been constructed on Turbék hill outside Szigetvár. Tonight, the heart would be stolen from them.

A small unit of around a dozen mercenary soldiers had finally uncovered the exact location of the holy relic. They had spent weeks meticulously planning a daring infiltration of the garrison and, tonight, all that patience and cunning was going to pay off. The captain of this rebel group was keen to reinforce the momentous importance of their mission.

'Tonight,' he declared, 'we play a pivotal part in realising the prophecy of Suleiman the Magnificent. The golden casket containing His Majesty's heart will be in our grasp before this night is past. The honour has fallen to us to reclaim the sacred artefact and ensure it gets into the hands of our one true leader, our fallen aga.'

The twelve Janissaries knelt in unison.

'Thirty days from now we must be in Dubrovnik, in time to meet a ship called the *Colossus*. It is more than two hundred and fifty miles of difficult terrain and hostile locals. While no word will ever be released of this appropriation, in the years ahead we will be celebrated for our role in returning glory days to the empire. For now, we will be hunted over every mile of our journey. Some of us will give our lives in the name of this endeavour. But we shall receive our rewards in akhirah. This will be the greatest honour of our lives. Brothers, I salute you.'

The soldiers stood as one and looked back upon their leader, pride shining in their eyes. The room was heavy with the weight of history. Nothing now would stop these men fulfilling their destiny.

10

June 10, 2012
Istanbul

Serkan drove north on the European shoreline road out of Istanbul. It was late, and the lights from the opposing Asian shore shimmered on the Bosphorus. Despite the hour he was in no hurry. He knew how this meeting would go. He had seen it many times before.

As the Mercedes glided past increasingly affluent neighbourhoods, he reviewed the activities of the last few days, checking and rechecking that all loose ends had been tied up. He was almost as obsessive in his eye for detail as his boss. Many thorough men who had come before him had been 'let go' because they weren't thorough enough. You had to be fanatical about the details to ensure no mistakes were made, and Duman Osman had a rigid zero-error policy.

Of course, things still went wrong, but Serkan wanted to be sure that they never went wrong on his watch. The motorbike hit in London a month back hadn't gone according to plan, but that wasn't his fault, and he had made sure that his boss knew that. Nevertheless, he had taken personal responsibility for executing the Oxford contract. There was no point in asking for trouble, and if you wanted something done properly …

That contract had troubled him. It had seemed

almost out of character for Osman. First, he'd gone to the trouble of trying to get Randolph to block his son's appointment to the DIVE project, and then when that didn't work out, Osman immediately commissioned a hit on the son. Why not just go with that option from the start? If it hadn't been so rushed, maybe it would have been better executed. And why then order the hit on the old man? He was a high-profile target, which was always going to attract unnecessary attention. Okay, Serkan had made sure it looked accidental, but still, why bother? Osman had just said that it was a loose end. Not for the first time, Serkan wondered whether his boss was beginning to unravel. For such a meticulous man, he had suddenly become alarmingly impulsive.

This brought him to the troubling events of the previous night. This contract had been carried out to the letter. An Istanbul society couple had been arrested on a drugs charge two weeks previously. They were released on bail, but word on the street suggested that they were in the process of plea bargaining in exchange for immunity. This might have been of no interest to Duman Osman whatsoever had they not been recently bragging about having Osman in their pocket because they had video proof of him carrying out an execution himself. The fact that they had commissioned this hit was conveniently overlooked. Osman had decided that he couldn't take the chance and instructed Serkan to take care of it. Personally.

It had seemed like a routine operation. A double assassination presented as a bungled home break-in and armed robbery. Serkan's information had confirmed that the couple would be home alone, and it was only after the second kill shot that Serkan heard the cries of the couple's seven-year-old son in the next room. Whilst the cover story window dressing was completed by the team, Serkan grabbed the bewildered and increasingly distressed child and hastily left the crime scene.

As soon as he had heard the first whimper, he'd known how this was going to end. Osman had a rare sensitivity around orphaned children. Some might have called it an Achilles' heel, others a redemptive quality in an otherwise entirely cruel and dangerous man. It was true that the boys he had taken in over the years were all from broken homes. It was also true that he had mostly been responsible for breaking them. Furthermore, their adoption or abduction, depending on how you looked at it, enabled him to introduce a refreshed version of the devşirme system of child slavery. The same one favoured by Janissaries in the fifteenth and sixteenth centuries. Many of the entrants into his growing army came through this system, Serkan amongst them.

But it wasn't just about a recruitment drive. It was more personal than that. Serkan had observed this on many occasions. He would never dream of trying to engage Osman on the subject. Yet what he witnessed had a tenderness about it that was entirely at odds with Osman's character. Something reparative, redemptive almost.

Over the years protocol dictated that any boy orphaned through a hit be taken to a safe house for twenty-four hours whilst more permanent arrangements were put in place. It was always boys. Osman had no interest in the recruitment of girls. The boy would then be 'presented' to Osman.

Serkan had slept alongside the boy all that night,

comforting him each time he awoke screaming, and soothing him back into fitful sleep. The crying triggered fragmented memories of his own childhood and abduction. Unlike the boy who was now in his care, Serkan had not been ripped brutally from a loving home, but more taken from a neglectful and abusive father. Nevertheless, it had been a violent kidnapping, and Serkan still remembered the shock and trauma. In many ways he was grateful to Osman for all he had provided, but overall his feelings for his boss and mentor were still riddled with ambiguity.

Serkan saw the turning he was looking for. Bebek was one of the most desirable residential districts of Istanbul. Maybe it didn't have the cachet of the Sultanahmet district, or the draw of Beşiktaş, but what it lacked in popularity it made up for in exclusivity. As soon as he turned, the car started the gentle climb up the shoreline slopes. The higher it got, the more desirable the properties became. After a couple of minutes, he slowed, punched a code into a handheld remote, and turned into a private road just as the discreet steel gates started to swing open.

The tyres of the Mercedes gave a satisfying crunch as they ran over the hundred-metre loose-shingle driveway up to the property. It was a vast contemporary villa of metal, glass, polished concrete, and slate. Serkan pulled up in front of the entrance and killed the low purr of the engine. He let out a long sigh and turned to the little boy sitting in the passenger seat. The configuration of the seat belt only reinforced his diminutive size and vulnerability. He looked close to tears again.

Serkan smiled. 'Zeki, don't cry. Everything is going

to be all right. I need you to be a brave boy for me now. Can you do that?'

Zeki wavered between the courage that had been asked of him and surrendering to the distress that he was feeling. Eventually he looked into Serkan's eyes and gave a small nod.

'Good boy. You are my brave boy. Now come. It is time to meet the man who is going to give you a new life. He is a very important man, so you need to be on your best behaviour. Do you think you can do that for me?'

The boy's eyes started to glisten again, but he nodded an assent, nevertheless. Serkan, who had killed more men than he could remember, with no remorse or anguish, felt a lump in his throat. He jumped out of the car and strode quickly round to the passenger side. After scooping Zeki up, he shut the door with his leg and punched another code into his remote device. The front door of the villa glided open, accompanied by a hushed electronic hum, as Serkan and his package slipped inside the home.

***

To say the villa was furnished and decorated with a minimalist eye would have been an understatement. Osman hated clutter of any kind. His needs for material possessions were few, and he found the lack of belongings positively liberating.

Serkan carried the boy through to the rear of the property and into the study. Unlike the frontage, which was dominantly glass to facilitate views across the strait, the study had no windows in it at all. Osman sat on a chair of chrome and black leather, by a gas fire, which, in the absence of any other illumination, lit up half his face, throwing the other half into shadow. A small, low-level matching table was positioned beside him. On the table were a magazine, a mobile phone, and a small dish of macadamia nuts. The accompanying nutcracker was conspicuous by its absence. There was no other furniture in the room. As Serkan entered, Osman seemed lost in thought, staring into the fire as he slowly rolled some brandy around in a large balloon glass.

Serkan lowered the boy to the floor, standing him three metres or so away from where Osman was sitting. He then retreated to the side of the room to wait. He knew better than to precipitate conversation. Finally, without looking up, Osman spoke in a soothing, gentle tone.

'So, tell me, Zeki, which do you think is best, chocolate ... or ice cream?'

Zeki appeared surprised that this man knew who he was. He looked across at Serkan, who nodded an assertion that he should respond. Zeki looked back at the man. He looked pretty scary, but this was a good question. A fine question.

He thought for a moment, then whispered, 'Chocolate ice cream?'

Osman turned and looked directly at the boy, a smile coming over his face.

'Very good. Good boy.' Osman paused, took a sip of his Armagnac, and then continued. 'Today, Zeki, your new life begins. And it begins with a new name. From this point on, and in honour of Suleiman's grand vizier, you shall be known by his original name. You will, henceforth, be called Sokollu. You will enter into a life of service and discipline. You will learn many things, and you will become a great man. One of an elite strike force. You will also have many friends, and they will all be like brothers to you. You will never have to worry about anything ever again. You will be in our protection. Forever. How does that sound?'

Zeki looked quizzically at the man. He wasn't really sure what he was saying, but it didn't sound like there was going to be any chocolate ice cream. In the absence of that, he could only think of one other thing.

'Sir,' he whispered, 'where is my ma ...'

'Your parents are gone. You will never see them again. But I can offer you something better. Something more profound. I am your father now. Your mother and your father. I am all you will ever need. You just have to trust me. That is all I ask of you. That you trust me. Do you think you can do that?'

Zeki continued to stare at the man. He didn't know what to say or what to do. He just wanted to be home in bed, with his mama by his side. He stared at the floor.

'Sokollu. Sokollu.'

Zeki looked up, realising that it was he who was being spoken to. Osman continued. 'Would you like to come over here and sit on my lap. Would you like a hug?'

At that moment Zeki wanted a cuddle more than anything else in life. He ran over to the man and jumped into his embrace.

Osman looked up at Serkan. 'Go now. Start making arrangements for little Sokollu. And mind, Serkan, I want him to know of honour, and faith, and brotherhood. Most of all brotherhood. Make sure he doesn't just learn how to kill.'

Serkan made the slightest of nods and exited, as an

older woman with a tight grey bun and a sorrowful demeanour entered the room. Her pale skin suggested she was far from home.

'Ahhh,' Osman sighed, 'and here is my trusty housekeeper right on time. Mrs Hart is going to take you now and get you ready for bed. But first, a little chocolate ice cream for Sokollu, I think.'

Zeki smiled, jumped down, and skipped over to the old woman, who looked so sad. She smiled at him and took his hand. As they were leaving the room, Zeki heard the sound of a nut cracking. He glanced back and thought he saw the man cracking the nut in his hand, but surely that wasn't possible.

As the door closed, leaving Osman alone again with his thoughts, he reached for the copy of *Vogue* sitting somewhat incongruously on the table. A striking woman in her mid-forties stared defiantly back at him from the front cover, alongside a caption that simply read 'The Relic Revolutionary.' He flicked through to the puff piece on Dr Solomon, director of the Cypriot Department of Antiquities. As he scanned the article a faint smile crossed his lips. He whispered to himself, 'Hello again, Dr Solomon. Our paths seem destined to cross once more. I think perhaps you may be able to help me in my quest.'

After dropping the magazine back on the table, Osman took another large mouthful of brandy, leant back, and closed his eyes. The holy relic he had spent much of his adult life searching for was now so close he could almost feel its presence. Its magic. Just a little more patience and the mythical heart of Suleiman would finally be in his grasp.

And then he would bring fire and brimstone down

upon this world.

***

Serkan had broken into a run the second he was out of the room. He just made it to the bathroom when he was violently sick in the toilet basin. He had seen countless appalling things in his life, many of his own making, but this new iteration of devşirme always instilled a horror in him. More than any other deed, his part in the kidnapping and recruitment of young children into the brotherhood made him question the path he had chosen the most.

11

November 13, 1629

Constantinople

Things quieted down in the pit in the evening. By this time the inmates had tired of taunting the new blood, and energy was dissipating. What little residual daylight leaked down to the pit base had long gone, and with it, prisoners' spirits also darkened. But the main reason that most pit residents turned in so early was that sleep was the only real escape that the prison offered. For those few stolen hours, inmates could break free of their chains, and escape to a better, or at least more human, place.

This night was no different from any other, with the exception of the unlikely couple who were creeping around the core, where their daring plan would commence.

Jabari offered some final words of advice: 'Emie, this is it. Remember, take your time; you will only get one shot at this. And please be quiet. You know what to do when you get to the top, right?'

Emir knew very well what Jabari expected of him, but he was unsure that he could fulfil this aspect of the plan. He would worry about that later. He elected to just nod confidently.

'Allah be with you, my boy. I will see you'—Jabari looked up to the faint distant light—'up there.'

Emir nodded again and crept over to the point in

the wall where he had decided to start. The beginning was trickier this way, but the other route offered greater difficulties higher up. He took one final look at Jabari, who smiled and crossed his fingers. Emir wished he hadn't looked back and turned his attention instead to the sheer wall before him.

The first step was a challenge in its own right. He had to crouch and then jump up to find the first handhold. If he missed it, or if it gave way, he would tumble back, and no doubt make plenty of noise in his fall. But he didn't. His right hand surely connected with the shallow hole in the wall. Quickly he swung his body so his left hand could find its intended purchase. His right hand had to move again before he got his first foothold, so he didn't hang around any longer than he had to, reaching up for the next grip point.

Jabari watched, unbreathing, as Emir scaled the steep face. The boy seemed like an erratic ant, darting this way and that. *Go on, my boy, go on*, he thought. Emir was already disappearing into shadow, but Jaba stood watch all the same. It was the least he could do.

Emir moved with all the confidence and purpose he could muster. Eventually the giant anchor loomed into view. It looked even more forbidding up close. As he pulled level with the anchor, the temptation to make the jump grew, but Emir had already calculated that he would fail if he jumped from here. Just a few more moves, and he would be perfectly situated. He reached up again with his right hand and found a secure chink in the rock. As he shifted his body weight and grip, a giant centipede crawled out of the fissure and onto his hand. Emir suppressed a scream, but he had instinctively let go of the hold, and his whole weight shifted onto his left hand. He scrabbled with both feet for another foothold. Eventually, one caught his right foot. He cautiously put his right hand back into the crevasse and quickly pulled himself up to his next position.

Below, Jabari watched some gravel and grit scatter to the floor. He looked through his fingers, waiting to see a small boy follow, but none was forthcoming. He shook his head. What had he been thinking?

High above, Emir had reached what he considered to be his optimum jump-off point. The anchor swung gently between ten and twelve feet away. Ten was a crazy distance. Twelve was impossible. Emir knew he had to time his jump exactly right. He looked over his shoulder at the giant mass, slowly rocking. If the timing wasn't difficult enough, he also had to make this jump backwards, as there was no way of turning his body round to face the anchor. He would need to let go with both hands to allow his legs sufficient bend before he pushed away from the surface into the dark.

Emir breathed deeply, let go of the rock face, and pushed away with all his might.

***

Jabari took one last look into the darkness and turned away. It was time for him to put his part of the plan into action. The boy hadn't fallen. That was a good sign, right? Maybe he was still scaling the wall. Jabari didn't know, but he couldn't wait any longer. He crept slowly, carefully round, back into his own territory and then across the dead-man's land and up towards the core structure. It was easy to navigate your way there, even in the pitch-black night of the pit, as the only light down here was within the core. A single torch flame licked at the darkness in the area where the three Bloodguard snoozed, awaiting the final cage trip before they could properly get some sleep.

Earlier, as food was being distributed, Jabari had slipped a small piece of gravel into the bolt hole of the gate facing his territory. Not so much that the key wouldn't return, but just enough, he hoped, to allow the bolt to be sprung back with a metal implement of his own fashioning.

Jabari knew the cage would be starting its descent any minute. He was running out of time. He reached inside his robe and pulled out the small black metal box Emir had seen earlier. He held the box reverentially and whispered down to it.

'Ah, my beauties, it is time for you to play your part.'

***

Emir flew through the air, desperately reaching for something to grab hold of. Had he miscalculated? Was he even now plummeting to his death? The fluke of the anchor suddenly loomed into view. Emir grabbed at it with his right hand and then swung his left arm round. He felt the anchor swaying with this newfound weight. He wasn't sure how long he would be able to maintain this hold, so he slung a leg up onto the arm of the huge metal beast. This allowed him to haul his body round into the palm of the fluke. He had made it. He breathed heavily, chuckling with excitement and relief. The sense of euphoria was invigorating.

After a few seconds to catch his breath, Emir turned his mind to his next task. He now needed to make his way to the central shank of the anchor. The end of the arm felt exposed, and Emir knew that the anchor would probably start to spin as it ascended. The giant maritime tool was of such scale that Emir could have easily walked along the arm, but his better judgement told him to go for the marginally safer crawling option. Emir was no more than five feet from the shank when the anchor suddenly jumped into life and started its slow ascent. Emir redoubled his pace and grabbed hold of the relative safety that the shank afforded in three quick moves. So far, so good.

***

Jabari had taken a calculated risk. If even one of the black assassin spiders chose to turn back towards him, he would be in real peril. They notoriously moved at frightening speed, but they also moved towards the light. Jabari opened the box and shook the three spiders through the bars into the core.

The spiders took a moment to come to terms with their unexpected freedom. Jabari held his breath, terrified of doing anything that might attract the attention of these deadly arachnids. And then, as if they shared a common sight, the three of them moved as one, scuttling towards the flickering torch, and the unsuspecting Bloodguard. A grinding of chains high above told both Jabari and the Bloodguard that the cage was on its way down.

***

Emir gripped tightly onto the shank and, as the anchor made its gradual journey up towards the surface, he reflected on his next role in this audacious bid for freedom. Jabari had been clear that he would have to find a way to handle the Bloodguard at the top of the pit. The only reason the final cage trip didn't bring the retiring Bloodguard down *before* taking his replacement up was that the official guards at the top of the pit didn't want the sweat of operating the cage if they didn't have to.

Jabari had therefore reassured Emir that he would only have to deal with the one man, and he would have the element of surprise. Emir still felt that when Jabari said 'handle,' what he meant was 'kill'. Emir wasn't sure he could do this, but time was running out. The rim of the pit was coming into view.

***

Jabari didn't stop to watch the progress of his beloved assassins but worked on the lock to his gate. He slid a sharpened and re-fashioned iron nail into the bolt hole and jiggled it. If he'd worked it right, there would be just enough spring left in the ratchet that with a little gentle persuasion, it would return to the open position. He rattled it with increasing desperation, but nothing happened. Desperately he gave it one last tug, but nothing. The lock was stubbornly refusing to move. It was over. If he couldn't get through the gate, the whole plan was destroyed. With a mix of anger and frustration, Jabari banged his fist futilely against the gate bars. The lock popped back with a resounding snap, and the gate swung slowly open. He was in.

He wasted no time and ran to the centre of the core. Two of the Bloodguard were even now twitching on the floor, the venom already beginning to exact its paralysing effect. The third man was retreating from his fellow Bloodguard, desperately scanning the ground in search of the deadly spiders. He looked up and saw

Jabari bearing down on him. The prisoner's crazed eyes told the Bloodguard that he was probably better off not taking this man on.

'Hold your run, Jabari, or I pull the emergency rope. You know this whole place will be locked down then.'

The Bloodguard was already backing towards the rope. Jabari realised he wouldn't cover the ground in time to stop him, so, with all his remaining strength, he threw the only thing he had available to him.

***

As Emir crested the surface, he saw the Bloodguard operating the wheels that slowly lowered the cage. Jabari was right. He worked alone. From further away came the faint sound of men's laughter. The official guards were distracted for now. As Emir rose, it dawned on him that if he could see the Bloodguard, then he might also be seen. He gripped the shank tightly and tried to hide behind it, but as he had anticipated, the anchor was slowly rotating.

The anchor came to a jarring halt. Emir looked up to see the Bloodguard gazing right at him. He was about to shout some sort of explanation, although nothing plausible came to mind, when the Bloodguard lit a small pipe and looked off to another dark point.

Emir realised that although the man was staring directly towards the anchor, he couldn't see the boy. Maybe if it had been a full moon, things would have been different. Emir started to believe that the gods were with them. His newfound optimism was quickly vanquished, however. He glanced across to the wall edge. It was at least twenty feet away. An impossible distance to jump. The pit was clearly wider at the entrance than at the base.

Emir stared at the gap with horror. He was stuck. He remembered that the anchor had swayed slightly when he'd jumped out to it. Maybe he could swing it over to close the distance. He tried to rock the huge weight, but, apart from its steady slow rotation, it didn't budge one inch closer to the edge. He looked around in desperation. There must be something he could do. Finally, he gazed upwards at the chain carrying the anchor. There was barely a drop of ten feet of chain from the pulley to the top of the anchor. If he could climb the anchor and those ten feet of chain, he could see an escape route through the block and tackle system.

He pulled himself slowly up the shank, past the balancing band, and onto the stock at the top of the anchor. He was almost there. He could do this. He grabbed the chain, and his palm slipped on the grease. The links were big enough for him to slide his small hands into them to gain extra purchase. He moved up the chain with agonisingly slow progress, but eventually he came to the pulley. As he reached out, the chain jolted back into life. The pulley moved immediately out of reach. The cage was coming back up, which meant the counterweight, with Emir on it, was on its way back down.

***

The black metal box hit the Bloodguard directly on the forehead, knocking him to the ground. Dazed, he continued to pull himself towards the emergency rope. Again, Jabari realised that he wouldn't get there in time. If the alarm was raised, he had no chance of using the cage to make his escape.

Suddenly the Bloodguard let out a small yelp, his eyes bulging with terror as he moved his hand to the back of his neck to feel the spider bite. It was the last feeling he ever had.

Jabari surveyed the scene. He knew the black assassin spider only had the capacity for one venomous bite at a time. It would be a full day before they were fully rearmed. However, sometimes a spider would space its venom amongst two or even three victims. They would still all die; it would just take a little longer. He couldn't see any of the little terminators now, but in truth, even if he did spot one, he wouldn't be able to evade it. He stepped over the third Bloodguard and pulled once on the rope. Once to bring up the cage. Twice to sound the alarm. He quickly stepped into the cage and swung the barred gate shut. Moments later he was making his ascent. *The worst is over*, he thought.

***

The anchor slowly made its return towards the pit base. Emir held on to the stock for grim death and wondered what would happen to him now. He couldn't stay on this thing forever. Below him the cage came into view. As the cage and anchor passed, Jabari stared incredulously at Emir. He gesticulated *what happened?* Emir held his hands apart to indicate that the jump was just too far. As Jabari disappeared into the darkness above, his last message was both palms out in a pushing gesture. The universal sign for *don't move*. Emir shrugged. Never had an instruction felt more redundant.

Jabari quickly pulled on the red frock coat he had

acquired from one of the paralysed Bloodguard. It was much too small for him, but it only needed to provide deception for a matter of seconds. As the cage surfaced, Jabari moved into the shadows and turned away from the Bloodguard manning the wheel.

Once the cage was stationary, the Bloodguard pulled out an oar with a large metal hook fixed to one end. He set the oar into a cradle, fashioned to make a crude rowlock. He then expertly swung the oar out to hook the cage. Once the hook had found a good connection to one of the cage bars, he slowly pulled the oar, and the cage began to swing across to the safety of firm ground.

As he pulled, he chewed on his pipe and complained absently.

'The dead haul was terrible today. Ten this morning and another six tonight. It's all right for you guys down there, but I'm doing all the lifting up here. It always seems to happen on my shift. You wait and see, my friend. You will have one or two tomorrow, nothing compared to my burden. Why do I always get the tough shifts? It's just not fair.'

Jabari opened the cage gate. He sent up a silent prayer of thanks that the guard had been too preoccupied with his own woes to notice anything suspicious and jumped the last couple of feet towards his unsuspecting brother in arms, hissing quietly, 'Stop your whining, you dog. You think you've had a bad day? Well, it's about to get a whole lot worse.'

With surprising agility, Jabari sliced his re-fashioned weapon across the guard's throat before he could cry out. Jabari pulled him close to his face. 'This is for every prisoner you have ever betrayed, you maggot.'

He pushed the man back and let go. The Bloodguard

flailed for something to grab hold of, but there was nothing, and he silently tipped over the edge and plummeted down into the abyss.

Jabari looked towards the recessed room, where the guards sounded like they had been drinking for a while. None thought to come out and check that all was well. He was in the clear. The exit was on the other side of the pit. He ran round the pit edge and started down the corridor of rock that would take him into the shroud of an overcast night. Freedom was his.

***

Emir gripped tightly to the anchor as it continued down. What else could he do? Finally, it came to a stop, and he was back where he'd started. Now what? The only option he could see was to climb back down to the base of the anchor, suspend himself from the arm to reduce the drop distance, and, well, drop. He knew he wouldn't clear the curved bars, but they might break his fall. It was worth a try.

He lowered himself down the shank all the way to the base and decided to make his way out to one of the palms at the end of the arm. If he waited for just the right moment as the anchor slowly swung round, there was a chance that he might survive the fall.

He was halfway out along the arm when the anchor started to ascend again.

***

Jabari saw the night's light at the end of the short tunnel. Freedom was within touching distance. His brother awaited. But what of the boy?

He stopped in his tracks. There was nothing he could do for Emir now. Better that one of them escape than none. Returning to the pit would be suicide. The guards would find the unmanned wheel any second. He didn't owe the boy anything.

Images of his own young brother, another Emie, infiltrated Jabari's thoughts. He absently pulled the red scarf from his pocket and mopped his brow with it. He stared at the scarf, and in that moment, he realised there was only one choice open to him.

He had to go back.

***

As Emir crested the pit rim, he saw Jabari operating the wheel. His heart soared. He knew his friend would never have left him behind. This time Emir hadn't taken any chances. He was already a few feet up the heavy chain, so when it came to a halt, he was ready to reach out to the block and pull himself up onto the system above. As he clambered overhead, Jabari stared up in trepidation. Emir had no fear. No thought that he might fall.

Jabari wondered at that quality, how liberating it was, and how quickly one lost it with age. Not for the first time he also thought how remarkable this boy was. In no time Emir was dropping to the ground beside him.

'I knew you wouldn't leave me, sir. You care about me too much.'

'Don't be such a fool. I just wanted my gold ring back. You don't realise, but I would be as good as dead without that ring. Anyway, I needed to be rid of this wretched scarf. I don't need the inconvenience of having to meet your mother. Here, take it.'

Emir clutched the scarf and pushed it deep inside his tunic.

'You were worried about me, sir. Admit it.'

'Come, Emie. We must away from this hell-hole while we still can. See that opening round the other side. There is the tunnel that will lead us out of this godforsaken place. Go on ahead, I will catch you momentarily. I just have to lock off the wheel to make sure the cage doesn't come flying back up.'

Emir nodded and scrambled along the vast pit edge to the exit on the other side. Jabari returned to the wheel and threw in the locking bolt. Nothing was moving now. He turned to follow after Emir, when a voice behind him shouted,

'Bloodguard. Why is the cage not returned? And why are you leaving your post? Answer me.'

Jabari looked ahead of him into the tunnel recess on the other side. He knew that Emir would be watching from the shadows. He smiled. A proper smile. A genuine smile from one friend to another. He made a subtle wave with his hand and dropped his head.

'By almighty God, you *will* answer me, you filthy pig.'

The guard slapped a hand on Jabari's shoulder. Jabari spun round and stabbed the guard in the stomach with his makeshift weapon. The guard screeched with pain, and immediately the sound of urgent movement came from the recessed rest area. The others were on their way. Jabari grabbed hold of the injured guard and the two of them wrestled, staggering unwittingly towards the pit edge.

Emir could do nothing but watch in horror. Jabari snatched one last look towards where he knew Emir was standing in the shadows. Summoning all his remaining strength, the Egyptian managed to break free of the guard's clutch. Feeling himself beginning to fall over the edge, the guard made one final desperate lunge at Jabari, catching hold of his tunic.

'Run!' Jabari yelled.

'*Jabaaaaa*,' Emir shrieked back, as the screaming guard toppled over the edge, taking Jabari with him.

And then, instinctively, Emir fled into the night.

PART 3
DISCOVERY

12

June 15, 2012
Oxford

Daniel and Paul drove back to London for the most part in silence. They had journeyed up to the funeral in Daniel's Defender, even though Paul was having to do the driving. It would be weeks before Daniel could get back behind the wheel. In truth, he felt so overwhelmed with conflicting thoughts and emotions that he was grateful to have Paul at the wheel.

Since hearing about his father's passing, Daniel had felt a growing sense of unease. The inexplicable rowing accident, right on the back of his own brush with death, just felt too, too … Daniel couldn't pinpoint what made him feel so anxious, but he couldn't shake off the disquiet. Paul had told him he was being paranoid, but Daniel was quick to riposte with the old adage 'just because you're paranoid, that doesn't mean they're not out to get you'. Daniel immersed himself deeper still into his feelings of loss and guilt, fear and disillusion.

He had never really expected to bury his father. Even though the overwhelming majority of people have to lay their parents to rest, it had never once occurred to Daniel that he would have to endure this ritual.

There were probably many reasons for this, but first and foremost was the fact that he had almost completely erased his father from his life. After the events of 1987, they had stopped all communication.

His mother had offered herself up as a peacemaker, then a mediator, then an arbitrator, and finally a simple conduit, but neither party seemed motivated to avail themselves of any of these roles.

They met briefly in 2005 when his mother was first diagnosed with vascular dementia, and again in 2009 when her deteriorating condition required her to be moved into a care home. Both parties blamed the selfishness and callous cruelty of the other for the deterioration of a wife and mother. Daniel had reflected that if ever there was a case for a person staying in a relationship out of a combination of duty, inertia, and fear, then his mother was it. He had hoped that maybe his mother would outlast his father and enjoy a new lease of life in her golden years, but sadly that wasn't to be. Although Daniel publicly loaded all the responsibility onto Randolph, in his heart he felt an enormous guilt for punishing his mother for the sins of his father.

The funeral was a quiet affair conducted within the grounds of the Fairlight estate. Randolph was to be interred within the private mausoleum that already housed the remains of his parents. Family, friends, colleagues: all were noticeable by their absence. Daniel was relieved that his mother wasn't in attendance. It was some small consolation that she was blissfully ignorant of her husband's passing.

Randolph's brother sent a telegram from far-flung Spain expressing his condolences and offering his apologies for not being able to attend 'owing to a previous longstanding commitment'. Similarly, some Foreign Office official had taken the trouble to fill in the blanks on the standard commiserations letter sent out to all current or retired senior diplomats, but no representative of Her Majesty's government chose to attend.

This left a handful of local village dignitaries whom Randolph had favoured with his support or custom, the grounds gardener, and the housekeeper. Daniel noted that neither of Randolph's direct employees looked remotely like shedding a tear at any point.

This pathetic collection of attendees—Daniel couldn't even think of them as mourners—was somehow made even grimmer by the inclusion of a senior member of the Thames Valley constabulary. After all, the death of a local luminary had happened on his watch. Publicly the police had declared Randolph's death as accidental, subject to a coroner's enquiry. In private they had expressed some misgivings to Daniel around the circumstances, but equally stressed that it would be very difficult to establish any evidence of foul play, let alone make a case for misadventure.

Daniel and Paul would have been the only other mourners present but for the surprise arrival of a most unexpected guest. As Daniel and Paul stood by the mausoleum, waiting for the hearse to arrive, Daniel felt something hard press into his back.

A low voice muttered, 'We know it was you that did it.'

Daniel spun round, his heart racing. The man facing him dropped his two fingers and gave a wide, genuine smile.

'Yousef? Is that you? I don't believe it.'

Yousef laughed as he threw his arms around the flustered professor. 'I knew you and your father didn't get on, but really, Danny, this is a bit extreme, don't you think?'

Paul raised an eyebrow and glanced across at the chief superintendent.

'Sorry, Paul,' said Daniel, 'you must forgive the gallows humour of this reprobate. Please let me introduce my oldest friend. This is Yousef Rahman, a partner in crime during my uni days.'

While Yousef and Paul did some introductory sparring, comparing headline notes on their mutual friend, Daniel took a closer look at his old uni buddy.

They'd met at Oxford, where Yousef was also studying anthropology. They had a shared passion for architecture, and Daniel ended up becoming an unofficial tour guide to Yousef on everything Oxford. They even double dated a couple of times. In their last year they drifted apart. Daniel had always felt that Yousef became quite radicalised in that period. Nevertheless, they kept loosely in touch through cards and the odd phone call and would catch up for a drink every couple of years when Yousef was back in the UK.

Daniel felt a bit bad that, in truth, he had lost track of Yousef's career path not long after Oxford. There had been talk of him joining the French Foreign Legion, but when Daniel had asked about this, Yousef had remained tight-lipped. He had always preferred to listen than talk.

'I can't believe you're here, Yous,' Daniel exclaimed suddenly.

Yousef gave his old friend a long look. 'I wanted to be here for you, mon ami. I guessed this would be a difficult time. And, if I'm being brutally honest, I also wanted to discuss something with you, Dan. Something important.'

Curious about what could be so important to bring

the Jordanian back to Oxford, Daniel was about to ask for more detail when the hearse suddenly swept into view.

***

The service had brought all of Daniel's conflicted feelings about his father back to the surface. While he felt abandoned by him, Daniel knew he had forsaken his father through his own inability to forgive. There was a specific event, from a childhood holiday, which he knew had scarred him deeply. Yet the dislocation he now felt wasn't just rooted in a couple of brutal incidents, but in a lifetime of being treated as a disappointment. The more his father had dismissed his achievements, the harder he had tried to impress him, to seek validation.

Despite it all, Daniel felt an overwhelming sense of failure and culpability. Would he ever get out from under his father's shadow, find his own peace, and become the man he knew he could be? Or would he continue to disappoint and fail those closest to him? Suleiman's heart flickered in a corner of his mind once again. Would his crusade to find the lost relic end in glory, or once again would he fall short? Finding it would be a triumph by anyone's standard. He could prove to himself and his late father, once and for all, that he was no failure.

Once the service was over, those gathered were quick to disappear. No wake had been arranged, and none was expected. There really was no appetite to celebrate this life. Despite everything, this made Daniel feel desperately sad.

Yousef had stayed, waiting to have a private word with Daniel. Paul noted this and excused himself, leaving them to it. Daniel smiled his thanks to Paul and poured two generous glasses of Glenmorangie for himself and Yousef. The two sank into a pair of Chesterfield armchairs and sipped quietly on their drinks. Finally, Yousef broke the silence.

'I don't have very long, so I'll get right to it. I've come here with a warning, Daniel. I think you could be in danger.'

'Me? What are you talking about, Yous? I'm a bloody anthropology professor, for Christ's sake. The most danger I meet is the occasional advances of an overzealous student.' Even as this dismissal was formulating, Daniel started to feel the truth of Yousef's words. He had known that something wasn't right.

'I can't say too much, Danny—even this warning may be putting you at risk—but I thought that, well, I owed you this much.'

'I don't understand. What do you mean?'

Yousef paused, selecting his words carefully.

'Okay, here goes. You're about to get a job offer. There's a shipwreck salvage operation currently underway off the coast of Cyprus. They're trying to recover a seventeenth-century Ottoman merchant ship. The biggest ship of its type ever discovered. It's called the *Colossus*. They're looking for a specialist consultant. An expert in the golden age of the Ottoman Empire. In short, they're looking for you. It's going to be very tempting to take it, Dan. Don't.'

Daniel waited for the explanation, but none was forthcoming.

'Is that it? Is that all you're going to say? Come on, Yousef, you can't seriously expect me to …'

'I'm sorry, Dan, that's all I can tell you.' Yousef

glanced down at his watch. 'Even being here puts us both in peril. You're just going to have to trust me on this. I'm sorry, I've got to go.'

Daniel stared open-mouthed as Yousef stood, put on his jacket, and walked towards the drawing room door.

'Yousef. Come on, don't leave like this. I don't know what you're worried about. You of all people should know that nothing on God's green earth would compel me to get on board a ship.'

Yousef sighed and turned back to give Daniel a rueful look. 'There's something else. Something that *could* compel you. None of the salvage team know this, but ... there's some chatter through certain backchannels that the heart of Suleiman the Magnificent may have been on board the *Colossus*. Don't be distracted if you hear anything like this, Danny. It's fool's gold. A mirage. A fiction designed to spring a trap.'

***

Two days after the funeral Daniel sat in his home study, trying to finish writing an article on Mehmed II and the conquest of Constantinople. He'd had sleepless nights trying to make sense of his conversation with Yousef. Could there really be a lead to Suleiman's heart coming his way?

The ringing of the phone, normally a source of great irritation whenever it broke Daniel's concentration, came as a welcome diversion that morning.

'Hello? Good morning, Professor Fairlight. My name is David Nightingale. I'm calling on behalf of a company called DIVE, Deepsea Investigation Venture Enterprises. I wonder if I might have a moment of your time to outline an opportunity you might be interested in.'

'I'm sorry, David, but whatever it is you're selling, I'm not interested. I don't want to be rude but ...'

'You misunderstand me, Professor. I'm calling about a job opportunity.'

As the penny dropped, Daniel felt a shiver run through him. Yousef had been right. What did this mean?

'Sorry, David, is it? Yes, actually, I was expecting your call.'

'Really, Professor, how so?'

Daniel's mind raced. How much of his conversation with Yousef should he reveal? 'A friend tipped me off, you might say.'

'Who might that be?'

'Yousef? Yousef Rahman. In truth he wasn't exactly encouraging me to take the position.'

'Really? I'm surprised to hear that. He's always spoken very highly of you.'

'Sorry. You know Yousef?'

'Certainly. He is our dive lead on the expedition.'

'I'm sorry, you've lost me. Are you saying that Yousef is part of this project?'

'Most certainly. A vital cog, you might say.'

As David continued to outline the 'chance of a lifetime' on offer, Daniel googled DIVE to check out their credentials. It turned out he was speaking to Sir David Nightingale, chief executive of DIVE. The website was very impressive. *These guys know what they're doing*, Daniel thought, as David started to wrap up.

'Listen, Professor, I'm sure you're a very busy man. Why don't I email over some materials? You can take a look, and then let's chat.'

As soon as the email arrived, Daniel scanned

through the material Sir David had shot across. He couldn't remember the last time his pulse had literally raced from a prospect, but this was something else.

From careful analysis and endless weeks of online cross-referencing, they estimated the *Colossus* had sunk around 1630. Although obviously eroded by time, it was still largely intact and amazingly recognisable as a vast shipwreck lying on the seabed. But by far the most exciting data concerned its potential cargo. Drawn from fourteen nations and civilisations, it was thought to include glass and jars from Belgium, Spain, and Italy; ceramics from Yemen; blue, green, and cream glazed jars from the Persian Gulf; and, perhaps most significantly, porcelain from the Ming Dynasty—potentially the earliest Ming porcelain to ever be found in the Mediterranean.

Whilst Daniel could tell that this cargo was a possible game-changer, he noted that the prospect of Suleiman's heart being among the artefacts wasn't mentioned once. It appeared that Yousef had been right in his assertion that the sacred relic was not within the project parameters. It wasn't even on their radar. What was it Yousef had said? *A mirage.*

Nevertheless, one line from the prospectus material really grabbed Daniel— 'Like a sunken time capsule, this major historical discovery provides the first tangible proof of a maritime Silk Road linking China, India, the Persian Gulf, the Red Sea, and the West. This find tells the story of the beginning of the modern world'.

Daniel had been working on his mental chalkboard in the background as he assimilated all of the material. Sometimes he just employed this technique to map out a way forward, as with his ill-fated London run, but on other occasions the chalkboard would appear when he had a decision to make. Chalk lines drew pictures of ancient galleons and contemporary dive ships, providing a constantly evolving backdrop to his evaluation of the merits of joining the team. He squashed down the sense of foreboding pooling in his gut and the memory of Yousef's worried expression.

'You had me at "sunken time capsule",' Daniel finally murmured to himself.

***

Later that same week, Dr Maria Solomon found herself alone in bed, in a private room of the new medical facility, the Near East University Hospital. She picked up a magazine and immediately put it down again. Maria didn't do hospitals and she didn't do waiting.

The room was all white walls and light oak. It said professional yet understated. Fully spec'd, yet minimalist. Reassuringly expensive, and entirely fitting for a woman of her status.

She had been the director of the Cypriot Department of Antiquities for three years now. She had always believed that she would follow her father into the medical profession, even undertaking a degree in medicine. Having become a doctor, she then took a master's in medical science. Her career seemed mapped out, and not a day would pass by without an old family member or friend of the family telling her how proud she would have made her father.

And then everything changed. She was invited by a French Cypriot boyfriend to join an archaeological dig in Larnaca, exploring the ancient city of Kition that lay beneath. The boyfriend didn't last, but the archaeology bug did. Another five years at university, in large part underwritten by her childhood inheritance, and Dr Solomon found herself on a very different trajectory. Her first paid work on this new career path was at the Cyprus Museum, as a receptionist.

And, as is so often the way, now she was director of antiquities, she began to wonder whether this was really what she wanted. Her naturally restless spirit had seen her seeking out fresh challenges over the last year or two. She had embarked upon a progressive programme of decentralisation of museum artefacts to local museums around the island. The Cyprus Museum was rightly proud of the fact that it housed only those artefacts found on the island, but Maria's ambitions stretched a little further. She was keen to make space to be able to accommodate Greek and Cypriot pieces from beyond Cypriot shores. Her real passion was Ottoman artefacts, given Cypriot history of Ottoman rule prior to British colonialism.

Her progressive ambitions had somewhat divided opinion, but she had never been much on people pleasing. When she further announced that she wanted to create a maritime archaeological department and museum wing, more eyebrows were raised in the ministry, although the press applauded the vison and ambition of the firebrand director.

She knew it was a conceit, but she had quite liked the 'firebrand' characterisation. She realised it didn't play well in the stuffy government corridors, but, if they couldn't take a joke ...

Maria appeared unstoppable in all her various pursuits, but a month ago all that had changed. In her thirties she had been diagnosed with bradycardia, a genetic disorder passed down from her father. Doctors reassured her that her slow heart rhythm was no cause for concern, prescribing a reduction in stress levels and a new medication regime. She embraced the latter element whilst dismissing the former.

This strategy finally caught up with her whilst she holidayed in Rome. A guided tour of the Unseen Colosseum, specially arranged by a fellow museum director based in Rome, was rudely interrupted halfway through when Dr Solomon suffered what was later diagnosed as a heart attack. She recuperated in the Salvator Mundi International Hospital in Rome until she was deemed fit enough to fly, at which time she was transferred directly to the Near East University Hospital in her hometown of Nicosia.

When her doctor recommended that she immediately have a pacemaker fitted, he did it with such assertion and urgency that her natural inclination to 'carry on regardless' was nipped in the bud. Nevertheless, she had proved a most impatient patient, as she waited for the operation to be organised.

Expecting the arrival of nurses to take her down to theatre at any moment, she jumped slightly when her phone ringtone of 'Mamma Mia' started to blare.

'That's enough to give me a bloody heart attack,' she murmured as she hit the accept icon.

'Hello? Maria? Is that you? It's, er, Daniel here. Daniel Fairlight.'

'Danny? What a surprise. To what do I owe this long-overdue pleasure?'

Daniel caught the sarcasm in Maria's tone. 'I know, I know. I promised to call, but, well, you know how it is —one thing led to another, and I never got round to it, then I felt embarrassed that I hadn't called and didn't have a good excuse, then ...'

'All right, all right. I will forgive you. Just stop with the pathetic excuses, please. So what finally got you to pick up the phone? Everything okay? You're not sick, are you?'

'No. Why would you say that?'

Maria rolled her eyes at how clumsily she had betrayed her own circumstances.

'No reason, so what's your news?'

While Daniel brought her up to speed on recent events in his life, Maria reflected on what might have been. Daniel really had been the nearest she had ever got to real love. She still remembered the demand she had hurled at him. *It's either Suleiman's heart or mine.* Something like that. She smiled grimly at the irony. Her naturally confrontational style had got her into more than one or two scrapes over the years, but she would always regret that particular ultimatum. She tuned back in.

'Sorry to hear about your father, Danny. I know you two had your differences, but still. Listen, Dan, I've got a meeting about to start. Can we pencil in a fuller catch-up in a couple of weeks?'

'Well, that's what I was really calling about, Maria. I think I'm going to be spending a bit of time in Limassol soon and thought we might be able to get together.'

'What the hell are you doing there?'

'I've taken a consultancy role on a marine expedition, and we will be based out of Limassol.'

'Hang on. Are you telling me you've taken a job on a boat? You? With all your hang-ups. How have they persuaded you to do that?'

'First of all, it's a ship, not a boat. And anyway, the work just sounded interesting. I was looking for a bit of a life change and this just came along.'

'All sounds very fishy to me, Danny. I don't think I'm getting the whole story here. Anyway, sure, you get your skinny white backside down to Limassol, and I will definitely come and see you. Meanwhile, I've really got to go. You take care.'

Ten minutes later Maria was being wheeled down to theatre. As she mused on the call from Daniel, she had a realisation that hit her like a thunderbolt.

'Of course,' she shouted out loud. The nurses looked down at her but didn't say anything. Maria smiled to herself. How had she not joined the dots straight away. There *was* only one thing that would get Daniel out to sea. He was still searching for Suleiman's heart. *You dodged a bullet there, my girl.* What on earth had she been thinking?

She was still wondering this when the surgeon asked her to start counting backwards from ten.

13

November 14, 1629

Constantinople Port

Emir felt like he had been running for hours. The pit was further out of the main city than he had remembered. The guards had given chase for a while but soon realised it was hopeless in the pitch black of night. He could see them with their torches, but they were never going to be able to make him out. Nevertheless, he ran.

As the guards turned back to deal with the bloodbath at the pit—four Bloodguard dead, as well as one of their own—they shouted out a choice selection of final threats designed to rattle the young boy.

'We'll find you. We know where you live. The whole city will be on your tail tomorrow. You can run, but you can't hide. We *will* find you. We always do.'

The threats gave Emir wings, even though he knew he was no longer being pursued. Were they right? Would he not be able to hide?

He finally came upon the outer wall of the city. Exhausted, he slumped down against the stones. The second he rested, the tumultuous events of the last few days came crashing in on him. What was going to become of him? He was completely alone, separated from his mother, on the run from the law, without a friend to turn to. A mixture of panic, distress, and overwhelming fatigue enveloped him, and he started to sob uncontrollably.

Emir saw no way forward, and no way out. His short life was over. He pulled out the red scarf and wept into it. And so, a child, utterly defeated and bereft of any vestiges of hope, cried himself into a dreamless sleep.

**

At five in the morning Emir was awoken by the distant call to prayer. He got to his feet and contemplated his next step. As is so often the way, a little sleep and a new dawn instilled some fresh momentum in Emir. Not hope maybe, but not despair either.

He looked along the wall and, in the absence of any better idea, started moving northeast along it. As he walked, an idea started to take shape. Something to give him a little purpose. He would find Jabari's brother and return the ring that had been entrusted to him. If this was to be his last act, it was a fitting one. Noble even. Slowly his aimless stroll became a purposeful walk.

As the sun gradually rose in the sky, another dismaying thought came to Emir. What if the ship had already set sail? He dimly remembered Jabari telling him yesterday that his brother's ship was sailing today. Was it only yesterday? That was what all the urgency was about. He quickened his pace, realising that he couldn't afford to think negatively. The ship would still be there. It had to be. He needed it to be.

Emir knew that the gates at the north end of the wall would already be open. A steady stream of traders would be flooding into the city, either delivering goods to a ship or more speculatively hoping to pick up some business along the busy southern bank of the Golden Horn estuary. His guess was that the *Colossus* would be near the mouth of the estuary, as that's where the biggest ships always seemed to dock. That could mean a walk of at least two miles. He glanced at the sun's progress. He was running out of time.

He moved easily through the gate, past the Blachernae Palace, and into the throbbing city he knew so well. Progress along the estuary was slow as the crowds swelled, but Emir continued with pace, weaving through the throng like some feral cat. As he passed through the Constantinian wall gate, he felt more positive. Now he was through the inner wall, there couldn't be too much further to go. He didn't even see the guard until he felt himself being lifted off the ground.

'And where are you going in such a hurry, young man?'

Emir summoned up his best indignation. 'Unhand me, you oaf. I am running errands for my mother, and if you cause me delay, you will have her to answer to. And then I won't be able to help you.'

The guard's fellow officers roared with laughter.

'Less of your lip, you little urchin. Now be still and empty your pockets. We have word that pickpockets are working in this area today. Let us see what contraband you might have acquired.'

Emir reached into his pocket with the righteous air of an innocent man and felt the ancient Egyptian gold ring on his palm. If the guard saw this, it was all over. Confidently Emir pulled out his pockets and held out his empty hands. The guard shrugged with disappointment. He had felt sure this little vagabond had something to hide.

'On your way then, boy, and don't let me catch you

loitering here again.'

Emir recalled a line he had once heard a much older boy use to sound bolder than he actually felt. Emir had been so impressed that he had committed the words to memory and enjoyed using modified versions of the quip whenever the situation presented itself. This was a perfect moment.

'Of course, Officer, and may I just say that I leave you on this fine morning feeling all the safer for your commitment and vigilance.'

'Why you …'

Emir ran off laughing. Never had he pulled off his father's vanishing coin illusion so effectively. And this time, with a ring.

It was barely seven o'clock as Emir approached the mouth to the Golden Horn, and the city was now teeming with industry and commerce. Emir knew this area particularly well, as it was a favoured daydreaming location for him. Watching ships set sail for exotic lands had often been a source of inspiration for Emir. Although he had always believed that his destiny was never to leave the city, he still dreamt of seafaring adventures like most boys of his age. Pirates and smugglers. Sea monsters the size of buildings and warrior tribes in the farthest corners of the world that would eat you as good as look at you. It made him giddy just to think of it.

As his mind wandered, he had been subconsciously making his way towards the first main docking point for ships as they approached the Golden Horn, situated in the old Prosphorion Harbour.

Without any warning, the ship came into view. Emir gasped. It was gargantuan, it was majestic, and most importantly, it was still there. Momentarily all Emir's troubles evaporated as he stared in wonder at this maritime marvel. Some crates were still being loaded, but all the other signs suggested that the *Colossus* was about to set sail.

A multitude of instructions were barked out on deck from a variety of different officers. Their voices could be clearly heard from the quayside. Crowds had started to gather to witness the epic departure. Merchants strode up the gangway, looking for all the world like they owned the ship. Landlocked loved ones shouted final best wishes. Small boats that Emir knew were called preventors were already positioned with giant ropes to help manoeuvre the giant ship away from the dockside.

The captain stood on the forecastle surveying the activity around him. A giant of a man, his long brown locks blended into a huge beard. Captain Barbarossa was a furious sight. Suddenly he bellowed across the ship's deck.

'Faster, you rabble. The wind is turning in our favour. I would be gone from here within the hour.'

Emir snapped back. He was almost out of time. How was he going to find Jabari's brother amidst all this frenetic activity? That's when he saw a man standing on the dockside bawling his own set of directives. He was obviously a man of some authority; maybe he would know where Shabaka could be found. Tentatively Emir approached the man, waiting for an encouraging window.

'Get away, boy. There are no jobs here, just accidents waiting to befall you.'

'Sir, if I might have a moment of your time.'

'That is the one thing where all my currency is spent.

Now away with you before you feel the back of my hand.'

'I'm sorry, sir, I can't leave. I have a duty to complete. The man that tasked me with this job paid heavily so I could be here. I need to find a man called Shabaka.'

'What do you want with him?'

'That is between me and him, I'm afraid.'

Shabaka eyed the kid. What was his game? How did he have Shabaka's name?

'You've got some nerve. I'll give you that. Well then, you've bought yourself thirty seconds, so talk. I'm Shabaka.'

Emir stared up at the man. How could he not have spotted the echoes of Jaba? Sure, Shabaka was a little leaner, maybe a little taller, but the face that stared down at him now was almost identical. The reddish skin, the piercing brown eyes. His head, rather than being close shaven, was completely bald, but that aside, his demeanour was a mirror image of his brother's.

He suddenly realised he was not prepared to say what now needed to be said. Not in the slightest. How did you tell a man that his brother was dead? Maybe he should start with some good news.

'I have something for you. I think it's important to you. I wanted to ...'

Emir's words failed him as he held out the ring.

Shabaka's eyes widened as he grabbed the jewellery. 'Where did you get this? Tell me quickly, boy, while you still have a tongue to speak.'

'I got it from your brother, Jabari.'

Shabaka's voice hardened like liquid iron turning to steel.

'Why have you got it? He would never surrender this

ring unless he was under duress. Be careful now, boy, very careful. Where is my brother?'

Emir's eyes started to moisten. Because this was a hard message to deliver, but also because he was confronting its truth for the first time.

'I'm sorry, sir. I'm so sorry. He's—he's dead.'

Shabaka moved quickly then, grabbing the boy and pinning him up against the warehouse wall. His eyes were wet also, but a blaze of anger shone through.

'You come to me with his greatest treasure in your possession and tell me he is dead. Why shouldn't I strike you down right here?'

'In truth, maybe you should, sir. I do feel that I have had some part to play in the loss of your brother. But before you exact your vengeance, I would have you know that he was my friend and protector. He died so that I might escape the Bug Pit. He died so that I might live.'

Emir appeared utterly deflated as he made this assertion, more to himself than anyone else. Shabaka sensed the grief within this boy and loosened his grip a little.

'I want you to tell me everything. Leave out no detail. I would know how my brother departed this world.'

***

Once the dam burst, Emir couldn't stop talking. He confessed to his ill-judged thievery, how he came to be caught, and the courtroom travesty. He described descending into hell and how Jabari befriended him. He chronicled the tortuous escape bid, and finally he recounted how Jabari sacrificed himself, allowing Emir to claim freedom.

'Yes, but how did you come into possession of his ring?' Shabaka probed.

Emir described the pact that the two of them had entered into, explaining how he came to have the scarf returned, but Jabari hadn't had time to take back his ring. Shabaka carefully sifted through Emir's words, as if trying to understand a puzzle. Finally, he nodded and spoke softly, more to himself than Emir.

'It wasn't just your life that he saved, my boy. He knew what to do to save my life also.'

It was now Emir's turn to try and decipher what he was hearing.

'I'm sorry, sir, I don't understand. What do you mean? How could he have saved your life?'

Shabaka seemed to realise that he had said too much, and, as a result, not nearly enough. He decided to change the subject. 'He killed four guards, you say.'

'Absolutely. Maybe more. Six or seven. In fact, I think it was more like ten.'

'Yes, ten,' Shabaka affirmed. 'That sounds about right. My brother may have died, but he went down fighting, killing ten of the dogs. Maybe more.'

'That's right, sir. That's how it happened.' Emir hesitated, considering the wisdom of returning to the earlier subject.

'He said that you also had a ring, sir, that they were a pair. That these rings were really important to you both. Is that right?'

Shabaka turned away from the boy and busied himself lighting his pipe so he wouldn't have to respond. Emir knew, as he always did, to hold his tongue. To allow this moment to breathe. Eventually Shabaka turned back and gazed down at Emir.

'Right, boy, we need to work out how to get you on this ship, and we need to be quick about it.'

'Oh no, sir. I'm sorry, but that can't happen. I must get home to Mama. She will be worried sick about me. I have to go. Right now.'

Shabaka knelt in front of Emir and placed his hands on the young boy's shoulders. He looked into his eyes and sighed. He didn't even know this boy's name, but Jaba had seen something in him. Enough to include him in his escape, and enough to entrust him with this commitment. One he had completed admirably. He composed his thoughts.

'What's your name, boy?'

'Emir.'

Shabaka smiled wistfully. Emir thought he knew why but said nothing.

'Right, now I want you to listen very carefully to me, Emir. You cannot stay here. You hear me. You cannot stay. If you were just a petty thief, they wouldn't bother about you at all. But now you're a prison escapee and, at the very least, a party to murder of prison officers. They will leave no stone unturned in hunting you down, executing you, and then executing your mother. I'm not saying this to frighten you—I'm saying it because it is a fact. If you stay here, you *will* die. Your mama ... will die.'

Emir stared at the Egyptian and saw the truth of what he said in his eyes. He looked up at the ship and then back over his shoulder at the city he had called home for all of his thirteen years. He felt the wheel of his life turning. What did his future hold? What would become of him? He looked back again, as if he might be able to catch his mother's eye. Maybe a wave. Some kind of goodbye.

Shabaka saw his turmoil.

'Listen, Emir. Tell me your address and your mother's name. I will make sure that word of your fate reaches her when it's safe. I promise you this as you made a promise to my brother.'

All of a sudden it had become really important to Shabaka to save this boy. To give the death of his brother some meaning, some worth, a little dignity perhaps. This boy might yet be Shabaka's salvation.

Emir finally nodded and stared back at his new protector.

'I will come with you. But you must make a promise as your brother did. You must promise to look after me. Not leave me or let me get hurt. Can you make that promise?'

Shabaka signalled his assent. He glanced up at the ship's open loading bay, middeck. It was now or never.

He took Emir's address details and quickly called to one of the dockworkers that he knew and trusted. He outlined the favour he needed, and the dockworker nodded immediately. Shabaka had looked after him more than once. The workhand gave Emir a reassuring wink and then disappeared into the growing crowd. Shabaka had already called over another man; this one looked like one of the ship's crew.

'This man is a friend of mine. He is a Christian, but you can still trust him. He will be looking out for you on the ship, yes? I will get to you as soon as it's safe.'

Emir nodded. Things were moving quickly. What had he agreed to? He could feel the panic rising. Shabaka grabbed his wrist and pulled him into the warehouse. He quickly described his plan to Emir. A plan that, itself, was only a few seconds old. Emir stared out across Constantinople one last time, not knowing if he would ever see his home again. There was no going back now.

***

He imagined that this was what flying was like. The container he had been squeezed into was filled with smaller chests containing oils and spices, together with large rolls of fabric: silks, cotton, and linens. It was the final consignment to be loaded onto the ship, and it was currently swinging thirty feet in the air. He couldn't see anything apart from needles of light breaking through the crate panels. This made the sensation of movement ever stranger. Being unable to anticipate the movements of the huge wooden box left him experiencing a strange floating sensation. Not altogether terrible, but still very disorientating.

Meanwhile his sense of sound was already compensating. He could hear sailors shouting instructions to each other, but behind that was an orchestra of other noises. Ropes stretching, pulleys squealing, gulls screeching, and, more distant still, the sound of distressed animals. Chickens and goats, Emir speculated.

Without warning the violent swinging slowed to a gentle rock and then a sense of returning to earth. Well, returning to something. The shafts of light disappeared one by one, and he was enveloped in a new level of darkness. Fresh voices were in dialogue, and this time he could make out words. Not just words but also their meaning.

There was some debate about where this last container should be positioned. One voice became dominant. Insistent that it be tucked in the far corner. Emir recognised the tone. Was that Shabaka's friend? Suddenly the box landed with what sounded like a resounding crash, from the inside at least. Emir sat perfectly still, not daring to move a muscle.

Slowly the voices dissipated until Emir was left in silence. He wiggled his hand in front of his face but couldn't make out even the most basic of movements. Abruptly a voice whispered right next to him. He jumped and let out a little gasp.

'Shush. In the name of God, Emir, you must be silent. If you are found now, you will be thrown overboard without any discussion. We must get out to sea before we can think about your leaving this crate. Do you understand?'

Is this a test? Emir thought. A trick. Should he answer or not?

'Emir? Answer me. Do you understand? Are you well?'

'Y-yes, I understand. Yes, I'm well,' Emir whispered back.

'Good. I will come back presently with some food. Don't go anywhere.'

Footsteps faded away, and for the second time in less than twenty-four hours Emir thought how unnecessary this instruction was. He looked around at his latest prison. He couldn't see anything, but he twisted his head around anyway. He felt doubt welling up inside him. What had he done? What was going to become of him now? He rested his forehead on his knees and sighed deeply. What would become of him indeed?

***

In the absence of the usual markers, Emir quickly lost track of time. Night and day blurred together. Shabaka's friend kept his promise and brought food and a small vessel for Emir to relieve himself in. Had the wait been an hour, or a day? Emir had no sense of it. His limbs started to ache, then seize up, as he had no room to stretch, let alone stand. His mind started to play tricks also. He saw animals in the crate with him, then people. His mama, asking him if he was eating well. His papa assuring him that he would be home soon. He wanted to reach out, to respond, but he dared not. Then the stomach pains came. Waves of gripping, squeezing pain. Was he dying? Was this what dying felt like?

On the third night, which may have been the thirty-third night for all Emir knew, he experienced his most vivid hallucination. His prison of blackness was broken as razor-thin shafts of light once again stabbed their way through the wooden panels. He heard voices approaching. The light flickered and guttered in a different way from the daylight he had seen before. He peered through a small crack in the wood. Two men stood not ten feet away from him. One held a flaming torch up high; the other was holding a metal box. They seemed so real to Emir.

The one with the box panted, 'Do you think it best to hide it down here?'

'Certainly,' the other replied. 'If we keep it in any of the cabins, it will be discovered. It is buried down here. There is no reason for anyone to go into the farthest reaches of the hold. It will be safe here. Trust me. Anyway, we have our orders.'

'If you say so, Mustafa. It seems risky to me, but you're in charge.'

'That's right, and don't you forget it. Nothing is going to go wrong, you hear me. People are relying on us. Great glory awaits us all. Just focus on that. We shall hide this box here for now and see if anyone finds it. I've put enough coin inside to tempt even the most devout. If it is found, it *will* be taken. If it's still here by the time we get to Dubrovnik, we'll know it's a good hiding place. Onur, I have heard rumour of a sacred artefact that is going to be smuggled on board in Dubrovnik. A powerful relic that will guarantee success for our mission.'

Onur stared blankly at his associate.

'You idiot. Hurry, hide that thing over there in the shadows.'

'Over there, where all the rats are scurrying about. That 'over there'?'

'In the name of Suleiman's heart. Give it to me, you excuse for a man. How you ever got recruited I will never fathom. I'm regretting negotiating for your place on board this ship already.'

The men moved out of view. Moments later the light disappeared. Emir marvelled at how real this picture had seemed. Even more real than when his mama had attended. He felt himself drifting back into sleep, and down into dark dreams. A Janissary was chasing him around the ship. No one else could see either of them. Jabari appeared beside the ship's captain and shouted, 'You know him, Emie. Remember. You know him.' Emir tried to answer, to ask Jabari what he meant, but he couldn't speak. His mouth was sealed shut, and his feet were melting into the deck. He could feel the Janissary's breath on his neck. There was no escape.

But then a blinding light shone down on him from

above. Was he being taken up to heaven now? Was he saved after all?

'Emie. Emie. Wake up, you're dreaming. You will wake the whole bloody ship with your cries. It's all right, you're safe. It's me, Shabaka. Emie, it's me.'

Emir squinted up at the light, and into the eyes of Shabaka. He smiled.

'What are you smiling for, you grinning fool?'

'Jaba called me Emie. Your brother called me Emie.'

'Well, *you* are my brother now, Emie. Now be quick; I have come to liberate you from this prison box. Tonight, you will sleep under the stars. And such stars the like of which you have never seen. Tonight, your new life really begins.'

14

June 29, 2012
Istanbul

Duman Osman prowled around his hotel room like a caged tiger. It wasn't the confines of the room that provoked him, though, but the dead time on his hands. He had always hated waiting. It seemed like such a waste. Of time, energy, potential, and productivity.

He sat down at the cheap desk that complemented all the other furnishings in the tawdry room. Osman was no stranger to sleeping rough, slumming it, but when it came to airline flights and hotels, he would, under normal circumstances, spare no expense. First class and penthouse apartments all the way.

But this night had altogether different requirements, and the two-star Hotel Ottoman ticked all the boxes. Payment in cash. No ID requirement. Nominal front-of-house presence, and lowbrow clientele, some of whom were clearly purchasing rooms by the hour. Just the name alone was too much for Osman to resist. The greatest empire the world had ever seen, reduced to a two-star knocking-shop. Was this hotel not the perfect metaphor for how Istanbul, Turkey, and the whole golden age of the Ottoman Empire had faded to become not much more than an historical footnote? How had his ancestors allowed such a fall from grace?

Of course, he knew about the betrayals that were at the heart of this appalling decay. If his brothers had been honoured and retained in the way that they should have been, then the world would be a very different place today. Lines on the map would be radically altered. But there was no use dwelling on past treacheries. There would come a time for reckoning. For now, Osman knew that he needed to focus on the very present opportunity. Providence had determined that he would be instrumental in leading the Turkish people to a new era of dominance and glory. It was his destiny.

In the meantime, when the compulsion came over him, he would seek out the company of sex workers. He didn't like this phrase. It was too functional. Too forgiving. Like what they did was somehow acceptable. Conventional even. It didn't convey their degradation or capture his abhorrence. Not that he liked the terms 'whore' or 'prostitute' any better. These were fallen women, plain and simple. They could not be forgiven, and they could not be saved. They could only be punished and eradicated. He had no interest in the sex. These sessions were about power and justice. Sure, he would brief Serkan to select women that would appeal to his tastes. His second-in-command knew what he liked, and always delivered. He also helped with the clean-up, which was useful. Osman had recently sensed some emergent reluctance on Serkan's part in fulfilling his duties. Almost a note of disapproval. He made a mental note to have a word with Serkan at the next opportunity. *Maybe a performance review is in order*, he mused.

He picked up the prospectus and marketing materials on his desk. DIVE didn't know it yet, but they were going to deliver unto him the means to finally call his people to arms, start the glorious revolution that had been so long in gestation. His people had been in exile for an eternity, but he would be their salvation.

He had been monitoring the pursuits of the DIVE Shipwrecks Project for some time, hoping against hope that they might stumble across materials that would be of interest to him. They would probably have got there a lot quicker if they had been in possession of his intelligence, but that was never an option. They needed to remain unwitting servants to his plan. And then, when his patience had been stretched to its very limits, site 127Qr came along. Site 127Qr. Truly the answer to all his prayers.

He flicked through to sections that focussed on the exploits of the *Triton*. A real warhorse of a ship, almost a hundred metres long and primed for serious work at sea. Rumour had it that the ship had been requisitioned by the Royal Navy in 1982 to act as a minesweeper in the Falklands conflict. Osman found the ship's war credentials particularly appealing. He longed to be on the ship himself, pulling the strings and overseeing progress, but that was an impossibility. He would have to settle for a more vicarious experience through the eyes and ears of others.

He clicked on his laptop mousepad, and the DIVE website came up. He selected the 'About Us' dropdown menu option and then scrolled to the latest entry, a profile of theologian and anthropology professor Daniel Fairlight. He scanned the introductory text. 'We are thrilled to announce that we recently secured the services of Professor Fairlight in a consultative capacity on the *Triton* dive at site 127Qr. Professor

Fairlight's pre-eminence in the field of Ottoman history and artefacts will prove invaluable in supporting this groundbreaking archaeological expedition'. Blah blah blah. Osman mused on the value of Fairlight to his own agenda. If his team hadn't bungled the London hit following Randolph's refusal to apply influence on his son, the professor wouldn't even be on the project. Now he was, would he prove an asset or an obstacle? *We will see*, Osman mused.

His phone vibrated. He glanced at the caller ID and elected to take the call. Before the caller could say anything, Osman jumped in. 'I only have a few minutes, so don't talk, just listen.'

'Sir.'

'I know you did your best, but Fairlight is in play now. We can't do anything more about that. Meanwhile, I need you to find another way to get our operative onto the ship. You understand what's required, right?'

'Yes, sir.'

Osman ended the call. He stared at the profile picture of Daniel on his laptop screen and considered the state of play. He had done everything possible to ensure that Professor Fairlight didn't join the operation, but maybe his involvement could yet prove beneficial. Undercover operatives could exploit his presence, and if all else failed, he still had the Cyprus Ports Authority as backup. Serkan had come through with a private number for Dr Solomon, and Osman had fed her just enough information to ensure that she would take his meeting. Once he saw her eye to eye, he knew he could tempt her to accommodate his requests. The opportunity to address a more personal issue at the same time was an amusing ... what was the phrase he was searching for?

'Fringe benefit,' he murmured with relish.

He returned to the paperwork and flicked ahead to the section on the *Triton*'s crew, but in his haste the papers slipped from his hand and spilled onto the floor. Not for the first time he cursed his false right arm, scooping the materials up with his more agile left hand.

Duman Osman had learnt to live with a prosthetic arm for the best part of forty years. Initially he had worn a wood-and-leather contraption that did little more than create the impression of an arm. Twenty years ago, he had replaced this with a lightweight carbon fibre arm that also attempted basic grip actions. But it was five years ago when Osman had what he liked to call 'a serious upgrade'.

Although the technology was still in its infancy, Osman applied some considerable persuasion to a leading surgeon in the field of bionic prosthetics. When he first heard about it, he dismissed it as fantasy science fiction for the pop culture generation. But when he started to google 'bionic prosthetics,' he was staggered at the amount of progress that had been made in the field, and what could now be achieved.

He underwent a series of experimental and entirely illegal operations, which involved implants inserted directly into remaining bone combined with painstaking nerve-reassignment surgery. After six months of painful rehab and microscopic gains, Osman started to be able to move his prosthetic arm, simply through his thoughts. Another six months and he was picking up needles off the floor.

Once in a while the mental pathways would get cross-wired momentarily, and he'd end up with papers all over the floor, but in the main he was now operating his arm without even thinking about it. The best part was that he had further encouraged his surgeon to make some calibration adjustments to the torque, push and pull settings, and limiters within his arm. And that did get him into some serious Steve Austin territory.

It was worth the inconvenience of a few broken crystal glasses and cracked iPhone screens to be able to crush the bones in a hand or lift a man's weight with a minimum of effort. His favourite trick, to attract attention or generally intimidate, was to crack a macadamia nut with his bare hand. He found that the application of three hundred pounds of pressure to a nut tended to focus the mind.

Osman had always subscribed to a 'rule by fear' philosophy. Forget hearts and minds; if you had them by the balls, they would damn well follow you anywhere. And if you had their balls in his particular vicelike grip, well, then you would see how far real loyalty got you. Not that inspiring visions and financial incentives didn't have their place. Much progress could be made with the right carrot, but soldiers who feared you would act without hesitation. As Capone famously said, 'Much can be achieved with a kind word, but more can be achieved with a kind word and a gun.'

Osman's thoughts were interrupted by a knock at the door. She was two minutes late. Something unforgivable in Osman's book. She'd soon learn the gravity of her error, Osman thought. He smiled as he flexed his prosthetic hand and considered which bone he should apply some justice to first.

'Good evening, my dear,' Osman said as he opened the door. 'You must be Paige. Please come in—we are going to have such fun together.'

***

Sometime later Osman heard the young woman's mobile phone ringing. He sat naked on the edge of the bed and reached into her red patent leather clutch. Her phone had an image of a baby as its wallpaper. The baby was eighteen months old.

The woman had picked the name Ruslan for her firstborn because it meant 'lion,' and he was truly her strong little man.

The phone bleeped again, indicating a message was waiting. Osman listened; it was from Paige's mother. She was saying how much she was looking forward to seeing her grandson this weekend. She finished by telling Paige to keep herself safe, as she always finished her calls.

Osman grinned, reaching over to the bowl of macadamias on the bedside table. As he idly cracked one open, an amusing idea came to him. He hit the camera function on the cell phone and took a picture of Paige. Despite the blood, you could still just about make out it was her. He texted the image to Paige's mother, and then carefully placed the phone back in her bag.

Yes, he thought, things are coming together nicely.

15

January 8, 1630

Dubrovnik

Emir had scampered up the rigging on the starboard bow of the *Colossus* as soon as he heard the 'land ho' cry from the crow's nest. Although the ship had never been more than one hundred nautical miles away from land so far on this journey, it was still exciting to know a destination was in sight. They would be docked in Dubrovnik before dusk.

They had been at sea for fifty-five days, apart from a three-day stop in Athens to refresh provisions and both deliver and acquire cargo. To Emir it had seemed like a lifetime. More had happened to him in the last two months than in his entire life.

On the first night that Shabaka had rescued him from the crate, he had slept on the deck. He'd believed that he was hallucinating—he could clearly see land on both sides of the ship—until Shabaka explained it. They had already crossed the Sea of Marmara and were now entering the Dardanelles Strait. Shabaka proudly proclaimed that this was one of the narrowest straits in the world, and only a captain and crew of the very highest calibre could navigate it. As they sailed through the pinch point of the strait at Cannakale, Emir gazed in wonder at the twin castles looking down on them from opposing banks. The ship glided through the gap and on into the Aegean Sea.

Shabaka told him to get his head down; tomorrow was going to be a long and challenging day. He had acquired a spare roll-up mattress for Emir, and the young boy crawled onto it, suddenly overwhelmed with fatigue. He lay on his back and looked up through the sails.

'You're right, Shaba,' he said, 'the sky *is* full of stars.' He was asleep before the last word left his lips.

***

Emir was roughly woken early the next morning by his new protector, who was ready to train him. Shabaka suggested that the red scarf poking from his shirt would likely disappear before many more nights had passed. He showed him a knot that could not be easily untied and then fastened the scarf around his neck. And there it had stayed.

To earn his place on the ship, Emir had to learn how all the ropes worked, their roles, and the knots employed for different purposes. Crew lives were risked daily, dependent on knots being fastened correctly and varying rope types being deployed appropriately.

Alongside deckhand duties, Emir was also tasked with rope maintenance. This wasn't as physically demanding as scrubbing the deck, but it still took its toll. Broken ropes needed rethreading, pitch was used to seal seams, and then pine tar would be applied regularly to protect the rigging against the weather. On many nights in the first month, before Emir's hands hardened, he would crawl onto his mattress with bleeding fingers. But he never complained. Instead, he would redouble his efforts the next day, offer to take the more mundane tasks away from other crew members, and work longer hours than even the most seasoned sailors.

After two weeks at sea, he had already garnered a reputation as a hard worker who didn't complain, and always did reliable work. He learnt quickly, and he never made the same mistake twice. Shabaka was amazed by Emir's work ethos. Jaba had seen something special in this boy too, he mused. Shabaka's plan was to make Emir an indispensable part of the crew long before he caught Barbarossa's eye, or indeed that of any of the senior officers.

Emir's efforts and natural charm meant that within the month he had become adopted by the crew. One so young and so small would not normally have a role on board, but this only further reinforced his appeal. After a week he was 'the boy with the red scarf'; after a month he was simply 'Red.'

The only crew members that Emir seemed unable to win over were Mustafa, the sailor with the dice, and Onur, Mustafa's friend. The one whom Shabaka had reluctantly given a position to when his brother's place became available. Normally Shabaka would trust his inner voice, which always had Jaba's tone and inflection, on any choice or decision he made. Any nagging doubt and he would pull out, irrespective of the information in front of him. Mustafa had been a rare exception. Shabaka hadn't trusted him then, and he didn't trust him now. Nor his friend. His hard tone with Emir only further convinced Shabaka that he had made a rare error of judgement with this one.

He would have let the both of them go at their first port of call in Athens, were it not for the fact that he'd lost four seamen on that first leg. It was not unusual to lose the odd sailor overboard, either through excessive drinking or inclement weather, or more likely, a combination of the two. Even more rarely, a falling-out could result in a sailor meeting a watery end, but this would only manifest on the longest voyages where tempers wore thin and tolerance thinner still. To lose four crew in a fifteen-day leg, with no challenging weather to speak of, was unusual. Unsettling even.

To compound matters, a merchant joining in Athens provided a recommendation of four crew he had previously sailed with. The merchant represented his endorsement direct to the captain, and Shabaka was presented with a fait accompli. He took his role as one of the hirers of crew seriously and prided himself on always being able to sort the monkfish from the minnows. These men seemed able enough, but they weren't his. He decided to roll with the waves on this occasion. You had to pick your battles with the captain, and he still hadn't declared his stowaway. Circumstances would force his hand on that front soon enough, but even Shabaka couldn't have seen those events coming.

Emir had continued to insinuate himself into the fabric of the ship whilst still going largely unnoticed by the officers. As well as becoming something of a mascot to the crew, he established rapport with the ship's merchant community. A diverse collective drawn together through common interests and mutual goals, the merchants hailed from around the Mediterranean: Italian, Portuguese, Spanish, Flemish and, of course, Ottoman.

They were drawn to Emir's friendly nature and tireless efforts to please those around him. For the merchants this meant that he became a 'runner'. When they required a chess set, he would run to the cabin to retrieve one. When their sherbet dispenser was dry, he would get fresh provisions. Their predilection for cups of sherbet was something that Emir quickly came to appreciate. The mix of sugar, lemon juice and rosewater, flavoured with musk and amber grease and infused from a bespoke brass dispenser, tasted like nothing Emir had ever experienced. Otherwise, he would make endless cups of coffee and appreciate the exotic beans that the merchants carried.

On one occasion, he watched a merchant perform a cheap card trick for his associates. They seemed impressed enough, but Emir had seen him palm the duplicate ace and thought the trader needed a bit more practise. He was wise enough to hold his tongue and applaud politely with the others, but when the merchant asked if anyone else could match his powers of illusion, Emir didn't hesitate. Within minutes he was pulling coins from merchants' ears, making them disappear completely, and then miraculously discovering them in spectators' pockets. The merchants marvelled at the trickery, calling friends over to witness the amazing illusions. He had earned himself a couple of coins before Shabaka noticed that he was drawing too much attention and quickly allocated him duties below deck. The merchants groaned. Entertainment on a ship was always in short supply, and anything in short supply carried a premium. Any storyteller or musician on board would be feted. But to have their very own magician amongst them. How fortunate.

In the absence of entertainment, the merchants fell into well-versed conversations. Their talk was mainly of their cargo, or the potential threat of pirates. Many would sharpen knives with stones they kept sheathed in bronze collars. Sometimes they would allow Emir to work the stone himself, a chore he really enjoyed.

As with the crew, there were one or two of the merchants who didn't fall under Emir's spell. One man in particular took exception to Emir. Initially, he had indulged Emir's inquisitive nature as the boy showed an interest in the depiction he was carving into his walking cane. The merchant's natural pride was encouraged by the boy, who'd learnt from an early age how disarming compliments could be. The merchant pontificated about how the first ship in his carving was a galiot, representing the superior Ottoman fleet, while the smaller second vessel was a Christian galley—a vastly inferior ship. The galiot had captured the galley and was towing it victoriously into harbour. Emir was genuinely impressed by the detail of the carving, but as he asked more about the Ottoman fleet's worldwide reputation, the merchant suddenly took exception to his questioning.

'You ask too many questions, boy. Away with you.'

Emir had learnt the fine art of retreat from his father. Where others might protest their innocence or continue pursuance of a strategy that was clearly delivering a diminishing return, Emir would recognise all the signs and make himself scarce. Something about this merchant unnerved him anyway, like they had got some previous unknown history. Like Shabaka, Emir had learnt to trust his instincts. There was something off with the merchant. He resolved to work on that riddle for a while.

Athens was another exciting chapter for Emir.

Shabaka taught him how to load and unload crates, and he learnt quickly. He could also leave the ship for a night and venture into the ancient capital of Greece. Under Ottoman rule it had slipped into what would prove to be a very long decline, but through Emir's eyes it appeared mythological, otherworldly almost. He marvelled at the ancient Greek legacy of buildings and monuments. He had thought that Constantinople was a breathtaking city, but nothing could have prepared him for the wonders and grandeur of this, one of the oldest cities in the world.

Shabaka accompanied Emir on his first shore leave and continued his education by introducing him to the questionable delights of a Greek taverna. Emir expressed some reservations about drinking alcohol, but Shabaka would brook no refusal. By Emir's second glass of wine, he completely saw the sense of Shabaka's words. By his third, he couldn't make sense of any words whatsoever.

The following morning, Emir felt fairly sure that he was dying. The more he expressed his concerns, the more his friends laughed. When he declared that he must have eaten something bad, they really started to roar. It was the first day on the *Colossus* where Emir barely pulled his weight. No one blamed him, but he resolved to never partake of alcohol again. A resolution that he kept until the day he died.

***

As the *Colossus* prepared to dock in Dubrovnik, Shabaka sat Emir down for an overdue conversation.

'Emie, tell me, how have you found your time on board?'

'Shaba. It's been the most exciting time of my whole life. I never dared to dream of such adventures.'

'Do you not miss your mama, Emie? Your home?'

Emir instantly lost his animation and stared down at his makeshift boat shoes that Shabaka had crafted for him. He immediately felt his eyes filling up at the thought of everything he had left behind. While he was occupied, he wouldn't think about these things, and he felt fine. But when he considered the weight of the choices he had made, they would rush in on him, suffocate him, and lay bare the thirteen-year-old boy that still dwelt within. Shabaka reached out and squeezed his shoulder.

'I know, Emie. It is hard to be away from home. Now listen to me: I want to tell you what our future has in store.'

Emir despatched his troubles with a speed that only a child possessed. He stared attentively at Shabaka. What wonders would be revealed to him now?

'Soon, we will dock in Dubrovnik. It has long been a tributary of the Ottoman Empire. This means that the city pays a monthly tribute to your great sultan. In other words, this is still part of the Ottoman Empire. But from here on in, Emie, we are going to be travelling much further afield. It is going to be a long time before we stand on Ottoman soil again. When we are done here, we will move further north until we reach the Italian city of Venice. Then we will sail around the Italian coast until we reach Naples on the western coastline. From there it's on to France and Marseilles and then Spain, Barcelona. Finally, we will head east towards my homeland, stopping in Tripoli before our final stop in Alexandria.'

Emir stayed attentive although he had never heard of any of these places. They sounded exotic and magical.

'Is Alec Sandra your home, Shaba?'

Shabaka smiled and felt a pang of real affection for the boy. The anguish of his brother's loss had been significantly diminished by the company of this remarkable young man.

'I was born in Cairo, but we were brought up in *Alexandria*. Not Alec Sandra.'

Prompted by Shabaka's use of *we*, Emir's thoughts returned to Jaba. Their time together had been fleeting and frenetic, but he missed his prison protector like he had been a lifelong friend. He felt overwhelming gratitude that Shabaka had filled the hole that Jaba had left.

'Shaba, can I ask you a personal question?'

Shabaka nodded, still smiling.

'Was Jaba really a prince? And does that mean that you are a prince too?'

Shabaka pulled him close to hide his tears.

'Yes, my brother truly was a prince. As for me, you will have to decide that for yourself in the fullness of time. Now listen to me, Emie, this is important. You have to make a big decision here. You can stay on the ship and continue on our six-month voyage, or …'

Shabaka paused. This was so much that he was putting on the boy. He wondered, not for the first time, where Emir's breaking point was. When would it all overwhelm this valiant child? Emir stared at Shabaka with eyes that betrayed his concern.

'… or I can arrange for you to get on a different ship. One that will take you back home to Constantinople. I know the boatswain on this ship; he would give you work and protection. You would get back home safely, that I can promise.'

Emir studied Shabaka as he spoke, horrified by this rejection. Something snapped, and he shouted at him.

'You don't want me anymore. You are trying to get rid of me. You promised to look after me. That you would never leave me. You promised, *you promised.*'

Shabaka shook his head and grabbed the boy's shoulders.

'No. *No*,' he shouted back. 'Listen to me, Emie. There is nothing that I would like more than for you to accompany me on this journey—see this voyage through to its conclusion. But it is going to get hard now, Emie. Food will become scarcer; weather conditions will get harsher. Are you sure that is what you want, when you could be home with your mother? I think it would be safe to go back now. You will have been away for a full seven score days by the time you return. They will have stopped their search for you by now. Think very carefully, Emie. There is no turning back from here.'

Emir stared out at the beautiful Dubrovnik skyline, bathed in late winter's setting sun. He thought about his mother and his home. He thought about everything that had happened to him since that fateful day at the market. It seemed years ago. A lifetime away. He looked back at his friend.

'I will return to my mother one day, Shaba. I have made that promise to myself. But not today. For now, my home is here with you. I want to see this through.'

Shabaka responded gruffly, not wanting to show his pleasure at Emir's choice. 'Fair enough. Remember, though, when the storms batter us like we are no more than gulls in the open sea, remember I warned you. Now, go belowdecks and bring up the ropes you have been working on. We shall need them to prepare the cargo winch.'

Emir grinned. 'You wanted me to stay. I can tell.'

Shabaka raised his arm in a mock threat, and Emir scuttled into the bowels of the ship, laughing as he went.

***

As Emir ran gleefully through the mighty ship, he was blissfully unaware of how quickly his destiny was taking shape in the shadowy backstreets of the Dubrovnik port area.

A soldier stumbled up to a dimly lit, heavy oak door. With one hand he retained a weighty sackcloth bag slung over his shoulder. His other hand made futile attempts to stem the flow of blood from a gaping wound in his stomach. The head of the arrow was still embedded in the Janissary's gut.

Unable to find the strength to reach for the bell chain, and unwilling to let go of either burden, he summoned up his remaining energy and smashed his head into the door. He then collapsed, praying that Allah would let him complete his duty before taking him.

After a few moments, the door swung open, and three heavily armed men pulled the soldier unceremoniously into the vestibule. A fourth man, the group's commander, knelt by the soldier. After releasing a robe from round his neck, he bundled it up and gently slid it under the soldier's head.

'Your journey is over, brother, your mission

complete. Rest now while we tend to you.'

One of the armed men also knelt and offered the dying soldier some water, but he desperately pushed it away. From somewhere deep inside he found the strength to try and speak. With shallow breath he whispered, 'Captain ... sent mess-message. Our duty has ... has been fulfilled. It is our honour to ... to ...'

'Take your time, my son.'

The soldier coughed up blood as he blurted out, 'No, must tell you. It is our honour to pass the heart of Suleiman into your hands. Now ... it is done.'

'Yes, my brother. It is done. I thank you. Understand, your aga ...'

'But,' the soldier wheezed, 'but, why?'

The aga frowned.

'Why what, brother? What still ails you?'

As the soldier uttered his final words, the four men bearing witness to his death stared with alarm at each other.

'Our captain asks ... with Suleiman's heart ... why, why were we not invincible?'

***

Emir scurried towards the aft of the ship. Whenever he moved among the merchants' crates, stepping carefully across the ship's timbers, he remembered his first days on the *Colossus*. His time in the crate seemed surreal. And like so many dreams, whenever he tried to recall exactly what happened, pieces were missing. Something felt just out of reach. Emir couldn't shake the feeling that he had forgotten something important, but the harder he tried to grasp it, the more it slipped through his fingers.

As he gathered a knot of ropes, he heard a distinct repeated tap against the ship's frame. He recognised the sound immediately but couldn't place it. It grew louder, accompanied by raised voices. Something in their tone told him to hide. He ducked behind the nearest crate and shrank into the shadows. He forced himself to take deep breaths and slow his heart rate.

The group came to a halt; the tapping ceased. Something stirred in Emir. A shrouded memory. Then he heard a clear voice.

'Mustafa. Check if it's still there. Quick.'

There were heavy footsteps and then a gruff confirmation that 'it' was indeed still there.

Like an avalanche, flashes of recollection pulled into focus and joined together. Emir knew who the man in charge was; he knew who Mustafa was; he knew what *it* was and exactly where *it* was hidden.

'Good, that's settled. We shall place our true treasure here in due course. It will not be found. Now remember, our most esteemed aga will be joining us, along with three Başhaseki. These men were generals in our army before they were banished. They reported directly to the sultan. They will not suffer fools. Everything must go according to plan. Is that understood?'

Emir heard three, possibly four voices of assent. He stilled his breathing. This was clearly an extremely dangerous conversation to overhear. He couldn't get caught eavesdropping.

'We shall meet here again tomorrow night, with our esteemed leader. We can give him encouraging news of our positive progress. And we will have the honour of securing that which has been lost to us for so long. Now, quick, back on deck. We are docking.'

Emir waited a full three minutes before he dared venture from his hiding place. He vividly remembered his vision in the crate. Seeing two men planning to hide a box. And now he knew that one of those men had been Mustafa. And the man he had just overheard giving the orders was the merchant who had been engraving the walking stick. It was the tapping of the stick he had heard before. But more than that, he now knew the true identity of the merchant. And he wasn't who he was purporting to be. Emir was breathless with the revelations. He needed to tell Shabaka right away. But what had he just been privy to? Who were these agas and Başhasekis? And what was the treasure of which they talked so reverentially? Again, he felt that something was just beyond his grasp. Something that might make sense of what he had just witnessed.

He heard his mama's voice telling him to leave well alone, but then he heard his father's voice saying *open the box*. The temptation was too much; he had to know. Quickly he crept to the plotters' hiding place. His hands swept around in the dark until they hit a hard surface. A metal box. Excitedly, he tried to open the box, and to his surprise the lid popped straightaway. It wasn't locked. He stared at the contents within.

It was more money than Emir had ever seen in one place. Gold and silver pieces. He gazed transfixed by the riches. Was this the treasure of which he'd overheard? He wasn't sure. Something wasn't right here, but what was it? He closed his eyes and calmed his pulse rate, breathing slowly in and out. This wasn't the treasure. It was a placer, a marker. Securing the space until the real treasure came along. He took one last agonising look at the coins and then snapped the lid shut.

As he returned the box to its hiding place, he felt the ship's hawsers mooring to the portside. They had docked, and he still had the cargo net ropes with him. Putting the jumble of troubling thoughts to one side, he dashed back up to the main deck.

By the time he got topside, the ship was a hive of activity. Crew ran in all directions. Merchants fretted on the stern buttresses and the forecastle, while the senior officers barked instructions out. Shabaka spied Emir hurtling towards him and held his hands out in a *where the hell have you been* gesture. A breathless Emir tried to explain, but there was just no time.

'Shaba. I must tell you something. It's important.'

Shabaka responded gruffly, 'It will have to wait. I've been searching for you.'

'But Shaba ...'

'Emie. Don't try my patience further. Just help rig up the yard and stay.'

Emir jumped over to the port side and attached the ropes that would manage the pulley system and lift the cargo net. He felt a little bruised. Shabaka had never spoken so harshly to him. He resolved to channel all his efforts into the job at hand.

The crew on the dockside had started to take the strain on the giant bag of ropes, called the 'net,' when one of the guide ropes slipped loose. The net, now untethered, swung wildly, and caught a sailor round the neck. The crewman lurched violently over the dockside, suspended by his throat. The slip ropes pulled tight around the weight of the man, as they were designed to do. He reached desperately to his neck but couldn't loosen the tightening knot.

Crewmen stood motionless, shocked rigid by this

unexpected turn of events. Emir, instead, pictured the angles and opportunities, as he had when faced with the pit wall. He instantly saw the best course of action he could take.

Grabbing a knife from a nearby merchant, Emir clambered furiously up the portside rigging, and flung himself onto the swinging net that was strangling the crewman. He caught the net just above the frantic sailor and slashed at the encroaching ropes.

Within a few seconds, the ropes violently snapped, and the sailor dropped into the waiting arms of his fellow crewmen below. A cheer went up, and Emir punched his fist in a victory salute, completely unaware that the integrity of the net was now compromised and no longer able to hold him.

In his moment of triumph, he suddenly plummeted down to the dockside. No one had anticipated this second body falling, and most eyes were on the recovering sailor. Two of the closest crew desperately tried to break Emir's fall, but he caught his head on one of the mooring posts before landing on the quayside.

'Shaba,' the closest sailor cried, 'come quickly, it's Red.'

Shabaka ran over to the port side and stared down at the horrifying scene below. The rescued sailor was already tentatively getting to his feet, but just along from the gathering crowd, Emir lay motionless. At first, Shabaka thought Emir's scarf must have loosened, as something red caught the sunlight. But it wasn't the scarf. Blood pooled from his skull onto the quay. Shabaka started for the gangway when an authoritative voice boomed across the silence.

'Shabaka. Would you mind informing me who that

child is, and what the thundering fuck he is doing on board my ship.'

Shabaka stared up at Captain Barbarossa and prayed for some convincing response to come to mind.

16

July 23, 2012

The Levantine Basin

'Professor Fairlight. Good to meet you. Come this way please sir. How good a swimmer would you say you are?'

Daniel had been anticipating this question from the moment that he accepted the position with DIVE. His role would be primarily office based in London, but he knew he would be required to spend significant time on board the *Triton* also. Not being able to swim would have been a deal breaker.

Fortunately, following the fateful events of 1987, Daniel had found an instructor doing an intensive course for adult beginners. He braved the ruthless sessions despite his fears, and felt his swimming improved significantly. Since then, however, he'd hardly been. If he was being honest, he'd never truly shaken off the inherent peril he felt in the water.

DIVE, however, made facing the water unavoidable. By the time he realised the full seafaring implications of his decision, it felt too late to back out. The company required him to pass a commercial sea medical with their team. Although he no longer needed the wheelchair, he felt that they weren't catching him at his best. He had pushed hard with Paul and his physio to step up remedial work on both his arm and ankle, but he was still far from firing on all cylinders. Fortunately, the team weren't concerned about the 'temporary setbacks,' being more focussed on overall fitness. Before the accident, Daniel had been his fittest in more than twenty years, and those needles still registered in his favour. With the pass stamp in the bag, Daniel hoped the major hurdles were behind him.

Until he heard about the 'Survival at Sea' course, which he was facing today. When asked about swimming, Daniel elected for a political but positive response.

'Good enough for your requirements, I hope, but no more than that in truth.'

Thirty minutes later, he was bobbing around in an Olympic sized pool with the other candidates. There was a remarkably realistic wave machine, augmented by three instructors operating hoses. Without the mandatory life jacket, Daniel never would have gone in the pool. It was hell. Only the vague promise of discovering Suleiman's heart kept him in the water until the instructor blew the whistle.

Between gulps of air, desperate determination, and the flaring pain in his still-healing arm, Daniel asked the crucial question. 'How did I do?'

'Well, Professor,' a broad Scottish accent came back, 'I canna see you making a late entry into the Olympics, sir, but I'm gonna sign you off all the same.'

***

Three days later, Daniel was in DIVE's HQ in London. He'd have a quick orientation session with Sir David before catching a flight to Limassol the following morning. The east end of London was pulsating with 2012 Olympics anticipation. Daniel felt a twinge of regret at missing a home Olympics, but the potential compensation was just too much to resist.

As Daniel jumped into the Addison Lee saloon, Sir David warmly shook his hand.

'Remember, Professor, you are on board to help provide some context for our discoveries. You'll develop some commentary on the wider significance of what we find, but you're also there to inspire the team. Give them a direct line of sight between the work they are doing in the most hazardous of conditions, and the higher purpose of our contribution. We are rewriting bloody history here, my boy, and you have hold of the pen.'

Daniel noted, once again, that no mention of Suleiman's heart had been made. Either Sir David's team was keeping that information close to their chest, or Yousef was right, and the project team was wholly unaware of the true potential of this salvage operation.

Upon arrival in Limassol, he was met at the gate by a vivacious woman in her mid-twenties who introduced herself as Jenny Brand. He needn't have worried that he might not spot his contact. What she lacked in overall stature she made up for in the hair department. Her small pale face and features were framed by a huge uncontrollable thatch of curly ginger hair.

'Everyone calls me Brandy, which sounds like some kind of porn name, but I'm stuck with it. Better than Ginge, I guess. I'm one of the dive team. Kal asked me to meet you. I'm the newest recruit, so I'm the one that gets all the gofer jobs.'

Daniel raised an eyebrow in mock offence.

Brandy spotted it and looked aghast. 'Oh fuck. Not that this is a chore, Professor. I didn't mean it like that. Shit, and now I've said 'fuck' to you as well. This isn't going well, is it? Sorry.'

Daniel smiled. 'Nothing to be sorry about, Miss Brand. As first impressions go, yours will live long in the memory.'

They both laughed, Daniel warming to the sheer energy of his new colleague. He was usually slow to establish new relationships, but he already knew that he and Jenny Brand were going to get on famously.

'Thanks, Professor,' she said, hailing a taxi, 'and please, 'Brandy'—none of this 'Miss Brand' bollocks.'

As they sped off towards the docks, Daniel quizzed Brandy on the team, and she showed little restraint in giving him the inside track on key players.

'Well, where to start? You've got two core teams: the ship's crew and the scientific crew. If we take the ship first, may as well start at the top. Captain Murphy was born on this ship, I think. He has a, er, complicated relationship with the vessel. Loves it, hates it. Protects it and brutalises it in equal measure. Mind you, he won't have anyone else say a word against the *Triton*. If you do, you're likely heading overboard.'

'I'll be a model of diplomacy.' Daniel had already wheeled out his mental chalkboard and was busily drawing up some kind of DIVE family tree diagram.

'Okay. His full name is Conor Murphy. Some of the crew call him Con, but for the rest of us'—she pointed between the two of them—'he's Cap or Captain. Then there's the first officer ...' Brandy fizzed through a list of names, ranks, roles, and responsibilities, providing flourishes of gossip and colour as she went.

'Is there going to be a handout on this orientation. I haven't been taking notes, and I'm beginning to think that this might be the most useful briefing I'm going to get.'

'You're all right, Prof.'

'Please, Daniel. Dan.'

'Sure Prof, that's going to happen. Anyway, those are the key players on the ship's crew side. All the others you'll get to know as you go along. Now, the project team. So, my boss is Kal. Khaled Farouk. An Egyptian. Lives for marine archaeology. Really knows his stuff. Bit of an academic. He's gonna love you.'

Daniel frowned in playful protest. 'I'll have you know I was considered for the Olympics in my younger days.'

'Whatever you say, Prof. Don't get me wrong, he's an action man too. Loves getting in the water any chance he can get. Constantly complaining that everyone else is having all the fun. He should try a shift or two of ROV maintenance—now that's a hoot.'

'Sorry, ROV?'

'Getting there, Prof, getting there. Don't jump ahead now.'

Brandy was off again, namechecking divers, maintenance crew, a restoration team, and a variety of other roles. Daniel was just deciding that he was going to have to get to know names, faces, and jobs as he went along when a familiar name suddenly popped up.

'The other key ROV pilot is Yousef Rahman. We think he's Jordanian, and he's definitely something of an enigma. But hang on, you know him, right?'

'Used to.'

'Well, maybe we'll finally get to see what's behind the curtain. You must have a bunch of stories to tell us about Yous, right?'

Daniel reflected on this while Brandy continued her

who's who. Yousef and he went way back, but he hadn't even mentioned he was part of the operation when he appeared at the funeral. He couldn't shake off the nagging feeling that Yousef wasn't being entirely open with him. Daniel resolved to have an honest conversation with his old friend at the earliest opportunity. At the same time he made a mental note to contact Maria whenever he next had a moment to see if they could arrange a meet. He didn't really hold any romantic notions anymore—he knew that he'd blown that a long time ago—but still, it would be nice to reconnect. As they pulled into the port area, he tuned back in on Brandy's energetic commentary.

'And that's about it. Which is pretty good timing, 'cos here we are, Professor, home sweet home.'

Daniel wasn't exactly sure what he'd been expecting, but what he'd imagined broadly fell into the Russian oligarch superyacht category. Lots of white and chrome, helipad, satellite instruments spinning, deck pool, that kind of thing. One look at the *Triton* and he realised that sundowner cocktails were going to be in short supply.

The ship was huge, and evidently not pitching to the cruise fraternity. She looked like she had a few miles on the clock. A functional blue-and-white livery, blue hull, white cabins: this was a commercial merchant ship that had clearly been customised to accommodate the very specific requirements of the DIVE Shipwrecks Project. Daniel swallowed, and not for the last time he wondered what he'd got himself into.

'Come on, Prof. Let me introduce you to Cygnus.'

As Daniel stepped onto the quay, crashing waves echoing from his childhood started to thunder in his ears. That familiar sense of going under the surface, helpless to respond, washed over him. He momentarily closed his eyes and regathered his balance and resolve before following Brandy onto the gangway and across to the waiting *Triton*.

***

Daniel had pictured some giant Greek fitness instructor ready to put him through his paces, but Cygnus proved much more formidable than that. The Remotely Operated Vehicle was, without a doubt, the star of the ship. The size of a small tank, the machine was a multipurpose marvel. Daniel surveyed the beast, made all the more impressive in its bright-yellow livery, and wondered what kind of investment had gone into building her.

Essentially a trenching support vehicle, originally designed to help lay seabed pipeline, Cygnus had been customised to perform state-of-the-art precision survey and marine archaeology work for the *Triton*. A dazzling array of hydraulic arms, propellors, filtration systems, brushes, claws, LED lights, thrusters, limpet devices, probes, suckers, blowers, and video equipment were all harnessed to a gigantic rig. Lights, cameras, and indeed, action, Daniel mused. And all this kit was designed to operate two kilometres below sea level. It was quite something to see up close.

'This way, Prof,' Brandy called. 'They're waiting for us to start the briefing.'

She led him quickly up some stairs and into the main control room below the bridge. About a dozen people sat in the operations centre, which was rammed with banks of control panels and monitors. Daniel felt increasingly like the proverbial fish out of water. He may as well have been on board the *Starship Enterprise* for all he knew. The group was in an animated debate about the timing of some event as Daniel slipped in unnoticed. Brandy gave a theatrical cough, and everyone turned to stare at the interloper. This was really going very well.

A North African man jumped up to save Daniel any further blushes.

'Professor Fairlight, I presume. Professor, I'm Khaled Farouk. I'm the project lead here, though you wouldn't think so given the level of respect I'm currently commanding. Please call me Kal. Ladies and gentlemen, please welcome our esteemed professor on board.'

The group provided a surprisingly warm set of cheers and whistles accompanied by enthusiastic applause. Daniel assessed Khaled, who would be his main point of contact. He seemed somewhat unassuming. Average height and build. Short dark-brown hair, light-brown skin, glasses, clean shaven. It was only when he smiled that his features came to life. Brandy had declared him as 'handsome without being striking,' which, Daniel thought, seemed a fair review.

Kal went around the room doing introductions, and Daniel put faces to the names and caricatures that Brandy had sketched out earlier. Before he could get to Yousef, the Jordanian jumped up and gave Daniel a big hug.

'Hello, my dear friend. It has been too long. I am so pleased to see you.'

Daniel smiled, sensing that Yousef didn't want the team to know about their meeting a few weeks earlier. At the funeral Yousef had worn a dark suit, but today he was back in a uniform altogether more familiar to Daniel. His tanned face looked weather beaten, reinforced by his ever-present stubble. His countenance was dominated by a large nose, but it was his eyes that Daniel would be able to pick out in a crowd. They were barely more than two sunbeaten slits; Daniel was always reminded of the actor Lee Van Cleef from the spaghetti westerns. And, of course, he was wearing the ubiquitous red-and-white keffiyeh scarf. As far back as college days Daniel could not remember a time when Yousef wasn't wearing his scarf.

As the old friends embraced, the room exchanged knowing winks and quizzical stares. Finally, a distinctive Newcastle accent piped up: 'Professor, hi, I'm Davy. We're all really looking forward to hearing some stories about your time with Yousef. He's famously guarded about his past, like.'

Daniel was about to explain that he probably didn't know much more than they did when Yousef chipped in.

'As you well know, I *could* share some of my mysterious past with you all ...'

'But then you'd have to kill us,' everyone chimed in, before roaring laughter ensued. *Maybe this isn't going to be so bad after all*, Daniel thought. He spent a little time getting to know some of his new companions, and then Kal suggested that Brandy show him to his cabin before they all congregated again for an early dinner.

'You join us at a very exciting time, Professor. This is going to be our first night-time deployment of Cygnus. Hence the early dinner. We'll be casting off in the next few minutes to make sure we are at the dive site in plenty of time.'

'I'm looking forward to it, Kal, and please, everyone,

it's just Dan.'

'Sure thing, Professor.'

Daniel reflected that the name thing was clearly a work in progress and, as he followed Brandy in search of his cabin, he mused further on Yousef's apparent subterfuge.

He was pleasantly surprised to find that he had his own accommodation. Pretty basic, but entirely acceptable. A bed that was a bit on the small side, a desk, a porthole, and even his own bathroom. *Bloody luxury*, he thought. As the engines fired up in preparation for departure, he wondered whether he was right next to the engine room, and he couldn't help but feel a frisson of excitement that he hadn't experienced for a long time.

He hoped the excitement would eclipse the nagging feeling that something wasn't right. Though Yousef had greeted him warmly, he couldn't really have been that pleased to see him. After all, Yousef was the one who tried to persuade Daniel not to accept this job, to avoid DIVE altogether. He had said it would be too dangerous, but everything so far seemed to be fine. Daniel felt any risk was worth taking if there was even the slightest chance of finding Suleiman's heart. *Maybe Yousef just wants to find it himself*, Daniel thought uncharitably. Then he shook off this suspicion; the last thing he needed was to become paranoid about a crewmate.

As the *Triton* approached site 127Qr and the deployment time of 22:00 neared, people started to focus. The laughter from dinner died away, and conversation became minimal. Daniel got the real sense of a team getting into the zone. Yousef would be the lead pilot for Cygnus this evening, and Daniel watched him and his co-pilot head towards what looked like a shipping container in the middle of the deck. It turned out that that was exactly what it was. The container housed a NASA-style control pod. Once the team went in, no one was allowed in or out. The ROV pilots would be controlling Cygnus remotely throughout the entire operation.

Captain Murphy had explained to Daniel over dinner that the *Triton* couldn't drop anchor at the site, as it was simply too deep. Once the ship was in position, he and his team would activate DP, or 'dynamic positioning.' This sophisticated computer-controlled system would make a constant stream of slight corrections and adjustments to the main propeller and three powerful side thrusters to ensure that the ship stayed exactly in the same spot. The *Triton* was tethered to Cygnus by a high-tensile steel cable and an umbilical cord that carried all the power and comms, so it was imperative that the ship maintain an exact location.

The captain also explained that the ROV would take two hours to make the two-kilometre trip to the seabed. It may be down there for three or four hours before returning. This was a period of intense concentration for the ROV pilots, who had to navigate currents, marine wildlife, and poor visibility while managing the ROV's tether as it cruised its way around the wreck, seeking out artefacts and freeing them from the silt.

Daniel had been invited on deck to get the whole visceral experience of the ROV deployment. He'd met some of the other technicians, ROV engineers, and divers over dinner and recognised three or four of them around him now. Davy, the Geordie lad who had asked about Yousef earlier, was operating a gigantic yellow crane, which was going to lift the ROV off the ship and settle her into the ocean. Three of his colleagues were providing 'eyes on the ground' to make sure nothing got caught up in anything else, Brandy amongst them. Kal, standing next to Daniel, leant over and shouted into his ear, making sure he was heard over the sound of machinery, wind, and the sea.

'Brace yourself.'

Daniel looked quizzically back at him, and the project lead winked. At that moment the crane swung Cygnus dramatically over the side of the *Triton*, and the whole ship listed to port violently. Everyone except Daniel had prepared themselves for this. Kal, anticipating Daniel's potential fall, grabbed hold of his arm.

'What the hell's happening?' Daniel screamed at Kal.

'Nothing to worry about, Professor. It's just a little initiation that the guys like to do when any newbies come aboard.'

The team members were all looking at Daniel now, laughing and applauding.

'When we move Cygnus out over the water, we significantly shift the balance of the ship, so it lists over accordingly. It'll right itself in a few seconds as Davy settles her into the water. I've seen people completely lose it. You did well.' He winked again and moved off to instruct the team.

Daniel caught his breath as an already familiar thought came to mind: *What the hell am I doing here?* Kal couldn't have known how much that jolt freaked him out, but he was really shaken as he glanced at the swelling ocean below. Once the *Triton* had righted herself, he wandered gingerly over to the port side to get a closer look at the ROV. She was even more impressive in her natural habitat. The craft's myriad of lights illuminated the water all around, creating an almost supernatural quality. The vast array of tools and devices blinked or rotated as each piece went through pre-flight protocols. It was like watching a giant robot slowly wake itself from hibernation. The sound of heavy metal on metal was augmented by a vast array of electronic fizzes and releases, like some kind of maniacal rock band tuning up. It was as menacing as it was majestic.

Once final pre-dive checks had been completed, the pilots blew the ballast tanks, and Cygnus started her slow descent into the deep. Daniel continued his gaze as the lights slowly faded. Cygnus was entirely in the hands of her pilots now.

***

Daniel watched one of the monitors in the control room which was directly linked to a live feed from Cygnus. Even with all the lights and advanced tech, Daniel wondered how the pilots were able to fly Cygnus down into the depths so confidently. There really was very little apparent visibility. *If you were on the M4 heading into London, you would have pulled over by now*, Daniel mused.

After a while the images started to all look the same to him, so he sought out Kal and asked what had been retrieved so far. With the pride of a parent discussing the achievements of his prodigious offspring, Kal went through the archived artefacts in some detail. Glazed jars from Persia, coffee cups from Yemen, Turkish pottery and cooking utensils, countless other ceramics —the list went on. The discoveries that excited the team the most included cases of a white substance that they believed was some kind of Arabian incense, two anchors, and two cannons, one iron and one brass. The team was confident there was a third anchor and more armoury down there to be found, even though the *Colossus* wasn't considered to be heavily armed. Just enough to flex some muscle towards any pirates showing an unhealthy interest.

Brandy called Daniel back over to the live-feed monitor.

'Professor, you might want to look at this.'

Daniel joined a group crowding around the monitor. Brandy explained what was on screen without ever taking her eyes away from the image.

'We think this might be our most exciting discovery yet, Professor. We won't be certain until we get specimens up, but chances are we're looking at some Chinese Ming porcelain.'

Daniel saw Brandy's eyes fill up. He glanced at Kal, who nodded, chewing on his unlit pipe. Daniel suddenly felt very privileged to be aboard the *Triton*. Not just because of her remit, but also to see the passion and emotion of the team. This really was what they lived for.

The moment was broken by Captain Murphy's arrival from the bridge.

'Listen up, folks. A lively weather pattern has just taken an unexpected turn and is now heading our way from the south. I don't like the look of it, and it'll be here in a couple of hours. You need to bring her up. Now.'

This clearly wasn't open for discussion. Kal hit an intercom button and started briefing Yousef in the ROV control pod on strategies to return Cygnus to the surface ASAP. Everyone else slipped into a well-drilled set of actions. Although Daniel didn't sense any panic, there was definitely a focussed urgency about the ship. Feeling both redundant and potentially in the way, he slipped back to his cabin.

Daniel spent a couple of hours writing up his first-day impressions and then tried to get his head down. After a further sixty minutes a combination of the storm symphony and a natural curiosity drew him back to the bridge. When he returned, the tone in the control room was quite different. His stomach dropped; something was wrong. Daniel listened to the tense voices and pieced together what had happened in his absence. On Cygnus's return journey, the umbilical cord had got entangled in something, and this had caused a loss of power to the ROV. She had nearly completed her return but was now stranded some fifty metres down. Brandy was the ship's strongest diver, so she had volunteered to go down to try and free the ROV. Meanwhile the storm had hit, and Captain Murphy and his crew were fighting to maintain their position. Brandy had already been underwater for twenty-five minutes. Daniel felt sweat run down his neck.

Yousef's deadpan tone came over the control room open speaker.

'Okay, she's done it, we have power. Cygnus is clear and free. We're bringing her up.'

The crew clapped and cheered, but Kal's voice cut through the celebrations.

'I'm not sure that's a good idea. Bringing Cygnus up —fully laden, mind—in this weather is going to be a roller coaster to say the least. Con, what do you think?'

The captain stared out of the window for a few seconds before responding. 'The devil, and the deep blue. I don't want to be tethered to her any longer than necessary in this weather, but I agree, bringing her up will be tricky.'

'Kal, we've got this,' Yousef cut in. 'We can bring her home. Just give us the green light.'

Kal looked back at the captain. 'Your call, Con.'

'Okay. I trust your people. Davy, are you happy to take the crane?'

'Just try and stop me, like.'

Daniel watched as the new plan was quickly patched together. Brandy was going to come up with the ROV. She would then attach the crane harness to Cygnus on the surface and ride up with it onto the *Triton*.

As the storm lashed against the ship, the two pilots quietly went about their work, sealed away in the ROV control pod. They had sent word down to Brandy to 'latch on to something and enjoy the ride' via the digital readout pad on the robot. It transpired that getting it to the surface was the least of their challenges.

As soon as the ROV broke the surface, Davy didn't waste any time swinging the crane into position. The *Triton* pitched violently in the waves. The harness was dropped, and Brandy quickly tethered it to the ROV mainframe. Daniel witnessed the operation from the relative safety of the bridge, alongside the first officer. He marvelled at the calm execution.

'Everyone appears so composed, like this is just a standard daily event.'

'They've trained for this, Professor,' the FO responded. 'It's this last bit that is going to test nerves.'

As soon as Davy got the green light from his eyes on the ground, he started the winch motor. Cygnus rose majestically from the sea, carrying a full haul and one additional passenger. She swung violently in the stormy conditions, but Davy just grinned and gave Brandy a thumbs-up. The *Triton* listed over to the port side, but Daniel was ready for it this time. The second the ROV reached clearance height, Davy started to swing her over to the ship's deck.

Everyone held their breath and stared rapt at the engineering manoeuvre on the port side. Only Captain Murphy looked out across the starboard bow of the ship.

He barely had time to whisper, 'Christ save us all,' before the giant wave hit.

17

April 27, 1630

The Adriatic Sea

Emir had spent three days in a coma on board the *Colossus* while the ship was docked in Dubrovnik. A surgeon was called on board, as the ship's doctor was really no more than a barber who knew how to stitch a wound. An anonymous merchant paid the doctor's fees.

The impact of the mooring post was directly on Emir's right eye socket. Despite the doctor's best efforts, he was unable to save the eye but dressed the surrounding wound and stemmed the bleeding. He advised that the boy was not to be moved, and, when asked what more could be done to shake him from his trance, he suggested warm blankets and prayer. Both were liberally forthcoming from crew and merchants alike.

Captain Barbarossa indicated that if the boy hadn't awakened by the time they needed to set sail, he would have to arrange for him to be removed from the ship. On the third day the captain suggested that it might be worth gathering some more supplies, thereby delaying departure by a day. This didn't go unnoticed.

Shabaka stayed by Emir's side day and night during their time in port, regularly removing his bandages and re-dressing the wound. The only time he left was when summoned by the captain. Barbarossa listened patiently to Shabaka's story of how Emir came to be on board. He sympathised with the loss of Shabaka's brother, and acknowledged the fact that, among many other contributions, the boy had saved a man's life. Nevertheless, he concluded, his authority had been wilfully undermined, and if he didn't exact some penalty, he would lose the respect of the crew.

Captain Barbarossa was a bright man. He had seen how much both his sailors and fee-paying passengers had taken to the boy. He also recognised that Shabaka was pretty much universally popular. He knew he was walking something of a tightrope. In the end he demoted Shabaka down to the rank of able seaman. The crew would see that he had taken action but had also been lenient in the circumstances. As for the boy, it looked as if he wouldn't have that problem for much longer.

Shabaka accepted his penance gracefully and retired back to the quarters that a merchant had gladly surrendered to accommodate the patient. And there he stayed. On the fourth morning in Dubrovnik, with barely two hours remaining before the *Colossus* set sail, Emir opened his mouth and whispered, 'Shaba.'

Two days at sea and he was able to get up and surrender the cabin back to its rightful owner with profuse thanks. As he cautiously walked out onto the deck, supported by Shabaka, he noticed that none of the crew were looking at him. They were all facing away. Suddenly they all turned round to reveal that each of them was wearing an eye patch. They cheered and clapped him back on deck with this tribute. One of the crew stepped forward and introduced himself.

'Red, my name is Antonio. I am the man you saved

on the quayside. We don't know each other well, but I shall forever be in your debt. I truly don't know how I will ever be able to thank you.'

Emir shrugged him off with a self-effacing mumble, but Antonio was having none of it.

'I am a proud Italian, and we take our responsibilities very seriously. In my country, if a man saves your life, you are beholden to him until that life debt is repaid.'

Emir wondered to what extent Antonio was playing to the gallery—all the crew were watching this scene unfold—but he smiled and placed his hand over his heart, nevertheless. After thanking the crew also, he escaped the attention as quickly as he could.

Later that day he was summoned to the captain's quarters. Barbarossa indicated that he felt that Emir had suffered sufficiently as to not warrant any further punishment. Nevertheless, he had been a stowaway on the captain's ship, and men had died for less. Barbarossa concluded by asserting that Emir would remain on probation.

'Don't vex me further, young man,' was his parting shot.

Shabaka watched Emir in the weeks that followed and often wondered just how much of the boy had been left on the Dubrovnik quayside. Simply put, his spirit seemed more broken than his skull. He continued to fulfil his duties diligently, and to a higher standard than many on board. It would have been difficult to find fault with any of his work, but it was clear that his enthusiasm had diminished.

The silence of a large personality is so much more deafening than the noise of petty men, and Emir's retreat into himself was deeply felt. As the days turned into weeks, crew and merchants alike tried to engage Emir, draw him back out of his shell. He was always polite, as his mama had taught him to be, but his heart no longer seemed to be in the voyage.

After some time, the men stopped their cajoling, sympathising, teasing, lecturing, or any of the other tactics employed to bring the old Red back to them. Most just felt sad for the loss of such a positive and refreshing force on the ship. Whatever their feelings, they universally decided that he was probably best left to his own devices.

Venice and Naples came and went without much incident. The crew attrition continued to be slightly higher than usual, and replacements were uncommonly available at each port the *Colossus* docked in. Shabaka might have paid this more attention if he was still fulfilling a foreman role, or if he hadn't been so distracted by Emir's melancholy, but as it was, these things went by unobserved and without issue or incident.

As for Emir himself, he was keenly aware that his withdrawal had significantly impacted the mood of the ship. He carried this burden around with him, and it further reinforced his growing sense of guilt and hopelessness. Guilt that he had let so many down. His mother, his prison protector, his shipmates, and of course, his best friend. He could feel himself slipping a little further into some abyss each day but had no sense of how to pull himself out. This was where his hopelessness stemmed from, but it was aggravated by a grim gnawing doubt in the pit of his stomach. A vague sense of real unease and apprehension.

Although to all intents and purposes he had fully recovered from his fall, with the obvious exception of the loss of an eye, he knew that his mind hadn't fully returned. There were big gaps in his recollection. He could remember Jabari, but nothing about the prison escape. He recalled meeting Shabaka for the first time, but not how he came to be on board this ship. He knew he had saved a crew member but had no memory of the actual incident. But of much more alarm to Emir was the nagging doubt that he had forgotten something else, something vital. Something that carried real threat and jeopardy. This too he bore like a millstone.

In Marseilles Shabaka resolved to confront Emir. Up until this point he had only adopted a nurturing approach and tone. But walking the streets of Marseille on their shore leave day, Shabaka decided to try and shake Emir out of the trance-like state that he had fallen into. The harsher his words, the harder his tone, the more it pained the Egyptian, but it appeared to have no impact on the boy. He just shrugged and nodded his acknowledgement. In the end Shabaka hugged the boy and simply pleaded with him to come back. Emir never uttered a word.

This had been Shabaka's last card. He had no other plays, and so resolved to continue to support Emir in any way he could but no longer press him to shake off his malaise. If the boy wanted to withdraw into himself, well then, he'd earned the right. And so, this distressing impasse prevailed, and probably would have continued for the remainder of the ship's voyage, were it not for an intervention from the most unlikely of sources, in Barcelona.

***

Merchant traders and crew alike always enjoyed a visit to the ancient Spanish city. It had long been overlooked as a trading port on account of it having no natural harbour, but everything changed when the artificial harbour of Port Vell was built in the fifteenth century. For the first time, large merchant ships could dock in Barcelona, even those the size of the *Colossus*.

A thriving community grew quickly around the new harbour, which provided diverse attractions and temptations for both traders and sailors. Most infamous among Port Vell's charms was the range of hospitality afforded at Casa Joaquin. The warmth of the welcome provided by the tavern's hostess, known as Valentina, was renowned across the Mediterranean.

Captain Barbarossa would never have stooped to frequent such an establishment. It was rumoured he had a long-term relationship with a courtesan in Barcelona who boasted royal connections. Yet he was keenly mindful of the fact that, during the course of a four-day stopover, most of his crew would indulge themselves.

Barcelona represented the turning point of many Ottoman merchant voyages around the Mediterranean, and this would be no exception. From the Spanish eastern coastline, the *Colossus* would set a course south-eastwards towards Tripoli and then on to Alexandria. As the ship started its long journey home, crew would focus on what they were returning to. As such, the furthest stop often represented the last port where sailors could indulge without compunction. Certainly, the large contingent from the *Colossus* that descended on Casa Joaquin on the ship's final night in dock had only one thought on their mind.

Shabaka insisted that Emir accompany the group rather than stay behind on his own. He reluctantly agreed when Shabaka said they were visiting a place where Jabari was something of a legend. Emir could see, even through his mist, that this particular pilgrimage prompted conflicting emotions in Shabaka.

As they entered the taverna, Shabaka placed his arm protectively around Emir's shoulder. The young boy stared open mouthed. He had seen many sights, gained many experiences on this journey, but nothing could have prepared him for this sheer assault to his senses. Exuberant music filled the room. Candlelight glittered in every corner. Faux temple architecture provided a dramatic backdrop to the whistling and screaming of the clientele. And of course, there was the ladies. The pervading aroma of sweet perfume provided a stark contrast to the equally distinct smell of a crew that had been at sea for many days.

Wherever Emir looked, there were beautiful women. Some danced on counters, others served drinks, many sat amongst the patrons, laughing and whispering conspiratorially. Most of them wore very little clothing; the remainder wore no clothes at all. Emir had never been so bewildered in his whole life. And this giddiness felt nothing like any previous experience. It was breathtaking, suffocating, intimidating, and utterly intoxicating.

Shabaka sat Emir in a quiet corner and strode over to the establishment's owner and hostess. When she saw him, she screamed and hurtled towards him with an alarming velocity. Shabaka was prepared and swung

Valentina in his arms. After she had finished kissing his face all over, he reached to whisper in her ear. Emir watched as her countenance changed completely, and he knew that Shabaka was telling her about Jabari. Her eyes glistened as she shook her head. Shabaka continued and then pointed towards Emir. He flushed and stared at the ground. What was his friend telling this imposing woman?

Slowly, over the next hour or so, every one of the women working in San Joaquin found a moment to come over to Emir and kiss him tenderly on the forehead. Many of them looked like they had been crying, but all of them gave Emir a smile of genuine affection. It seemed that, to honour Jabari, they all wanted to commune with the boy who had known him last. Although Emir was ill equipped to decipher the complex emotions at play, he was mindful that this alien custom was an important one.

Finally, Valentina herself appeared at Emir's side and pulled up a chair next to him. Shabaka watched from across the chaotic room as the infamous brothel madam took Emir's hands in her own. She leant forward and gently stroked his face. As the minutes passed, Shabaka could see the formidable woman quietly talking to the young boy. When he started to cry, Shabaka had to resist a nearly overwhelming urge to run over and comfort him. Instead, he just continued to watch. Eventually Emir's tears dried, and he started to nod in some kind of assent or understanding of Valentina's words. Eventually, she stood and, like her girls before her, she kissed him gently on the forehead and then left him with his own thoughts.

Shabaka stared at the boy, wondering what had

been discussed, and whether this had been a dreadful mistake. Finally, Emir lifted his head and looked across the crowded room into Shabaka's eyes. He held his gaze for a long time. And then he smiled. It was a grin that Shabaka hadn't seen in the longest time. One he hadn't been sure he would ever see again.

Emir had come back to him.

Over the next few days, as the *Colossus* embarked on its long return journey, Emir did become his old self again. He walked a little taller and gave as good as he got when the crew turned to teasing him again. He didn't talk at all of Valentina or what had passed between them in Casa Joaquin that night, but he would always carry her tender words and generosity of spirit in his heart.

***

Emir continued to struggle with the holes in his memory, and the subsequent nagging sense of unease. He felt that if he could just remember, fill in those missing pieces, then he would truly be himself again.

On the fourth day out of Barcelona, Shabaka was pleased to notice Emir once again toying with some of the merchants and tricking them out of a few coins. A large, particularly vain and pompous merchant by the name of Agostinho had joined the voyage in Dubrovnik. He had been observing Emir from a safe distance for a while and now stepped forward.

'I can see your tricks with ease, my boy. You may fool these idiots, but you can't fool me.'

Emir nodded and bowed, his confidence and quick wit fully restored. 'I wouldn't even dream of trying to deceive a gentleman of your stature and clear intelligence, sir.'

Agostinho smiled approvingly and turned to leave.

'Perhaps I could give you the opportunity to fool me, sir.'

Agostinho realised that, with the eyes of the group upon him, he couldn't now decline the boy's challenge. 'Nothing would give me greater pleasure,' he declared, returning to the circle.

Emir turned over three empty coffee cups on the rough fruit box in front of them. He pulled out the coin he had just won and put it under one of the cups.

'I am going to move these cups around. If you can tell me which one has the coin under it when I stop, you can keep the coin. You can't lose. It's my coin.'

The merchant weighed up the proposition. The boy was right—it wasn't his money, so he had nothing to lose. He nodded. Emir moved the cups around, finally coming to a stop with the three cups back in a line. He looked up enquiringly at Agostinho.

'You make it too easy, boy. The coin is under that cup.'

Emir lifted the central cup, and sure enough, there was the coin. The group sighed in collective disappointment that Agostinho had outmanoeuvred Red. Agostinho laughed triumphantly and grabbed the coin. Emir looked dejected, but then suggested that a gentlemen would certainly give him a chance to win his money back. Agostinho quickly assented. This was too easy. The coin was placed, the cups were moved, and the merchant pointed derisively at his chosen cup. The outcome was the same. Agostinho picked the correct cup and took a second coin from Emir.

'How many coins have you got left, Red?' Agostinho

enquired, seeing an opportunity to make a nice little profit at the boy's expense.

Emir reluctantly emptied out his pockets. He put eight akçe on the table. 'That's everything I have,' Emir mumbled.

Agostinho placed a large gold Portuguese coin on the box. 'This is worth all of your meagre coinage, and some more besides. See how you do with some real Portuguese money.'

A number of the merchants counselled Emir against the proposition. Agostinho clearly had the better of him. Emir stared at the gold coin for a long time but finally picked up his coins and made to leave.

'I knew it. Nothing but a cheap fraudster. Look at him run away when presented with a proper wager. Boy, I'll make it easy for you.' Agostinho placed a second gold coin on the table. Emir stopped and slowly returned to the growing group of curious spectators.

'I wouldn't dream of taking a second coin,' Emir declared, theatrically replacing the new coin into Agostinho's tunic pocket, 'but I will take up your original challenge.'

Agostinho smiled with self-satisfaction. Emir lined up the cups and placed the gold coin under the middle one. Slowly he moved the cups around, eventually bringing them back into a straight line. Agostinho pointed to the middle cup.

'You are an idiot, boy. This cup has a chip in it. We all know the coin is there.'

Emir lifted the cup to reveal ... nothing. Agostinho, eyes blazing, pointed to a second cup. Emir lifted this one also. It was empty. Most of the merchants started to laugh. Agostinho, embarrassed and furious, slammed his hand over the third cup.

'You have cheated me. This coin is mine.'

'What coin?' Emir responded.

Agostinho lifted the third cup to reveal nothing.

'What is this? What have you done? Tell me, boy, or you're going overboard.'

'I don't have it, sir. Look.' He reached deep into the Portuguese's thick black beard and pulled out the piece of gold. The group roared their approval and asserted that the merchant should give the boy the coin. Emir smiled and handed it back to Agostinho.

'I don't need this, sir,' he declared disarmingly.

'Whyever not, boy,' the merchant responded. 'It is more money than you would normally make in a month.'

'Because you see,' Emir responded, laughing now, 'I already have the other five gold coins you had in your pocket.'

Agostinho lunged forward to grab the money, but Emir was too quick, already spinning round to run away.

He would have made good his escape but for the fact that he instantly collided with a giant of a man and fell back to the ground. He glanced up at the merchant, who held his walking stick in hand. In the blink of an eye, all the missing pieces in his head flooded back into focus. He remembered everything.

He stared at the merchant and wondered how he hadn't realised earlier. Or had he somehow forgotten? This was *Kazim*. The Janissary who had arrested him in the market. But what was he doing here? Kazim eyed the boy too, as if he also was struggling to make a connection. It seemed to just elude him. Instead, he pulled Emir to his feet.

'Where were you off to in such a hurry, young man?'

Emir was about to respond when another merchant —the one who'd given Emir his cabin during his coma— stepped in.

'Red was just having a little fun at Agostinho's expense, and if ever a boil needed lancing it's that one.'

The group fell about laughing again. Agostinho was puce with rage and stared purposefully at Kazim. The Janissary shook his head almost imperceptibly, and then joined the laughter of the group.

'You're right there, good sir, and no mistake,' Kazim acknowledged. 'Well, I'll say this for you, lad: you've got some balls. Go on, you scoundrel, away with you. You must have some duties awaiting you.'

Shabaka, who had been monitoring the situation, saw his cue, and stepped in.

'You are not mistaken, sir; he's got ropes that need attending to.' And with that he dragged Emir out of sight. Once they were safely hidden from view, he turned to Emir.

'Emie. You need to be more careful with your trickery. If just one of these men thinks that you're cheating them, you will be in front of Barbarossa, and you know how that will go. Promise me now, no more playing for money. Just to entertain, yes? Emie, are you listening?'

Emir was staring past Shabaka in a daze.

'Emie, what is it? You look like you've seen a ghost. What the hell is wrong with you?'

Emir looked up at Shabaka, his mind still racing to catch up with the flood of memories and revelations.

'Shaba. I can remember. I can remember everything.'

He paused, trying to work out where to start. 'Shaba, there are things I have to tell you. Things I've learnt. Things I've seen. Maybe, I think. I'm not sure. I think there is some mutinous plan being hatched on board our ship.'

Shabaka looked exasperated. 'You have a wild imagination, Emie. It will be your undoing if you aren't careful.'

'But, but ...'

'No buts now. We have plenty of time to talk. Now, you need to rest.'

Emir almost protested further, but, in truth, he needed some time to order his thoughts. All the pieces were back in play, but it would take a while to join them back up and work out what they meant. He nodded an acknowledgement at Shabaka, grabbed his rolled-up mattress, and headed down into the cargo hold.

As he lay down, knowing there was no chance he would sleep, Emir catalogued his fresh insights. He breathed deeply, slowing his heart rate right down, and summoned up a space in his mind where he could work. He pictured an empty parchment spread out on the captain's desk. He had stolen a moment some weeks back, as he was running an errand for one of the officers, to take a look in the captain's cabin. Now, he conjured up the detail of that room again. There were books and papers everywhere, bottles of strange-coloured liquor, maps and pictures on the walls, a bed four times the size of Emir's mattress, and, in the middle, a giant desk, covered with more maps and brass navigational instruments.

Except now, in his mind, the desk was empty save for a blank parchment. Emir started laying out his thoughts. Kazim was on board. Kazim was a Janissary. A senior Janissary. Emir had seen Kazim in secretive conversation with the one called Mustafa. And, earlier, he had seen Mustafa and another—Onur, was it?—down in the cargo bay when he was hiding in the crate. He had thought it a hallucination then, but he knew it to be a fact now. The two men had been seeking out a place to hide something. Something of real value. Emir could picture where they had hidden the box. He could see it. He remembered seeing the riches within. But this wasn't the real treasure. It was a decoy. A substitute? Something.

His mind locked those facts in and moved on. He had witnessed another illicit meeting. Also down here amongst the cargo crates. More men this time. And they were talking about other, perhaps more senior recruits joining their ranks in the ports along the way. But who were these men, and why were they operating in secret? Kazim had been the leader at that meeting also. And he'd talked about treasure.

Emir looked up from his vision and stared at the space which the two men had originally identified as the 'optimum' hiding place all those weeks ago. He glanced around. He was alone. What better time to check whether his recall was true or scrambled? He skipped over towards the shadowy recess he remembered from before. Rats scampered around his legs to make way. He felt blindly around the hull floor. Nothing. Had he been mistaken? If he was wrong about this ... maybe he'd imagined the whole thing. Or dreamt it up when he was unconscious. His hand hit something that wasn't wood. He pulled back some sacking and gave an involuntary gasp as the corner of a stunning gold, jewel-encrusted casket was revealed. He sprang away, as if he had been scorched by it, and scrabbled furiously back to his mattress. That was not the dull metal box he remembered seeing before. Not at all.

Desperately Emir tried to process this new information. The box *had* been replaced, and by something much more valuable by the look of it. What should he do with the knowledge he now had? Where next? As these questions circled, Emir drifted off into a fitful sleep. By the time he awoke, a plan had taken shape in his mind. He would keep his powder dry for now, keep a careful eye on Kazim, and tell Shabaka the whole story when he'd got it figured out. He still had time.

***

The *Colossus* made good time towards Tripoli, and crew conversations started to turn to themes of home. Emir had attempted on one occasion to share his most recent discoveries with Shabaka, but his friend had been uncharacteristically dismissive.

'Not all this again, Emie. Please. I thought we'd put this behind us. All this foolish talk of treasure and scheming at every turn. I won't entertain any more of this nonsense.'

The closer the ship edged towards Shabaka's home, the quieter and more withdrawn he became. Normally an ebullient character, the Egyptian invariably influenced the climate of the room. He had a larger-than-life, almost heroic quality that Emir adored. He eyed his mentor carefully. Emir had so much to tell him, secrets and revelations that had become a great burden to him, but he could see that now was not the time to take Shabaka into his confidence.

'What's wrong, Shaba? You're very quiet.'

Shabaka shook himself from his musings and looked across at the boy whom he had witnessed transform into a young man over the last six months. Jaded as he was, he had experienced a life at sea as if for the first time on this trip, seeing everything through Emir's wide eyes. He felt rejuvenated and revitalised, once again tasting the thrill of a seafaring life that had long been absent. He felt reborn in Emir's company and thanked Allah that Jabari had delivered the boy to him. This left him feeling all the more guilty at the decision he had reached.

'Come over here now, Emie, so we might talk.'

Emir had grown accustomed to this ritual. When Shabaka had something serious to say, he would always start by making sure that Emir was fully focussed; then he would ask him a big question.

'We've become close these last many months, Emie, good friends, wouldn't you agree?'

Emir nodded, already wondering where this was heading.

'I have marvelled at how you have grown on this voyage. You truly are a fine seaman. I would be proud to sail alongside you at any time. More than that, you have become a fine man, even at your tender age. Your mother would be immensely proud of you.'

Emir flushed at this unusual eulogy from his friend.

'Family is important, Emie. The loss of Jabari has made me realise just how important. Voyaging with you has been one of my life's most special moments, but I feel the pull of my family more keenly now as we approach my home city. For that reason, I have made a decision. I am going to finish my journey in Alexandria.'

Emir stared at Shabaka, dumbfounded. Shabaka realised he needed to be plainer still.

'Emie, I'm not sailing on with you to Constantinople.'

Emir started to shake his head. 'No. No, no, no, no. You can't. You have to stay. You don't understand. I need you. We all need you. You can't do this. I won't let you.'

'Emie, please. Don't make this any harder than it already is. We will still have some time. I'm going to show you the most amazing things in my hometown. We will have a fine time, but … you need to know, Emie, I've made up my mind.'

Emir stood up and looked furiously down at his friend. He felt betrayed, angry, and utterly devastated.

'You promised you would never leave me. You promised,' he spat out. Before Shabaka could respond, he tore down the deck and into the retreat of the cargo bay. The Egyptian didn't call after him, but his eyes filled up. The boy would come round. He just needed some time.

Emir ran until he ran out of ship. Once again, he found himself in the dark bowels at the aft of the *Colossus*. He leant his head against one of the beams and waited for his anger to subside. He wanted to cry, as he had done many times on this voyage, but he wouldn't allow himself that release. Couldn't allow it.

Instead, he thought about the story he had been trying to tell Shabaka. The Egyptian had dismissed his fanciful tale of a mutinous plot as nothing more than the product of an overactive imagination. When Emir had gone further and speculated that the heart of

Suleiman the Magnificent might actually be on board, Shabaka had been more firmly dismissive.

'Emir. You must be careful what you present as a truth. Otherwise, when you really do have important information to impart, people might not so readily believe you.'

Emir had been hurt by this reproach but resolved to work even harder to try and get the proof that he clearly needed.

Now, as he reflected on all that had passed since the incident in Dubrovnik, a smile came to his lips. When Shabaka heard the whole story, he would have to stay. He had caught a glimpse of a golden casket. Surely he now had the evidence to back up his outlandish claims. He just had to make sure that he got all the details right. Didn't leave anything out. He breathed deeply and slowed his pulse right down, as he had done so often before.

He still had a few weeks before they docked in Alexandria. Everything would work out once he got the telling of his tale straight.

PART 4
ENDEAVOUR

18

August 18, 2012

The Levantine Basin

Daniel and Yousef sat in the Cygnus control pod, staring at the relay images of the ROV repair work going on outside. The engineers had done an amazing job of making the submersible robot serviceable only three days after the storm. Nevertheless, glitches remained, and further troubleshooting work was required after each dive.

'I still wonder how such a sensitive and fine-tuned piece of kit like Cygnus survived at all, to be honest,' Daniel reflected.

'You would be surprised how resilient she is,' Yousef responded. 'Remember, she is diving to around two kilometres on every run. You've got to be pretty robust to keep that pace up. She has to deal with all the detritus that any strong currents chuck up down there, not to mention the attentions of some of the more predatorial marine life. And on top of that she has to cope with me piloting her. Actually, come to think of it, you're right, it's a wonder she's still in one piece.'

Both men were keenly aware that this polite conversation was papering over a tension between them that had been seeded in their meeting at Randolph Fairlight's funeral. Daniel wanted to have it out with Yousef but feared what damage may be done to their relationship. If he was honest with himself, he feared hearing the truth even more. So, the fragile interaction continued.

They both smiled ruefully, observing in silence the correction and adjustment work that Brandy and Davy were methodically working through. They had finished the on-deck maintenance and were now going through a series of tests with Cygnus in the water. Looking at the images took Daniel right back to the storm.

He had been pretty shaken up by the events of that night. In the ensuing days, Kal had to provide a lot of reassurance to persuade Daniel to stay with the project, let alone stay on the ship. No one had been lost that night but, in truth, no one could quite believe it.

'I still can't fully get my head around what happened, Yous. How did we not all perish?'

Yousef continued staring at the screen, frowning a little.

'It was what you English like to call a 'perfect storm.' I don't mean the actual storm; I mean the coincidence of several factors coming together at exactly the same moment. In a thousand dives that would never happen again. Cygnus getting tangled'—Yousef counted the elements on his fingers—'the weather changing direction, the ship listing with the weight of my baby out of the water, the additional weight with the load and a diver, the abnormal wave hitting at that exact moment. All those things coinciding. It was just a freak event. That, or someone up there is trying to tell us something.'

Daniel nodded. He had heard this commentary more than once from Khaled and Brandy over the last couple of weeks.

'The bizarre thing is that I remember those

moments in vivid detail. I remember thinking, okay, so this is how I go.'

'I'll tell you this, Danny. We would normally be leaning at about a ten-degree angle when the ROV is hanging over the side. Doesn't sound much, but as you well know, you can definitely feel it. Well, when that wave hit, we were already nearer twenty, and my estimate is that the wave knocked us to well over forty. Anything beyond that and we would have capsized for sure. It's only the captain's quick thinking that saved us.'

'What do you mean?' Daniel probed. This was new information to him.

'When that wave hit, he was the only one that saw it coming. Well, him and me. But he was the only one that was able to respond. He grabbed the DP stick and swung the bow away from the wave at the last minute. If he hadn't done this, we would have lost the ROV and half the crew for sure.'

Daniel chewed on these new facts. 'I'm not sure that is particularly reassuring.'

'But that's the point, my friend. It should be. There are two things to focus on here. First, it was a freak event. One in a million. Seriously. And second, you're in good hands. The best. That's why we're all still here to talk about it.'

'I'll take your word for it. Listen, Yousef, can I ask you something?' It was the first time Daniel had managed to get Yousef alone, and he couldn't let the opportunity slip away. 'About what you said, at the funeral ...'

'I'm not sure what you mean.'

'About Suleiman's heart, the danger—'

Yousef's phone vibrated, and he turned away to read

the message.

'Saved by the bell,' Daniel said ruefully.

Yousef changed the subject. 'So, what's excited you most about what you've seen since you got here, Professor?'

'Oh, don't you start with that professor shit.' Daniel leant back. 'Frankly, I don't know where to start. I mean, just the ship. Let's take the wreck. You guys are dating this thing as sinking around 1630. Well, if you're right, that changes everything. A ship of this size. All the assumptions we've made about the Ottoman Empire being in significant decline by this date would have to be revisited. Then there is the cargo. It looks beyond doubt that there were goods on board from as far afield as Jingdezhen. I mean, how is that even possible?'

Yousef smiled. 'Well, as you know, the *Colossus* didn't sail there herself. Much of her burden was loaded in Alexandria. The cargo had already made an immense journey from China, through southern India, then down to the Persian Gulf. From there round to Mocha and up the Red Sea, and then on up to Suez. From there the cargo had to be transhipped to Cairo, before being ferried up the Nile to Alexandria. No Suez Canal back then, mate. And only then did it get loaded onto our ship. What an amazing journey, eh?'

'Exactly. It really is like finding a new planet.'

'I don't know which I'm looking forward to more, Professor, the book or the lecture series.' Yousef feigned a yawn.

Daniel shook his head and put an imaginary gun to his temple. 'Right now, I don't know where to begin. It's all quite overwhelming. When you finally get to exhibit this stuff, no one is going to believe that these artefacts have been at the bottom of the ocean for the best part of four hundred years. They have been preserved unbelievably well.'

'Yeah, it's the stuff that's buried in the mud and the silt that has fared the best. It doesn't look much when Cygnus uncovers it, but by the time it's been cleaned and restored, well, some of the goods look brand new. Have you had a chance to look at that walking stick that came up yesterday?'

Daniel leapt to his feet. Whenever he got really excited a childlike enthusiasm would kick in.

'I know. Unbelievable, right? The detail. The engravings. And *so* well preserved. Just take that one item. What mysteries will it reveal to us, Yous? What do the engravings mean? Who owned it? Was it part of a shipment or a personal possession of someone on the ship? Maybe the captain, who knows?'

Yousef smiled wistfully at his old friend. 'I do wonder sometimes whether it's entirely healthy, you know, digging up the past, literally. You never know what you might find.'

Daniel moved to theatrically object when the buzzer sounded, indicating that a digital message had been received from one of the divers.

'Ha. As you said, saved by the bell.' Yousef grinned.

He scanned the message and then indicated to Daniel that Davy had hit his time limit. He was coming out but wondered whether Yousef would mind suiting up and running some checks while Brandy finished her final tweaks. This was quickly followed by a message signed off by Brandy, which questioned both Davy's commitment and his parentage.

'Sorry, Danny boy. Can't leave you in the pod. Not

licensed and all that. God knows what havoc you'd wreak given ten minutes on your own. We've only just fixed the bloody thing.'

Davy came back once more asking whether Yousef wanted him to stay in the water until he subbed him. Technically no diver was allowed to be in the water on their own. Yousef gave him the 'all clear' to exit, and Brandy typed, 'At last, a little peace.'

As the men exited the container, Daniel glanced at his watch and at Yousef's back as he moved away. Yousef had said he was in the best hands and on the best ship for this voyage. But Daniel couldn't quite relax, couldn't quite get past the fact it might not be the sea or the storms that he needed to worry about. Yousef was hiding something, and he had to find out what it was.

**

I can help you find it. The boy's voice kept shouting this line. Daniel stood on deck. A storm was raging all around. He thought he could see the boy at the other end of the ship, but as soon as he started to move towards him, a giant wave swept Daniel clean overboard. He took a desperate breath as he sank beneath the waves. Frantically he reached and clawed to pull himself above the surface, but his strength was waning. His lungs started to scream out for oxygen, and the familiar terror descended. He was going to drown. No one would save him.

Suddenly a piercing siren sounded, and Daniel sat up in his bed, gasping for air. The noise was deafening. He swung his feet onto the reassuring 'dry land' of the floor and focussed on calming his breathing. Gradually his heart started to slow.

Only then did Daniel fully grasp that the siren hadn't been in his nightmare. It was still wailing. He desperately tried to remember the emergency drill he had been given by Brandy when he'd first arrived. *If it's safe and you're in calm waters, make your way to the deck.*

Daniel stepped onto the deck. In stark contrast to his dream, the waters were calm. There was no storm. But something was amiss. Cygnus was harnessed to the crane and floating in the ocean, but no one was on deck at all. He ran up the short set of steps to the control room and burst through the door. The scene inside was shockingly still.

Brandy lay on the main board table, motionless. The top half of her wet suit had been pulled down. The ship medic was administering mouth to mouth. Yousef desperately gave chest compressions. Everyone else in the room stood frozen, staring with horror at the unfolding scene.

'When will that bloody AED be ready again?' Kal screamed.

As if to answer, the machine indicated a 'Shock Now' status. 'Clear,' Yousef shouted by way of response, and the medic stepped back. Yousef pushed the 'Shock' button and the charge pulsed through the two pads stuck to her bare chest. Her body tensed and briefly reflexed before returning to a supine position.

'Again,' Kal urged.

Yousef looked up at him and shook his head.

'That's eight times now, sir,' the medic whispered. 'She's been out for nearly thirty minutes. We've got to call it.'

'Again. Please.' Kal's voice broke as he entreated, unwilling to accept the medic's call. He just wasn't ready to lose one of his crew.

Panic seized Daniel as he frantically looked around the room. Davy rocked back and forth on a chair, tears streaming down his face. The rest of the team huddled together, unable to bear witness, but equally unable to look away. Captain Murphy stared on grimly.

The medic placed his hands on to Yousef's, stilling his compression movements.

'That's enough, son,' he breathed quietly, 'she's gone now.'

Yousef stopped his motions and bowed his head.

Kal's expression hardened. 'I want to know what the *fuck* happened here, and I want to know right now.'

'It's my fault. I killed her.' Everyone looked across to Davy. He was staring at the floor and shaking his head. 'I should never have left her in the water on her own. It's my fault.'

'Yousef?' Kal barked at the Jordanian. 'Is this true? Was Brandy in the water alone? *Well?*'

Yousef had been staring at Davy, but now he returned Khaled's accusatory glare.

'Yes, that is right. I gave the 'all clear' to Davy. I was coming in to replace him. His time was up. Brandy can't have been in the water alone for more than two minutes. But it was my call, not Davy's. I made the decision. Danny, Professor Fairlight, he was there. He saw the dialogue trail. He can confirm it. I'm responsible.'

Everyone's gaze shifted to Daniel, who was numb with despair.

'Professor?' Yousef prompted.

Daniel looked across at Yousef, then nodded reluctantly.

Khaled walked slowly over to Yousef. 'So, tell me exactly what happened when you got in the water. Exactly.'

'After I'd given Davy the green light to return, I went straight to the kit room to suit up. Then I went onto the dive platform and dropped in. Brandy was working round the other side, so I just started completing the checks that Davy had requested. After a minute or two I tapped out a message to Brandy on my wrist panel, just asking how long she had to go. When I didn't get a response, I made my way round. I wasn't worried. You know how the comms panels are, pretty erratic.'

People around the control room nodded.

'As soon as I saw her, I knew there was a problem. Her harness straps were entangled with the ROV cage. It looked like she had become more caught up as she tried to free herself.'

'Okay, but she still had plenty of oxygen in her tank, right?' Kal realised that his anguish at losing Brandy had distilled all too quickly into anger, and he was now trying hard to regain a more measured approach. His tone become less accusatory, more clarifying.

'Right. It looks like something blocked her supply. That's all I can think of.' Yousef shook his head, seemingly unable to comprehend what could have happened.

The ship medic had quietly watched this premature postmortem, but now interjected.

'Khaled. Kal. I know we are going to have to work through all of this in the fullness of time. No one wants to know more than me how we have lost a soul on my watch. But ...' He paused, scanning the room. 'For now, may I suggest that we all take a moment to just honour the passing of a friend and colleague.'

Kal stared defiantly at the doctor, but then he nodded. Davy got unsteadily to his feet. Daniel couldn't believe someone so vibrant, funny, and intelligent as Brandy could really be gone. His mind raced through his own accident, his father's death, Yousef's warning, and now this—was he just being paranoid, or was there something seriously wrong here? He shoved the thoughts aside for now; Brandy deserved his respects in this moment.

Numbly, he lowered his head with everyone else, as they turned towards Jenny Brand and prayed.

***

Later the team got together to open a bottle of spirits, toast their lost colleague, and reminisce a little. Alcohol was strictly forbidden on the ship but, as it was Captain Murphy who opened the bottle, no one was of a mind to object. It seemed particularly appropriate that the bottle was a twenty-year-old Remy Martin cognac.

One of the crew took the opportunity to quietly slip away, returning to his cabin. There he retrieved a personal mobile phone connected to a secure line. He clicked on the address bar and selected the only name on the list. After identifying the message icon, he then typed out a brief sit-rep to his boss.

Situation under control. Girl eliminated as per your instructions. Cover still intact. Please advise on next move.

19

April 28, 1630

The Mediterranean

Emir and Shabaka were too close to let their falling-out over Shabaka's decision come between them, both choosing to place what was in their hearts to one side and enjoy the time they still had together. Shabaka made no further mention of his deep desire to embrace his family, and Emir kept his own counsel concerning his fears of mutiny.

They agreed, instead, to spend as much time together as possible in Alexandria. Due to the considerable amount of cargo being loaded onto the *Colossus* in the Egyptian port, and the additional trading demand, the ship would be docked for at least six days. Emir planned to use that time to persuade Shabaka to continue with him to Constantinople. He was sure his friend would change his mind when he heard all that Emir knew—with the evidence to prove it.

Following his revelations and recollections a few days out of Barcelona, Emir had become much more focussed and alert to anything that seemed amiss. Anything that just didn't fit the picture. He continued to keep his anxieties to himself, fearing that if he shared the information he had so far, it may be dismissed again as just wild imaginings of a young boy. Shabaka had already more or less accused him of crying wolf, so he needed to pick his moment. He would only have one more chance at this.

As it turned out, the voyage from Barcelona to Tripoli, despite being the longest leg to date, proved wholly uneventful. No more crew were lost. No further secret assignations took place in the hold. Emir gave both Kazim and Agostinho a wide berth, maintaining vigilance from a safe distance. Kazim caught his eye once and gave him a look that was both penetrating and perplexed, as if he too were trying to remember something.

Emir wondered how he hadn't recognised the Janissary earlier in the voyage. Certainly, Kazim looked far less ostentatious than he had during their last meeting in the marketplace. His beard adornments were gone, as was his colourful Janissary costume, but still, he was a striking figure. All Emir could put it down to was that he hadn't expected to see Kazim on the ship, and their exposure to each other had been brief. He only hoped that these principles would apply the other way round. It seemed unlikely to Emir that Kazim would remember something as inconsequential as the arrest of a young market thief, but there was no point in taking any chances. As things turned out, this was a philosophy he would have done well to remember.

***

One night Emir had an overwhelming urge to check if the casket he had glimpsed was still in place. Upon stealing down into the darkest recesses of the hold, Emir found the spot where the treasure had been concealed. For a second time he pulled open the hessian sack and reached in to retrieve the casket. This time he lifted it clear of the recess it was hidden in. Emir's mouth dropped open as he withdrew a stunning golden casket, encrusted with jewels and glistening, even in the dark of the hold. It was even more magnificent than he had remembered. After a long period of just staring at the relic, Emir started looking for the latch that would open it. Suddenly he heard a distinct and familiar tapping on the hull.

A dim glow grew at the other end of the hold as the tapping grew louder. Gripped with fear, Emir rapidly replaced the casket and silently withdrew deeper into the shadows just as Kazim appeared. He held a flambeau in one hand and his cane in the other. Accompanying him was Mustafa. They stopped at the exact spot Emir had been moments earlier. Kazim knelt and pulled out the small chest, stroked the lid reverentially, and returned it. Emir stood not eight feet away, aware that the flickering of the torch risked exposing him. Kazim continued to kneel as if in prayer, and then he spoke.

'Mustafa, hear me now. The moment is almost upon us. Soon our aga will gather us and share his plans. He intends to tell the men about the heart of Suleiman. He says he wants to reassure them, but all he wants is the glory and the adulation. He intends to tell them that they are invincible with Suleiman's heart in their possession, but he has secretly confided to me that he has started to question the veracity of the legend. His conviction is waning. There was a time when he was a great leader, but today he is little more than a bumbling fool. The fiasco with that boy—the way he brought attention upon himself just to satisfy his own ego. Pathetic. People think his disguise on the ship is just a cover, but the truth is, he is not the man he once was. I will not risk this mission failing under his leadership. So, when the time is right, we will arrange for a terrible accident to befall our aga. And then I will take command.'

He looked up at Mustafa. 'Are you with me?'

Mustafa nodded. 'Always, sir. You can rely on me.'

Kazim nodded pensively, gave the casket a final pat, stood up, and strode back down the hull with Mustafa scampering behind.

Emir didn't move for an age, as the sweat poured down his forehead. If he had been just a minute later, or Kazim a minute earlier, the game would have been over. And, Emir reflected, it was anything but a game.

As Emir lay down on his mattress that night, he felt absolutely shattered. He tried to decipher these latest disclosures. Who was this aga, and what was this fiasco with the boy that Kazim had mentioned? Maybe the secrets were weighing heavily on him; maybe it was just the come down from the adrenaline rush he had just experienced. Either way, he didn't sleep a wink.

***

The stop-off in Tripoli proved entirely routine. When they set sail again, the mood on the ship was unusually upbeat. The winds and the weather had been kind to them. Piracy had been absent, and they were ahead of schedule. Talk turned to all the rumours about the exotic cargo slated to be loaded in Alexandria, and seamen allowed themselves to make plans for returning home.

Emir had taken to sleeping behind the crate he had originally been smuggled aboard inside. He liked the darkness and the solitude. And it was there, on the second night out of Tripoli, that the final pieces of the puzzle fell into place.

He had been asleep for little more than an hour when he was awakened by the hum of a group speaking excitedly in hushed tones, and the flicker of torchlight beyond the cover of his crate. Careful not to move into the light, Emir silently shifted his position to see what was going on. The group numbered around twenty men. Emir recognised both crew and merchants amongst them. Emir caught snippets of the conversation.

'... who is in charge here ... has this group been checked for infiltrators ... when will we make our move ... is it true that we have it in our possession ...'

One voice cut through all the others with its authority rather than its volume. It was a voice that Emir knew well.

'Silence, men,' Kazim instructed. 'Time is short. Our leader approaches now.'

An imposing figure stepped into the circle that the group had formed. Immediately every man knelt and bowed his head. Emir stared open-mouthed at the scene. The man commanding this deference was Agostinho, the merchant he had crossed.

'Rise, brothers. You all have earnt your place here. None need bow before me.'

Agostinho surveyed the group, nodding with pleasure. He acknowledged one or two individuals like long-lost friends before addressing the gathering.

'You know who I am. I will continue to use my alias whilst we remain on this godforsaken ship, but you all know my true identity. I was your aga before, and I am your aga still. I had the privilege of being the supreme leader of the Janissary corps, and I will lead them again.

I continue to honour our last true sultan, Suleiman the Magnificent.'

Murmurs of *inshallah* ran around the group.

'And my heart still belongs to the great Ottoman Empire. My exile at the hands of the foolish boy sultan, Osman the Second'—he spat the name out—'does not diminish my belief, nor my devotion to the empire. I know many of you have suffered the same fate, and I honour you for keeping the faith and joining us here on this mission.'

Emir's mind raced, trying to assimilate this new information into the picture he had already built up.

'… and the empire owes everything to the corps. There would be no empire without us. And yet we have been discarded, disgraced, and disrespected these last few years. And already we see the empire fading, becoming less, without our guiding hand. Under the reign of Osman's weak brother, Murad, we have seen plague and famine beset our mother country and our home city of Constantinople, while we have had to watch from afar, exiled by the very people we served and protected. I for one can bear witness to these travesties no longer. It has fallen to us, the forsaken, to reinstate the empire to its former glory. Are you men with me?'

The group reverentially pledged their commitment. The aga continued, outlining his plan. The Janissaries would wait until the *Colossus* had left Alexandria before taking the ship as their own. Merchants would be thrown overboard, and crew would be subjugated to their will. Once the ship had finally docked in Constantinople, the Janissaries would insinuate their way into the sultan's court, under the pretence of being merchants offering exotic goods from the Far East. Once inside they would overcome the court protectorate, assassinate the sultan, and assume control of the empire. Existing Janissaries would be given the opportunity to join this new republic, or face execution. The aga finally paused, having outlined the plan in some detail. For any doubters in the group, he had one more card to play. He smiled in anticipation of the impact he was about to have.

'I know many of you will be concerned that we are few and they are many. How will we possibly overcome our opponents? I want you to remember that we are the best of the best. I look around me, and I see a battalion that could not be equalled anywhere in the world. And …' He paused to further reinforce his point. 'We have something that no other army has. Something that makes us invincible. Something that instils a divine right in us to rule.'

Emir noticed Kazim giving Mustafa a knowing look.

'A few months ago, the Hungarian chapter of our brotherhood reached out to me with incredible news. I was sceptical to begin with, but now I know the truth of their words. A discreet unit of my very best warriors was despatched to Szigetvár on a scouting mission. Meanwhile, we hatched a plan that allowed us to gather key officers from across Europe, as well as providing cover upon our return to Constantinople. That plan turned out to be the *Colossus*. My elite unit reclaimed a long-lost prize in Szigetvár. They spent many difficult weeks smuggling it overland to Dubrovnik in time to load it onto the *Colossus*. Many of your brothers fell to make this moment possible, and I honour them.'

As he spoke, Kazim joined him in the middle of the

circle carrying a large box shrouded in a hessian sack. He dramatically pulled the hessian away.

'Warriors, brothers, I give you the holy relic that legend has spoken of. The artefact that was thought lost. The last light of hope for every Ottoman. You want reassurance that we will win this fight, and I give you the heart of Suleiman the Magnificent.'

The men dropped to their knees and held up their hands, gasping in wonder at the ornate golden casket being held aloft by Kazim. Shining gold, ornately carved, and decorated with jewels of every colour, it was staggering to behold. But it was the contents of the casket that had so enraptured the assembled.

'As you all know from legend, any ruler who possesses the true heart of our greatest sultan will command the will of our people. Brothers, we cannot fail in our task.'

The group eventually disbanded, having replaced the casket in its hiding place, this time securing it under some loose boards. Emir lay behind his crate in the pitch black, with only the rhythmic sound of the waves massaging the ship's hull to accompany his racing thoughts. Finally, he could see the whole terrifying picture. His friend had to believe him now. As soon as he could snatch a moment alone with Shabaka, out of sight and earshot of anyone else, he would tell him everything.

***

It was day four in Alexandria. No one had been given even a single hour of shore leave. The crew had worked in shifts around the clock, moving cargo off and then onto the *Colossus*. Emir hadn't had a single moment alone with Shabaka, and he knew that time was running out. The Egyptian was still contracted to conclude his service on the *Colossus* in his home city.

On the fifth day Shabaka was finally granted some personal time. Emir wasn't. In his desperation he approached the captain personally, pleading for some time ashore that day. Barbarossa, whilst quietly respecting the boy who had won over his crew, claimed he needed every pair of hands he could get at this stage. Emir persisted until the captain caved and said that if Emir could persuade another crewman to forgo their leave, he might take their place.

'Good luck with that, my boy. You will need more than sleight of hand to pull that trick off.'

A short while later, Captain Barbarossa watched Emir walk down the gangway with Shabaka. He thought, not for the last time, that he really should stop underestimating this boy. Antonio, the flamboyant Italian whom Emir had saved, was happy to allow Emir the shore time in his place.

The pair went into one of Shabaka's favourite coffeehouses, bringing fond memories of the Constantinople coffee scene flooding back for Emir. The Egyptian was smoking a new craze in Egypt, imported from India, called hookah. The strange pipe with its glass vase and ceramic pot made for a very exotic image. Emir declined the hose; he was too nervous to do more than drink coffee.

They sat quietly under an awning outside the coffeehouse, each lost in his own thoughts. Shabaka was building up the courage to reaffirm his decision to finish the voyage here. He formed his opening gambit in his mind and began to speak.

'So, Emie, my friend—'

'Stop. Just stop,' Emir interrupted. 'First listen to what I have to say. Shaba, please, you owe me that much. Just listen, and then if you still decide to stay, I won't test you further.'

Shabaka took a long drag on his shisha, blew out a plume of smoke, and slowly nodded.

'All right my friend. I will hear your tale, but you should know that I will not be turned about on this. The loss of my brother is weighing heavily on me now. I need to be with family. I need to be home.'

It was Emir's turn to nod sagely. How could he deny his friend this choice? He decided in that moment that he would share everything with Shabaka and seek his counsel, but he would not press him to change his mind. If Emir truly was a friend, he should respect his companion's decision. Of course, he needed to be with family. Emir only hoped that he himself would live long enough to see his own flesh and blood.

And so, he poured his heart out, recounting every detail of the conspiracy he had uncovered. From his first run-in with Kazim to the clandestine meeting some two weeks ago. The plot to assassinate the sultan and the gathering of an exiled Janissary battalion. The sailors murdered to make way for undercover Janissary recruits, and the true identity of Agostinho. Shabaka's expression was inscrutable, his face stony as he listened.

Emir deliberately saved the most shocking revelation to last. Slowly he described the presentation of the golden casket and what lay within. Even as he described this detail, Emir's confidence and conviction faltered. Hearing this story out loud, for the first time,

Emir felt doubts creeping in. Had he really witnessed all these things, or were some of them imagined? Had he leapt to fantastical conclusions without really checking the evidence? Did he really believe this himself? Instead of bringing his story to a triumphant conclusion, he found himself running out of steam and surety.

Shabaka saw that Emir was waning and stepped in. 'That has been a heavy burden for you to carry on your own, my friend. Especially for one so small.' Shabaka knew Emir needed comfort now. He could at least take the weight from the shoulders of this child. 'I thank you for trusting me with these details. I am shocked and appalled by your story. I would like to take a moment to consider everything you have said before I give you my counsel.'

Emir nodded. He could see where this was going.

'So, while I let your bloody tale of treachery and villainy percolate, I will share something of my own.' Shabaka took another long draw on the shisha, as if considering where to begin.

'You once asked me about my brother's ring, the one you returned to me. I would share that story with you now. As you know, there are two rings. An identical pair. When my brother and I were not much older than you, my father sat us down and showed us these rings, and how they fitted cleverly together to make one larger ring. He told us that they were ancient Egyptian rings. They are centuries old, and, I believe, priceless. But that doesn't truly describe their worth. The real value of these rings'—Shabaka pulled the two rings off his finger at this point and placed them upon the table—'the real value is in the relationship between the two. You see, my father was told that these rings could never be truly separated. They would always find a way back to each other. My father and his brother each had been given one by their father. He said the rings would make sure that the brothers never separated. And so it was, until my uncle passed, and then my father gifted the rings to Jaba and me.

'Many times in our lives, when one or other of us was in difficulty or lost to themselves, the rings would find a way of pulling us back together. I have come to understand that they embody a lifelong relationship between two souls. A loyalty and devotion. They are connected, and in being so, they create a powerful bond between the two wearers. A never-ending circle that cannot be broken in life. And in that way, you cannot put a price on these rings. Jaba understood this. He knew that the ring must return to me in the event of his death. And, with your kind help, it did.'

Emir looked at Shabaka, then down at the pieces of jewellery. A tear rolled down his cheek as he thought about his friend Jaba.

'What will become of the rings now, Shaba? Who will you bequeath them to?'

'Ahh. Yes. A good question. Well, this one'—he picked up one of the pair—'this one I shall return to its place on my finger. As for this one, this one is for my soul brother. This one is for you, Emie. We are as one now, my friend. You're bound to me.'

Emir stared open-mouthed at his friend. 'Does that mean ... ?'

'Yes, Emie, it does.'

Two days later the *Colossus* set sail from Alexandria with much fanfare. Two friends stood together on the port side of the grand galleon, watching the crowds waving and screaming enthusiastically. They looked ahead to a lifetime of shared voyages and adventures.

How could they have known that this would be the final, fatal voyage of the *Colossus*?

20

October 23, 2012
Limassol

'I'm just saying, she might be the answer.'

Khaled looked sceptically at Sir David Nightingale on his video satphone. Since the terrible accident, Sir David had been a constant source of support to Khaled, but this recommendation seemed a bit premature. He wasn't sure if he was ready to replace Brandy. If he would ever be.

The mood on the ship since the loss of Jenny Brand had been subdued. Davy took it the worst. His spirit seemed broken. He castigated himself to anyone prepared to listen. Most of the crew were sympathetic and made time to hear his confessions, before attempting to persuade him that no blame could be assigned for this terrible accident.

Khaled also carried a heavy burden of guilt. It was his team. His project. His responsibility. The first month had been the worst. The operation was inevitably suspended while a routine investigation took place. Brandy's body was transported to Limassol, where a postmortem confirmed what everyone already knew—that she had drowned.

Two officers from the Marine Accident Investigation Branch flew out from the UK to co-ordinate an inquest. Interviews were conducted on board and, whilst both Davy and Yousef were reprimanded for breaking protocol on the buddy system, the MAIB recorded a verdict of accidental death.

Whilst Davy sought out absolution from fellow crew members, Yousef withdrew further into himself, becoming increasingly detached from the group. Even Daniel was finding it difficult to get anything out of his old friend.

After a month of watching his crew floating more adrift than any ship, Khaled had a decision to make. Shut the operation down indefinitely or push on. Sir David had made it clear that he would back Kal's choice. Khaled appreciated the vote of confidence but knew it would be a big setback for DIVE if the project was mothballed. Obviously from a financial point of view, but also from an archaeological standpoint. Once the engines were shut down, it would take a long time to get them running again.

Finally, he brought the whole team together to check their appetite to continue. They were all still under contract, but Kal knew that imposing project continuance on a grieving and reluctant group would be futile at best, dangerous at worst. Nearly everyone spoke: about Brandy, about how they felt, and about their aspirations going forward. Only Yousef stayed silent. Kal was surprised by the strength of feeling amongst the team. The overwhelming expression was one of sorrow, qualified by a real determination to see the project through.

Even Davy spoke up. 'Look, I know my voice doesn't count for much round here right now. I will never forgive meself for what has happened, like. I just want to say, I miss Brandy like hell, but you can't shut us down now Kal, man. If we leave it here, not only will it be unfinished business, but we'll also all be left to work through this stuff on our own. To honour Brandy, let's get this thing finished.'

Kal knew that no matter what he said, Davy would always punish himself for Brandy's death. What Kal chose to keep to himself, though, was that he couldn't entirely say the same about Yousef. He had known the man for a long time, and really admired his work, but he had made a bad call. Yousef's behaviour since had neither been helpful nor, if he was honest, conventional. *We each manage grief and guilt in our own way*, Khaled reflected.

'I'm with Davy,' Daniel chipped in. Everyone murmured their agreement. As before, only Yousef remained quiet.

Kal nodded and agreed to push forward. As he closed the meeting, he was told there was a video call coming in from the UK, and he could take it in his cabin.

'She's been recommended by one of our non-execs,' Sir David said. 'You're a head down, a diver short, and your team could do with some fresh blood. Her CV is pretty bloody impressive, Kal. Got to be worth taking a look, old chap, wouldn't you say? No pressure, mind; it's entirely your call. I'm just saying she might be the answer.'

***

Kal met the young Turkish woman in a small café on the seafront promenade of the city of Limassol. The crew knew the port well, but this was not one of their regular haunts, and that was why Kal chose it. He wanted to meet her alone, before anyone else even knew that he was considering bringing a new member onto the team.

He'd perused her CV at length beforehand, so this was much more about style and fit than qualifications. Nevertheless, her credentials were impeccable. Over five hundred diving hours and extensive experience working specifically with ROVs and in the field of marine archaeology in general, but what really piqued his interest was her academic profile. She was an honours student in studies on the Ottoman Empire and had published numerous papers and two books on the subject. Her specific area of interest was the Osman dynasty of sultans. She certainly ticked all the boxes on paper.

'Mr Farouk. It's a pleasure to meet you.'

'Khaled. Kal, please.'

'Sure thing, Kal. I'm Banu.'

'The pleasure is all mine, Banu. Sir David couldn't speak highly enough of you, and your bio makes for impressive reading.'

'Thanks, Kal. I always worry that I must read like the world's dullest woman. Plenty of qualifications but pretty far down on your party invitation list. You can just imagine— "We must get Banu along; her thesis on the role of Janissary development in the decline and modernization of the Ottoman Empire really gets the party started".'

Khaled laughed and thought that he hadn't done that in a while. He studied her a little closer. She had an athletic build and a deep, warm tan, and her eyes were jade green. She wore her dark hair in a short, punky cut. Her smile seemed so natural, and her self-deprecating manner endeared her to him instantly.

'You are too modest, Banu.'

'I kid you not, Kal. But enough of my woeful social

life—I want to hear all about the DIVE project. It sounds super cool.'

Khaled found her passion infectious. They talked excitedly for over an hour before Banu said, 'I sense I might be running out of time, Kal, and there was something else I wanted to put on the table. Well, declare, really.'

Kal nodded solemnly. She had been too perfect. Here came the stinger.

'It's obvious that I want to join your project, but to be completely honest, there is another driver that I haven't been entirely up front about.'

Kal braced himself.

'You see, I'm a bit of a fan of Professor Fairlight. A bit more than a fan, really. He's kind of like, well, how can I put this without sounding like a complete psycho? He's kind of a hero of mine. Not in an "I watch you when you're sleeping" way, I should clarify. More in a "I've read all your books and attended all your lectures" kind of way. So, anyway, when I heard that he had joined the project, I was thrilled. Well, that's probably a bit of an understatement. So, there it is, full disclosure. I'm a Fairlight groupie.'

Relief flooded through Kal. 'So, if I offered you the position, as well as getting an experienced diver and another Ottoman expert ... I would also get to watch you give our professor a run for his money.'

They laughed and continued their banter for some time, until Kal stood to leave.

'Banu. It has been a real pleasure getting to know you. I do hope that you will join us on our little adventure.'

Banu jumped out of her seat and impulsively hugged

him. He smiled and blushed a little.

'In truth, Banu, you had me at "super cool".'

***

Banu exceeded all of Kal's hopes and expectations in her first few weeks on board the *Triton*. Her knowledge and expertise around the ship, Cygnus, and general diving duties were everything her CV promised and more, but that wasn't the half of it. She engaged a cautious and reluctant crew so infectiously that their mood reclaimed its previous buoyancy. They all said what a find Banu was. Even Davy seemed to regain some of his natural Geordie swagger. Kal couldn't believe his good fortune, but perhaps the biggest plus was with Daniel.

They circled each other at first, keeping a cool distance, Daniel unsure on where Banu fitted, Banu mindful of Daniel's credentials and reputation. But soon their academic debates became less polite and more animated. Banu reminded him of their interaction at his last lecture.

'That's it!' Daniel declared. 'I knew I knew you from somewhere. You asked great questions.'

After a month they were burning midnight oil on a regular basis, debating everything from the ethical merits of the devşirme system for Janissaries to who was the greatest sultan. It was clear that they were the perfect pair to tackle the DIVE project together and were raring to go for the next stage of the project.

***

If the crew had not been so distracted by the frenzy of positivity Banu provided, they may have paid more attention to the increasingly withdrawn state of Yousef. Whilst the Jordanian fulfilled all his duties reliably, he no longer seemed interested in being part of the team. His naturally guarded air, which had been the subject of banter in the past, now became much more pronounced.

Also, far from falling for Banu's charms as the rest of the crew had, Yousef seemed to resent her presence, even treating her with something bordering hostility at times. When Daniel, already feeling protective towards his new protégé, tried to gently question the motives of his friend, he was met with a brick wall. Daniel's patience was wearing thin. First Yousef gave him that strange warning at the funeral, then he was guarded on board the *Triton*, and now he was rude to Banu for no good reason. What did Yousef think he was playing at? The more Daniel ruminated on it, the more he knew he had to confront Yousef. And sooner rather than later.

21

January 18, 2013
Nicosia

Dr Solomon stared out of the window of her chauffeur-driven Mercedes at the blur of wet buildings and pavement going by. She glanced up; the enthusiastic winter rain showed no sign of breaking, as had been forecast. She began to regret taking the meeting.

It was dusk in the Cypriot capital, and the neon signs flickered into life and shimmered in puddle reflections. It was only a short drive from the ministry offices to her destination, little more than a kilometre in fact, but at this hour it could still take thirty or forty minutes to traverse the city. Some of that was down to the inevitable rush-hour traffic, but she knew that the real delay would be prompted by the need to cross the UN buffer zone, leaving the Republic of Cyprus and crossing into Northern Cyprus.

Maria shook her head. Nearly twenty-five years after the Berlin wall had finally come down, Nicosia remained the world's last divided capital city. Why had the world forsaken her beautiful island? Sure, nations had unanimously chosen not to recognise Northern Cyprus as a sovereign state—with the exception of Turkey, obviously—but where was the action? The embargoes, the protests, the political pressure. Old men with failing sight and diminishing memories, looking the other way, she thought, and shook her head again. As a proud Greek Cypriot, Maria Solomon was desperate for her country to be unified once more, for it to be healed and rehabilitated. But, if she was honest, forgiveness wasn't in her own heart. How could she expect the country to let go of the past, when she herself continued to harbour a smouldering resentment for what the Turkish people had done to her. To her family.

She felt no malice towards Turkish people per se. Some of her closest colleagues in the ministry were either Turkish or Turkish Cypriot. Hell, her last boyfriend had been from the occupied northern territories, as she continued to insist on calling the Turkish section of Cyprus. But the atrocities in the wake of the 1974 coup d'état couldn't be forgotten. Shouldn't be. She had had firsthand experience of the rape, torture, and pillage that the Turkish forces had liberally indulged in on those sweltering days in August of '74. Others might forgive and forget, but she never would.

She felt herself stiffening and clenching and looked out of the window once again, seeking some distraction. The brutal memories and bitter emotions were never far beneath the surface for her, but she had tried hard in recent years to not let them command her. As her driver took a hard left into the one-way system, she glanced at the Cyprus Museum on her right. With its faux Roman façade, it provided a distinctive landmark and a welcome diversion for the director.

It had been six months since Maria had had her pacemaker fitted, and after an initial period of nervous caution, the director had found her stride again and hadn't looked back. She recaptured the 'firebrand' characterisation that the *Vogue* article had suggested and resolved to push through her innovations at an even quicker pace.

She reflected that if it hadn't been for that celebrated magazine article and the ensuing media coverage, she probably wouldn't have received the mysterious meeting invitation that she was currently en route to keep. The man hadn't given much away on the phone but was very clear that it involved a 'game-changing' discovery in Cypriot waters.

She felt a buzz in her handbag and reached inside for her phone. It was just a text confirming her booking at the Landmark Hotel that night. She lived ninety minutes outside the city and, although she would get chauffeured home, she enjoyed booking the occasional stayover in the luxury of the Landmark. She always carried an overnight case and always stayed in the same suite. The staff was both attentive and discreet, two qualities that Maria particularly appreciated.

She glanced up to see that they were now approaching the border patrol checkpoint on Ledra Street. She always felt a shudder whenever she crossed the buffer zone. The unoccupied no-man's land was a constant reminder of past conflicts. It was generally referred to as the 'green line,' a nickname attributed to General Young, commander of the British forces in 1963 who, following a fresh outbreak of tensions, delineated a line on a map, separating north from south, with a green pencil. The director never used the casual sobriquet, although she was pleased to see that the sit-in Occupy Buffer Zone movement had finally been moved on. Although she agreed with their politics, she had no time for the aesthetic of passive protest.

As the car crossed over the UN-controlled zone, she

made a promise to herself that she had made a hundred times before and never once kept: to not look up at her old family home as they passed by. The Louisiana-style building stood at the northern point of Ledra Street, its distinctive galleries making it a popular tourist snapshot. She failed as she had failed so many times before, glancing up at the last minute, eyes glistening and bile rising in her throat. The sight of her childhood home never failed to break her heart. Would the events of that night nearly forty years ago ever stop haunting her?

The director forced herself to transfer her gaze, staring instead at her reflection in the privacy screen in front of her. She pulled out a tissue and dabbed at her eyes, careful not to smudge her eyeliner. Maria was a striking woman whose appearance belied her forty-five years. Her long, dark tousled hair framed a well-sculpted face in a Mediterranean olive tone. Her prominent cheekbones and full lips had prompted many people to remark on her similarity to the Italian film star from the fifties and sixties, Sophia Loren. She prided herself on still being able to turn heads when she entered a room and continued to enjoy the attention of men on a regular basis.

The intercom speaker crackled into life. 'We're approaching the Büyük Han now, Doctor.'

'Thank you. If you could just drop me at the eastern entrance, please. And then if you don't mind hanging around. I shouldn't be more than fifteen minutes.'

'Of course, ma'am. Will you be returning to Kornos this evening?'

'No. The Landmark tonight. Then you're done.'

The rain obligingly desisted just as the Mercedes

glided to a halt, and Dr Solomon stepped out of the vehicle. She had made it clear to her driver when he first started working for her that she didn't want him to open doors for her. She had never been dependent on anyone, and she wasn't going to start now. She could open her own damn doors.

***

The Büyük Han, which literally meant the Great Inn, was a caravanserai that was built by the Ottomans in the sixteenth century. Initially constructed as a stop-off point for weary travellers, it had also spent periods as a prison and a refuge. Today it housed a thriving arts centre, including galleries, cafés, and shops. It was Maria's favourite building in the city. She particularly loved the tranquillity of the central courtyard and the distinctive little mosque within.

Her mystery caller had instructed her to head round to the eastern entrance, where he would meet her promptly at six. The last vestiges of twilight dramatically silhouetted the building's skyline, and as the dark descended, the director felt some nerves taking hold. What had she been thinking, coming here alone? She pulled out her phone to call her driver and say she was returning, when a large figure stepped out of the shadows.

'Dr Solomon, I presume?' Duman Osman lifted his fedora slightly in greeting.

'You have me at a disadvantage already, sir, as I don't even know your name.'

'Please forgive me, Doctor. I would never normally be so rude, especially to such a formidable and beautiful woman, but I'm afraid I will have to withhold my identity for just a little longer. If and when we come to some understanding, I will be more than happy to make myself an open book to you. Now please, follow me; I have taken the liberty of preparing some refreshments.'

Maria eyed the stranger as she considered her next move. He had been civil, polite, complimentary without being sycophantic. He spoke with an authority and confidence that she always liked in men. He was certainly physically imposing—six three, six four maybe, and toned to match—but he didn't seem threatening in his disposition. She decided to play her hand a little longer.

They walked in through the eastern gate and on into the courtyard where Maria felt so at peace. The storm-clouds had finally broken, and the cool air was a welcome relief. She took a moment to bask in the space once again. Enjoy its serenity and understated grandeur. The grey cobbling on the ground was beautifully offset by the series of sand-coloured arches that ran round all four sides of the square. But what made the courtyard most striking was the second run of galleried arches above. All this elegantly simple architecture beautifully framed the bijou mosque situated in the centre of the courtyard. The mosque itself was octagonal in shape and stood on a series of small pillars located at each of the eight corners. The sandstone walls contrasted with a simple grey clay dome.

Osman strode directly towards the mosque, pulling a large brass key from his pocket. Ignoring the steps up to the main entrance, he opened a door at the side of the building and beckoned her inside.

'I am sure you have been in this space many times

before, Dr Solomon, but I still think that what I am about to show you will come as a bit of a surprise. A pleasant one, I hope.'

He stepped across to the opposing wall and pushed against two adjoining stones. A section of the wall swung open, revealing a further space behind. He beckoned to his guest to follow him through to where a circular staircase wound down to a lower hidden level.

'When the Ottomans created this building, they thought to incorporate a safe room, in case of unwanted visitors. It remains a secret to this day, with only a handful of people being aware of its existence. My work affords me certain privileges, and access to this room is one of them. Can I offer you a glass of wine, Dr Solomon?'

Maria stared around the torchlit room, completely unaware of her slack-jawed appearance. She was utterly dumbfounded by this discovery. 'I-I-I don't really know what to say. Are you seriously telling me that this room has remained a secret to the whole world for over four hundred years?'

'Around four hundred and fifty, actually. Well, put it like this: if the director of the Department of Antiquities for Cyprus doesn't know about it, who does?'

Osman handed over a glass of dark red wine, smiled, and waited for the director to regain her composure. She took a large mouthful, immediately thinking that if he wanted to drug her, this was how he would do it.

'Please, have a seat. I've much to tell you and little time to cover the ground.'

Maria sat herself down and took a deep breath. The man sat down opposite her, smiled, and poured himself a glass. As if sensing her concern, Osman took a sip and looked down at the ground, considering what to say next.

'Dr Solomon. I have shown you this room as an act of good faith. I am sure you will appreciate the risk I am taking in sharing a secret such as this with someone in such high public office as yourself. I do it to impress upon you the gravity of my business and the sincerity of my offer.'

She was fully back in the room now and keen to re-establish her position of authority. 'And what might that offer be, Mister … ?'

Her host smiled again and winked.

'Patience, Doctor, all in good time. But first I must acknowledge the, the … how is it? An elephant in the room.'

Maria looked around. 'It would have to be a pretty bloody small elephant.'

The man ignored the comment and pushed on. *Not one for humour then*, she thought.

'You are astute enough to recognise that my accent is not Greek Cypriot, or even Turkish Cypriot. I was born and brought up in Istanbul. I am Turkish. I am keenly aware of your family history, Dr Solomon, and I just wanted to say how vehemently I denounce the atrocities of my fellow countrymen. I hope you will not judge me in the same light as those dogs. They do not represent what Turkish people stand for, and I can only offer my profuse apologies and condolences.'

Maria knew that her biography was well reported, but it still threw her whenever a stranger addressed her past tragedies. She nodded and bowed her head, utterly oblivious to the sheer scale of Osman's bold deceit.

'And now we have that unpleasantness out of the

way, let me, how you say, cut to the chase. I am aware of your ambitions for the Cyprus Museum and your personal interest in all things'—he gestured to the room around them—'Ottoman. Well, I have in my possession detailed information on a maritime excavation taking place more or less in your waters, which is going to make headline news around the world.'

Osman paused to allow this information to sink in. His guest placed her half-full glass of wine back on the table and leant forward.

'Even as we speak, this seabed dig is recovering treasures from a seventeenth-century Ottoman merchant shipwreck. The cargo is going to change the whole way we perceive the Ottoman Empire and includes riches from as far afield as the Far East. It is, if you will forgive the metaphor, the holy grail of shipwrecks.'

'Surely this dive is already a matter of record on our books.'

'Certainly, goods are being declared at Limassol, but the project asserts that it is operating in international waters, an assertion that I know you can overturn.'

'How?' Maria challenged.

'Ahhh, and so we come to the rub. I am in a position to furnish you with all the details you need on the shipwreck project and the leverage to assert Cypriot jurisdiction. This information will enable you to seize all goods from this recovery. Hundreds of artefacts that rewrite history and illuminate the voyage of an incredible Ottoman galleon. From a career point of view, it's a game-changer. But ... in return I want you to commit to me that I may reclaim one item from the haul.'

'Reclaim?'

'Yes. I have reason to believe that one particular artefact is a long-lost family heirloom, which is rightfully mine. But to be plain, Doctor, whatever the legitimacy of my petition, the price for my information is that this item be gifted to me with the minimum of fuss or examination.'

'And what is that item, sir?'

'That is a private matter, but I will say this. There will be many more valuable artefacts in this recovery than the item I require. This is not an issue of financial gain, but more of a sentimental attachment, you might say.'

Maria sat back, draining her glass. She slowly crossed her legs and noticed his brief glance down at her toned calves. She enjoyed knowing that she invariably had the upper hand against the men she negotiated with. She clinked the side of her glass with one of her many gold rings as she weighed up the proposition. Finally, she stood up to address the man opposite her.

'Okay. *If* you check out, and *if* you have the information you say you have, and *if* we are successful in asserting our rights of jurisdiction, and *if* there really is a recovery project of the scale that you are describing, then yes, I will allow you to retain one item.'

'That is a lot of ifs, but no mind—your caveats do not concern me. As long as I have your assurance, in writing of course, then I do believe we have an agreement.'

He also stood, stepped forward, and took her hand, then bowed down to kiss it.

'I will have to know your identity, of course.'

'As soon as the papers are drawn up, Doctor, I will be

most happy to make your proper acquaintance.' Again, there was a glint in his eye as he said this.

Maria scanned him again. He was maybe a bit older than she had first judged, but he was undoubtedly in good shape. 'I can have the basic agreement drawn up over the next couple of hours. Maybe you would like to join me at my hotel a little later. We can go through the details and perhaps celebrate over a glass of something?'

'You are most gracious, Doctor. I have a previous commitment this evening, but I will try to move it. If I can, I would be more than happy to accept your kind offer.'

Maria pulled a card from her bag and placed it into the hand of the tall, imposing stranger.

'This is my card; the hotel name and room details are on the back. And please, call me Maria.'

Osman stood in the shadows of the Büyük Han, watching Maria Solomon get back into her car. He mused on the fact that she had no clue as to his identity. He would enjoy revealing who he really was in due course, which would, inevitably, mean that once her usefulness was spent, he would have to kill her.

22

May 7, 1630

The Levantine Basin

Emboldened by Shabaka's decision to stay on board and provide support, Emir urged that they approach the captain before the *Colossus* set sail out of Alexandria. Knowing that Barbarossa would need considerable persuading, Shabaka counselled Emir to proceed cautiously. This fell on deaf ears as the boy's adrenaline rushed. *Surely, the time is now*, Emir thought. With every passing minute they risked the traitors slipping through their fingers, or worse, putting their mutinous plan into action.

Emir approached Captain Barbarossa less than an hour before departure. He got as far as the third step up to the poop deck before he heard the captain's thunderous tone.

'The next man who does anything to risk delaying our departure further will feel the weight of my bastinado on their feet, so they won't be able to walk for a week. Do I make myself absolutely clear?' he bellowed.

An hour later Emir stood beside his friend waving at the crowds on the quay and reflecting that maybe a more measured approach might be no bad thing after all.

***

On board, the crew were distracted by talk of what

the substantial cargo from Alexandria held. Merchants were unusually tight-lipped, and this only fuelled the rumours that the *Colossus* held treasures from the Far East: magic potions, flying carpets, miracle cures, and never-before-seen precious stones and metals.

All the gossip gave Emir and Shabaka little opportunity to hatch their own secret plans. Only on the third night out of Alexandria could they sneak into the cargo hold undetected. Shabaka had been closely monitoring Agostinho and Kazim, amongst others whom Emir identified, watching for any suspicious behaviour for himself. Whilst no further covert meetings had taken place, the Egyptian witnessed enough furtive nods, looks, and gestures to suggest a clandestine operation may be underway.

Apart from Emir's accounts, the only material evidence they had of potential foul play was the casket that Emir had spoken of. Even that only presented circumstantial evidence, but Shabaka knew they needed something tangible to support their outlandish story. Even a man of Egyptian descent such as Shabaka had, of course, heard the legends of Suleiman the Magnificent, and the supernatural power associated with his missing heart. It had always seemed fanciful to Shabaka, but the truth of the legend wasn't at issue here. If the men who had acquired it believed in its powers, that would provide a substantial foundation on which to build a revolution.

As they approached the darkest recesses of the cargo hold, Shabaka secretly prayed that Emir's story had been, at least in part, embellished by the wild imaginings of an impressionable thirteen-year-old. He still had no idea how they would convince the captain that he had a potential mutiny on his hands, let alone that it was a platform for revolt and treason.

They stumbled blindly in the dark until they reached the spot where Emir knew the casket was hidden. He lit the smallest of flames, just enough to see by, and beckoned to his friend to pull back the loose boards. Shabaka lifted two wooden battens away and immediately saw the sacking that Emir had described. Eagerly he lifted out the package. After placing it down with a care bordering on reverence, Shabaka removed the hessian cloth to reveal the casket.

Shabaka found himself momentarily unable to breathe. He stared down at the box, caught in the spell of its majesty. It was so much more than Emir had described. The ornate gold caught Emir's flame, reflecting it back into Shabaka's countenance. He was entranced.

Emir finally broke the spell. 'Do you think we should open it?'

Shabaka looked up at him from his kneeling position. His hands were shaking. 'I'm too afraid,' he whispered.

'What, in case there isn't anything inside?'

'No,' Shabaka replied, 'In case there is.'

'We have to know, Shaba. We *have* to.'

Shabaka slowly nodded his assent. He tried opening the lid, but it wouldn't budge. He couldn't see any locking device or keyhole. How did you open it? Closer examination revealed an intricate layer of interlocking bolts. It appeared to be some kind of puzzle box.

'I've come across these before, in the souks of Persia. Unless you know the trick, it cannot be opened,' Shabaka said, resigned.

'Let me try,' Emir said, sliding the box in front of him. He stared at it for a long time. Shabaka thought he had gone into some kind of trance. Just as he was about to shake him from his daze, Emir suddenly snapped into action, moving and sliding bolts with purpose and assuredness.

Less than a minute later, they both heard an audible click, and the lid sprang open. The man and the boy both leant over to behold what lay within. Eventually Shabaka gave a wry grin.

'Well, I guess that's not altogether surprising, my young compatriot.'

'I guess not,' said Emir, with a philosophical tone.

As Shabaka made to close the box, the two of them heard sounds of conversation. Distant, but growing. Silently Emir slid all the bolts back into place, seamlessly reversing the sequence he had just used to open the casket, and gestured to Shabaka to replace the wooden panels. Shabaka put the casket back into the sackcloth, but before he could tuck it back into its compartment, Emir lifted it out of his hands. Shabaka stared at him incredulously, then, as he grasped Emir's thinking, vigorously shook his head.

Emir nodded firmly. He couldn't leave the casket behind again. There was simply too much at stake. Shabaka shook his head, more ruefully this time; replaced the wooden battens; blew out the candle; and followed Emir as he retreated behind the nearest cargo crates.

No sooner had they hidden than two men came into view, one carrying a torch. They continued to speak conspiratorially, in hushed but anxious tones. It was Mustafa and his sidekick, Onur.

'If Kazim knew that we were down here, death would be the very least of our concerns,' Onur whispered desperately.

'Well, he won't, will he. That is, as long as you don't tell him. And I'm of a mind to think that you won't, you old scrote. Now stop your bellyaching and pull out the casket. I have to see what lies within.'

'You know what lies within. They told us what bleedin' well lies within. Isn't that enough for you?'

'No. I need to see it with me own eyes. Now, a little less whining and a little more divining.'

Onur scrabbled over to the spot where Emir and Shabaka had been moments earlier and pulled up the boards. And just as Shabaka had, he too stared down in amazement, unable to speak. Finally, he looked up at Mustafa.

'It's gone. The casket. It's gone. The sacred heart of Suleiman the Magnificent is lost. What will we do now? What on earth is our aga going to say?'

The man holding the torch snapped, 'He won't say nothing, 'cos he won't hear nothing, 'cos we ain't gonna say nothing. You got that? We were never here. Now put those boards back quick, and let's get out of here sharpish.'

The two men quickly covered their tracks and hastily retreated back down the hull.

Finally, their sounds faded away.

Shabaka grabbed hold of Emir's shirt. 'Are you mad? What were you thinking, Emie? Now they know that the casket has been taken, they will turn the ship upside down to find it. We are doomed.'

'Steady, Shaba. I admit that I didn't expect that discovery to happen quite so quickly, but this was going to happen sooner or later. We still have the edge.'

Shabaka stared at Emir, doubt written large across his face.

'We have the box and the upper hand. You heard them; they're not going to say anything. They wouldn't dare. They would have to admit that they were breaking the rules. That's not going to happen. We are still at the wheel, Shaba. We decide what happens next.'

Shabaka looked down on the boy and once again was struck by his maturity and pluck.

'Kazim was right about one thing, Emie.'

'What?' Emir responded indignantly.

'You *have* got some balls.'

***

Deep in the cargo hold, the two of them stayed behind the crate a while longer to make sure that neither of the men returned for another look. Emir showed Shabaka a space he had fashioned for hiding the casket. It was significantly more discreet than the original bolthole, and slowly Shabaka's confidence returned.

Once they carefully placed the casket in its new hideaway, their conversation turned to next steps. They knew they were on borrowed time. Any advantage they had, hung by the slenderest of threads. Whatever they were going to do to foil the plot needed to be done now. Emir argued again that it was time to approach the captain and share their information.

'Not yet, Emie. We need more allies first. People more receptive to this news who also have the captain's ear. Our message will be lent credibility by the standing of our messenger.'

Emir started to pace with frustration.

'Who then, Shaba? Who can we trust? Who can we get to, that will get us to the captain?'

'I think I know just the man,' Shabaka said, staring back down the ship's hull, into the darkness. 'The boatswain. He is known to me. He joined the ship in Constantinople, he is fair and approachable, and'—Shabaka smiled for the first time since they had come down into the hold that evening—'he is favoured by our captain.'

The two of them finalised a plan and split up.

An hour later Shabaka approached the boatswain. The officer listened intently for a couple of minutes as Shabaka gave an outline of what he knew, before stopping him, as another officer approached.

Once the officer had passed, the boatswain indicated that it was too dangerous to carry on the conversation so openly.

'We shall meet later, when the ship is asleep—say at the second bell of the middle watch at the bow of the ship.'

Shabaka hesitated, then responded. 'There is another who will join me, the boy, Red. He is the one that uncovered the plot. He has more detail and more firsthand account than I. You need to hear this story from him.'

'Shabaka, I know the boy you're referring to. He's a good lad, but I'm uncomfortable involving him at this stage. He's just a boy. If something were to happen, I wouldn't forgive myself.'

'I appreciate your concern,' Shabaka acknowledged, 'but you must hear it from him. I cannot do it justice, and I cannot risk you not believing what we have to tell you. He must come.'

The boatswain grimly nodded his assent but impressed upon Shabaka that no other party should be involved at this stage. Having finalised arrangements, the men casually parted, the senior officer shouting some spurious directions after Shabaka as he retreated.

Shabaka shared key aspects of the meeting with Emir and then suggested that they meet at the bow ten minutes before the allotted time.

'I prefer to be in good time rather than be late, Emie. Now, I have other preparations to make, so I shall see you at the bow. Agreed?'

Emir nodded, and the two separated.

***

Ninety minutes later they found themselves by the lantern at the ship's most forefront position, wondering if the boatswain was actually going to turn up. They didn't have to speculate for very long, as he stepped into view.

'Shabaka. So, this is your boy, Red, right?'

'My name is Emir, sir, though you may call me Red.'

'Well, Emir, I understand you are the man with all the answers, so why don't you take me through what you know. And take your time, lad—don't miss anything out, all right?'

Emir glanced across at Shabaka, who nodded reassuringly. After taking a moment to assimilate his thoughts, Emir then launched into his story in hushed tones. Over the next fifteen minutes he repeated all the information he had shared with Shabaka: the run-in with Kazim, the furtive meetings, the real identity of Agostinho, the crew replacements, the casket and its shocking secret. He finished by summarising the events from earlier that evening.

The boatswain listened attentively, shaking his head with each new revelation.

When Emir had said everything he could think to say, he stopped. There was a pause.

The boatswain stared at him, for a long moment, before finally responding, 'First, I must thank you for bringing this to my attention. You've done the right thing. I must also commend you on your bravery and your valour. And in one so young. You should be very proud of yourself. In truth, you have done little more than confirm some fears that I was starting to harbour, but now we have some proof of this treachery, and with that I am confident that we can nip this thing in the bud.'

Shabaka and Emir nodded, encouraged by this positive assertion. The officer continued, 'But first things first. Let us secure the casket.'

Shabaka frowned. 'Sir. The casket is perfectly secure where it is. It will not be discovered. Surely we need to gain the captain's ear at the earliest opportunity.'

The boatswain stared down towards the deck. Finally, he lifted his head and gave an almost indiscernible nod.

Shabaka saw the gesture and realised too late that some deception was at play. Before he could react, he felt the blade push into his back. Onur stepped into the light.

Shabaka turned to Emir. 'Emie, *run.*'

As Emir struggled to comprehend what was happening, he felt the officer harshly grab him round the throat. He was helpless to intervene as Onur pushed Shabaka over the prow of the ship. A second later there was a splash as Shabaka's body hit the water.

Emir tried to scream and free himself, but the boatswain held him, enveloping him like boa constrictor. Tears of rage sprang to his eyes. In an instant, his plan had been overturned and his companion had been murdered right in front of him. He stopped his struggle and went limp in the officer's grip. It was over.

He stared defiantly at Onur as the sailor stepped forward, wiping the blood off his knife as he approached.

PART 5
CONSTITUTION

23

January 18, 2013

Nicosia

'Dr Solomon. It's a pleasure to welcome you back, as always.'

'Thank you, Jean-Pierre. How's your family?'

'They are all well. Thank you for asking. Your usual suite?'

'Thank you.'

Maria felt entirely at ease and at home whenever she checked into the Landmark. It wasn't just the staff, although she couldn't fault them. They were attentive and engaging, without being intrusive, but it was more than that. She felt an affinity with the hotel itself. A connection, almost.

For a start, they were the same age. The hotel had launched in 1967 and had quickly become the most prestigious hotel in Cyprus. It stood for luxury, elegance, and professionalism—qualities that Maria Solomon admired greatly and also liked to think that she embodied.

She opened the door to the executive suite, dropped her overnight Louis Vuitton bag on the opulent super-king-size bed, kicked off her Christian Louboutin heels, and slipped into the thick, luxurious hotel bathrobe.

As she poured herself a large glass of her favourite Rioja from the bottle that was always provided in her room, she thought, not for the first time, that she really was drinking too much these days. A couple of glasses during the week 'just to take the edge off' had gradually become a bottle a night. But wine didn't count, right? It's not like she was doing a bottle of Jack every night. It didn't affect her ability to work, and it didn't seem to be creating any health issues, so what was the problem?

She flopped into the sofa and gazed out of the panoramic window at the twinkling Nicosia skyline. In the summer she would sit out on the balcony and watch the sun go down, unless she had company, of course.

Maria's thoughts drifted back to the earlier meeting. Why had she invited the stranger back? What compulsion made her do these things? She suddenly had an overwhelming sense of loneliness. Was that it? Was she just lonely?

She had much to be grateful for, and much to be proud of. A celebrated career. Rewarding work. Financial security and independence. A lifestyle hallmarked by luxury brands and first-class experiences. Good genes that meant she still looked great. She could still have her pick of men. She could please herself, and for the most part, she did.

She poured herself another glass and wandered up to the window, lost in her thoughts. The question she found herself returning to more and more these days was, with this enviable lifestyle, why was she angry and unhappy so much of the time? This was the life she had chosen for herself, wasn't it? She had everything she had ever wished for, and now she was starting to wonder whether she had wished for the right things.

The interview she had done for *Vogue* had asserted that she may have been a product of her background in the choices that she made and the characteristics that she had developed. At the time she had strongly refuted this viewpoint. Her choices were those of a strong, modern, independent woman. The tragedy in her life did not define her. She wouldn't let it.

But now, she wasn't so sure. She had lost her family as a child, and she had chosen to not have any family of her own as an adult. She had grown up without any children around her, and she had no close friends in adulthood. She had lost everything once, and now she curated artefacts for a living. Gathering old possessions to fill empty, soulless rooms. She had witnessed the worst that men could do, and now she would never let a man get close. Intimate, sure, but not close.

Idly she googled DIVE to see if she could fill in some of the blanks in the narrative of her anonymous stranger. As she casually scanned the 'Key Personnel' drop-down menu, wondering whether she might have come across any of the executives, her jaw dropped as a familiar face suddenly popped up. 'We are thrilled to announce that we recently secured the services of Professor Fairlight …'

Maria stared at the picture of the one man she had ever truly loved, while her brain fizzed as she tried to calculate all the connections and implications. This was the project Daniel had mentioned in his call the day she had her operation. She should have guessed. Why hadn't Daniel called back to set up his suggested Limassol meet?

She resolved to try and make contact with Daniel tomorrow. Meanwhile she actioned instructions to get the *Triton*'s salvage cargo seized, thinking that if her anonymous benefactor had his eyes on what she now suspected he did, then she was going to have to disappoint him.

Was there still a chance for her and Daniel? She dismissed the sentimental notion. Following their breakup, she had reconciled herself to the fact that she was destined to lead a solitary life. One not without its pleasures, but, given the long shadows cast by her childhood trauma, a solitary one, nevertheless.

She emptied the bottle and returned to the comfort of the sofa. Was it too late to change, to make different choices? Could she finally outrun the tragedy of her past? A tear ran down her cheek. She closed her eyes and started to drift, the wine giving her a familiar buzz. She tried to conjure up some happy thoughts, some positive affirmations that she could cling on to, but as she slipped into uneasy sleep, her mind skipped back through the years, like tumbleweed running down a war-torn boulevard, to her childhood and, inevitably, to the horrors of 1974.

***

The small mercenary squad of six elite soldiers slowly progressed down the boulevard. They had offered their services to the Turkish military during the first invasion of Cyprus back in July but were now operating under their own cognisance. Whilst the men broadly shared in the ideology of Pan-Turkism, they had no interest in the positioning of this invasion as a 'peace mission' operating in response to the Greek coup d'état only one month earlier.

This second invasion had begun two days ago, on August 14, and was making painfully slow progress towards its predetermined target of taking control of everything north of the green line. The July operation had resulted in a meagre 3 per cent occupation of Cyprus. This push was destined to capture 36 per cent of the island.

For this unit, though, even the numbers were irrelevant. This was about ethnic cleansing, plain and simple. Removing Greeks from the island to allow Turkish occupation. The unit had much greater ambitions than an occupied Cyprus, but that was the long game. For now, this cause was as good as any for keeping your hand in.

The squad sergeant lifted up his fist, signalling to the squad to pause while he surveyed the scene in front of him. They had come to a junction. It was late in the evening now, but the last vestiges of light still left you exposed in open areas. He had heard that a Turkish M47 tank had been taken out less than half a mile from here earlier, and he was proceeding with uncharacteristic caution now.

On the other side of the junction, Ledra Street began. They were no more than two hundred metres from the green line. The young sergeant pulled out some binoculars and slowly scanned the route ahead. Something caught his eye, a flickering light coming from the first-floor gallery in one of the buildings ahead. He turned to the soldiers behind him.

'You three go left; you two follow me to the right. We'll meet at the foot of that building over there. Something tells me that Greek arrogance has provided some entertainment for us. Watch your marks as you go. And quiet.'

The sergeant was barely twenty-five, but his assured authority and passionate commitment to the cause made him a natural leader. These men had already committed much more than just their service to him.

The squad slowly made their way around the junction, scanning for snipers or potential ambush locations. They regrouped at the foot of the building, which appeared to be a domestic dwelling. Two of the squad picked up a piece of concrete rubble, whilst the rest checked their ammunition levels. The sergeant pulled a small vial from his pocket and sniffed some of the contents deep into his nostril. The effect of the opioid was immediate. He laughed maniacally as the lump of concrete was swung violently into the front door.

The door gave way easily, and the squad slipped inside. They scanned the ground floor, consisting of a kitchen and various utility rooms, before ascending to the first floor. Despite their heavy boots and cumbersome weaponry, they moved largely in silence.

The sergeant was the first to step into the living room. Across the room stood a man and woman clutching a boy of around fourteen and a girl of maybe ten years. The woman stared at the soldiers defiantly whilst the girl shook with terror. The boy looked angry and petrified in equal measure. The husband stepped forward, putting up both his hands in a gesture of supplication.

'Sir. Please. I am a man of medicine. I bear you no ill will. I am not armed. We are no threat to you or your men. Please take whatever you want but leave my family. We have no quarrel with you.'

The sergeant lifted his pistol and shot the man directly in the forehead. His wife screamed and clutched her children still closer, as her husband fell to the floor.

'The girl is of no use to us. Get rid of her.'

One of the men grabbed hold of the young girl, who started to scream. The mother desperately tried to intervene, but she didn't have the strength. Her daughter flailed desperately as the soldier grabbed her round the waist.

'Shut her up. Now,' the sergeant spat out, then took another deep snort of his drug.

The soldier pulled out a knife and expertly sliced it across her throat. She fell, silenced, to the floor alongside her father.

The sergeant had already turned his attention to the boy.

'Today is your lucky day, young man, as I've decided to let you live. In that way you will be able to recount how the dominance and virility of Turkish men pleases your women in a way that your own men never could. Hold him.'

Another of the soldiers grabbed the boy without a moment's consideration, gripping him with an arm around his neck.

'If you turn away, you will only make it worse for your mother. You two, take her to the table. Show her what it feels like to have a real man inside her.'

The remaining two members of the squad dragged the wife and mother across to the dining table, ripping her clothes from her as they went. They also acted completely dispassionately. This wasn't even sport; it was duty.

The woman cried out, 'Please, let my son go, and I will let you do whatever you want to me. Please, let him go.'

'You miss the point, sugar tits,' the sergeant responded. 'We are doing this in order for the boy to see it.'

As the woman was brutally defiled, the sergeant carefully watched the boy, whose terror had now cooled to a piercing anger. Despite his mother's screams, he never once took his gaze away from that of the sergeant. For fifteen horrifically long minutes, the boy stared with righteous hatred at the squad leader.

What the sergeant didn't know, couldn't have known, was that the boy maintained his steely gaze in order to stop himself from looking at the wooden panels directly behind where the sergeant was standing. The panels hid a small cubbyhole area that had long been a favourite hiding place for his seven-year-old sister, and for the entire duration of the shocking ordeal, his sister stared through the cracks, desperately trying to muffle her agonising sobs.

Finally, the sergeant, now dangerously high, called his men off the brutalised woman as he strolled over to the table.

'Don't worry, sugar tits, I'm not going to sully myself with your stench. Your work is done.'

He pulled out his pistol and shot her in the temple. The boy screamed with rage, deciding that this was the time to make his final defiant gesture. He pulled out a grenade that he had been holding under his coat the whole time and hurled it at the sergeant. Deftly the squad leader caught it and nonchalantly threw it towards the safety of the open gallery onto the street, but the grenade exploded as it left his grip. The soldier nearest him caught the blast full on and died instantly.

The sergeant turned back to the boy with a crazed

look in his eyes, grinning wildly.

'Well, that's more like it. Good lad. Well played.'

The other soldiers stared aghast at their leader. One of them finally spoke up. 'Serg-Sergeant Osman. Your arm. Sir, your arm, it's gone.'

Osman looked down at his side. Such was the level of opioids flowing through his system that the horrific injury had barely registered on his pain dial. It was severed cleanly at the elbow. He shook his head with a perplexed look of disbelief before returning his gaze to the boy. One of the soldiers ripped a section of the tablecloth and fashioned a tourniquet for the sergeant, whilst he continued to stare at the young boy. Finally, he brushed the soldier away.

'Brave boy. You have earned my admiration and respect.' He paused, as if considering his next move. 'Time to move on. Kill him.'

Two of the soldiers unshouldered their HK11 light machine guns and emptied fifty rounds into the young boy, ripping his body into pieces. The squad quickly scanned the room before following their sergeant out. A framed certificate, dislodged from its screw in the wall following the gunfire, dropped as the last soldier was exiting the living room. He caught it with a reflex action before it could hit the floor. Lighting a cigarette, he casually scanned the copy. It was nothing more than a first-aid course distinction certificate in the name of Maria Solomon. He shrugged, dropped the frame, and left.

It would be another six harrowing hours before Maria finally ventured from her hiding place.

***

Maria was woken from her troubled sleep by the ping of her phone announcing a text message. She was disorientated, but still pleased to have been woken. The dreams were always the same: after the horror she'd crawl from her hiding place, only to be grabbed from above by the monstrous sergeant. She would scream until she woke. She was grateful that the phone had intervened before her dream's conclusion.

Feeling dehydrated, she reached for one of the bottles of sparkling water on the coffee table in front of her. As she took a long swig, she unlocked her phone to take a look at the message.

It was from an unattributed number and read, 'Managed to free myself up. Will be with you in ten mins. Hope we still have something to celebrate. Bringing bottle.' She was no longer in the mood and on the wrong side of a bottle of Rioja, but he was on his way. *Just a quick drink*, she thought, *and then I'll wheel out a migraine or something*.

She quickly changed out of her bathrobe into the evening outfit she'd packed. It seemed overly provocative now, but she didn't want to get back into her work suit, so it would have to do.

Next Maria booted up her laptop and checked to see whether the documents she had asked to have drafted had been sent through. The first was a variation on the standard NDA. If this man really had the intel he'd said he had, she didn't want him selling it to other interested parties. The second outlined the agreement they had reached earlier, and just required a name to be inserted and digital signatures to be applied. She had no intention of presenting this to her stranger until she got a few more answers, but it was in her back pocket if she needed it. Having quickly proofed the documents, she connected her portable printer to the laptop with a USB lead and left it to sync.

She wandered over to the mirror in the hallway and took a close look at her reflection. Maybe a bit puffy from the sleep, but not bad. She applied some fresh lipstick and reached into her handbag for the travel bottle of Chanel. At that moment there was a confident rap at the door. She did one last check in the mirror, sprayed a fine mist of perfume, and walked through it to the door.

Her potential business partner stood nonchalantly in the doorway, reading a text. After a moment he looked up and then smiled as if just remembering where he was. Maria found it unusual and not a little unnerving to be treated in such a casual, borderline dismissive manner. Nevertheless, it also triggered a sexual desire in her that she had thought to be pretty dormant this evening.

He held up a bottle of Dom and raised an eyebrow, as if to say, 'Am I at the right party?' She ushered him in, and he strode straight towards the laptop and started to scroll through the draft documents.

Already feeling on the back foot, Maria pushed past the man's taut, muscular frame and took a seat at the desk, quickly typing in dates and outstanding details. Stopping at the name field, she looked up over her shoulder and raised an eyebrow questioningly.

He nodded, briefly glancing at the copy one more time, before responding, 'Dr Solomon, my name is Osman. Duman Osman. Pleased to make your acquaintance.'

The surname, common as it was, made her shiver. It

was a name that came to her every night. Nevertheless, she shrugged the feeling off and typed in the name across both documents. She then closed the docs, saved them as PDFs, and hit print to provide copies for the man she now knew to be Duman Osman.

She spun round on the swivel chair, turning her palms upwards in an 'all done' gesture.

'Right, Mr Osman, as you can see, all the paperwork is in order, and I have already filed an instruction to detain the *Triton* when it next docks in Limassol. However ...'

Maria paused. Getting slowly back to her feet, she weighed up how best to call out this man's economy with the truth, whilst still keeping him onside.

'I've been doing my own research since we last spoke. It's led me to believe that there might be more to this "family heirloom" than you were strictly sharing with me.'

Osman pursed his lips as he opened the champagne but said nothing. Maria realised that she was going to need to speak more plainly than she had hoped.

'I noticed that Professor Fairlight has joined the team.'

'You know him?' Osman interjected, seemingly rattled for the first time.

'Enough to know that only a very specific artefact would lure him out to sea.'

Maria picked up a champagne flute and held it out for Osman to pour. 'I guess what I'm saying is ... we may need to renegotiate, Mr Osman.'

Osman smiled knowingly. 'It's your show, sugar tits. Whatever you say.'

The colour drained from Maria's face as she heard

the seedy term that had also followed her down the years. The acrid smell of gunpowder and blood mixing with sweat and cheap cologne filled her nose. She shot a look at Osman's right hand. At the Büyük Han he had been wearing gloves, which, whilst a bit eccentric, hadn't seemed out of the ordinary to her. But now the gloves were off, and she could plainly see that his right arm was a prosthetic.

A lifetime of grief and fury erupted inside Maria as the horror of coming face to face with the man who had so brutally taken her family from her took hold. She summoned up all her strength and poise to ensure she didn't betray her ragged thoughts and emotions to her nemesis.

'I'm glad you feel that way. Please take a seat in the lounge. I just need to powder my nose, and then I'm sure we can still come to a mutually beneficial agreement.'

Osman shrugged as Maria picked up her handbag and walked purposefully but slowly to the bathroom. She closed the door and stared at her reflection in the mirror. *I will not allow this man to take my life a second time*, she thought. *This time will be different.*

She pulled her mobile phone from the bag and brought up Daniel's contact details. She desperately wanted to call but knew this would be too dangerous. Instead she frantically typed a short message. 'Think u may be in v real danger. Must speak. Ctc me urgently. M.'

Replacing her phone in her bag, she flushed the toilet and walked as casually as she could out into the suite.

Osman called out to her from the lounge, 'Grab the bottle on the way through, hon, I could do with a top-up.'

Maria walked coolly over to the desk where the ice bucket sat and pulled the bottle out. Her eyes were tearing up, but her mind was calm, collected. She had waited all her life for this moment; she would not fail now. Could not.

She strolled into the lounge where Osman was sitting in an armchair looking out towards the Nicosia skyline. With a single powerful movement she swung the bottle with all her force, connecting with the side of Osman's head. Osman slumped. Maria had seen too many horror movies to think about sticking around. She kicked off her shoes and ran for the suite door. As she exited, she heard a scream:

'BIIIITCH.'

She didn't look back but headed straight down the corridor towards the elevator lobby at the end. Once she was safe, she would contact the police. He wouldn't escape justice this time.

With ten yards to go, the elevator doors opened ahead of her, and a man stepped purposefully out. His stare told Maria what she had already feared. He was Osman's man. Without breaking stride she barged into the emergency stairs door and ran through. Behind her she heard Osman's roar.

'Serkan. Get her. She mustn't escape.'

Maria leapt down the stairs, taking the steps three at a time. She could hear the man gaining on her but didn't dare look back. She never saw the fire extinguisher coming as it smacked into the back of her neck, sending her sprawling down a full flight of stairs.

Serkan trotted down to where she had landed in a crumpled heap. From up above he heard Osman cry, 'Is she dead?' Serkan checked her pulse at the neck and the wrist. Nothing.

'Yes, sir, she's dead.'

'Be sure, Serkan.'

He checked again. 'There's no pulse, she's gone.'

Osman staggered to the top of the stairwell and slumped up against a wall. He peered blearily down the stairwell at the grim scene below. This was going to work out all right. It was certainly inconvenient, but not a deal-breaker. With no evidence of foul play, the Cypriots would still run the red tape interference at the port. The good doctor no longer offered a route to his prize but, no matter; things would just have to be resolved on board the *Triton*.

'Replace the extinguisher, Serkan. Then clean her room of any evidence. Disable the lift, too, so it looks like she had to take the stairs. I'll see you in reception. That bitch has been a stone in my shoe for far too long.'

Even as Serkan was exiting the stairwell, Maria's imperceptibly low heart rhythm was still being supported by her pacemaker. After about a minute she started breathing, so lightly it could barely be noticed. Just before she slipped back out of consciousness, she promised herself that she would survive Osman's clutches again, and live to see him suffer.

24

March 3, 2013

The Levantine Basin

The *Triton* had journeyed back to Limassol for one of its bimonthly stock-up and shore leave visits. The sun was out, spirits were up, and some leisure diving was being arranged.

'Come on, you'll enjoy it. Just ten minutes in the water. I promise, Danny, you'll love it. Please. Pleeease.'

Daniel smiled at Banu. This had become a familiar entreaty, and he had to admit, he was enjoying the dance. As Daniel had matured over the years, he had grown to appreciate certain things which he felt he had maybe taken for granted in his youth, and chief amongst these was the kindling of a new friendship.

Over the past few months, Daniel had felt that connection again, for the first time in a long time. If he was honest, he hadn't felt this way since Maria. And given how that had finished, he was very tentative in his moves now. Initially he had made sure to keep things on a professional level, adopting a somewhat stilted formality in their interactions. Apart from anything else, he had noticed an exotic ring on the third finger of her left hand and had naturally assumed she was spoken for. Even when Kal put him right, he maintained an appropriate distance. When it came up in conversation, Banu just shrugged and indicated that it warded off unwelcome attention. Daniel felt that her expression as she spoke about the ring whilst turning it round her finger suggested that the jewellery had more significance than just a convenient prop, but he didn't pursue it.

Banu graduated from reverential student to feisty colleague, and Daniel enjoyed the ride at least as much as the young woman. She was witty, passionate, challenging, relentless, even maddening on occasion, but there was no doubting the gravitational pull between the two.

Daniel mused that it seemed at times that the only thing they didn't have a shared passion for was Banu's love of the sea. How could he possibly explain his loathing, no, his deep-rooted fear of open water?

'It's not gonna happen, B. There is a very good reason why we evolved out of the sea four hundred million years ago to become land-based mammals. We're not meant to be there.'

He had quickly taken to calling her B and enjoyed the fact that he had a pet name for her that no one else shared. She had gone from Professor to Prof, to Daniel and then Dan, and finally Danny.

Banu sat on the edge of the diving platform, preparing to enter the water.

'Your loss, Prof. Whatever's stopping you coming in, it sure as shit isn't four hundred million years' worth of evolution. You academics will have your little mysteries. No worries. Gonna play with some real men now.'

And with that she was gone. Daniel smiled at the space she had just vacated; then he slowly shook his head. He hated to admit it, but deep down he knew he was falling for her. He probably would have already declared his feelings to Banu, but some niggling doubt was stopping him.

From the moment he had realised she was the impassioned 'student' at his London lecture, he had felt conflicted about her motivations. Was she genuinely happy to just be part of the expedition, or did she have her own hidden agenda? Was he alone in harbouring a secret desire to discover Suleiman's heart, or was she also privy to the intel he had? The more Daniel wrestled with his suspicions, the more he kept returning to one core concern. Was he going to lose out on love for a second time due to his fixation on all things Suleiman?

To add to his growing sense of paranoia, he continued to get discouraging news from Nicosia. First he had received a very uncharacteristic and alarming text talking of danger, and then when he tried to contact Maria, he was told that she had had an accident in the hotel she was staying in. Fell down a flight of stairs while heavily intoxicated. None of it added up. Maria continued to hover between life and death in a coma at Near East University Hospital. Even if Daniel could have got to Nicosia, he wouldn't have been allowed to see her. He had contacted the Cyprus Police and advised them of the text she sent, but as soon as they started asking questions about her circumstances, he realised that he really didn't know her anymore.

***

Later that afternoon he and Banu sat together in what was grandly referred to as the Archive Centre but was actually nothing more than another sea container bolted down to the deck.

Every piece retrieved from the seabed was

meticulously cleaned, treated, catalogued, and then carefully stored in the Archive Centre. Half the space had the look of a high-tech laboratory, whilst the other half was essentially a walk-in vault, where all the artefacts were stored securely.

Captain Murphy had insisted on the security, as he didn't want the gaze of suspicion falling on any of his crew in the event of a piece going missing. Kal readily agreed. The haul was literally priceless, and the responsibility for its safekeeping sometimes weighed heavily on his shoulders. Both Kal and Daniel had a set of keys, but there was a manually entered signature required every time the vault was accessed, supported by a digital timecode record of the gate being opened. No one resented the security—they all felt protected by it.

Daniel watched Banu typing in a detailed description of an elaborately decorated dish that had been part of yesterday's retrieval. Images of the plate appeared on her screen. Even with this relatively mundane administrative task, her excitement was palpable. She was utterly absorbed by what she was doing, appearing completely entranced by the piece in front of her.

Daniel smiled at her focus and cast his mind back to her earlier diving invitation. Suddenly, surprising himself as much as Banu, he mumbled, 'I can't swim.'

'Sorry?' Banu looked up quizzically.

'I felt I owed you an explanation for my resistance to joining you in the water. I can't swim.'

'Oh.'

'Well, I say I can't swim. That's not entirely true. I can probably do a length in a pool unaided, but that's about it.' Daniel shrugged sheepishly.

'How did you pass the Survival at Sea appraisals?'

'Barely.'

Banu nodded slowly as she processed this confession. It explained a lot. Daniel's reticence had always felt out of character to her. She shrugged. 'Okay. No biggie. So, accepting a seafaring position seemed like a really good idea because … ?'

Daniel nodded. 'Mm, yeah, fair point. Well, first, in my defence, history will attest that at least three-quarters of the crew that manned the *Colossus* were unable to swim.'

'Yeah, but they were unable to drive automobiles, either. I mean, you know, that was four hundred years ago, Danny. Speedos and water wings were in short supply. What's your excuse?'

Daniel could see that although Banu was teasing him, she was also curious. Something didn't stack up, and she could sense it. He stared at her for a few seconds, mulling over a choice, before finally responding, 'I had swimming lessons as an adult, you know, enough to be able to splash about in shallow water without completely embarrassing myself. But if you put me into open water at sea, I just wouldn't survive. The terror would take hold. It's like, y'know, everyone has a default fear dream. Something we can't control. Falling, suffocating, buried alive, enduring a whole One Direction concert, that kind of thing.'

He smiled lamely. Banu just raised an eyebrow.

'Mine is drowning. But not just drowning. In my nightmare there is water for as far as you can see in all directions. I'm trying desperately to tread water, but my head is dipping under. I'm getting more and more tired.

I can taste the salt water that's starting to seep into my mouth. And then I feel this massive swell of panic. The more I thrash about, the more I start to sink. I try to hold my breath, but my lungs are screaming out for air. It starts to go dark, and then I wake, gasping for breath.'

Banu frowned and pulled an expression of empathy. 'You know there are courses that can help you overcome that fear.'

'It's too engrained, B. Too carved into me. I know it's not rational, but it's hardwired now. And, if I'm honest, it's attached to other stuff that I've never dealt with, and never will now.'

Banu leant forward in her chair and reached out for Daniel. She didn't say anything, just looked deep into his eyes and gently squeezed his hand. Daniel looked down at his hand in hers, and an overwhelming rush of emotion washed over him. Without looking back up, he quietly spoke. 'I'm going to tell you something now that I've never told anyone. Not a living soul.'

Daniel closed his eyes and slowly found himself drifting back to the events of a summer day in August of 1973.

***

The summers in those days just went on for ever. The days were sun bleached, endless, and carefree. It was 1973, and Daniel was seven. The summer holidays were already four weeks in, but the big event was still to come. This year the family holiday would be to the Canary Islands. This meant nothing to Daniel, although his father proudly asserted that it was far enough away to avoid 'the Costa Del Sol riff-raff.' For Daniel it just sounded exotic and distant. And you got to go on a plane. He was beside himself with excitement.

As an only child he had been used to amusing himself, playing both cowboy and indian. Sure, he had some friends, but he mostly stayed close to home during the holidays. And he was fine with that. He could lose himself into whatever fantasy took hold.

But the family holiday was going to be a special time. It meant that he would get to spend time with his father. Mum would do her own thing, sunbathe and read books endlessly, but he would have his father all to himself. It was going to be perfect.

In a rash moment earlier in the year, Randolph had promised to teach his son to swim on holiday. In truth he was a bit irritated at Daniel's lack of progress on a whole host of fronts, and swimming had become a symbol of wide-ranging underachievement that Randolph simply wasn't going to tolerate.

In reality, Daniel was carrying a well-hidden apprehension about the much-touted swimming lessons. The previous year there had been a school trip to the local swimming baths, and, when no adults were looking, Barry, the class bully, had pushed Daniel's head underwater. He was probably only under for five seconds, but it was time enough to believe that he was drowning. The helpless feeling of being held under as his need to take a deep breath became increasingly desperate, had stayed with Daniel.

But this would be different. He was with his father. It was safe. It would be fun.

Randolph was as good as his word. On the first full day of the vacation, the father and son were amongst the first to venture into the hotel pool. Randolph patiently stood two metres from the edge of the pool, held out his hands, and encouraged his boy to swim towards him.

By late morning, Randolph became aware of younger kids staring at Daniel's pink water wings, as they literally swam rings around the boy's father. Pink, Randolph thought, what the hell had the boy's mother been thinking?

And so, the vicious cycle began. Randolph became more irritated and impatient. Daniel, sensing this, became increasingly anxious and unable to let go, which, in turn, further fuelled Randolph's frustration and growing sense of shame at his son's weakness.

By lunchtime Daniel's father had given up. Both parties were relieved that the ordeal was over. Daniel retreated into his own imagination, and Randolph retreated to the swim-up bar.

Two or three days went by with Randolph barely speaking to his son. Daniel was aware that something wasn't right but was too young to be able to process it. One morning, he walked in on a row between his parents. His father was shouting at his mother, 'If he doesn't learn now, he'll find himself out of his depth for the rest of his life. You're always too soft on him.'

The remainder of the holiday was cast into shadow by a brooding tension. Daniel felt that things could snap at any moment, and all he wanted was for everyone to be happy. He spoke less and less in case he would be the one that triggered an explosion. Mealtimes became unbearable in their fragile silence.

And then, with two days of the holiday remaining, everything changed. Randolph's mood lifted, and the clouds parted. Everything was going to be all right after all. Daniel's father even agreed to taking out one of the pedalos for hire on the beach. Daniel had studied them enviously throughout the holiday. They looked like the most fun you could possibly have.

As the father and son slowly cruised away from the shoreline, Randolph assuming the lion's share of pedalling duties, Daniel imagined himself aboard a giant pirate ship. If you looked straight ahead, all you could see was the horizon. You could be in the middle of a giant ocean. It was an intoxicating illusion for a seven-year-old boy.

After ten or fifteen minutes, Randolph tired and stopped, allowing the pedalo to drift while he lit a cigarette. He took a long drag and then looked across to his young son.

'Do you know one of the magic things about the ocean, Daniel?'

Daniel stared wide-eyed at his father, as he slowly shook his head.

'The ocean is full of salt, and salt makes you float. It really is like magic. Look, just dip your hand in the water and taste it.'

Daniel leant forward and plunged his hand gleefully into the cool seawater, before sticking two fingers into his mouth. The taste made him wince, but he smiled too. This was amazing.

'See? And some oceans have more salt in them than others—they have more salinity. There is a sea near a place called Jordan which is so saline that you can sit on the water and read a newspaper. Can you believe that?'

Daniel was laughing at this image, and that made Randolph laugh. Soon both man and boy were roaring with laughter as their pedalo drifted on. Daniel couldn't have known it, but this would be the last moment of pure shared joy that he would ever have with his father.

Finally, Randolph stopped laughing, took a final drag on his cigarette, and flicked it into the sea.

'So, do you want to see how much you float in this water?'

Daniel enthusiastically agreed. This was a grand experiment, and it still felt a bit like a magic trick.

'Okay, well, take that silly life jacket thing off. It won't work if you wear that. Then you can just slip into the water and hold on to the pedalo.'

For the first time Daniel looked a little wary. He felt his old anxiety rising up, but he didn't want to break the spell with his father. After a moment of hesitation, he unbuckled the life jacket and followed his father's instructions on the easiest way to lower himself into the sea. He gently slipped into the cold water, careful to keep a tight grip on the rope trim on the side of the pedalo.

'You bob in the water much more than in a pool, right?'

Daniel wasn't sure he could feel any difference, but he nodded just the same.

'Right, now let go and tread water like I've taught you. Just keep moving your arms and legs in that circular motion, and you'll be fine.'

Daniel hesitated, assessing the risk. The pedalo was right there. He could easily reach back if it started to feel too difficult. This was going to be okay. Better than okay, maybe.

The second he let go of the rope, Randolph pedalled vigorously in reverse. Within a few brief seconds the craft was a good five metres away from the young boy. Daniel started flailing his arms wildly.

'Daddy. DADDY.'

'Stop being such a baby. Just move your arms like I taught you and swim over to me.'

Daniel tried to focus, attempting the front crawl and achieving something approximating a doggy paddle. Slowly he started to move forward. It was working. He was swimming. Three metres away. Two. Daniel gasped with the elation of his achievement.

'Stop doing that silly baby crawl, boy. Swim properly.'

Randolph engaged the pedals again, this time opening up a ten-metre gap. Daniel immediately started to panic. He screamed at his father to come back. Barry the bully appeared in front of him, laughing and splashing water in his face.

'You're going down, Fairylight, and this time, you're not coming back up,' he sneered.

Daniel felt himself tiring and starting to drop. His father had lied. The seawater didn't keep you up. As his head went under, he heard another voice: 'Hang on, kid, I've got you.'

There was a splash behind him, and then a strong arm grabbed him round the chest and under his chin. The last thing he remembered before passing out was his father's commanding voice:

'Leave him be. He's fine. Leave my son alone.'

***

Banu had released Daniel's hand as he recalled the story, but now she reached out again. She paused, waiting to see if he would continue. Eventually she decided to break the silence.

'So, what happened?'

Daniel grimaced ruefully. 'Well, spoiler alert, I didn't die.'

They both smiled, relieved to have broken the tension.

'Another couple on a pedalo had been nearby. They had seen my distress, and the guy had dived in to rescue me. By the time he pulled me from the water into their boat, I had already come round. They brought me back to shore.'

'What did your dad do?'

'He muttered some thanks and maintained he was on his way back and that I was never in any danger. I think I would probably have adopted that truth, but I'll never forget the look on the other guy's face. He said, "Whatever you say," but the look was one of absolute admonishment. It was an expression I knew well, even at the age of seven. I have no doubt that Dad's truth was one of "tough love," but tough love can kill you. It wasn't long after that that the nightmares started.'

They sat in silence for a moment, both reflecting on Daniel's conclusion. Eventually Banu tried to shift the mood. 'And here you are, some forty years later, still bobbing around on the open sea. What's that all about, Professor?'

Daniel recognised the tease in her tone. He knew the honest answer involved his obsessive search for the heart of Suleiman, but he wasn't quite ready to share that motivation with Banu.

'You know what, B. I think I've just realised something. The truth is that I have spent my whole life in my father's shadow. Trying to seek his approval. Striving to live up to his standards. I've been trying to cover those ten metres my whole adult life. He died recently, and the next choice I made was to come here. Maybe this is my way of moving on, y'know, getting some closure, taking control, whatever you want to call it.'

Banu turned her chair back round to resume her cataloguing work. 'Good for you, Danny. I can't think of a better reason to be here.'

She started typing in more information, absently adding, 'I guess I'm here because of my dad too.'

'Really?' Daniel responded; his curiosity heightened.

'Yeah. He taught me to dive. If I'm honest, he has been the driving force behind everything I've ever done, everything I've ever achieved. My parents split when I was young, my dad raised me. Have you any idea how unusual that is in Turkey? He calls me his 'special girl,' which is really embarrassing sometimes. I have been brought up to believe that I can achieve whatever I set my mind to. He has been a pretty tough taskmaster over the years, but also my greatest advocate. I can't complain, especially after what you have described. My father has been great.'

'Sounds like you guys have a solid relationship.'

'Oh, don't get me wrong, we have some major disagreements. I'm talking monumental rows, but, yeah, he's always been there for me. It sometimes feels like I'm living out his aspirations rather than my own, but if it hadn't been for his relentless pushing, well, I'm not sure I would have amounted to much. I am the product of his ambition, not my own.'

Daniel frowned. 'Sorry B, I'm not buying that. You seem so driven, so focussed, so talented. Surely you should be owning your successes.'

Banu spun her chair back round to look at Daniel. 'I

know what you're saying, Danny, and that's very sweet. Sure, I feel good about what I've done, what I've become, but you've got to understand that even today, being a woman in Turkey is still a struggle. Without male patronage you ain't going nowhere.'

'What do you mean?'

'For such an ancient country, Turkey is still very much trying to work out what it wants to be. Since the end of the Ottoman Empire, we have struggled to establish a modern identity, you know, our place in the world. It sometimes seems that we have lost all of what made us great and just retained the darker bits. Especially if you're a woman.'

Daniel sensed that they were straying onto thin ice but was also intrigued at the picture Banu was painting. He raised an eyebrow and turned his palms upwards, suggesting he was waiting for further expansion.

'Oh, I don't really want to open up that can of worms. I've found in the past that if you get me going on this subject, you can't shut me up. I've lost friendships over it. Suffice to say ...' Banu paused, gathering her thoughts. 'The irony is, Turkey led the way in Europe when it came to speaking up on political rights and equality legislation. But the gap between the rhetoric and the reality is frightening. We still face significant discrimination when it comes to employment and education. Female participation in employment is less than half the European average. Just getting a basic education is so much harder for Turkish women. Then there is the child marriage outrage, the domestic violence, rape and murder within the home. Turkey continues to pretend that femicide is a nonissue in our country by not measuring it. If the data isn't there, it can't be true, right?'

Banu had risen to her feet now and was pacing.

'But the reality is that the murder rate of women has exploded over the last ten years, something like a fifteen hundred per cent increase. Not fifteen per cent, fifteen *hundred*.'

Daniel also stood, stepped towards her, and put an arm on her shoulder. 'B, I'm sorry. My ignorance has hurt you. I feel embarrassed that I'm not better informed.'

Banu shrugged and smiled weakly. 'No need to be embarrassed. But if you really want to hear about this stuff, I'm more than happy to continue my rant over a cup of coffee.'

'Sure. I'd like that.'

***

A fellow crew member watched the couple walking along the deck before he picked up speed in the ship's utility dinghy. As he sped off towards the Limassol port, he speculated, not for the first time, on what the professor's true relationship with the Turkish girl might be. They looked for all the world like they were taking a promenade on board a cruise liner.

She was becoming an unwelcome distraction. An inconvenience even. He shrugged. The intelligence he had been getting recently made him think that events were going to start to escalate pretty quickly from here on in. He could worry about the girl later. For now, he had to be on his game. Ready.

His training had taught him to always be primed for the unexpected. He could take a guess at how things were going to go down, but there was always a curve ball. No matter how anticipatory you were, you still had to plan for the unknown.

He had volunteered to do the major supply run this evening. It gave him time and space to think, but it also provided the ideal cover for the meeting he had arranged. No sooner had he moored up at a quiet end of the marina than he hit redial on his phone, walking briskly past the castle and on along the promenade.

After confirming his arrival, he ended the call and continued the seafront walk. The palm trees rustled in the evening breeze, skateboarders cruised by, and laughter could be heard from the cafés serving the promenade. The operative was oblivious to all this. His mind turned over like a tumble dryer, gently moving all of the variables over and over, speculating on how things were going to play out.

Ten minutes later he arrived at his assignation. The café was quiet apart from a swarthy hulk of a man, squeezed into a metal chair on the outdoor patio area. His jet-black forehead shone with sweat even though the sun was almost below the skyline. He smiled as the man approached, heaving his bulky frame out of the chair. The two men stood facing each other silently for a moment. Finally, the operative spoke. 'What country do you hail from?'

Together, they both uttered the age-old response: 'Legio patria nostra. The legion is our country.'

They laughed and embraced warmly.

'Bosco, you are a sight for sore eyes, comrade,' the operative said as he took a seat, picked up the carafe of water already on the table, and poured two decent glugs into each of the glasses already half-full of Ricard. He watched the spirit cloud and then looked up again at his old compatriot.

'You too, my old friend,' Bosco responded. 'It's been too long. I am glad to see you so well. Maybe a little heavier around the middle, eh? But it suits you. Especially now you are a middle-aged man.'

The two men had spoken but not met since the project went live some months back.

'So, where've you flown in from? Are you basing yourself back home in the Côte d'Ivoire now?'

Bosco spat on the ground. 'How dare you insult me. As you know only too well, I am *français par le sang verse* —French by spilled blood. France is my homeland now.'

'Okay. So, where are you living?'

'Well, yes, the Ivory Coast.'

The two laughed again and fell into an easy conversation reminiscing about daring adventures in the French Foreign Legion, particularly shared tours in the Lebanon and the Gulf War. Inevitably, as more recent skirmishes were referenced, the names of lost friends came up. Both men fell into a comfortable silence, staring at their drinks. Finally, the operative lifted his glass.

'The toast is the same as always, my friend. To absent friends and fallen comrades.'

The two soldiers clinked glasses and downed the contents before returning to their own thoughts. Eventually the crew member glanced at his watch and leant forward to have a more private word.

'I'm running short on time, Bosco. Let me just check a few things off the list.'

Bosco slipped immediately into military mode. 'Sir.'

'Are the men ready?'

'Check.'

'Are they briefed?'

'Check.'

'Are they on standby to move?'

'They can all be here within twelve hours, sir.'

'Firearms?'

'Check, I have a local contact. I've arranged a full complement of auto and semiautomatic weapons. We're good to go, sir. Just waiting for your call.'

'Good. That's good. This operation will need to run like clockwork, Bosco. Precision timing. In and out. No one can ever know it was us.'

'Sir, I'm telling you, the men are ready.'

The crew member stood up. 'I know. You've never let me down, my old friend. Wait for my signal.'

The hulk of an Ivorian threw a quick salute, but his superior was already briskly walking away.

An hour later, the fully loaded utility dinghy was pulling up alongside the *Triton*'s cargo bay entrance. Crew members hustled over to help unload the supplies. Davy leant over the edge of the ship railing and shouted down to the dinghy below.

'Where the hell have you been, like?'

'Your girlfriend was complaining to me that she was feeling unfulfilled in the bedroom. She asked me to pick up some marital aids for her,' the man in the dinghy shouted up.

Davy smiled, shaking his head. 'You're a funny bloke, Yousef, a really funny bloke.'

25

May 8, 1630

The Levantine Basin

Emir watched Onur walking towards him. If the boatswain hadn't been gripping him tightly round the neck, he would have collapsed onto the deck. Shabaka was gone. *Gone.* He felt numb. He had been through so much, overcome so many obstacles and setbacks, only for it to end like this. He was so tired he just wanted it to all be over. As he waited for Onur's blade to end his tribulations once and for all, the last thought that came to him was that he would now fail in his promise to his mother. In his dreams he had seen himself returning triumphantly to her, rescuing her from poverty and finally gifting his red scarf to the woman who had sacrificed so much for so long. None of that would come to pass now. He closed his eyes and awaited his fate.

'Stand down, Onur. We still have need of this wretch.'

Emir opened his eyes to see a look of surprise and no little disappointment on the sailor's face. The boatswain continued.

'He knows where the casket is, idiot. If it was left to you, you would have him overboard with that other scumbag, and then think about asking questions later.'

Slowly Onur's expression shifted to one of partial understanding.

'And the clouds part,' the junior officer continued, enjoying his assertion of superiority. 'Allah save us from imbeciles and idle bones.'

Onur, with the insult flying high over his head, proceeded to nod wisely. 'Of course, sir. He knows where the casket is. Dead men can't talk, sir, isn't that right?'

The boatswain shook his head in despair. *Where did we get these people from*, he thought, as he lashed Emir to the sailor.

'There, now at least there is no chance of you losing him. Take him below to show you where the casket is hidden. Once you have it in your hands, and only then, you can dispose of him. Do you understand?'

'Yes, sir. You can leave it to me. It will be a pleasure to rid ourselves of this urchin. He marches around the ship like he bloody owns her. Red this, Red that. I can't stand him.'

'Do you think you will be able to handle a thirteen-year-old boy with one good eye on your own, or will you need some help?'

Missing the sarcasm, Onur simply offered further reassurances that he was up to the task, as he checked the stretch of leather tying his wrist to that of the boy.

'Once you're finished, make sure there is no trace of the body, and then bring the casket directly to my cabin. Got it? No dilly-dallying. Straight to me.'

The sailors had been speculating that a storm was brewing, and Onur had to admit there was definitely something in the air. He nodded an acknowledgement and started dragging his hostage back down the deck, towards the stairs that led to the lower levels and the cargo hold. Emir put up little resistance. All his fight and passion had gone overboard with his friend. He felt nothing but defeat and dismay. He didn't care what became of him now. He had come so far, but now he felt he had nothing left to give.

'Which way, boy?' Onur said, prodding him with the blade he still held in his favoured right hand. Emir shrugged and unenthusiastically pointed to the darker recesses behind the final crates. Onur felt a frisson of excitement at the prospect of being the one to reclaim the sacred prize. He would be rewarded well for this, he knew. He moved quickly, yanking at Emir to keep up.

Behind the final crate, Emir pointed to an area with extra straw over it. Onur took out another lash and tied Emir's free hand to one of the crate rings, before releasing his left hand from Emir's. The tie would keep Emir well out of reach as he retrieved the casket. He wasn't as stupid as people said he was, he thought to himself.

He brushed away the detritus to reveal boards beneath and immediately saw that one looked loose. Rushing now, after a quick glance to check on the boy, he pulled away the boards to reveal a large box in a cheap sackcloth bag. His breath quickened and his brow started to sweat as he pulled the heavy casket from the sacking.

It was more magnificent than he could ever have imagined. Onur felt intoxicated by its mere presence. He might have stared at it for the remainder of the night had Emir not broken his reverie.

Emir's thoughts had returned to a conversation with Shabaka that seemed like a lifetime ago, but in fact was only a week earlier in Alexandria. Emir had been talking about his mother, a favourite topic of his, when Shabaka had interrupted: 'You talk about your mother a lot. Don't get me wrong, it's always nice to see a boy honouring his mother. But I'm surprised you never talk about your father.'

'Why would I?' Emir responded. 'He left. He's absent from my life. We may as well be strangers.'

'I'm not entirely sure I agree with that, my young friend.'

'What do you mean? He left. That's all there is to it.'

'I think he is with you always. I think he is in you, more a part of you than you may want to admit.

'You see,' Shabaka continued, 'I see your mischief when you tease the merchants. I see your cunning when you do your illusions. I see your agility when you appear caught in a trap. Your courage in the face of adversity. Your charm when you need to engage. Your daring when a risk needs to be taken. And your ingenuity when you find yourself in a tight corner. So, I guess my question is, where do all those qualities come from?'

At the time Emir had simply shrugged again and moved the conversation on, but now, with tears in his eyes, he thought about the wisdom that Shabaka had shared with him. He wondered whether his father would have been proud of him, and this thought hardened his resolve.

'Onur. That means being good, right? An honourable man. Have I got that right?' Emir had decided to go out on his own terms. He would not bow down to this scum. He owed it to fallen friends to die with dignity and valour. He would not give this pathetic man the pleasure of seeing his fear. He glared indignantly at the conspirator.

Onur stood up, assuming the most dignified posture he could muster. 'Yes. That is right. My parents knew I would be a noble man. An important man who deserved a name that people would look up to.'

'How disappointed they must have been, then, when their boy turned out to be nothing more than a coward, a cheat, and a liar.'

Emir had done his best to break the strap that trapped him to the crate, but it had not budged. He knew these were his final moments. He would not plead or scream.

Onur showed a flash of anger, but then he smiled. He was going to enjoy this. He placed down the casket and pulled a larger, jagged dagger from his belt. He would carve this boy slowly. Maybe make a night of it. He was skilled in torture and knew how to keep a man alive for many hours whilst still inflicting enduring wounds.

Emir bowed his head. He would not cry. His father's image came to him, saying, 'Don't worry, my son, they'll never catch me. I always find another way out. Just when you think you're trapped, that's when a different door opens.' His father winked at him.

'Not this time, Papa,' Emir whispered as he braced himself for the blow.

Instead, he heard the unmistakable sound of a body falling to the floor. He opened his eyes. Onur was lying at his feet with a dagger in his neck. Blood was gushing from the wound. He was completely motionless. A voice spoke from the shadows. It was a heavy accent, but Emir vaguely recognised it.

'I am Italian. When my life is saved, I owe a life debt. Tonight, I pay what I owe.'

A man stepped out from behind the crate.

Emir stared at him, as his mouth dropped open in surprise. 'Antonio?'

'Yes, Red, it is the one and only Antonio.'

Emir gawped disbelievingly at the extravagant Italian man whose life he had saved all those weeks ago on the quayside at Dubrovnik.

'How, I, what, I mean, I don't understand. How did you come to be here?'

'Red, my friend, I have been watching over you these long months. A life at sea can be a dangerous life, and I promised myself that if you were ever in trouble, it would be I, the great Antonio, who would save you. Earlier tonight I saw you and the big Egyptian meeting with the boatswain and this piece of shit. I never trusted either of them, so I thought I might just tag along to see what kind of trouble you had got yourself into. I'm sorry, I could do nothing for your friend'—Antonio paused and bowed his head momentarily—'but I swore that I would save you, even if that meant sacrificing my own life. Fortunately, it didn't come to that.'

As he babbled on about his heroics, he pulled a small knife from his belt and cut through the leather strap restraining Emir. Antonio's excitement and verve were beginning to infect Emir. He felt his taste for the fight returning, if only to honour his friend. Friends. He had lost two brothers, both of whom had sacrificed themselves so he might live. This was no time for self-pity. He found himself with refreshed resolve. He would not allow this mutiny to happen, let alone the broader treasonous plot that he had overheard.

'Antonio,' he whispered urgently, 'there is something I need to do right now.'

'Then Antonio will help you.'

'You can't, Antonio, I must do this alone. But I do

have a favour to ask of you.'

'Anything, my friend. I don't know what you're mixed up in. I know you well enough to know that you will be on the right side of it. How can Antonio be of service?'

Emir stared at the suave Italian. It struck him that, in this whole crazy adventure, when he needed it, there had always been someone there to help him. Truly his was a charmed life.

'You are a good friend, Antonio. I need you to get rid of Onur's body. No one must suspect any foul play. If they do, then all is lost. Can you do that for me?'

'It will be my pleasure to despatch this filthy dog to a watery grave.'

Emir nodded his thanks. He gathered up the casket in its sackcloth bag and started off towards the stairs. His mind was racing. First, he had to find a new hiding place for the casket. Somewhere no one would ever suspect. He had an idea, but it was risky and fraught with difficulties. He shrugged. It would have to do.

Once the casket was safe, he would then need to find a way of getting to the captain without any of the Janissaries seeing him. From here on in, he would have to assume that everyone else on board was part of the plot. That simply couldn't be true, but it was the only safe way to progress.

Approaching the stairs, he noticed that the ship was rocking much more vigorously than it had been earlier. He glanced back at Antonio, labouring with Onur's body in the shadows, and sent a silent prayer for his safety.

As he mounted the stairs, some seawater spray slapped across his face. In the distance he heard another voice shouting, 'There's a storm coming. Truly a fierce tempest.'

He ducked his head against the wind. 'Ain't that the truth,' he muttered to himself.

PART 6
INTREPID

26

April 26, 2013

Limassol

Banu and Daniel stared out across the bay at the Limassol port. The *Triton* had taken to dropping anchor a mile or two out, rather than docking in port. It attracted less attention, required less paperwork, and provided greater privacy. Kal said it also enabled a quick getaway 'if things ever got hairy,' and Daniel sensed he was only half-joking.

They were back for more supplies. Yousef had volunteered for supplies duty last time out, and Daniel put himself forward for this run. He'd accompanied others enough to know what needed doing, and he could do with some time alone.

This phase of the project was nearing its end. Most of the artefacts that had been discovered had either been recovered or registered for later retrieval. The latter involved a painstaking process of being photographed and measured, having their position recorded, and being catalogued into the database. The cataloguing process was critical, especially for items remaining on the seabed for later recovery. Without proper provenance, DIVE had no proof of rights to ownership.

Whilst you could never be sure with an operation of this scale that everything had been found—in fact, the only thing you could really be sure of was that not everything had been discovered—Kal had made a call that 'it will be slim pickings from here on in'. With that broadly agreed, the operation was now running final ROV flights and completing the cataloguing process.

Things were coming to an end for this crew, and the mood had palpably shifted. Daniel had put this down to the inevitable blues that came with completion and conclusion and admitted he was feeling more of a sense of impending loss than he had anticipated. His time on the ship had become so much more than an assignment. He sensed that this was going to prove a life-changing experience for him.

But there was something else. Tensions had begun to resurface. Banu, in particular, had become more testy, more abrasive, and more impatient. Daniel observed that from the moment she had come on board, she had been the climate control for the ship. Her engaging personality and infectious passion had re-energised a team in grief, and now her more erratic behaviour was having an equal but opposite effect.

It had culminated in a full-on meltdown two days earlier, during the last dive. Tensions between Yousef and Banu had become particularly fractious. They had both been spoiling for a fight for a few days, and as the night's haul was being transported from Cygnus into the Archive Centre, a delicate operation in its own right, things finally boiled over.

Now, with the afternoon sun beating down, tempered by a welcome Mediterranean breeze, and two days having past, Daniel decided to attempt some delicate probing of his own.

'So, B, what happened the other night? I mean, one minute everything was cool, and then ...'

He let the observation hang, having learnt to be

comfortable with silence over many years.

She sighed and removed her sunglasses. 'It was nothing. I was just tired and irritable. You know, time-of-the-month stuff.'

Daniel stared at the marina in the distance. 'You know, I am world renowned as being a marketing man's dream. I'll purchase just about anything that is dangled enticingly in front of me ... and even I'm not buying that.'

Banu laughed. Daniel thought it was nice to hear. He'd missed it.

'You wanna take another run at that, hon?'

'All right, all right.' Banu put her arms up in the universal sign of surrender. 'You deserve a proper explanation; I'll give you that.'

Banu took a deep breath, then slowly blew air out, processing where to start. 'You've probably noticed that Yous and I haven't been getting along.'

'The way I heard it, a Russian satellite crew had phoned in that they were worried about you two.' Daniel was deliberately trying to keep it light. He had learnt enough about Banu to know that if you pushed even a little harder than she was prepared for, she would simply shut down.

Banu laughed again, more heartily this time. A real laugh. 'Right. This is difficult for me to say to you, Danny, but if we're plain speaking, I just don't trust him. I know you guys are friends, but he's just got too many secrets, too many no-go zones. There's something not right there, mark my words.'

Daniel looked her in the eyes, and he could instantly tell that she was sincere in her concern. He dropped his head. Yousef was a friend, and he would never want to betray him, but if he was being completely honest with himself, he had also been carrying reservations about his old college compatriot. Nevertheless, he wasn't sure he was ready to completely give up on his friend just yet.

'Okay, let's just say for a minute that his privacy issues may be hiding deeper secrets. I still don't get what snapped that night.'

Banu sighed with exasperation and turned to face Daniel head on. 'It was the casket. You must have seen. The way he was manhandling it, well, it was just … unprofessional. Almost like deliberate sabotage. He could have damaged it. Destroyed everything.'

'Hang on, B, hang on. I didn't see anything like … wait a minute, what do you mean, he could have destroyed everything?'

'Oh, come on, Danny, don't make me say it.'

'Say what?'

'The casket. Come on, are you telling me you aren't thinking the same thing I am? Seriously?'

Daniel decided to employ the silent treatment again. He had an idea what she was going to say, but he needed to hear her say it.

She looked at him, exasperated, then pulled him close and whispered in his ear. 'The box we've got catalogued as artefact 1309 and locked up behind that gate is Suleiman's casket. The sacred casket that, legend has it, holds his heart and the will of the Ottoman people.'

She pushed back and stared defiantly at him.

'Now hang on just a minute. Let's not get ahead of ourselves here. Are you seriously saying … ?'

'Forget it. I wish I'd never mentioned anything. I thought you would be more honest with me, Danny.'

Daniel could feel things slipping away. Banu was shutting down, maybe permanently. 'Don't pull away from me, B. You can trust me. Just ... just give me a moment here.' Daniel knew there were concerns still unsaid. Important concerns. He still wasn't completely sure of her motivations, let alone where the two of them stood. 'I tell you what, why don't you accompany me on the supply trip. Let's get away from everyone else and have a proper heart-to-heart. What do you say?'

'Heart-to-heart. You're gonna go with that?'

'Sorry, no pun intended, honest. Come on. Let's go somewhere where we can really talk.'

Banu hesitated, and Daniel could see some calculating going on behind her eyes. Eventually she nodded. 'Okay, you're on.'

***

An hour later they were sitting inside an unassuming Cypriot taverna. The wooden tables were beaten and stained from decades of abuse, the pictures on the walls were cliched at best, and the service was far from attentive. Despite all this, or perhaps because of it, the place had a certain charm. More importantly, it wasn't on the crew's preferred list. They were away from prying eyes and eavesdropping ears.

Daniel poured two glasses of red wine from a carafe as he mused upon how best to recue on their earlier conversation. *Oh well,* he thought, *I'm always being asked to dive in, so here goes.*

'I want to be really clear here, B, so let me just check that I am understanding you correctly.'

Banu nodded solemnly.

'You think that, and I can't believe I'm even saying

this, you think that the box we recovered a few weeks back is, in fact, the fabled casket of Suleiman the Magnificent that, legend has it, contains the enduring heart of the sultan himself. Am I getting this right?'

Banu, stared into Daniel's eyes with a burning conviction. 'It is.'

Daniel threw up his arms in exasperation. 'How can you say that, how could you possibly know?'

'I just know.'

'No, no, no. You're going to have to do a whole lot better than that, B. Let's just assess the facts for a moment. We recover a box. It is a beautiful and ornate box. It looks incredibly precious. Gold, jewels, the lot. The amount of scale means that we can't even open it at the minute. We literally have no idea what is inside. It will take weeks of careful treatment to remove the scale. But let us say ...' Daniel was on a roll now, giving Banu no chance to jump in. 'Let us just say, for a moment, that it is indeed a Suleiman artefact. If that is the case, and it's a *huge* if, *if* that's the case, what the hell is it doing on board an Ottoman merchant ship heading *towards* Istanbul? And even if we can establish *why* it would possibly be on board the *Colossus*, how can we remotely know what it might contain?'

Banu held his gaze. 'It contains the sacred heart of Suleiman the Magnificent, and therefore the power to lead our people back into days of glory and redemption.'

Daniel was about to tear into what seemed like a hopeless reach to him but was halted by Banu's use of 'our people.' He paused.

'I'm sorry, B. I appreciate how much this legend means to you, and how important it is to the Turkish people as a whole. I didn't mean to come across as dismissive. But surely you must see we're dealing with myth and legend here? Not reality. You can't really believe that his heart is in there, and it controls the will of the people? Please, you can't believe that?'

Banu reached out and took his hands in hers. A single tear ran down her cheek. 'You're asking all the wrong questions, Danny. It doesn't matter what I believe. If the people *believe* this to be true, then it is true. Don't you see? We have been waiting for a sign, something to bring us together, rekindle our belief. If we believe that this is that sign, then it will have the desired effect. This has nothing to do with ancient legend and everything to do with present hope. Look around you. Some of the most powerful and compelling beliefs in the world are founded on faith and faith alone. What's inside the box doesn't matter. That isn't the point. What we *believe* the box contains, however, matters a great deal.'

Daniel slowly nodded. 'So that is what you meant by "he could have destroyed everything".' Daniel put Banu's words from the other night into quotation marks with his hands. 'You don't want to risk the illusion being broken. The curtain getting pulled back.'

'Danny, I'm not saying it is an illusion. Who knows what's in there? I'm just saying *if* it's just a myth, let it be one we can still unify around. You, of all people, should want to protect the legacy of Suleiman, the legend of our last great sultan, the golden era of the Janissaries and the Ottoman Empire.'

'Oh, don't get me started on the Janissaries,' Daniel blurted out.

Banu looked at him quizzically. 'What is it with you and the Janissaries? Why have you got it in for them so much? What have they ever done to you?'

'Where to begin? They were the product of a brutal slave system. They manipulated the government to suit their own ends. They extorted money from their own sultans. Through their greed and indiscipline, they became a law unto themselves. They repeatedly murdered sultans who tried to challenge them. Their general abuse of power—I could go on.'

'Or ...' Banu interjected, 'the first elite military outfit in world history. No Janissaries, no SAS. A committed group whose loyalty was betrayed. And yes, you're right, the product of a brutal slave system. There are always two sides to the story, Professor; you should know that.'

Daniel smiled and raised his glass. 'Touché. You always seem to have a different perspective, Banu. I love that about you. But it's more than just knowledge I sense. You're invested. This stuff is really important to you. You take it so personally. Why is that? What am I missing?'

Banu's eyes started to glisten again. 'I was brought up to believe that Turkey is its own worst enemy. We could be a great nation. We have been, and we can be again. Instead, we are characterised by our worst traits. It hurts. I want to be proud of my people, not ashamed. And I want to make a difference, not just talk about it.'

Daniel pulled his chair round so it was alongside hers.

As he took her hand in his, she closed her eyes. 'I know this sounds crazy, but I was brought up to believe that I can change things, and maybe this discovery is the way I'm going to do that.'

She opened her eyes and stared at Daniel with a look

of desperation. It was more than Daniel could bear. He put his arm around her and cradled her head against his.

She looked up at the man who was trying so hard to console her. Despite her best efforts, she knew she was falling in love with him. Their eyes locked, and months of suppressed passion started to spill over. As they kissed, she let go of everything else and simply allowed herself this moment.

***

Back on board the *Triton*, at the exact moment that Daniel and Banu were finally surrendering to their feelings for each other, one of their fellow crew members was returning to the privacy of his cabin. As soon as the door was shut, he returned to his phone conversation.

'Listen. I can't really talk. In a minute or so I'll be missed. We're now at high alert, repeat, high alert. New intel suggests that we will need to be ready to make our move in approximately two weeks' time. This is the news we've been waiting for. My next call will be a call to arms. We'll need troops ready to scramble within thirty minutes ...'

After a further minute of clarifying exchanges, the operative ended the call. He stared ruefully at his phone, considering the implications of his directives. He didn't fear the fight; he had been here many times before. He wasn't worried about the manoeuvre. He would have elite soldiers around him. In truth, his only concern was that he might not personally get the chance to kill his nemesis on the *Triton*.

He promised himself that when the firing began, he

would take that shot first.

27

May 8, 1630

The Levantine Basin

Across the behemoth of the *Colossus*, crew were busying themselves, preparing for the coming storm. Sails were exchanged for heavier storm sails, and rigging was reconfigured. Everything that wasn't already fixed was lashed down. Instructions and admonishments were shouted across the deck. Most of the merchant passengers had retreated to their cabins, but some still gathered on deck to share concerns and reassurances. 'The worst was yet to come,' one would say. 'This ship is too robust to ever sink,' another would assert. 'A fully loaded ship is the safest ship,' was a popular straw to clutch at.

Up on the poop deck, Captain Barbarossa bellowed directions and orders to his junior officers. Despite the shouting he appeared calm and controlled, knowing that panic was quickly instilled and even quicker to spread. If he was worried, no one would have guessed it.

Over the next thirty minutes, as every soul on board prepared for the onslaught to come, Emir put his plan into action. His deepest fear was being caught in the act of stowing the treasure when no explanation could possibly get him off the hook. But such was the frenzy and diversion all around him that he was able to complete his task without any interruption.

For the remainder of the day, Emir made himself as

scarce as possible. He no longer trusted anyone on board —apart from Antonio, who was nowhere to be seen— and he couldn't risk falling back into the hands of the mutinous Janissaries. He had no option but to disappear until he could be sure of getting some time alone with the captain.

And so it was for the next few hours that Emir found himself back in the very same crate that had carried him aboard the *Colossus* six months earlier. Sitting in the dark, feeling the ebb and flow of the waves, he reflected on his journey. Friends he'd made. Friends he'd lost. Lessons both learned and spurned. The things he had seen and the experiences he'd gained. He looked back at the child who made an ill-judged call to steal a scarf for his mother, and he could hardly recognise that boy in the person he had become.

He twisted the ring on his finger and thought about Shabaka. How would these rings ever find their way back to each other now? He resolved to throw his ring overboard at the earliest opportunity. Maybe the wild sea would enable their union one last time.

As the hours passed, Emir became aware of the ship listing less violently, the wind howling with less ferocity. Had the storm passed? He had experienced much more tempestuous weather in his short time at sea. Was this not meant to be the storm to end all storms? Finally, his curiosity prevailed. Staring through the slightest cracks in the crate, he could see no light, make out no movement. If the storm really had passed, then surely this was his moment. With danger abated, the captain would have retired to his cabin to do whatever it was that captains did in their cabins. If he was to engineer a moment alone with Barbarossa, then now was surely that moment. He took a deep breath and pushed up on the lid of the crate.

The hold was quiet, deserted. The ship still rolled enthusiastically, but with nothing like the ferocity of a few hours earlier. Tentatively, furtively, he crept up the stairs that ascended to the lower deck. Crewmen were strewn all around, drained from the day's demands. Mostly they were sleeping, or simply staring into mid-distance, reflecting on the challenges that the storm had presented. Others talked in low tones. As Emir moved on, staying in the shadows wherever possible, he wondered at how lucky they had been. No one talked of casualties or losses or mourned the passing of a friend. Truly they must have had the might of Poseidon himself sheltering them from the storm this day.

Emir glanced up to the poop deck. The captain was nowhere to be seen. It was as Emir thought. He would be in his cabin, recovering from the day's exertions, or planning for whatever challenges the following day might bring. As Emir approached the quarterdeck that led to the captain's cabin at the aft of the ship, he felt his nerve start to shred. This was a monumental risk. There were too many variables, too many unknowns. What if the captain wasn't alone? What if he didn't believe Emir? What if *he* was a Janissary? This was a mistake.

Emir turned to retreat the way he had come. Out on the main deck he saw two merchants approaching. One of them was Kazim. Emir was hidden in the shadow right now, but once they stepped out of the moonlight, they would see him instantly. The two mutineers paused to debate some point. Emir didn't need a second invitation. He sprinted to the end of the corridor and knocked loudly on the captain's door.

He heard movement within, and then after a brief pause an unmistakable voice boomed, 'Come.'

***

Emir slipped quickly inside the spacious cabin. Sitting imposingly at his desk, completing entries into his logbook, was Captain Barbarossa. Emir glanced quickly around. They were alone. One less worry.

'Red, my boy. To what do I owe this pleasure?'

Emir had no idea where to start. Shabaka had said to him, 'You can't just blurt this tale out.' He racked his brain for a good way to start. Maybe some polite talk of the weather first.

'The storm didn't seem as bad as was feared, Captain.'

'That was nothing but a collop, young man, the main course is still to come. This isn't the lull before the storm, but the hush before the hurricane.'

'Hurricane?' Emir blurted out with alarm.

'I have seen this once before—a cyclone, a hurricane, whatever you want to call it. A storm to soften us up, followed by a period of unsettling quiet when we are in its eye. The gods' rage is yet to come, boy, mark my words.'

Emir stared desperately through one of the portholes, trying to make out the oncoming destruction, but all looked relatively calm.

'Are we going to go down, Captain?'

Barbarossa looked at him with penetrating eyes, as if trying to decide how much he should share.

'We are in the lap of the gods, Red. What will be, will be.' He leant across his desk and stared even more intensely at Emir. 'But something tells me that you haven't come here to discuss the weather.'

Emir took a deep breath. He anxiously twisted the ring on his finger. What he would give to have Shabaka with him now. He heard something his father used to say. 'If something needs to be said, say it plain and have done.'

'Captain, I've uncovered a mutinous plot on your ship. Janissary troops have sneaked on board, disguised as crew and merchants, and they plan to take control of the vessel. Once docked in Constantinople, they will use our cargo as a way of gaining access to the sultan's court, where they intend to overthrow his government.'

Barbarossa smiled. 'That's quite a claim boy. Remember now, I have warned you before not to vex me. Can you prove the validity of your story?'

'Yes, sir. I have proof. But first I must give you all the facts.'

'Be quick, Red. One way or another, we have little time to be dallying.'

Emir had told this story before. He knew it by heart. Once again, he would have to start on the day that the *Colossus* set sail, but this time he knew he had to focus on the key facts. And so, he spun his tale. The clandestine meetings, the 'recruiting' of exiled Janissaries at each stop along the way, the revelation of their plans for both mutiny and treason, and the casket that held Suleiman's heart. He culminated in the events of the previous night, and the loss of Shabaka. Finally, he was done. He waited to discover his fate. Would he be believed? Was he already talking to the enemy?

Barbarossa had listened intently to Emir's story without interrupting. Now he stood and stared down at the boy. 'So show me.'

'Show you what, sir?' Emir exclaimed, confused.

'Show me the sacred relic. That would appear to be the only tangible proof you have. So, show me. Now.'

Emir felt himself trembling in the presence of this giant of a man. He had never felt so intimidated, but from somewhere deep inside him he summoned the courage to respond. 'No.'

Barbarossa stared open-mouthed at this defiance. 'What do you mean, no?'

'I mean no, I won't show you. I can't.'

'Why not?' the captain enquired with surprising restraint.

'I have to know that I can trust you. That you're not one of them. Otherwise, this will all have been for nothing. I can't risk handing it over until I know you are who I hope and pray you are.'

Barbarossa smiled and nodded slightly. 'Good boy. Brave boy,' he said quietly, pulling a ring off his finger and placing it on the desk. 'I know you are telling the truth. I know because I've already heard this story. You *can* trust me, and I *can* prove it.'

Emir barely heard the captain's words as he stared at the ring on the desk. 'Where did you get that?' he hissed.

Barbarossa smiled again and glanced across the cabin. Emir followed his gaze in time to see a figure step out of the shadow. Emir felt a lifetime of emotions well up inside him and couldn't stop the tears coming. Through the choking in his throat, he gasped, 'Shaba?'

28

May 1, 2013
Amathus

Serkan had always enjoyed operations that took him to Cyprus. Osman's right-hand man had originally been born in the Turkish Republic of Northern Cyprus, and over the years he had come to appreciate the whole island. When Osman directed him to establish an appropriate location for his much-anticipated military briefing, Serkan immediately thought of Amathus.

Five miles east of Limassol, just a short run along the shoreline, lay the ancient royal city. No one had been able to date when the city was actually founded, but in modern times several ruins had been revealed, including the striking citadel, with its columns and arena. Serkan may have been interested to know that it was also a favourite spot of Dr Maria Solomon, who had authority over the site in her role as director of antiquities for Cyprus. Not that she was in any position to tell him this.

Tonight, the private gathering had been made even more dramatic with medieval-style fire torches surrounding the citadel, throwing shadows and casting flickering light against the ancient stones. Hidden speakers played centuries-old Janissary marching music. The distinctive sound, powerful drums and shrill horns, suggested a mood of glory and triumphalism.

Standing in the arena was a group of around thirty men. The music imbued a shared sense of passion and camaraderie amongst them. They were colourfully garbed in traditional Janissary military dress—long tunics of differing hues, sashes, ornate footwear and the distinctive börk headgear. They were all armed, some with traditional weapons—bows, blades, and muskets—others with more contemporary hardware. Above their heads each soldier, for that was most definitely what they were, held a procession torch.

Moving amongst them, informally inspecting them, Serkan reflected on the events that had brought them to this place. He wasn't afraid of getting his hands dirty for the cause. Was it really a year ago that he had disposed of Randolph Fairlight as punishment for his refusal to bring influence down on his son, Daniel? In the end that hadn't proved a problem. It seemed to Serkan that Osman always had a plan B, but in recent months he had become increasingly unpredictable in his choices.

The mood amongst the troops was a heady mixture of anticipation and affirmation. A journey through the centuries was arriving at a watershed moment. The glorious story of the Janissary corps was on the brink of a pivotal new chapter. These men were the chosen ones who would usher in this new dawn. They all appreciated the privilege and the responsibility.

Abruptly the music ceased. Their leader was approaching. There was no cheering or clapping. No trace of poor discipline. Instead, each man took a knee in unison and bowed his head in silent prayer and thanks.

Duman Osman walked onto the small stage that

had been erected for him. He had spent his whole life building to this moment. He surveyed the platoon kneeling before him, saying nothing for nearly a minute. He was wearing a wireless microphone hooked over his right ear, which allowed him to address the group without raising his voice. He needed to be heard, but he wanted it to feel like an intimate conversation, secrets shared with a select few. Finally, he spoke.

'Kaşık Kardeşliği. Brotherhood of the Spoon. We are bound by a comradeship that has lasted through the centuries. We have eaten, slept, fought, and died together in the service of our sultans and our beloved empire. And now, brothers'—he paused, eyes glistening with the significance of the moment—'the time has finally come for us to rise again.'

On cue the soldiers stood to attention. Each, if checked, would have been able to present a small wooden spoon nestling in the plume holder of their börks. It was a symbol of their commitment, and as such it was a sacred item. When their leader called upon them as a Brotherhood of the Spoon, they knew they were being called into service.

To many these simple implements may have appeared faintly ridiculous. Certainly incongruous. Ruthless warriors brandishing spoons. But that would be missing the point. The utensil was a symbol of their unbreakable bond. It spoke to the communion the men shared when they gathered around a meal. The stories they would tell. The honour they would pay. The connection they felt. It wasn't the spoon, but what the spoon stood for.

Duman continued, 'For too long now we have been downtrodden. For too long now we have been forgotten, castigated, subjugated. Well, the time has come to say, no more. Since the fourteenth century we have protected and expanded the Ottoman Empire. We built a reputation as the finest military corps in the world.

'As early as 1595, the authorities started trying to retire us. Disrespecting us. In 1622, the feeble Sultan Osman the Second blamed us for his defeat against Poland and tried to disband us. He failed, and it cost him his head. In 1807, Selim the Third tried to replace us with a different army. In the end he failed, and it also cost him his head. And in 1826, the greatest of all insults against us happened, as Mahmud the Second issued a fatwa against us, trying to get us disbanded. When we protested, we were slaughtered. Six thousand brothers murdered in the Auspicious Incident. The rest of us strewn to the four corners.

'They thought they had eradicated us forever. But even as they began to weaken and diminish, so we started our long journey to redemption. The brotherhood grew, generation on generation, always underground, waiting for our moment. For nearly two hundred years, our secret army has grown. We have infiltrated the senior ranks of every recognised militia in the world. We have a seat at government tables in the West and the East. Like a fire that has been banked, we have continued to burn and smoulder, waiting for exactly the right conditions to burst into cleansing flame once again.

'And we are right to want to wield this firestorm. Punish those who have promulgated this appalling persecution. We have never been compensated. The atrocity has never been recognised by our leaders. We were betrayed by the very people we served and protected.'

Osman paused again, feeling that familiar swell of anger that threatened to overwhelm him. He would never come to terms with the injustice of it all. The brutal slaughter of his brothers.

'Well, all that is about to change. We are the new order of Janissaries. Many of you have come through the resurrected devşirme system. You have been plucked from ordinary lives and trained to become elite soldiers. Would any one of you want to return to your old life, to be the person you were before we made you what you have now become?'

Not one soldier moved a muscle.

'Of course not. You are exactly where you are meant to be. Standing on the brink of greatness. Each of you is a lieutenant in our army. Each of you has platoons of your own, who will be called into action imminently. You are each charged with carrying these momentous messages to your own troops. It has been my great privilege to be your leader. To bring you all to this glorious point. I am an Osman. I am directly connected to the House of Osman and the Ottoman dynasty. No one can doubt my credentials.'

Osman paused yet again. Once he made these announcements, there was no going back. Wheels were set in motion. The new rise of the Ottoman Empire would be unstoppable. The world would never be the same again.

'Tonight, brothers, I have summoned you to say that the destiny we have been praying for has finally arrived. One week from now, we will have the sacred casket of Suleiman in our possession.'

Finally, the discipline of the platoon started to crack.

Soldiers glanced shocked at each other amidst gasps. One or two returned to their knees.

'We will have the casket, and we will have the heart of the last great true leader of our country. And ... we will have the hearts and minds of the people.'

Soldiers started to cheer and whoop. Some hugged as the importance of the moment sank in. Serkan, standing to one side of the stage, didn't share in this release. He hoped that Osman had calculated the retrieval of the casket correctly. That their agent on board was going to come through.

'We will put a new sultan in power. A sultan directly descended from Mehmed the Sixth, who was also betrayed. With a rightful leader on the throne, and the will of the people at our back, we cannot fail to rise again and take our rightful place as the dominant force in the world today. No army can defeat us while we carry the heart of Suleiman the Magnificent.' Osman screamed out his last line, testing the limits of the sound system. *'We are invincible.'*

All of the soldiers fell to their knees and offered up prayers. Osman glanced across to Serkan and nodded. Serkan took to the stage to address the squad.

'Brothers, hear me now and hear me well. Our great leader General Osman has brought us to this moment. He promised us power and glory, and now you see we will have it. We will gather again in this place exactly one week from now. At that point we will have the casket, and we hope that our new sultan will also join us. From here, each of you will then be despatched to rally your own platoons. Our sleeping army will be woken. We will be heard. Let me talk you through the plans ...'

***

As Serkan continued to provide instructions to the group, Osman walked away from the lights, through the ruins, and up the hill. He felt drained. Utterly and completely exhausted. He had carried the burden of this responsibility for so long. He had foregone so much. But now it would all be worth it.

He sat on a large rock and felt the night breeze on his face. He took out one of his faithful Maltepe and cupped it against the wind to light it. Taking a deep drag, he reflected on his journey to this point.

He thought about his family. His estranged brother, and the bad blood between them. His mother, little more than a whore as far as he was concerned. She cheated on her husband repeatedly, cuckolding him in a way that brought social embarrassment and public shame. Finally, she left them. Osman's distrust and distaste for women could be traced back to the overwhelming sense of betrayal he had felt when his mother left.

His father had always been an angry man. Short of temper and quick to administer punishment. But after the humiliation brought on him by his wife, he started to rage against the world. He neglected his young sons, and turned his back on an uncaring society, before graduating to paranoia and conspiracy theories, magnified through the bottom of a bottle.

Looking back, Osman was not surprised that he was recruited into the resurgent Janissary movement. He was ripe for the picking. He didn't care that technically he had been kidnapped. Anything had to be better than the life he had been left to live.

He thought about his mentor, the man who had first

suggested his true lineage and the path he needed to take. The man who had tutored him in the ways of the Janissary, brought the warrior out in the boy, and then honed those skills into the discipline and focus of an elite fighting machine.

He thought about the men he'd killed to gain the position he was now in, and the women he had brutally murdered, simply because he could. He knew his actions were questionable, but he also knew that the end would truly justify his means. Hadn't Suleiman himself murdered those closest to him? Great men made great sacrifices.

Then he thought about his own son. The arguments they had had. The words exchanged that could never be taken back. He thought about how much his son's hatred towards him had hurt. The ongoing feud about his Janissary movement. The terrible fight that had culminated in his own son drawing a knife on him. He had only meant to disarm the young man. He had never meant to stab him, let alone flee, leaving him to bleed out.

And throughout all of this he had kept the faith. Believed that his moment would come. And now it had.

He wondered how he would possibly wait one more week before fulfilling his destiny. Then he thought again about all the soldiers who had gone before. Those who had made the ultimate sacrifice. Truly he was standing on the shoulders of giants. And now, as the stars aligned, he would join that great pantheon. A lifetime of dedication would be recognised.

There was no stopping him now.

PART 7
BOUNTY

29

May 8, 2013

Limassol

'Sir David, I'm sorry to trouble you so late, but we've got a bit of a problem.'

Kal had been putting off this call for as long as possible, hoping he would find a solution, but in vain. Things had been going so smoothly; Kal should have suspected that a curve ball was coming.

During the course of the archaeological project, Kal had arranged for the *Triton* to dock in the Limassol port on three occasions. This allowed the recovered artefacts to be transferred from the ship and transported on to DIVE storage facilities in both the UK and the US. The first two instances had gone without a hitch. Appropriate paperwork was completed with the Cyprus Ports Authority, who showed very little interest in the cargo itself.

This final transfer of cargo was the most critical, both in terms of scale and value. Kal had deliberately held back the most significant recoveries, testing the attitude and protocols of the ports authority with more modest declarations. Everything had gone like clockwork, and he had no concerns about this trip. In fact, he had made a point of getting to know some of the key authority staff, building a co-operative and friendly relationship with them. This was just another routine transfer.

But from the moment the *Triton* docked in port, at about six in the evening, it was clear that things had changed. For a start, there was a welcoming committee at the dockside. Ports authority agents insisted on boarding the *Triton*, as was their right, to inspect the freight that had been prepared for transfer.

At first, aside from showing a much greater degree of interest, they followed the same protocols and adopted the same friendly manner. Paperwork was completed and signed, and the cargo was transferred to the dockside. At this point things started to unravel quickly.

Additional officers appeared from nowhere, and Kal was instructed, in a far more officious tone than had previously been used, that these goods were being seized by the Cyprus Ports Authority. Initially, Kal could get no clarity as to the rationale or authority behind this action, but eventually he was provided with paperwork that accused DIVE of illegal excavation.

Several key crew members had observed the debate, mindful that it wasn't their place to get involved. However, once an accusation was articulated, tempers frayed, and emotions started to boil over. As voices rose, Kal spotted an officer he had established a particularly good relationship with over the past few months sitting alone in his office. The officer had looked reluctant to get involved, taking a back seat throughout the confrontation. Kal casually wandered over to the man and enquired as to whether he could shed any further light on what was going on. After a lot of shrugging and wringing of hands, Kal finally received the intelligence he needed—the ports authority had been instructed by the Cypriot Department of Antiquities. Apparently, they had been given a tip-off that the *Triton* was excavating in Cypriot waters. To make matters worse, there were also suggestions of intelligence indicating that DIVE had employed unethical marine dig practices and intended to sell antiquities for profit, rather than donating them to an appropriate museum.

At this point, Kal finally understood that this was a political issue that wouldn't be solved on the Limassol dock that night. Immediately he shifted his strategy. He had already sought out Conor Murphy earlier, asking the captain whether they could relocate the *Triton* to its usual offshore position, if they could gain some kind of ports authority clearance. Once he'd explained that although all the artefacts had been seized, all the provenance data and cataloguing materials were still on board, Conor had immediately agreed. It would make life more difficult for the authorities if they wanted to gain access to the ship again, and, as Kal had often said before, it might just facilitate a quick getaway, or at the very least, buy them some valuable time. It may result in a fine, but this was too important. Kal had asked the captain to be on standby.

The project lead took a calculated risk, asking his ports authority contact if he'd look the other way while Kal's team moved the *Triton* offshore to secure DIVE records and kit. He placed a large wad of euros on the desk. Money available to Kal for exactly this reason. The officer eyed the banknotes and shrugged.

'We've already seized all the goods. I wouldn't want us to be difficult about this. You have two hours, Mr Farouk, and then we will need access to the ship again. If it isn't here, arrests will be made.'

Kal thanked the man for his understanding and

diplomacy. As he left the office, he looked across the warehouse to Conor, who was standing by the doors. He gave him the slightest of nods.

With the ship soon to be safely out of reach, Kal asked his project co-ordinator to help calm the crew down and take a little heat out of the situation. The two of them spent the next hour reassuring team members that there was nothing to worry about. Simply misunderstandings and red tape blowing things out of all proportion.

Finally, Kal made the call he had been avoiding for most of the evening. Sir David was very interested to hear about the tip-off but could also see the futility of Kal's position.

'Khaled, my boy, you've done all that you can do. More. This is not going to get fixed overnight. I fear, in fact, that it may take many months. But we have right on our side here, and in the end we will prevail. It's up to me now to open up some political channels and leverage some of my contacts. Meanwhile, I want you to now focus on the welfare of our people. Let's not allow this to boil over. Am I making myself clear, Khaled?'

'Absolutely, sir. I'll report back on what conclusions are reached tonight. In the meantime, I will focus on extracting the crew. Night, Sir David.'

Kal looked up from his phone at the scene unfolding in the ports authority offices. Raised voices were on the brink of turning into raised fists. He could really do with some of Daniel's counsel about now. Where the hell *was* Daniel?

***

Sir David had been woken up by Khaled's call, and,

not wishing to disturb his wife further, he had quickly slipped into a dressing gown and retreated to his office downstairs to continue the conversation. Once he was reassured that Kal would manage things appropriately at Limassol, he concluded the call, already realising that it would not be his last of the evening.

Even as Kal described the drama, Sir David had started jotting down names of people who could intervene on his behalf. Key political influencers. This was tiresome, but nothing to be overly worried about. Although he'd said to Kal that it could take time to sort this mess out, in truth, he hoped to have profuse apologies from the Cypriot government landing in his inbox before his wife woke in the morning.

So intent was he on searching his contacts app that he didn't sense the figure slipping out from behind the ornate curtains. As the blade pressed firmly into his back, David Nightingale froze. A voice whispered in his ear, 'Duman Osman sends his apologies. Sadly, your services as chief exec are no longer required. Accept this as your severance payment.'

The last thing Sir David heard was the swish of the traditional Janissary sword just before it sliced his head clean off.

***

Daniel had watched events unfold from the sidelines. He saw that Kal was up to his eyes trying to manage an increasingly volatile situation but didn't really feel he had anything to offer. If Kal needed help, he would ask for it. He noted with interest Kal's quiet word with Con and the captain's subsequent departure with a handful of his crew. Daniel was tempted to follow and offer his support to the captain but, realistically, what could he do?

As he stood there, wrestling with an increasing sense of helplessness, he felt a hand slip into his. He turned to see Banu looking up at him with an expression of anxiety bordering on fear. He was just about to volunteer that this didn't seem like the ideal moment for a romantic exchange when she spoke up.

'Danny, I need to get back to the ship—will you come with me?'

Daniel looked at her doubtfully. 'B, I'm not sure what can be done there. It seems like Kal might need our support here a bit more. It's all getting a little heated, don't you think?'

'Danny, we *have* to get back to the ship. It's important.'

'What's so important, Banu? What's wrong? You've gone white as a sheet.'

Banu hesitated, looked around to check if anyone was nearby, and then pulled Daniel's head down to hers so she could whisper in his ear.

'Not everything was transferred off the ship.'

Daniel stared incredulously at her.

'What are you saying, B? This is the last of it. I personally oversaw the transfer. There isn't one item still on the *Triton*. They've seized the lot.'

Banu looked away, appearing to weigh something up in her mind. Finally, she turned back to Daniel.

'Not everything came off the ship. One item is still on board.'

Daniel looked uncomprehendingly at Banu. Slowly it dawned on him what she was saying. His expression turned to one of horror. 'Banu, please tell me you haven't stolen the casket.'

Banu put her palms up defensively. 'Of course not, Daniel. You know me better than that. I'm just protecting it. Look what would have happened if I hadn't tucked it away.'

Daniel couldn't believe what he was hearing. 'Tucked it away? Can you hear yourself, B? It isn't a pint glass from a pub which you just took a fancy to. It's a priceless artefact. You had no right.'

'Danny, please. You must trust me. Would I be talking to you now if I planned to steal it? There was a time maybe ...' Banu drifted off for a moment, reflecting on her choices. 'But now my focus is purely on ensuring this doesn't fall into the wrong hands.'

'And who, pray, are the right hands?'

Banu stared intensely at Daniel. 'Professor. Will you help me or not?'

'Oh, it's "Professor" now you want something.' Daniel smiled. 'Of course I'll help you, B, you know that. I'm not saying I approve, but, hell, lead the way.'

The two casually wandered around the edge of the vast offices towards the exit. Once outside they picked up the pace towards where the *Triton* was docked.

If they had looked back, they might have noticed one of their colleagues also exiting the building before following them, making sure to stay in the safety of the shadows.

***

The pair turned the corner to where the *Triton* was docked and froze. The ship had disappeared. It took a few moments before either of them could process what they were seeing, or not seeing. It was like some crazy

David Blaine illusion. It had to be there. Eventually Daniel attempted some levity.

'I'm sure this is where we parked it, honey.'

'Not funny, Danny.'

Daniel continued to stare at the space where a sizeable ship had been, then it suddenly clicked. 'Hang on. I think I know where it is. I saw Kal having a very covert conversation with Con earlier. I couldn't work out why he was wasting his time talking to the captain, but I've just realised …'

Banu finished his thought. 'He was telling him to move the ship. Get it away from the dock.'

'Exactly, and I think we can both guess where it is.'

'Right, so, what now?' Banu asked desperately.

'Con will have left the utility dinghy nearby so Kal can get back to the ship. Come on, quick.'

The two of them dashed to the next dock inlet and, sure enough, the boat was waiting there. Without even hesitating, they jumped in. Daniel fired up the engine with the keys that had been left in the ignition. He was far from expert in handling the dinghy, but he had established sufficient proficiency to give him the confidence to go out onto the water, albeit cautiously. Gently he steered the boat round and started to manoeuvre out of the dock.

'Maybe we should stop somewhere on the way for a picnic?' Banu volunteered sarcastically.

Daniel decided not to respond but edged the throttle forward a little. The bow of the boat rose in the water as it picked up speed. Neither of them spoke as they headed out into the darkness. There was so much to say that saying nothing seemed like the better option.

Five minutes later, they saw the lights of the *Triton*,

reassuringly anchored in its usual position offshore. Their relief was palpable. They pulled round to the dive platform and secured the boat to the ship. Daniel didn't enjoy negotiating the ladder up to the deck but tried not to focus on his fear, and pushed on, getting it over with as quickly as possible.

He pulled himself onto the deck. Banu was right behind him.

'We should let the captain know we're on board,' he whispered, not really sure why he was whispering.

'First, we retrieve the casket; then we can talk to the captain. Follow me.'

Daniel had little option but to comply. He assumed that they were heading for Banu's cabin, but when she started towards the main deck, he realised that wasn't the case. They stopped at the archive container.

'Open it up, Danny. You've got the keys.'

Daniel did as he was told. 'I don't get it. There's nothing in here, B. I did a final sweep myself. Everything from the vault is gone.'

'Who said anything about the vault?'

They stepped inside, and Daniel went to switch on the lights.

'Leave them,' hissed Banu. 'Let's not attract attention right now.'

She stepped over to a bank of monitors and reached up to the largest one, on the far right of a row of screens.

'That one doesn't work. It packed up a week or two ago. Don't you remember?'

Banu ripped the screen away from the case. Instead of the usual chaos of wires and boards, the cabinet was filled with a knapsack. Carefully Banu pulled the bag out and set it on the nearest free desk space. She unzipped the bag to reveal the casket, now wrapped in heavy polythene. They both stared at it, aware that the next choice they made would be one with far-reaching consequences. Gently Daniel took Banu's arm.

'Come on, B. Let's go and talk to the captain. I'm going to say that I held this back to ensure its safety. No one will question my motivations. I promise you this will get to where it's meant to. I promise.'

Banu looked suddenly deflated. Her eyes started to well up. She made a slight nod of assent. Daniel put the casket back in the bag, zipped it up, and carefully slung it over his shoulder. He put his free arm around Banu, and they made their way up to the bridge.

Before he even opened the door, Daniel sensed that something was wrong, but by then it was too late. They stepped inside to see motionless bodies strewn all over the floor. Daniel instantly recognised some of the crew, including the first officer. Before he could take in anymore, a hand grabbed his arm and yanked him further inside. Banu was bundled in behind him.

It took Daniel a moment to assess what was actually going on. There were five, maybe six men, dressed completely in black military-grade body armour, complete with balaclava hoods. They were all heavily armed. Shell casings were strewn all around, and the air was thick with smoke. Blood was pouring from the bodies on the floor. Then Daniel noticed the captain. It was obvious that Con had taken a beating, but he was still standing, albeit only just.

Captain Murphy stared at the intruders with utter disdain. He knew the situation was hopeless. There was no point in pleading or bargaining. All he could do was to go out on his own terms. Daniel noticed a hardening resolve in his eyes as he spoke up in a measured, authoritative tone.

'I don't know who you arseholes are, and frankly I don't care. For the last time, get the *fuck* off my ship.'

The soldier nearest him pointed his gun at Conor's head, awaiting a direction from one of the others. The sergeant nodded, and the soldier pulled the trigger without even looking. The dull thud of a bullet exiting a silencer still made Daniel jump. The captain crumpled to the floor.

Daniel protested wildly. 'Stop this madness. Whatever you want, you can have it, but for God's sake stop the killing.'

The soldier nearest Daniel swung the butt of his automatic machine gun into Daniel's gut, snatching the bag off his shoulder at the same time. Another of the squad grabbed Banu from behind. Not one word had been uttered by the invaders. The man that shot Con now turned his gun on Daniel. He closed his eyes.

'Don't hurt him,' Banu cried.

The soldier held his gun in position, once again awaiting direction. After a long pause Daniel heard the soldier reholster his firearm. He opened his eyes to see the leader give quick and decisive hand signals to his unit. The ops team exited the bridge silently, dragging Banu with them.

Quickly they moved around to the stern of the ship, where they had secured two dinghies and placed temporary collapsible rope ladders. They silently returned to the boats with the casket and their hostage. One soldier remained on board, holding Daniel at gunpoint.

One of the boats fired up, and Daniel saw three of

the team speeding away with Banu on board. As their eyes caught one final time, the soldier guarding Daniel grabbed his collar and dragged him to the edge of the ship. With panic rising, he struggled violently, but the soldier was prepared for this resistance and tightened his arm around Daniel's neck. He felt consciousness start to slip as the soldier pivoted round and hurled him over the side of the ship in one clean movement.

The last thing Daniel heard before he hit the water was the distant sound of Banu's scream.

30

May 8, 1630

The Levantine Basin

Emir stared at the apparition of Shabaka. This could not be. His friend stepped forward and smiled.

'Emie, it's me. I survived. It is good to see you, my friend.'

Emir finally accepted what his eyes were telling him and leapt into the big Egyptian's arms. They embraced tightly, neither being able to speak with the emotion catching their voices. Eventually it was the captain that broke the moment.

'Red, I'm sorry I didn't tell you earlier, but I needed to hear the story from you unprompted to see whether it lined up with what your friend has already told me. Now I believe each of you and owe you both a debt of gratitude for the courage you have shown in uncovering this deceit and bringing it to me.'

Emir nodded while still looking perplexed. He turned back to Shabaka. 'I don't understand. I saw you die. How … ?'

Shabaka chuckled as he reached over to the captain's desk and picked up his ring. He looked at Emir with a glint in his eye.

'I told you once, my friend, these rings can never be parted. They will always find a way.'

Emir looked down at his own ring and wondered at

the power these rings must possess. More magic than in any of his illusions.'

'But still, you were stabbed. You were thrown overboard.'

'I remember you telling me once that your papa always had an escape route in case things went south. A safety net, he called it, am I right?'

Emir nodded at the fond memory. 'Yes, that's right.'

'Well, I had my own safety net. You should never go into a situation that you aren't sure you can get out of, Emie. Once we had arranged where to meet, I manoeuvred the external maintenance rigging round to that side of the *Colossus*. Nets and ropes aplenty. My thought was that if you or I went over, there would be a fair chance that the rigging would catch us.'

'But I heard you hit the water,' Emir said, perplexed.

'Yes. Things didn't quite go to plan. I missed the rigging and did hit the sea. Fortunately, there were three or four trailing ropes, and I managed to grab one. Pulling myself back up proved a bit more of a challenge, I'm not as fit as I once was, but I didn't dare shout for help. My only regret was that I had to leave your fate in your own hands, but I've seen enough of your character to know that you would endure.'

Emir was shaking his head at the extraordinary turn of events being related to him.

'What about your wound? I saw you stabbed.'

'A scratch. The blade barely punctured my leather jerkin.'

Emir was about to interrogate Shabaka further, when the ship listed badly to the port. The captain's log box flew off the desk. Everything else was necessarily secured, but Captain Barbarossa had been completing the day's entry, recounting the events of the storm, before Shabaka and then Emir arrived. As the ship righted, he picked up the brass box and sat back down at his desk.

'Gentlemen, I invite you to continue your reunion over there in my cabin chairs. I have to complete some final entries for the log. Please be patient.'

Twenty minutes later Captain Barbarossa closed his logbook and placed it, together with some other papers, inside the brass box, then locked it with a large brass key before stowing it securely. After he threw the key into a desk drawer, he looked back at his guests.

'Right, gentlemen, the time has come. My plan is to bring together a handful of men I know I can trust. Men who I personally selected. Men who have been on the entire journey as well as previous voyages with me … and then we will restrain the mutineers one at a time. By the time they realise what's happening, we will have sufficiently depleted their numbers such that we can confidently overcome the remainder.'

Shabaka interjected. 'Well, they are already down by one in number. I despatched one of the traitors before I came to you, sir. Mustafa. He is the dog that brought that fool Onur on board. Needed to fix me a little retribution.'

The *Colossus* rolled violently again. The wind mounted a fresh assault outside. The captain looked grave.

'If we are about to be hit by what I think we are about to be hit by, then all of this may become irrelevant. Even the most motivated traitors can't mount an attack from the bottom of the ocean.'

Emir looked genuinely terrified. He was an excellent

swimmer, having grown up in a port, but he didn't fancy his chances in these seas.

'And if I'm not mistaken, she's very nearly here.'

The two men and the boy, who had matured unrecognisably over the last six months, stood quietly for a few moments. They contemplated the magnitude of what Barbarossa had just said. The captain was the one to break the silence.

'You promise me this casket is safe, Red?'

'Yes, sir. It won't be found.'

'Then that is all I need to know of it for now. If we survive the night, I will expect you to surrender it to me. I will need some tangible proof if I am to detain these men, many of whom are men of good standing in Constantinople. In the meantime, I think all of us are going to have our hands full over the next couple of hours.'

Shabaka pulled Emir to his side. 'You stick right by me, Emie. I don't want you out of my sight.'

Barbarossa interjected, 'And the two of you can stick right by me. I can't afford to lose either of you to this thing. Right by my side, do you hear?'

Shabaka and Emir both nodded vigorously. If any man was going to survive this ordeal, they'd put their money on the captain.

'Right, so listen up. You already know that most of the sails have been stowed. Only the fore topsail and the jib are still raised. If we are to have any chance of steering into this thing, we're going to need them. I will pick a couple of men I know I can trust, and who you would think twice about picking a fight with, to stay with us. Then I'll place another four at the prow to try and protect the sails for as long as possible.'

The ship was rolling with increasing resolve. They were definitely on borrowed time.

'Shaba. You will be with me at the wheel, following my instruction. Red—Emir, sorry—you will be between us. Shaba, if we're to have any chance of beating this thing, we have to sail at an angle. That means we'll keep turning into the wave, right?'

Shabaka nodded his understanding. He was good at the wheel and was happy to have the responsibility.

'We have to keep moving and keep our rudder in the water. If not, we will surely perish. Now, last thing. Many men will lash themselves to the ship. Normally I would support this tactic, but if the ship goes down, then it will take you with it, and ...' he paused to contemplate what he was about to say. 'I think there is a good chance that the *Colossus* will surrender herself this night.'

Barbarossa held out his hand in a gesture of comradeship. Emir and Shabaka placed their hands on top.

'May the gods be with us, gentleman. Now, let us see what she's got, shall we?'

***

As soon as the trio emerged onto the deck, it was clear that the time for any subtle execution of plans had long since passed. The storm had re-established its grip with frightening speed. Over the course of less than a minute, a relative calm had been replaced by utter pandemonium. This was to be survival of the fittest, pure and simple.

The *Colossus* was taking on vast amounts of water, and the crew desperately tried to bail it back out. It looked to Emir like a completely futile task, but what else could they do?

Spray lashed at their faces constantly as the grand ship creaked and groaned against the battering it was now enduring. The howl of the wind made it really difficult to hear any words, even if they were being barked out right by one's side.

For a moment, Emir caught the eyes of the boatswain, who looked at him with an expression of shock, but the moment was fleeting. The hurricane demanded their total attention. The officer thought that he would deal with Emir later. As it was, this was his last coherent thought, as a wave knocked him straight over the siderail and into the roiling waves below.

As Emir attempted to take the scene in, he himself was smacked by another wave. He would have surely suffered the same fate as the boatswain had it not been for Shabaka's quick thinking. He grabbed the boy and swung him round, using the force of the wave to carry Emir to a new purchase point.

Again, Emir looked around, trying to grasp the gravity of the situation. It seemed hopeless. How could they possibly survive this? As the captain had predicted, many of the crew were lashing themselves to the body of the ship, hoping this would stop them from being thrown overboard. Other crew members had already met their fate. Emir saw Antonio floating face up in the water on deck. The deep wound across his forehead would have rendered him unrecognisable were it not for the distinctive green, white, and red sash that he always wore round his waist.

The howl of the wind ripped away the screams of

the men. Only the hurricane and the sea could be heard now. Even the ship's protestations were silenced by the deafening roar of the onslaught.

Slowly the two men made progress towards the poop deck, more or less carrying Emir between them. As they reached the wheel, the sailor manning it looked towards his captain with despair. He shouted something Emir couldn't catch. The captain nodded and put a hand on the sailor's shoulder. Even Emir could see the gesture expressed a mixture of reassurance and acknowledgement. It said, *You've done your best, son. I'll take it from here.*

The captain took the wheel, immediately attempting to turn it back into the storm, but the resistance made it impossible to move.

Shabaka turned to Emir, screaming into his ear, 'I need to help him. Stay close. I have a way off this ship.' He turned back to the captain and grabbed the port side of the wheel, adding his considerable might to the task. With both men applying every ounce of strength they could muster, the wheel started to turn.

Emir stood back, recognising he had little to contribute here. As the hurricane continued, he suddenly had a moment of clarity. This ship was going down. He needed to retrieve the casket or, at the very least, ensure that it couldn't fall into traitorous hands.

As Emir moved to head back down to the main deck, Shabaka turned his head and glared a look of disapproval. It clearly said *don't move.* Emir shrugged and mouthed 'I'll be right back.' He knew that Shabaka didn't dare leave his post, so with a reassuring hand to his heart, he headed back down into the bowels of the ship.

31

May 8, 2013

Amathus

Daniel barely had time to gulp any air before he felt the shock of the water's impact. Immediately, he felt himself starting to sink. He kicked hard, and his head broke the surface of the water sufficiently for him to take another desperate gasp of air.

He knew he had only seconds to live. He had found treading water in swimming shorts tough enough, but now he was fully clothed, and he could feel the saturated fabrics weighing him down. In that instant his clear thought was, *This was always meant to be. This is my fate. I was always destined to drown.*

And then his schoolboy nemesis Barry was there in front of him again. Taunting him. His father was shouting reprimands and recriminations at him. He was already tiring and felt himself sinking down for a final time when Banu's voice came to him. *Don't leave me, Danny. I need you now.*

He kicked up again, desperately fighting against the inevitable. Despite everything that he was experiencing, he felt his mind still a little, and the empty chalkboard came into focus. Feverishly the white lines explored potential routes to safety, before erasing them as unworkable and starting over. The chalk was telling him what he already knew. There was no salvation to be had here.

In those moments, Daniel found a new clarity. Time stretched as he witnessed his life's events as a set of lightning-quick scenes. He thought about his failures. His failed relationship with his father. How he subsequently failed his mother. His failed affair with Maria. And how even his successes had become failures. He wasn't the hero he knew people wanted him to be. He was the victim that he had allowed himself to become. How apt, then, that his final act would be to fail another. To fail Banu.

And then he heard another voice. A child's voice. It spoke directly to him. *It isn't over. You still have time. There's always a way.* He just had to fight for it. He could still be the man that he wanted to be. The man that others needed him to be.

Daniel reached deep down and found the strength to power himself to the surface again.

He heard the drone of a distant outboard motor. Then he saw a spotlight sweeping back and forth across the sea. Was he imagining this? Had they returned to finish the job? Suddenly he felt a hand grabbing hold of his armpit and pulling hard. How was this possible? He felt himself being pulled from the water into the safety of a boat. Coughing and spluttering from the water that had started down his throat, he slowly opened his eyes to try and make out the identity of his saviour. His sight gradually came back into focus, and he stared incredulously at the man looking down at him.

'Yousef? Yousef, is that you?'

'Yes, my friend, it is me. You are safe now.'

'How are you here? I don't understand.'

'I followed you and the girl out of the offices. I

thought you might need some help.'

Daniel snapped back into focus. He felt a surge of energy, like he had been reborn. There was still time. He could still step up. Make a difference.

'Banu. They've taken her. Yousef, we must save her. Did you see which way the boats went?'

'Don't worry, my friend, I know exactly where the boats are heading. Hold on just a moment; I need to make a call.'

Daniel stared at Yousef, bewildered. He started to speak but Yousef put up his hand in a silencing gesture.

'Bosco. The package is en route, as expected. I need men on the ground at the rally point in the next ten minutes. Over.'

He listened to the brief response and then ended the call without any further dialogue. He turned back to his friend and smiled.

'Danny, I've got a lot to catch you up on, but for now let's see if we can rescue your lady.'

Daniel sat fully upright in the boat. He had so many questions he didn't know where to start. Finally, he identified the most pressing one.

'Where is she?'

As Yousef gunned the boat into high gear, he shouted back, 'Amathus.'

***

Yousef and Daniel raced to cover the five-mile distance to Amathus as quickly as possible. The two friends valiantly fought against the cacophony of wind, engine, and pounding water to have a seriously overdue conversation. Daniel searched out some dry clothes and waterproofs that had been stowed on the dinghy previously. As he changed, he stared at Yousef, once again having to reappraise his friend. He was beginning to realise that there was more to Yousef than met the eye. Much more.

The Jordanian explained, 'I've been tracking a criminal, a guy called Duman Osman, on and off for a number of years. He's wanted for multiple murders, wartime atrocities, child kidnappings, sexual assaults … the list goes on. I know this because, in short, I run a, er, "renegade" crew of ex-military men. I select projects that offer some financial return, whilst also allowing us to do some good. It's black ops stuff. Strictly off the books.'

Daniel nodded, more in disbelief than anything.

'I secured a position on the *Triton* after getting fresh intel that Osman had taken a non-exec role with DIVE—and had *also* infiltrated the ship's crew for his own ends. When I heard that DIVE was going to approach you with a job offer, of course, I tried to stop you. Who knew how dangerous this mission was going to get?'

Daniel desperately tried to keep up, as Yousef hurled one huge piece of news after another at him. Nothing really made sense, and then Yousef mentioned the missing jigsaw piece.

'Osman is obsessed with Suleiman, and the whole legend around his heart.'

Daniel interrupted. 'That's what the men who kidnapped Banu must have been doing on the ship. They took the relic with them. Yousef, they've got Suleiman's casket.'

Yousef looked at Daniel, contemplating this new piece of information. 'That's what I guessed. If I'm right, those are Osman's men. And that means *he* now has his hands on the casket. Tonight, he is gathering his troops at Amathus to brief them on his plans. My sources tell me he will be activating a series of large-scale military operations. There will be at least thirty elite officers there, and if he really is in possession of the casket, then that means ...'

Yousef trailed off, but Daniel finished the thought: 'He has no need of Banu.'

The men stared grimly at each other. Yousef spotted some distant lights on the shoreline where they were heading, and immediately he throttled back the outboard motor to a low purr.

'What are we going to do? There's just two of us. We can't leave Banu in this monster's hands. His men are ruthless.'

Yousef cut through Daniel's increasingly urgent concerns.

'Don't worry, my friend. Do you think I would allow us to get caught up in a gunfight without bringing some firepower of my own?'

Daniel looked penetratingly at Yousef. 'Who are you, and what have you done with my friend?'

***

They reached the shore in time to see moving lights further up the rise ahead. Yousef told Daniel to sit tight while he did a quick reconnoitre. In truth, he didn't want Daniel to hear the details of his next call. The professor seemed spooked enough as it was. Bosco confirmed that Yousef's squad of eight men was in position. He also indicated that he had sight of thirty-three men and one woman. Yousef gave some final instructions, then rang off as he returned to Daniel.

'Right, I've identified an optimum vantage point. Stay low and follow me. If you see any men, don't panic; they're with me. Can you handle a gun?'

Daniel had grown up with guns around him. He never really developed a liking for them, but he knew which end to hold.

'Sure. No hotshot, but right now I'd prefer to have one and not need it than need one and not have it.'

Yousef handed over a Glock. After checking the safety was on, Daniel pocketed the pistol, hoping that he wouldn't have to use it. They crept slowly up the hill, following the glow of light on the brow ahead.

As they approached the top, Daniel hissed, 'So, where the hell are your men? I thought you said we'd see some of them. Are you sure they're here?'

'We passed within two metres of three of them on the way up, Dan. Don't worry, they'll make their presence felt soon enough.'

They ducked lower still and then crawled the last few metres to the point that Yousef had selected. As Daniel caught his breath, he peered down into what looked like some ancient ruins of a small amphitheatre, lit dramatically with fire torches. He couldn't believe what he was seeing.

Around thirty men were gathered in the arena. They were standing at ease but not easy. They were clearly military. They waited silently, expectantly. Daniel scanned the scene for any sign of Banu, but she was nowhere to be seen. Yousef nudged him and pointed to a soldier who was standing on the stage. Daniel studied the man, and a look of recognition came across his face.

'Isn't that Davy?'

Yousef nodded and pulled an expression that said

'welcome to the party, pal.' Daniel looked perplexed. Yousef leant over and whispered, 'He was Osman's plant on the ship. He murdered one of my team. Brandy was one of ours.'

Daniel was reeling as the revelations kept coming. 'Brandy was with you?' he asked incredulously.

'Yep. And she's not the only one I've lost in this operation.'

'But why did he kill her?'

'Who knows. Maybe her cover was blown. Maybe she was protecting my cover. We'll never know. Davy has been feeding Osman information all along. Tonight, I avenge Brandy's murder. Whatever else happens next, that Geordie fuck goes down.'

As Yousef voiced this commitment, a well-built man joined Davy on the stage. His stature only partly explained the presence that oozed from him. No one could be in any doubt that he was in charge. The men snapped to attention in unison. Davy retreated a couple of steps to a small pedestal erected stage right.

'Osman,' Yousef whispered. Daniel stared intently at the man. There was something familiar about him.

Osman stood in front of his men proudly, eyes glistening. He looked down on his brothers. No traditional costume or ancient weaponry was on show tonight. The squad was all dressed identically in black ops combat gear, complete with state-of-the-art firepower. This was no ceremonial gathering. This was a military briefing, plain and simple. Osman stood beside a simple throne that had been positioned centre stage.

'Tonight, we summon up the great leaders from the House of Osman, beginning with Osman the First. On through Mehmed the Conqueror, Selim the Resolute, and, of course, Suleiman the Magnificent. All the way up to our last sultan, illegally deposed, Mehmed the Sixth. This pantheon of the greats in Ottoman history are with us tonight. They look down on us and honour us for our endeavours.'

The squad gazed adoringly at their leader, knowing their place in Ottoman history was now assured. Many of these cold-blooded killers had tears in their eyes. The sense of destiny was palpable.

'Tonight, the final pieces that we have waited so long for are finally with us. Our patience has been rewarded. Our sacrifice recognised. Our devotion answered.'

Osman couldn't resist a smile as he savoured his next words.

'Brothers, I promised you a sultan for our times. A sultan who can lead us all. A sultan who is directly related to Mehmed the Sixth and, as such, has rightful claim to the throne. Tonight, I make good on that promise. Serkan?'

'Serkan is Osman's second. A killing machine,' Yousef whispered, continuing to fill in the gaps for Daniel.

Osman looked across to a series of ancient columns. Daniel and Yousef followed his gaze. Serkan emerged from the shadows, escorting with him the heir apparent to the throne of the Ottoman Empire.

Daniel's and Yousef's mouths dropped in unison as the figure stepped into the light.

***

Dressed in radiant white, starkly contrasting with the black combat gear of the troops, Banu walked onto the stage. Duman gazed upon her adoringly. It was a look that only a proud father could have. She walked to his side, and he knelt, subjugating himself to his future monarch. Immediately, every man in the squad followed suit. The symbolism of leadership transfer was clear to all. After reverentially kissing her hand, Duman rose and turned back to address his troops. In unison, they stood also. Davy stepped up to Banu's side. Daniel thought it was unclear whether he was there to protect her or restrain her.

'My daughter comes before you today to claim her rightful place on the throne. In the spirit of the Sultanate of Women and the honourable Hurrem Sultan, wife to Suleiman the Magnificent, she makes her claim.

'Following the despicable expulsion and subsequent exile of our last sultan, Mehmed the Sixth, he sent a declaration to the Caliphate Congress asserting that he had never waived the right to reign. Even at the moment of his death he was still the rightful ruler of our people. Today, my daughter, his great-granddaughter, steps forward to usher in a new era of glory and dominion.'

Daniel was reeling as he tried to keep up with the astonishing narrative that Osman was spinning. This was Banu's father? The man of whom she had spoken so adoringly.

Osman continued, 'I can prove her heritage, and that proof will be forthcoming in due course. Our long night of waiting is now finally at an end. Tonight, we can finally reunite a true leader with the sacred instrument of leadership. The sacred artefact that commands the followership of our people. Finally ... we have the heart of Suleiman the Magnificent in our hands. Serkan.'

Osman's faithful ally strode for a second time from the shadows onto the lit stage, and this time he carried a heavy box in his hands, wrapped in deep-red velvet.

In truth Serkan had misgivings about this part of the proceedings. He had tried to persuade Osman to open the casket moments earlier, away from a fanatical audience, but his leader was having none of it. 'They deserve this moment as much as we do, Serkan. It must be revealed as part of the ceremony.'

He placed it on the small pedestal. After a brief pause, and following a nod of instruction from his boss, he pulled a stunning golden box from the velvet bag and placed it reverentially back on the pedestal.

'Suleiman's casket,' Daniel whispered to no one in particular. An expression of horror came over his face as he then watched Serkan take out some crude tools and start to butcher the casket. They were simply going to force it open.

'I don't believe it. That is a priceless artefact, and they're just going to hack away at it.'

'The casket is worthless to them, Dan. It's what's inside that they care about,' Yousef responded. 'Brace yourself now, Danny. Things are going to escalate very quickly from here on in, I suspect.'

Daniel looked across at Yousef quizzically. He was about to explore exactly what Yousef meant when a roar of anguish made him physically jolt. He looked back towards the stage to see Osman holding the casket open. Whatever was inside, it wasn't what he had been hoping for. Serkan took a couple of steps back from Osman. He had been caught on the wrong side of one or two of Osman's rages in the past and was attuned to the early tremors.

Suddenly, one of the squad raised his semiautomatic machine gun, directing it towards a point on the surrounding skyline. 'I just saw a scope flash sir. Two o'clock.' The entire squad shouldered their weapons and pointed in the same direction.

'And away we go,' Yousef muttered. He raised his own weapon and found Davy in his sight. He wasn't about to let him slip away. He realised that thirty men, high on rhetoric and pumped for action, weren't going to allow their better selves to get in the way for very long. A single shot rang out, heralding a cacophony of gunfire.

***

What seemed like an hour of relentless gunfire was actually a chaos of less than three minutes. Davy was the first of the Janissaries to react, as Daniel recalled. He made a calculated call that Banu was not a target and promptly grabbed her to use as a human shield. Putting his arm around her neck, he whispered something in her ear and started to retreat off the stage. Meanwhile, six or seven of the Janissaries dropped almost immediately in the first volley of fire. The remainder scattered in search of cover.

Shots seemed to rain down from all sides of the arena, so finding shelter was almost impossible. Yousef still hadn't fired a shot. His finger hesitated over the trigger as he tried to get a clear shot of Davy. The rest of his team was relentless in their onslaught.

The second Osman saw Davy's move, he pulled his pistol from his shoulder holster and aimed it squarely at the Englishman's head.

Daniel distinctly remembered hearing Serkan scream above the racket of gunfire, 'Duman! It's over! Don't be a fool! *We have to escape.*'

Davy shifted his angle to block Osman's line of sight. Yousef didn't need a second invitation. His shot hit Davy directly in his left eye, killing him on impact. As his grip released, Banu stepped forward. Oblivious to the peril all around, she made no attempt to run for cover. Instead, she simply stared in fury at Osman.

Osman held his daughter's stare, seemingly weighing up his next move. Finally, he grabbed the casket and fled from the arena. Serkan knew where Osman was heading and immediately gave chase.

Daniel surreptitiously glanced across at Yousef. The soldier looked pretty preoccupied. He hesitated for a moment, then rolled away from the position they had taken, back down the incline. As soon as he could, he stood, pulled out the pistol Yousef had given him, and chased off in the direction that he last saw Osman heading. A new sense of purpose and drive had hold of Daniel now, but more than that, he was acting without fear. He realised in that moment that fear of failure had defined his life. Well, no more.

Daniel caught up with Osman on the beach. It turned out he had taken a bullet in the leg, and it was starting to slow him down. In the distance, he saw boats with flashing lights approaching. Multiple smoke cannisters had been deployed, and a thick purple haze blew eerily across the sand. Faintly, Daniel thought he could hear the whine of a helicopter engine.

Daniel shouted at Osman to stop and fired a warning shot over his head. Osman came wearily to a halt and slowly turned round.

'Professor. We meet at last. My daughter is a great admirer of yours, I understand.'

'Just put the casket down, Osman, and you can go. I have no desire to get into a gunfight with you. You must see that it's all over. Your guy Serkan was right about that.'

Once again, Osman seemed to be considering the choices available to him. He took a step towards Daniel. Alarmed, Daniel took his gun in both hands in an attempt to signal that he meant business. 'That's far enough, Osman.' He hoped he sounded authoritative. He felt anything but. This was new territory for him.

Osman paused, staring intensely at Daniel. 'I think in the end, Daniel, your father was proud of you.'

Shocked and rattled, Daniel focussed on trying to retain a calm tone. 'How would you know? You don't know anything about my father or our relationship.'

'Oh, but I do. I have been doing business with Randolph for more than thirty years. He's the one that introduced me to David Nightingale. It was one thing taking out that irritating Brand woman, but without Nightingale's influence, I wouldn't have been able to get my own girl onto the *Triton* as her replacement.'

Daniel desperately tried to process what he was hearing. 'Banu was working undercover for you? I don't believe it. She must have been coerced. I don't even believe that she is your daughter. Her values are so ...'

Daniel's voice petered out as he tried to make sense of everything he was hearing.

'Oh, but she is, Daniel. I can assure you of that. Children don't get to pick their parents, do they? You should know all about that. Are you your father's son?'

'Maybe you knew him, but that doesn't mean you

know me. You don't.'

Duman sighed deeply. 'I am reaching for my cigarettes. Don't get twitchy now.'

He reached into his trouser pocket and pulled out the distinctive red-and-white soft pack of Maltepe cigarettes and his Zippo. He lit the cigarette and took a deep drag. During this process he never once relinquished his grip on the casket. He looked out to sea, his gaze stretching for miles, momentarily lost in his thoughts.

'It's not easy being a father, you know. We want the best for our children. We want them to be the best they can possibly be. We want them to not make the mistakes that we made. We do terrible things to give them legitimacy and opportunity. We hope that the end will justify the means.' He paused again to draw heavily on his cigarette. 'Randolph understood that. And, at the end, he realised that he'd paid too heavy a price.'

'What do you mean, "at the end"?' Daniel spluttered. 'Were you there at the end? Did you … did you kill my father?' Daniel's voice was thick with emotion now.

Duman took a final drag before flicking the half-smoked cigarette onto the beach. 'Yes, well, not exactly. Serkan completed the assignment, but I gave the order.'

Daniel was shocked at his own emotional response. He hated his father. Why did he care? But he found he did. His father had been a monster, but he had also been his dad.

'Why?'

'He became an inconvenient loose end. You see, I won't let anything, or anyone, get in my way, Professor. My work is too important. I know that Banu has feelings for you. She was the last pure thing in my life. Unsullied by my choices. Untainted by my past. And now I have lost her trust and her love. I saw the look in her eyes tonight. She no longer believes in me. I think ... her affections have shifted. That's a pity. I might have enjoyed having a son-in-law. But if it's between you and me, Professor, well ...'

Osman gazed at Daniel, seemingly trying to calculate his next move. Suddenly he looked less strong, less commanding. Less sure. Daniel stared into the eyes of his nemesis and saw despair. In that moment he looked utterly defeated.

Finally, he spoke. 'I have failed. Failed my people. Failed my forefathers. Failed my children. Failed my men. But most of all, I have failed my sultan. I have failed Suleiman.'

Just as Daniel thought that Osman was resigning himself to defeat, he seemed to snap out of his reverie. In a flash, he had unholstered his own pistol and now pointed it directly at Daniel.

'I don't think you are going to shoot me, young man, and I don't want to kill you either. I like you, Daniel. Something tells me you might still be my best route to the heart of Suleiman. This isn't over yet, Professor Fairlight. Not by a long chalk. We'll meet again, but until then, I leave you this gift.'

Osman stooped and reverentially placed the golden casket of Suleiman onto the sand. After a brief bow of his head, he spun away and ran as fast as his leg wound would allow towards the chopping sound of the waiting MD500E helicopter.

Daniel watched him slowly disappearing into the violet mist. In that moment, he experienced a rush of thoughts and emotions. He thought about his father, and whether there really had been some chance at redemption for them. He thought about Suleiman and his reach across the centuries. He thought about Banu, and the fact that he might never now get the chance to tell her that he loved her. To prove to her that he was worthy. And he thought about Osman's deluded sense of destiny. *This isn't over yet.*

Daniel started to run.

***

Osman allowed the noise of the helicopter rotors to guide him through the shroud coming from the smoke canisters. He could hear that his pilot had got the chopper primed for lift-off. As the main rotor blades momentarily dispersed the haze, Osman saw Serkan standing by the cockpit door. In one hand he held a gun pointed at the helicopter pilot. In the other he had a semiautomatic machine gun pointed directly at Osman. He stared defiantly at his boss, slowly shaking his head.

'It's all gone too far, Duman. You've allowed your obsession to cloud your judgement. It's time for a new man to step up and finish the job.'

'*Stand down, soldier,*' Osman screamed. 'You would be nothing without me. I have taught you everything you know.'

Again, Serkan shook his head. 'No, my friend, you have taught me everything *you* know. I'll take it from here.'

Osman lifted his gun, but Serkan was ready. The short burst of machine-gun fire ripped Osman's prosthetic arm clean off. He howled in agony.

'You see, old man? It is my time now.'

Serkan raised his gun again to finish the job. Osman

braced himself for the rain of bullets, but instead he heard the clap of a single shot. The bullet hit Serkan in the centre of his chest. He stared in shock at the rapid spread of blood across his shirt. As he fell back, his hand clenched onto the machine-gun trigger. Osman lurched to one side in an attempt to avoid the spray of bullets. He tried to right himself, but he could feel his injured leg starting to give way. Desperately he surged towards the haven of the helicopter, becoming disorientated in the chaos of swirling dust and pain and gunfire.

Osman's vision cleared just in time to see the tail rotor as he ran headlong into it. His head and upper torso were instantly reduced to a bloody pulp.

In the clearing mist, Serkan raised his head to try and make out his assailant. Daniel stood, still holding his gun at shoulder height. Serkan smiled, and his body dropped.

As Daniel wrestled with the fact that he had just killed his father's assassin, his attention shifted to the helicopter pilot. The Janissary manning the controls held one hand out in a gesture of surrender. In his other hand he held a radio microphone. He never took his eyes off Daniel as he continued to talk urgently into the radio.

Slowly, Daniel retreated from the chaotic scene. Away from the howl of the rotor blades, still running at lift-off speed. Away from the carnage and back down the beach, pausing only to pick up a golden casket.

***

Dazed and bewildered, Daniel had little recollection of making his way back to Yousef's vantage point. But he did remember what he saw when he arrived. He would never forget the image of broken and brutalised bodies everywhere. He didn't want to look, but he had to. He was searching for her. He scanned the battle zone over and over, but no Banu. The remnants of her ceremonial white robe could clearly be seen, but no Banu. She had vanished.

Yousef started to shake him. 'Danny, snap out of it. What happened with Osman?'

'He's dead.'

'Good man. Didn't know you had it in you. Did anyone see you?'

'No, well, the helicopter pilot, I guess.'

'He'll be one of Osman's men. You don't need to worry about him. Okay. Now listen really carefully, Danny boy.' Yousef took the Glock back out of Daniel's hand as he completed his instructions.

'I can hear the cavalry coming. Always bloody late, but better late than never, I guess. Anyway, we can't be here when they arrive. In fact—and this is really important, Dan—we were never here.'

Daniel stared at a man that he hardly knew. He could feel the shock enveloping him. He started to tremble uncontrollably as the evening's events crowded in on him.

Yousef grabbed him roughly. 'Get it together Danny. If you don't calm down, you're gonna end up in prison for killing a criminal that the world could well do without. Focus on that.'

Daniel forced himself into his breathing exercises, and slowly his equilibrium returned. He stared at Yousef. 'Why did you do it, Yous? What's it all for?'

Yousef shook his head, knowing that he wouldn't be able to get Daniel to understand even if he had a lifetime to explain, let alone the few remaining seconds.

'I do it to pay a debt. I do it to try and right some of my many wrongs. To balance things out a little.' Realising he sounded more virtuous than he deserved, Yousef added with a twinkle in his eye, 'And for the money, of course. We shouldn't forget about that.'

'What money?' Daniel interjected.

Yousef smiled conspiratorially. 'Let's just put it like this, Danny. If, when the time comes to do a full inventory check of the *Colossus*'s burden, you happen to find that you're one item short, please don't search too hard for it.'

At that moment there was a deafening roar as a helicopter flew directly overhead. Both men ducked instinctively.

'We only have a minute or two left, Danny, so listen up.'

Yousef continued to outline the story that Daniel needed to adopt, before giving him a bear hug and readying to go. Bosco stood waiting at a respectful distance. As Yousef looked at him, Bosco held up two fingers. Yousef winced. Two of his men were down. Two more casualties. This op had come at a heavy price. Like the rest of the squad, they would not be found here, but they were lost to Yousef now.

As he started away, Daniel called after him, 'Will I see you again?'

Yousef paused, thought for a moment, then shouted back, 'Take this number. Don't write it down, just commit it to memory. If you ever really need me, brother, call it. I'll be there.'

***

'And that's everything, Detective.'

Daniel wrapped up his statement. He could hear Yousef telling him to keep it short and sweet. Stick as close to the truth as you can. The best deceptions are the ones that are almost true. But don't say any more than you have to. The more extraneous detail you provide, the less convincing you'll become. He knew he was suppressing his shock and there would be a price to pay later, but for now he just had to get through this.

'Anything else to add sir? Any detail that might help us?'

'Like I said, I saw Banu getting kidnapped. I followed her to the ruins. By the time I got there, all hell was breaking loose. I found the casket on the beach, and I retrieved it on behalf of DIVE Recoveries. Then you guys turned up.'

'What about the girl? You said that you followed her to Amathus, but there is no sign of her anywhere. Plenty of other bodies, but not her.'

'I can honestly say, Officer, I have no idea where she went. By the time I got up to the peak, there was no sign of her. She just vanished.'

Daniel felt his voice breaking. This last statement was the truest thing he had said throughout the whole interview, and the one that hurt the most. Banu was gone from his life. Like Suleiman's heart, she had disappeared.

32

May 8, 1630
The Levantine Basin

The *Colossus* groaned and creaked and screamed as the tempest continued to batter her. Emir heard wood straining and breaking over the storm's own protestations. Her heavy load and gargantuan stature were in her favour, providing much-needed stability and stamina. She was also in the hands of a master mariner in the form of Captain Barbarossa. But still she shrieked as the hurricane relentlessly pounded her frame.

Emir made slow progress towards the casket's hideaway. It was impossible to anticipate the violent swings of the ship. In such unfortunate circumstances, all Emir could do was brace himself to be bounced around like a marble on a bagatelle board.

Finally, he found his way to the entrance he was looking for. He was back at the captain's cabin. He had been the last of the three to leave it, so he knew the door wasn't locked. Nevertheless, it resisted his push. He tried again, this time with all his might.

The door opened, releasing two feet of water at floor level. A section of the ceiling had ripped away, and water was gushing in every time the *Colossus* rolled into the waves. Emir could see that there were only minutes remaining before this cabin would be completely submerged.

Well, it seemed like a good idea at the time, he thought to himself. When he had first emerged on deck with the casket earlier, the storm had proved a great distraction to all, including Captain Barbarossa. His cabin was the perfect hiding place. There was limited access to his quarters, and the sheer audacity of the move made it unlikely that anyone would guess this location. And the captain was clearly otherwise occupied.

Now he moved purposefully over to the captain's desk. Waiting for a slightly more stable moment, he jumped up onto the desk and reached into the heavy netting that dressed what was left of the ceiling. The box, wrapped in its hessian sack, was still there.

He pulled it down and jumped from the desk in one movement, making straight for the door. And then a fresh thought popped into his head. Despite the violence flexing all around, he felt himself calming and picturing a new ploy in his head. He saw how it would play out, just as he had envisioned his escape route from the Bug Pit a hundred lifetimes ago.

Yes, that would work. He returned to the desk and pulled open the drawer he had seen in his mind. There was the key, just as he pictured it. He then pulled the brass box from its secured position on one of the shelves.

Without hesitating he opened the brass box to reveal the captain's leatherbound logbook and papers. He then turned to the casket. Again, Emir pictured the release sequence in his head and swiftly repeated it with his hands. The casket opened immediately.

When Emir had first opened the box with Shabaka, he hadn't been sure what he would find. He had imagined a pulsing bloody heart, but instead there was just another box, and this one had no opening. It had been sealed up completely. Protected from unsolicited access. Impervious to everything, even water. As he now picked up the inner box, he was in no doubt that he held the heart of Suleiman the Magnificent in his hands. He trembled at the enormity of the moment.

The crack of further wood splintering brought him sharply back into focus. Without missing a beat, he placed the captain's logbook in Suleiman's casket and returned all of the bolts. Quickly he completed the operation by placing the sealed unit containing Suleiman's heart inside the captain's log box, locking it, and pocketing the key. With the switch complete, all that remained now was to place the casket, with Captain Barbarossa's logbook inside, back in the stowage point where the brass box had been. Then he could leave with the captain's box safely in his possession.

As he picked up the casket, he heard a ragged voice behind him.

'Put that *down*.'

He wheeled round. There, drenched and breathless, stood Kazim. The Janissary officer had cast a shadow over Emir throughout this voyage. From the moment he had arrested him in the marketplace, through the various suspicions and seditions on board, he had, more than any other figure, embodied the threat that Emir had uncovered. And now, at the last, he was here again. He looked at Emir with an expression of utter loathing and contempt.

'You have been a stone in my boot for far too long, boy. I will not allow this storm to deprive me the privilege of taking your life, you can be sure of that. But first, the casket. Hand it to me now. Gently.'

Emir knew that as soon as he did that, he was as good as dead. He searched his mind for another play, an escape route, but nothing came. And then, just as he was about to surrender the casket and take his chances, the hurricane made its own intervention. A wall of water ripped the side of the cabin clean away. Both man and boy were now exposed entirely to the full wrath of the storm.

Emir saw the chance, however slim it was, and hurled the casket towards the opening. Kazim screamed with anger and desperation and dived after it without thinking. Amazingly he managed to place a hand upon the casket before it got swept away. He grinned and looked back at Emir.

'Nice try, boy,' Kazim sneered, relishing the moment.

He lifted up the casket and turned to address his unfinished business with Emir, but the storm had unfinished business of its own. Another mighty wave crashed into the hull. Splintered wood flew everywhere. Kazim couldn't keep hold of the casket and reach for safety at the same time. He made his choice, and the sea embraced both soldier and casket. Kazim's final scream was snatched away by the storm.

Panic rising, Emir suddenly realised that he was losing vision in his one good eye. Everything was going dark. He reached up to his eye, which felt warm, wet, and sticky. He put a finger to his tongue and tasted the unmistakable tang of blood. He scooped up water from the floor and flushed out his eye. The saltwater stung, but he could see again. Above his eye he felt a splinter of wood protruding from his forehead. Without thinking he tugged it out. Immediately more blood started to pour from the wound. His silk scarf was loosely tied around his neck. He slid it up over his face and tightened it round his head.

Emir grabbed the brass box, which had tumbled to the floor, and half walked, half swam out of the cabin and up the corridor towards the deck steps. He scrambled up them as best he could, returning to the carnage on deck.

The *Colossus* was barely recognisable as a ship any longer. Bodies were strewn in all directions. Wreckage washed across the top level, leaving havoc in its wake. Waves continued to crash onto the deck. Emir looked up to the wheel point. Unbelievably both the captain and Shabaka were still at their post, valiantly continuing to try and determine the direction of the ship.

As Emir headed up the steps to the poop deck, another terrible sound came from behind him. He glanced back to see the main mast cracking. As it started to lean, he realised that the wheel was right in the middle of its trajectory. He screamed at Shabaka, who, miraculously hearing the warning, stepped instinctively back from the wheel for a second. The mast missed him by inches but struck the captain directly.

The wheel spun furiously, no longer being submitted to the will of the two men. Shabaka reached down to the captain, but it was clear that the blow had been fatal. Even in the middle of the chaos, Shabaka took a moment to honour his captain. He had sailed under many, but none better.

Emir stood and watched the scene, not knowing what else to do. He had placed any last vestiges of hope in the skill and experience of Captain Barbarossa. What would become of them now?

Emir hunkered down by his friend, trying to find some small reprieve from the hurricane's relentless onslaught. After placing his brass box down for a moment, he pulled the ring off his finger and grabbed Shabaka by the shoulder so he could make himself heard in one ear.

'You should have this back now, Shaba. The rings belong together. You have been a good friend to me. The best. I couldn't have wished for a more worthy companion. You have shown me such things, and now I am happy to die by your side.'

Shabaka stared incredulously back.

'Don't be a fool, Emie. This isn't over yet. Always have another escape route. Just when you think you're trapped, that's when a different door opens. Isn't that what your papa always taught you?'

Emir smiled through the tears and the spray. It was true. But this was a truly hopeless situation. He appreciated Shabaka's relentless optimism and his attempt to reassure, but the *Colossus* was going down. There was nothing else to be done now. As Shabaka got to his feet, pulling Emir up with him, the boy deftly slipped his ring into one of his friend's pockets. It was the right thing to do, and that was all that was left to him.

'Anyway,' Shabaka continued, 'you've been on this ship far too long. Look at you. You look like a pirate, what with your eye patch, and now that red scarf tied round your head.'

Emir laughed, despite himself. Shabaka grabbed Emir's arm and started back down the steps. Emir desperately held on to the brass box with his free arm.

'We must head towards the forecastle. If we get separated, we will both be lost. Don't let go of me, Emie. Do not let go, you hear?'

As the ship continued its slow, painful death, the incongruous pair battled their way through the waves, the bodies, and the detritus towards the prow of the ship. The large Egyptian man and the slight Turkish boy would not be separated. They had been through too much.

As they reached the ship's prow, the *Colossus* had already started its final surrender. Shabaka lunged at the jib sail, letting go of Emir for the first time. In the same instant, the bowsprit that had pointed the way for the mighty ship over countless voyages started to crack. Shabaka seemed to have sensed this coming, as he smiled back at Emir.

'Quick, Emie. Jump over here. The bowsprit and jib sheet will give us our own vessel as she goes down. Trust me, this will work.'

As if the *Colossus* had been waiting for her cue, the mighty ship started heeling over on its port side. The additional strain proved decisive in breaking the bowsprit free. Shabaka felt the movement and held out his arm. Emir looked on, amazed, as Shabaka rode the ship's foremost stay and sail.

'Grab hold of me now, Emie. Drop the box, you'll need both hands. *Now, Emie. Now!*'

Emir hesitated. He looked back down the ship. A figure shouted and waved furiously. It looked like the captain, but that wasn't possible. Was it? Emir shouted, *'It isn't over. You still have time. There's always a way.'*

Emir wiped blood from his eye and looked again. The apparition was gone. He glanced at the precious cargo he carried. He had gone through too much protecting this sacred artefact to lose it now. He stared back at Shabaka. He couldn't surrender the casket. He knew there was only one choice he could make.

***

Two hundred yards below the hurricane's brutal assault, the sea was still experiencing its effects. Calm by comparison with the carnage above, it was nevertheless being unusually churned and disrupted.

Pieces of the *Colossus* were starting to land on the seabed. A mass of shattered wood littered the area for a mile around. Sections of mast and sail, splintered barrels, and shredded rigging. Bodies, whole and broken, evidenced the fury at sea level.

Amongst all this flotsam and jetsam that told the story of the destruction above, a golden box, more of a ceremonial casket really, landed with a thump and partially buried itself in the disrupted silt. The casket had its own story to tell, of course, but it also contained the final story of the *Colossus*.

Five minutes later, and a hundred yards further along, another box also hit the bed. There was nothing grand about this one. Plain and functional, it certainly wouldn't catch the eye. Nevertheless, it remained visible right up until the point that the hull of the *Colossus*, complete with most of its cargo, crashed down onto its final resting place.

It would be nearly four hundred years before any of this wreckage would see the light of day again.

33

May 8, 2014
London

The British Museum had always been Daniel's favourite London museum. Yes, the V&A had its beauty, the National History Museum its grandeur, and the Tate Modern its moments, but for sheer tradition you couldn't beat the 'World's Museum,' as Daniel liked to call it.

The classical Greek architecture, the columns, the pediment, the reading room, even the Great Court combined to create an environment that was its own museum piece. The Great Court was something of a new kid on the block in its latest millennial incarnation, but it still had a certain charm, Daniel would reluctantly admit.

And, what with it being tucked away in the heart of Bloomsbury, it was only half a dozen stops on the tube from home. What was not to like?

For a while it had looked like the *Colossus* exhibition would be curated in the National Maritime Museum in Greenwich. In many ways a logical choice. Then at the last minute the British Museum stepped in. This was a real coup for DIVE.

As their chairman said at the time, 'There's nothing wrong with the Maritime, old chap, but nothing beats the cachet of the Brit.'

Overlooking the somewhat jingoistic undertone,

Daniel had to agree. He had kept his aspirations to himself. He knew he didn't have a seat at this particular table but was secretly thrilled when the change was made official.

For a while, the switch appeared to be threatening the launch date of May 8, but in the end, after the inevitable mad scramble that accompanied the launch of any live event, the eighth was locked in. For the crew of the *Triton* this had become a particularly resonant date. Not only was it exactly a year after the black ops team lay siege to their ship, killing all of the ship's crew, kidnapping one of their number, and stealing Suleiman's casket, but many now believed it was also the date that the *Colossus* sank. Whilst it was impossible to be sure, it had become 'fact' amongst the team.

All of the science crew were in attendance that night, as guests of DIVE. Given the shocking loss of life a year earlier, including the horrific murder of their CEO, it was a bittersweet occasion for many of the team, particularly those who had worked closely with the *Triton* crew.

Daniel was particularly happy to see that Maria had accepted his personal invitation. She had been instrumental in cutting through the red tape and ensuring that all items recovered from the *Colossus* were returned to the DIVE corporation. When Daniel had called, he couldn't tell her everything that had happened, but he told her enough for her to know that her nemesis was gone from her life once and for all. The closure she had needed for so long was finally hers. It would take a while, but she felt sure that she would get there. A new man was on her arm at the launch, and when Daniel nonchalantly asked who he was, Maria teasingly responded that she thought he was 'the one.' Daniel thought Maria looked fully recovered from her ordeal and subsequent coma, but more than that, she looked genuinely happy. He was happy for her.

Daniel scanned the room, feeling rather uncomfortable in his black tie. A familiar voice spoke up from behind him.

'Hope you feel a lot better than you look in that monkey suit, Professor.'

He turned to see his old friend and doctor, Paul Atterbury.

'Always concerned about my welfare, Doctor.'

'That's my job. Seriously buddy, how you doing?'

'Fine. Running ten kilometres a day. Cut out sugar. Getting my eight hours a night and my five a day. I'm good to go.'

Paul smiled and slowly shook his head. 'That's not what I meant, and you know it.'

It was Daniel's turn to smile ruefully. He gazed across the room, wondering how much of his inner turmoil to share with his friend. 'I'm all right, mate, honest. Yes, I still find myself looking for her in a crowd, and yes, not a day goes by without me thinking about her and what might have been. I have so many unanswered questions. Was she there under duress, or had I been duped all along? Was she really who Osman claimed she was, or was that just the ravings of a lunatic? Did she really have feelings for me, and if she did, why did she just disappear? I mean, I've stopped actively searching, but I still feel like I'm on the quest, even today. That can't be healthy, right?'

'There's no right answer for this stuff, Dan. Everyone processes in their own way and at their own speed.

When you are ready to move on, you will.'

Daniel shook his head again and slipped comfortably into a piece of well-worn banter with his mate. They both knew he was using humour to distract, and they were both okay with that.

'You know, I've never actually seen any certification from you. Are you really a doctor? Have you got any qualifications at all, or is this all just a scam? I'm sure I saw you stacking shelves in Tesco the other day. Come on, admit it. You don't know one end of a stethoscope from the other.'

'Okay, I admit it. I've just been fleecing you this whole time. Then again, I'm as much a doctor as you are a writer. This latest book, *The Colossus*, not exactly a page-turner, is it?'

'You mean this latest *award-winning* book, I think you'll find. It's got lots of pictures in it, right up your street, I'd have thought. Twenty-nine ninety-nine in all good book shops. Make sure to pick up a copy when you exit through the gift shop, sir.'

'Thirty quid? That's outrageous ...'

Paul was just warming up, but Daniel had clocked someone else he wanted to get a minute with.

'Sorry, would love to continue this highbrow discussion, mate, but I've just spotted someone more at my intellectual level. Enjoy.'

Chuckling quietly to himself, Daniel moved slowly through the crowds. He wondered how long he would have to stay before he could slip away without raising any eyebrows. Not before the speeches he guessed. Or the presentation. He was honoured that his account of the recovery of the *Colossus* had garnered so much praise and recognition, but he had never learnt how to get comfortable with the ceremonies.

He glanced back to see whether his mate had already taken his opportunity to exit through the gift shop, and suddenly, there she was. Banu.

Across the other side of the room, she stood perfectly still, staring straight at him. She had changed her hair, but he would have recognised her anywhere.

The two of them held their gaze for a few seconds, but then Daniel broke the spell by starting to move towards her. Immediately she shifted and disappeared from view. He wanted to shout out to her to stop, but he knew he couldn't. He pushed through the crowd as quickly as he could without appearing rude, exited the room, and ran to the gallery edge. Scanning the various stairs and corridors leading off in different directions, he saw no sign of her. She'd gone.

Slowly he walked back into the room, still trying to process what he had seen. Had it really been her? Had she been waiting for him to see her? Was she ready to be found? Maybe there was some hope after all.

***

Back in the main exhibition hall, he made his way over to the central exhibit, where he had seen Khaled standing a moment or two earlier. He waited for Kal to free up from the latest in a seemingly endless stream of well-wishers and gave him a light-hearted salute.

Kal beckoned him over.

'Quickly, save me from all this adulation,' he whispered conspiratorially.

'You love it,' Daniel responded scathingly.

Kal shrugged. 'Yes, I do.'

The two of them stood in silence for a moment,

staring at the twin exhibits in the centre of the room. Kal looked at Daniel, clearly trying to find the right way to pose a question.

'What?' Daniel said. 'Spit it out, what is it?'

'I was just wondering whether you ever hear anything from Yousef?'

Daniel rolled his eyes. If he had a pound for every time he got that question.

'Kal. Come on. If I had heard, would I tell you? Don't put me in this position. Look, I'll tell you this. I haven't seen him since that day. I get the odd cryptic postcard which may or may not be from him, but apart from that …'

'Will you ever tell me what really happened that night?'

'I wish I had more to tell. Frankly the whole thing is a bit of a blur now.'

Kal could see that Daniel wanted to change the subject, but he wasn't quite done yet. 'I heard that an ornately carved walking stick with a shipwreck provenance was recently auctioned on a black market site. Sounded a lot like our one that went missing. Went for two million apparently. You wouldn't happen to know anything about that, would you, Professor?'

Daniel looked shocked. 'You have me mixing in some terrible company, Khaled. I have to say, I'm a little hurt.'

Khaled shook his head with an air of resignation. He wandered over to the two pedestals cordoned off that presented both the exhibition's centrepiece and its most intriguing story. Daniel followed.

Each pedestal supported a glass cabinet. Within one cabinet lay a priceless casket of gold and jewels of every hue. In the other cabinet there was a battered brass box etched with the initials *A. B.* Daniel glanced at Kal.

'Do you think we will ever understand the secrets contained in these two boxes?'

'I hope not. The secrets are what make them so alluring. Anyway, they have already given us so much. We have the heart of Suleiman the Magnificent, preserved for all time. We have the captain's logbook cover that, from his final engraving on the back, gives us the exact date that our ship went down. And we have the initials that tell us who the captain of the *Colossus* was on that fateful voyage. The legend of Alparslan Barbarossa made manifest. What more do you want, Professor?'

'I want to know how the logbook ended up in Suleiman's casket and his heart ended up in Barbarossa's log box. Don't you want to know?'

'No, no I don't. You know, I once saw a magician make the Statue of Liberty disappear before my eyes. It was one of the most amazing things I had ever seen. And then they showed us how he did it. I didn't feel enlightened, I felt cheated. Pulling back the curtain only ever leads to disappointment, Dan.'

Kal grabbed two glasses of champagne from a passing tray and handed one to Daniel. He raised his glass.

'These artefacts have given us so much; they deserve to keep their secrets. Here's to the *Colossus*, and all who sailed in her.'

The two men clinked glasses and then stayed a little longer, gazing upon the intertwined exhibits, and wondering what really happened.

EPILOGUE

September 12, 1633

Constantinople

Three years after the sinking of the Colossus

The boy couldn't have been more than ten, maybe eleven. He sat on a stone block beside the well. This was his favourite spot. He found that you had a great view of the whole market, and occasionally a mark would come and stand right by you to take a drink of water. What he had learnt was that if someone walked into your space, they were much less likely to be aware of you than if you had walked into their space. This made picking much easier. But not today.

As the sun reached its zenith, he wondered whether it was time to call it a day. He was hot and frustrated. He hadn't had so much as a single pick all morning. As he jumped down from the block, adjusting his peaked cap to the direction of the sun, something caught his eye. Over the years he had developed an intuition for spotting anything incongruous. Anything out of the ordinary. Anything that plain didn't fit. And this definitely fell into that camp.

Exiting the north side of the market, an unlikely pair walked together. The younger man looked Turkish and stood out from the crowd, if for no other reason than his dazzling eye patch, which appeared to be adorned with a multitude of jewels. The older man, his companion, didn't look from round here. Libyan possibly. Maybe Egyptian. Some part of the glorious empire. He looked battle worn, hardened, and yet weary, simultaneously.

The boy was about to dismiss the unlikely looking pair when something else caught his eye. The younger man had something red fluttering from the makeshift bag slung over his shoulder. A silk scarf maybe? Ordinarily the boy wouldn't have bothered to cross the street for such meagre pickings, but it had been a particularly barren morning, and he hated to return to the den without some booty or other. He decided, if for no other reason than he had no conflicting plans at this exact moment, to track the pair as they continued up the slight incline away from the market. The scarf looked an easy lift, so, why not?

He picked up his pace to get closer to the two companions. This was a good spot for a pick. Quiet. Not many unwanted onlookers. Multiple exit routes. Now was the time to make his move. He accelerated again, but suddenly the older of the two travellers halted while the younger companion continued on. The boy, only some ten feet behind by now, knelt down quickly, to remove an imaginary stone from his shoe. What was this all about?

The boy watched as the younger man stepped away from the road and approached an unassuming door to a dwelling that looked in worse condition than that of the boy's own lodgings. He continued his pretence of adjusting his shoe, trying his best to look inconspicuous, as the young man glanced back briefly to his companion and then knocked on the door. He was just about to knock again when the door opened.

An older woman answered. Dressed completely in black, she looked to have had a hard life, but still retained a striking appearance. She stared at the young man suspiciously. They spoke for a few moments, and then the woman's demeanour suddenly changed. She threw her arms around the man and started to weep.

The older companion, who had stayed back a respectful distance, also appeared to be in tears as the young man reached to his bag and pulled out the red silk scarf, then loosely tied it around the woman's neck.

The boy looked on for a moment longer at the curious scene. He had missed his moment. Taking a closer look at the scarf, he decided it probably wouldn't have been worth it anyway. It didn't look particularly good quality—quite old and badly worn. He shrugged and started back down the hill. Something about the moment he had just witnessed left him with a bit more of a spring in his step. Maybe he'd put in a couple more hours. You never knew what the day might bring.

Today might be the day when all his fortunes changed.

The End

AUTHOR'S NOTE

Someone once said that truth is stranger than fiction, but not so popular. As I write this, in the strangest of times, that has never felt truer. But what I also think is that the best fiction feels like a truth. It has the ring of truth about it. I think I agree with Yousef's philosophy that the most convincing lies are the ones that incorporate the most truth.

I have inevitably taken one or two liberties within these pages—there is no beach to speak of in Amathus—but even these liberties are laced with a certain truth.

Let me be very clear, if only to ward off any enthusiastic legal teams, The Colossus is a work of complete fiction. All the diverse characters described within, and all their various exploits, experiences, and adventures are pure figments of my imagination. However, like all the best lies, The Colossus takes its inspiration from many engaging truths.

There was a famous and feared elite Ottoman military unit called the Janissaries, who, after a series of falls from grace, were abolished in the Auspicious Incident of 1826.

There was a colossal Ottoman merchant vessel which sank to the depths of the Levantine Basin around 1630. The ship was carrying goods that provided invaluable proof of a maritime Silk Road linking China, India, the Persian Gulf, the Red Sea, and the West nearly four hundred years ago.

There was a landmark archaeological maritime expedition, with a mission to recover the wreckage of that ship, along with eleven other vessels.

The Cypriot Department of Antiquities has seized the cargo recovered from that excavation mission, accusing the expedition of illicit excavation and violent extraction. As I complete this book, the standoff between the Cypriot authorities and the British research and recovery team continues.

There was an attempted military coup in Turkey called Operation Sledgehammer that was uncovered in 2010, when more than forty senior officers were arrested and then formally charged with attempting to overthrow the government.

And finally, Suleiman's heart, together with other organs, was removed from his body after his death, and buried on the site of the siege at Szigetvár in Hungary, whilst the rest of his remains were returned to be interred in Constantinople.

In 2016 the ruins of Suleiman's tomb in Hungary were finally discovered.

No heart was found.

ACKNOWLEDGEMENTS

When I first set sail on this voyage I honestly thought I had booked a berth for one. I was travelling alone. There are certain things in life which are best done on your own with the door firmly shut, if not locked. Reading a book, for example. Like an idiot I thought this was also true of writing one. How wrong I was. Sure there are many, many hours where it's just you and that pesky blank page. Writing can be an intensely lonely experience: one filled with self-doubt, feelings of vulnerability, and isolation. It's easy to conclude that you are indeed cast adrift on a raft built for one, facing all the perils of this journey alone. It turns out this couldn't be further from the truth. Who knew?

There have been so many travel companions on this trip that I know I won't remember them all. For those I overlook on this page, I hope you felt my appreciation at the time and apologise for my failing memory now. As for the ones I do remember, my heartfelt thanks for your support and encouragement, without which I would have jumped ship many times over.

First to my wife, the shining star that is Paula, thank you for being my first reader and for your unfailing encouragement. I love you everything. While I'm talking family I also need to thank my parents, John and Enfys, for introducing me to the giddy world of books, having both been librarians in their careers. My mum was the first to correct my grammar. She wasn't to be the last, but more of that later. Also thanks to my bro, Adam, for keeping me honest and encouraging me to write. And, of course, my son, Luke, who was the first to give me a positive review. He found time to read an early manuscript despite the arrival of his daughter and my granddaughter, the gorgeous Lily Enfys. I guess his wife, Nicci, also deserves an honourable mention for facilitating that particular arrival. She only took nine months to deliver something perfect, which puts my three-year project into considerable shade. Respect.

To my early Reader Group, thank you for agreeing not only to put time aside to slog through a very leaky first draft, but also provide invaluable feedback. Every comment, every observation prompted an improvement. So a big thank-you to Mike and Nicky Macleod, Andrew Kukielka, Richard and Liz Pepper, Paul and Gaynor Atterbury (yes, there is a real Paul Atterbury, who sadly bears no resemblance to my Paul, whatsoever), Tom Squirrel, Phil Basset, Rob Lewis, Barry Dyer, Deborah Hart, and Simon Jacobs. Special mentions go to Lucy Adams for kick-starting me again, Neal Basson for sharing his publishing journey, Susi Pasqualini for arguing the toss on every comma in this book, Vicki Griffiths for having the guts to tell it how it is, and especially my good friend Mike Harper, for going above and beyond on both multiple read-throughs and generous feedback.

All of these people have been great cheerleaders as well as giving me a wonderful reader perspective, but I have saved my most profound thanks for the professionals I have collaborated with on this publication. First to

Reedsy, the online brokerage house for world-class publishing professionals; you welcomed me in and helped me find some wonderful collaborators. Thank you to Stephanie Chou for your warmth, humour, and patience in guiding me through the copy edit and some perilous formatting; to Megan Katsanevakis for creating artwork that helped me fall in love with *The Colossus* all over again; and to Vickie Boff for taking on the daunting task of helping me reach as many readers as possible.

But most of all I have to thank the brilliant Holly Domney, my amazing editor, cheerleader, coach, counsellor, therapist, and confessor. You took my words seriously and laughed at my jokes. Holly, you made every page of my book better than it had any right to be. You rock. And yes, I know I should have used less words here.

Finally, a shout out to the Tuscan Six and the Spicy Girls. You know who you are. I love you all. Even you, Paul.

ABOUT THE AUTHOR

Simon Wright

Simon Wright was born, raised and continues to live in and around the Home Counties of London, England. He has forged a career as a leadership and brand consultant, advising and coaching business leaders internationally. When challenged on his credentials as a writer he cites a school commendation for creative writing and winning the Jane Austen award for achievements in English at his sixth form college. He acknowledges that other writers have more prestigious credentials. Simon's first book, The Colossus, is volume one of a series and was inspired by a Guardian article concerning a real life shipwreck salvage operation. As a middle aged, middle class, white male living in southern England Simon feels uniquely qualified to guide us through a century spanning high seas Ottoman adventure. He suggests that, through meticulous collaboration, he has managed to create a highly readable book, but also admits that the Oxford comma continues to keep him awake at night.

COMING SOON...
THE TWIN RINGS

An English professor and a Muslim boy reached across the centuries to protect the sacred heart of an Ottoman sultan.

Now they must build an even stronger bond as they race to uncover a secret that could change the course of humanity.

Two rings, forged in Ancient Egypt, link man and boy, legend and truth, ancient and modern.

Daniel and Emir face their most formidable adversaries yet, as they risk everything they hold dear to save a treasure for the ages.

Can they overcome impossible odds to secure a future for us all?

See overpage for a preview of book 2 in The Red Scarf Series

Chapter 1
May 8, 1630, Levantine Basin

The giant merchant ship was in her last death throes. Brutalised and battered by the raging storm, the *Colossus* shrieked and groaned as she was torn asunder. Most of the crew had been consumed by the angry sea, the rest lay strewn about the ship's wrecked remains, beaten and broken by the tempest.

Only one man and a boy still clung to the ship's remains, hanging on to their lives by the slenderest of threads. The man, around forty years old, was an Egyptian; his friend, a Turkish boy, was barely fourteen. They had met on board this gargantuan Ottoman vessel, and now appeared destined to go down together with the ship.

During the course of their six-month voyage, they'd faced many daunting challenges. The boy, Emir, had lost an eye saving a fellow crewman, discovered a priceless relic, uncovered a mutinous plot and narrowly escaped murder. The man, Shabaka, had been stabbed and thrown overboard, assumed dead. Time and time again the two compatriots had overcome adversity. Forged by these tribulations their friendship had become something more. A deep-rooted kinship born of respect, admiration, and a real affection. Shabaka had come to love the boy like he was his own son, and Emir, for his part, worshipped his friend and guardian.

They had travelled so far, endured so much. But now, in these final moments, as the Colossus prepared to surrender herself to the depths, all seemed lost. Not even a miracle could save these kindred spirits from the sea's cruel rampage. Surely.

***

'Now Emie, now,' Shabaka howled over the wind's fury. As he compelled Emir to make the jump, he reached into his pocket for his trusty knife. If his wild plan had any chance of working, he would need to be ready to slash any remaining ties that continued to bind the front section of the ship to the main vessel. His desperate hope was that the bowsprit and accompanying jib sheet would become entirely freed from the hull before the mighty galleon succumbed to the depths.

His hand fell on something unexpected as he rummaged around in his pocket, trying desperately to locate his dagger. Something that didn't belong in his pocket. Something that made his blood run cold.

Shabaka pulled out the ring he had given to Emir less than a week before as a symbol of their comradeship and commitment to each other. One of an identical pair. Shabaka knew the rings bound their wearers. Made their lives inseparable. Unbreakable. Shabaka stared down at the ring with horror.

His mind raced. Emir was no longer tethered to him. His plan had been built on the belief that they were irrevocably bound by the rings. As long as each wore his piece, the rings would not let them become separated. They would endure.

Moments earlier Emir had tried returning the ring to him. Of course, he'd refused, but Emir must have slipped the ring into Shabaka's pocket, believing that they were already doomed. He stared desperately at the boy he had come to love, imploring him with his eyes to take the leap of faith before it was too late.

'Please Emie. You must jump,' he implored.

Emir appeared strangely conflicted for one always so decisive and quick to action. Blood continued to pour from Emir's earlier head injury, seeping through his red scarf bandage. The scarf was precious to Emir, symbolising a deep-rooted conviction that he would return one day to his beloved home city of Constantinople, and to his mother. Shabaka wouldn't let him die before Emir's dream was realised.

Emir still gripped a metal box. They both knew that the plain brass box hid an extraordinary secret. Contained within was the sacred heart of Suleiman the Magnificent which, legend suggested, held power over the Ottoman empire. In that moment Shabaka understood. Emir had endured so much to protect the relic that now he simply couldn't bear to relinquish it. His relationship with the heart had shifted from duty to destiny.

He wanted to shake Emir and knock some sense into him, but instead, despite the howling chaos all around, he stilled himself and looked deeply into Emir's eyes. He could feel the bowsprit starting to break away beneath his feet, but he resisted the panic and spoke.

'Emie, it's over. The heart is safe. You need to let it go Emie. Right now.'

As if to punctuate his entreaty, a silent fork of lightning skewered the heart of the ship, instantly followed by a deafening roar of thunder. The force of the strike ripped the remains of the ship's hull in two, and hurled Emir into the air. Instinctively he released the box and miraculously Shabaka grabbed his unencumbered hand and pulled him tightly into an embrace.

Such was Emir's obsession with Suleiman's heart that he might still have hurled himself after the brass cabinet, and into the pounding waves, but the shock of the lightning strike had knocked him out.

As the last vestiges of the mighty vessel slipped below the swell and surf, Shabaka's roughly improvised raft slipped free of its mooring. Without the relative stability of the huge ship, man and boy became even more susceptible to the sea's tantrums. As they continued to be buffeted and bounced around, Shabaka desperately attempted to tether them to the unlikely craft.

Confident that Emir was well secured Shabaka now collapsed down next to him, all remaining ounces of energy spent. He looked down forlornly at the unconscious boy and clasped one of his small hands.

'Stay with me Emie. Our story isn't done yet. There is more to be written. Don't you dare die on me now.'

Printed in Great Britain
by Amazon